Book 1:
Blessing of
The Mother

Antonio R. Belizario
©

Prolog

Doctor Oloo says you're gonna be fine, said Isaiah.

I think that guy used to wash dishes at Cracker Barrel, said Troll.

When he first got here he had to, said Mingo. But he's a great doctor.

Isaiah stood next to the hospital bed besides Wilhelmina, who sat staring at her black husband, The Troll. Chrysanthemum sat at the foot of the bed in the Lotus position with her eyes closed in meditation as did Ivy, though she and Tiffany-Dawn were on the floor playing with the toddlers Silas and Elias. Silas was Ivy's son, Elias was Safflower's son, and Troll was the father of both boys.

Safflower paced impatiently. She and Wilhelmina were of one mind.

They were all married to the Troll.

All of the women wore baggy tie dyed, homemade muumuus, which they preferred to wear when they were not at home, where they usually wore nothing. They and Troll were domestic nudist, and at home enjoyed the pleasure of nakedness.

All three carried stainless steel SIG Sauer P229R DAK 9mm Parabellum semiautomatics, that held twenty bullets apiece. Chrysanthemum carried a stain less steel Smith and Wesson 357 Magnum, with a pearl handle and a six inch barrel, as well as a Glock 17 with a 33 round capacity in a shoulder holster. Wilhelmina carried an old Smith and Wesson 38 caliber snub nose revolver which she'd used many times before. It once belonged to her dead father.

All five women carried their guns in old scuffed up hip holsters and wore wrap around Cammo Kevlar vests and helmets. The helmets were disguised with head wraps. Each woman carried a Khukuri war Knife in a scabbard on the opposite hip.

Counter snipers were positioned on the roof knock-off Boomerang Sniper detection system purchased in Mexico City. Moon and a squad of his Cedar Crest Crew soldiers armed with P90s, illegally loaded with armor piercing bullets, as well DIY Laser Dazzlers, and a were guarding the outside, as well as the room's door, even though Isaiah had a crew of well armed guards keeping the facility secure. A friend of the family and something of a hood rat, he was a close friend of Trolls. Even so, Trolls friends were angry and were spoiling for a fight.

Why are we sitting here like ASHOLES? Said Safflower. Let's go find whoever did this.

Let's follow Willy's lead, said Ivy. Let's calm down.

Chapter One

The hospital room had the moody air of a bunker under siege. The women were camping out in the room; sleeping bags and backpacks attested to that. They were impatient to get him home, where they felt better able to protect him and themselves without the aid of outsiders. The doctor and nurses were frightened to enter the room, and had to be brow beaten by Isaiah to do so.

Troll was waylaid and ambushed by the Trinity River, where he'd gone fishing with his buddy MaGoo, after he was left alone. It was the largest Urban forest in the USA, and muggings were not unheard of there, yet they were still angry. He was attacked a viciously beaten by masked assailants. Though he killed three of the assailants with his Khukuri, and mortally wounded the other two, his wives wanted the survivors found.

It was the first time the peaceable Troll killed anyone, and he was a little overwhelmed by the goriness of what he'd done.

All of a sudden Troll was no longer seen as a granola munching hippy pacifist, if he ever was. He and all his wives wore long dread locks, but were no ganja smoking Rastas. As modest as he was, as peace loving as they seemed, they walked to the beat of a different drummer. Self styled Sephardic Orthodox Jews, who practiced what they called Ancient Judaism, they were fighters.

They were urban micro-farmers, green-simple living domestic naturists/nudists, who mostly went barefoot, practiced Veganism, ate barehanded from one communal plate, slept communally, and were also polygamists. He and his wives were also pot smoking, wine and beer drinking cottage industry black hippy capitalists. Re-cycle, re-use, re-purpose, repair and rebuild was their living philosophy. Many people considered them flakes.

Just about everything in their lives from how they dressed to how they bathed was done as a conscious decision about how to live sustainably, without marring nature.

They ran a housing rehabbing business, and an Antique shop, where he and his wives repaired old furniture for resale. In addition, they made and sold rustic twig furniture, and also sold wreaths, dried herbs, berries, teas, mushrooms, and nuts all harvested from the Forest. With the exception of Safflower, they also made copper jewelry for sale.

Their store served as a type of clearinghouse-community center for West Redemption community of hippies. Not so secretly, he produced gourmet beers and wines for sale.

It was surprising to some that, even if peace symbols were much in evidence, neither he or his wives were truly pacifists. Anyone who tried to trouble them did so at their peril. They were no victims. A very real part of their idiosyncratic lifestyle was being prepared to protect themselves and family from those who might view hippies, especially black ones, and nudists as targets for abuse, or in the case of nudist women, targets for sexual assaults. It surprised many to realize that though they were naturist-nudist, they on the whole were not only not pacifists, but were always well armed.

Their home and compound had a second yard, that wrapped around the main yard, and it was patrolled by several attack dogs.

Maybe now he was viewed as a target for unknown assailants, who might come back to finish the job, as well as a payback target for the friends or associates of the men he killed. Wilhelmina's brother, Angus, upon finding out from her about the attack, soon after, cleaned the site, but would not reveal the identity of the assailants.

The Communion Police were not called in.

Though close to Isaiah and the Westia Fellowship, not to mention the SWC, Troll and his wives were not gang members.

No one knew who tried to murder Troll. Was it anti-nudists? Haters of Polygamists? Someone trying to muscle in on his fledgling beer and wine making operation? Anti-Semites? Was it his former friends in the SWC? Why had they turned on him? Where had MaGoo gone? Was it MaGoo who had him beaten? Or did he sell out Troll?

It seemed MaGoo had a lot to answer for. So did Angus and the SWC.

Someone was going to pay.

They were in a "private recovery facility," that was unlicensed and catered exclusively to members of the Westia Fellowship. Everything about it, from the antiseptic smell, to the bed and furnishings and medical equipment said Hospital. Possessing most of the features of a large residential clinic, if not a hospital, for all intents and purposes it was. The corridors were bright lit, patients and visitors sat in waiting areas, orderlies pushing wheel chairs and gurneys were in evidence, as well as nurses and a doctor dressed in scrubs, sporting stethoscopes. It even boasted a small pharmacy and surgery room as well as a roof top organic vegetable and flower garden.

It was a ten unit apartment building, which had been derelict until Isaiah purchased it for back taxes, through a dummy corporation set up by her sister in law Rosy. It was re-habbed by Troll as a General Contractor, with a large crew of illegal's he hired, for a very hefty fee. The painting he did personally with Wilhelmina, Chrysanthemum, and Tiffany-Dawn. He was paid a small fortune by Isaiah in cash. Then it was set up as a secret Hospital by Isaiah and her husband Mingo. They named it Nameless.

He worked on a part time basis as the properties maintenance man when no money was coming in. Thereafter he became a preferred General Contractor for Isaiah, and Rosy.

It never dawned on him that he would become a patient there. Most of the patients, ill or injured, were on the run from rival gangs, or were in America illegally and would not have been safe at a regular hospital. Security was provided by a private company. It was staffed by heavily armed uniformed gang members moonlighting as guards.

The rooms were large and sun filled, the grounds were manicured, and most important, it was surrounded by thick thorny hedges and a security fence, and was gated. It was a fortress.

The one Doctor, Erick Oloo, and the nursing staff, were Kenyans without papers, who had no licenses to practice in America and were happy to practice off the books for the generous wages Isaiah paid. Doctor Oloo was a skilled Physician from Nairobi, Kenya, who fled to America after offending a powerful Mungiki leader, who ordered him killed. He fled secretly to the Redemption and worked as a dish washer, until Isaiah, who's mother knew him, offered him the position of the facilities one and only physician , albeit an unlicensed one.

They were all working off the books, though well protected from Immigrations. It wasn't what they preferred, but it was better than many other alternatives. Isaiah's mother, a Kenyan, secretly ran the facility, though she worked at Communion General as a neo-natal nurse.

One of Trolls eyes was swollen shut, and he had a split lip, not to mention a few broken ribs.

Wilhelmina's face was frozen with fury as she looked at him. The other women deferred to her and allowed her to talk for them, which for Safflower and Chrysanthemum was unusual. She was the one among them who survived several gun fights, and more importantly, she was Trolls lawful wife.

Even though they all carried guns and knew how to shoot, among them she was the only one who had ever killed, and it was not once, but many times.

Her eyes, one blue and the other hazel, seemed very frightening to Isaiah at the moment.

Once she managed a gas station convenience store, Toot 'n Tote'm, which was located next to Loop 12, on the Eastern edge of the Redemption, North Texas' largest city. It was considered the premiere Southwestern City. It was not far from where she was raised, and still called home. It was the neighborhood from which Bonnie and Clyde sprang, a notorious spawning ground for gangs, gangsters, and bandits. It was outlaw country.

Toot n Tote'm was a franchise run by a frugal owner to put it kindly. Few knew that, for reasons known only to her, Rosy, something of a chief financial officer for what she laughingly called Isaiah's Mafia and cult, owned it and several other Toot n Totem's through several proxies.

The Manager was one Mister Pattle. He viewed the eerie Wilhelmina with fear, and tried to avoid her if possible.

Even if the convenience store did a great deal of business, he had a rule: one shift one cashier. It was always notoriously understaffed. She worked the late evening shift and often over night by herself. Being right next to Loop 12, it was a tempting plum, a good lick, for stick up artists. Once they did the deed, many of them reasoned, you hit the Loop, hightailed it down to twenty or thirty-five, ditch the boosted ride, and if you were wise enough to wear a mask, you were a lick to the good.   So it was said among the wolf packs that specialized in convenience store rip and runs.

The problem was Wilhelmina. She failed to grasp their views.

The store policy was simple: give them the money. Wilhelmina knew enough hoods to understand that it was not that simple. Her policy was not to get killed.

Unfortunately for several of them, it was the misfortune of several stick up boys that she worked the hours that she did. Dusk to Dawn was the best time to do a lick. No one wanted to work those hours, even if the store was locked, and business was done through a bullet proof windows for most of the shift. The fact was that but for the occasionally robbery, it was a quiet and peaceful shift to work.

Wilhelmina, shy, took on the shift gladly. After all, when cops cooped in the parking lot, it was relatively safe. Receiving a few dollars above the minimum wage, she liked her job and did not intend to lose it. She reasoned that all would be ok if she wore a bulletproof vest.

Late at night, when she locked the door and only did business through the cashier window, she practiced her draw with a Smith a Wesson snub thirty eight with a four inch barrel. It was long enough for gunfights, short enough for a fast draw. Once it belonged to her black father, who died a hero's death in the Nam, allegedly. She also packed in her pockets several loaded speed loaders. Neither her older sister, Tiffany-Dawn , or her older Brother, Black Angus, had any use for it. Each preferred Sig-Sauer 9 millimeter semi-autos with high bullet capacities. Wheel guns were for dinosaurs, they said, but Wilhelmina loved the gun.

The reliable wheel guns made Wilhelmina feel more secure, so she preferred it, though she carried a Glock 9 millimeter tucked in a concealed holster in the small of her back. She also carried a little Stainless Steel Bauer 25 automatic in her boot.

Seemingly cold blooded, virtually emotionless, and a cracker jack shot, she was an accidental gunslinger. When her brother, Black Angus, called Big Red on the streets, taught her how to shoot she was ten; back then she was a lousy shot.

One thing I know for sure, Little Red, her brother once said in utter frustration.

What? She asked.

You'se the lousiest shot I've ever seen, sis.

Well maybe I need glasses, Bow-bow.

Maybe you do!

Maybe I'll get some!

Maybe you should!

Maybe I will! I'ma go in the Marines jus' like Daddy and win the Congressional metal too!

Maybe you should learn how ta knit!

Why?

Why? Cause maybe could be shootin' ain't in your future, said her brother, who at the time was fourteen.

Maybe I don't see you making A Marine!

Maybe I'll learn to shoot as good as you, Black Angus! She said.

Whatever, he said laughing at her, and mussing her red hair.

Quit, you big dumbass!

Black Angus and Tiffany-Dawn raised her and each other in a spavined, white colored clapboard ramshackle three bedroom shotgun shack with peeling paint, that always needed a paint job, behind a tattered picket fence, in the far West area of the Redemption, a few blocks from Loop 12. It had been in their family for a few generations. All three lived there together until she moved in with Troll. Soon thereafter her sister moved out too.

Her Mother, Matilda Cromwell-Smith, who was called Honey Buns, rode with the SWC, Steel Wheel Confederates. Her people came with her from the Island of Aruba when she was ten, but she grew up in Brooklyn, New York, in the Fort Green Projects, among the Jamaican enclave. Rastas were scum to her.

With a warrant out for her arrest, on a charge of attempted murder, she moved to north Texas with her brood, where she had cousins, after an unfortunate incident involving her, and a butcher knife, and an obstreperous randy ganja smoking Rasta neighbor, who did not know how to keep his hands to himself. She purchased a bone hilted razor sharp Bowie knife at a pawn shop in East New York, on Sutter Avenue, and took a Greyhound all the way to Texas.

Sharp Bowie knives became her favored weapon of choice thereafter. She was good in a fight, but armed with a Bowie she was lethally deadly. With a flick of the wrist she could cut a throat, with a stab and a twist she could lay a belly open. With a fast thrust she could pierce a heart. A swift slice across a forehead could render an opponent blind with their own blood. It didn't take much for her to draw her knife, and she believed that if it was drawn it could not be sheathed until it got a good taste of blood.

All three of her children saw her work her magic. All three viewed her with fear.

Wilhelmina came to dislike her mother bitterly.

As Texas newbie's, they rattled around couch surfing among relatives in North Texas. Mostly they viewed the volatile psychopathic woman with fear, and were more grateful to see her back as she left than her smiling face with its glittering psychotic miss matched eyes as she arrived. Eventually they ended up staying in the roomy shot-gun shack that became their home with an old childless widower uncle. The girls had their own room, Honey Buns slept in the enclosed porch in the back. They made themselves at home. A miserly Pullman Porter, the Uncle died soon thereafter, out of aggravation with Honey Buns antics, some said.

Many of the neighbors wondered how a spry, relatively healthy man died so suddenly, but there was nothing to justify their suspicions, other than their view that the circumstances of his death were fishy. That Honey Buns gave him a large shot of insulin that he did not need was never considered by the coroner.

Wilhelmina dearly loved her uncle. Though child she knew there was something suspicious about his death.

As it turned out the house was left to the three children in his will, but Honey Buns received a life estate. There upon Texas became home. In North Texas, she quickly developed a love for American made Semi autos hand guns, which her Uncle left her plenty of. There was great elegance to simply gunning someone down with no need to fight. Yet she always loved the feel of a Bowie on her hip and more so in her hand. Just about anything made her grin and laugh, but she had a propensity for violence, and a mean streak. Beer and Ganja kept her mellow, but she was no weed head or barfly. She loved a good time and excitement with one man of her choosing; she was no crow eater or whore either. Even so, high heel boots, fishnet stockings, plaid halters and faded denim daisy dukes were preferred mode of dress. Her hard body and flat abs showed those clothes to good effect.

What with the big hair and the garish make up, many men mistook her for a working girl, and earned themselves a handsome scar for the mistake.

A point came when she Badly cut a member of the SWC for being too quick with the hands. Payback was in order. The club President, McNeil, who fancied a ruthless crime lord, sent their best knife man, a murderous psychopath, by the name of Boot, who acquired his skills as a knife man in prison, not to take her out, but to settle the score and put her in her place. After all, were they not knife men? How could they sit back and allow some crazy island chick who might be a Negress to kick the ass of a SWC member in a knife fight for goosing her curvaceous ass so wantonly displayed? Hell, it was a white man's right, circumstances allowing…

The two met. He bought her a drink. It was a pretext. She ordered Wild Turkey. They chatted. They danced. They sized each other up. He liked her perky ass. She thought he was hot and liked to give 'im sass. She knew why he was there, and didn't care. She was amused. He found her amusing. They decided to negotiate hands on.

They left the bar on his Harley. Negotiations commenced in a Motel 6 room. A rousing, vigorous, climax to the negotiations led them to make peace. Days later they left the room, stiff sore and happy. There was no going back. Weeks passed. McNeil demanded action. She became his lady. The club President argued with Boot about his choice of chick. They met in a lonely back alley to discuss the matter. Foolishly, McNeil came alone. In an effort to resolve their differences amicably, Boot cut the Club President's throat from ear to ear with a straight razor, after Honey Buns first snuck out and stabbed him repeatedly in the liver.

Thereafter Boot elected himself as the replacement, at the suggestion of Honey Buns. A few old stalwarts who wanted to preserve the clubs democratic traditions unfortunately found themselves with their backs to Honey Buns, as she wielded a Mossberg twelve gage loaded with buckshot while she rode on the back of Boot's hog. Others were found knifed or with slit throats. And so the issues of democratic process were silenced.

He introduced her to the SWC as his chick. No one raised objections about a yellow-boned, red haired Negress with eerie looking mismatched eyes began to treat the club as if she owned it. She was their unofficial Queen after that.

Isaiah and Mingo, in their early twenties, were by then over lords of North Texas streets. They realized that neither Boot or Honey Buns were empire builders. So they held back but made it clear that their tribute had to be paid, no excuses. SWC was not foolish enough to buck the Westia Fellowship. They paid tribute.

But that was in North Texas.

Long before that, She took up with a devilish, well endowed black Marine, of legendary rowdiness, from East New York. Tall, dark, and wild, named Bartholomew Cromwell, he kept her more than satisfied. He demanded head every time the little head was up, which for him seemed to be all the time. She gladly complied so long as head was not all he wanted. She lived a good life with him, when they weren't drunk and battling, until he was sent to the Nam.

They had three children, one after the other. She was quite happy that the pretty little whelps came out as pale skinned as her, with flaming red hair, though they resembled their father in their features. Indifferent to children, though kind to her whelps, she had little time for a brood of three. She had them because she did not practice abortion. After the birth of Wilhelmina, with her man at war, she had her tubes tied, and proceeded to have a good time. She loved her husband but couldn't stand the boredom of being a grass widow.

None of her children ever forgave her for her open faithlessness to their father, who they idolized.

No one knew if the swaggering she-devil was mostly black, or mostly Mexican, or Puerto-Rican, or mostly demon, but she was generally regarded as white trash. She had a mane of flaming red hair, and a face covered in chocolate freckles. Strangely, one of her eyes was brown and the other was blue. So too, it turned out, were those of her three children.

The paleness of her skin and the Caucasian cast of her features and her vapid arrogance of manners made it easy for her to pass as a white woman.   Not intending to live her life as a second class citizen, she did exactly that. Better to be white trash than a nigger, she reasoned. She preferred being with white men, thereafter, since she found that they were more generous and tended to have more money. She also found them easier to manage.

Yet she could fly into a rage in a flash, and out came her Bowie knife, so she didn't want unmanageable men.

Most of the time she stayed with her boyfriend, Boot. Wilhelmina called him Heel for as long as she could remember. She hated him bitterly. He was a great big, foul mouthed, racist, homophobic, closeted bisexual, weed smoking lout, with greasy, stringy black hair and a full beard, who loved proclaiming to anyone that his woman had to have mucho black in her with a sweet round ass like Honey Buns, though she hadn't much in the way of tits. Even so, they were still bodacious tatas to him.

This here ass is as sweeter'n Honey Buns! He proudly proclaim, patting her on the curvaceous derriere.

She developed the reputation of having the finest looking ass in the West Redemption, rivaled only by that of her eldest daughter, Tiffany-Dawn. In a neighborhood of anal loving ex cons, that won her many admirers.

Wilhelmina fortunately was not so blessed.

Honey Buns thereafter was her mother's her nick name.

Hush ya foul mout', na, ya piece a white trash! She said with a smile when he boasted of her pretty rump. She spoke with a thick Aruban accent, though she was by her family raised in America.

He shamelessly proclaimed that a stint in the big house down in Huntsville left him with a pronounced proclivity, predilection and taste for the stemming of the rose, although he preferred to do it with a clean woman, preferably a colored one, generous of posterior, or Mesikan with some colored in her. Though at times it left her sore, if he liked stemming the rose, she too liked to have her rose stemmed by her wild man, given enough saliva, K-Y or Vaseline.

She also loved to suck sour green pale pickle, and he loved to have the sour green pale pickle sucked. Even so, she made certain to make him think that she considered him a perv, and half a fag.

What he never said to any one was that he also liked eating her furry burgers, and licking her hairy, funky arm pits and tonguing as well as licking the odorous rose too. Further, he liked having her lick his pink rose, and he liked to have her stem it with a big green cucumber. Those secrets placed him in Honey Buns' power, though he was quick to threaten to slap the shit out of her if she publicly disrespected him. But she was quick to prick pricks and dicks with a Bowie knife, as need arose. On many an occasion she gave him a handsome cut or two, landing herself in jail over night, and him in the ER, though he never pressed charges; so mostly all he did was to make threats.

Boot ran the SWC as well as Hell's half acre, as their neighborhood was called. And in as much as she ran Boot, she really ran the SWC and the neighborhood, so nobody messed with her or her kids.

The three red headed pale skin black kids grew up around the SWC. They grew up considering themselves white, and so being accepted by SWC members. They had cute round little noses, which seemed neither black or white. Their hair was slightly kinky, though red, and their lips were full, but that made them hardly remarkable. It was easy for them to be passed off as white. They were so accepted by the SWC. It was made up of what the ungracious called a motley crew of white trash and their no good Mexican friends.

Wilhelmina hated the leather clad, motor cycle riding saddle trash, red neck bums, beaner bandidos, deceitful pistoleros, and their skanky muchachas and women; she hated her slatternly Mother, despised Boot the Heel, and told them so frequently. Her Mother loved it. She threw her head back and laughed whenever Wilhelmina told them off.

My little red head snot is a rattler, nah! Honey Buns would chortle.

He found her sarcasm amusing.

The apple don't fall far from the tree, Boot like to say about Wilhelmina.

Boot saw to it that she got her father's 38 when she turned 16.

Boot, degenerate though he was, was a kindly man when it came to children, and was indulgent of his red headed step kids. When he came around he always had a fistful of peppermints for them. He allowed no one to treat them rudely. Frequently he took pains to not swear in their presence, or to behave rowdily around them. Since he shot blanks, he had none of his own. In his own way he saw them as his.

It seemed that her hood childhood amongst motorcycle hoods consisted of riding down to jail in the back of Boot's Ford F-150 Super cab pickup with the other children to bond her mother out for cutting someone. She remembered too summers of endless cook outs and barbecues in empty lots and backyards, of her mother's cat fights, of keggers, and of ducking around drugged up, drunken brawling bikers and their sluttish women.

Angus, loved the SWC, and idolized Boot. He treated Angus like a son. From him Angus learned to ride a chopper, drive anything, fix any engine, chop-shopping, gun-Smith-ing, and the art of dealing of Meth.

Boot was also a part-time Pastor to the two wheel riding devils he led. Wilhelmina found that laughable.

It was he who named Angus Big Red.

Tiffany-Dawn too loved but despised her slatternly mother and tolerated Boot, though she viewed him as an usurper. To his credit, he never touched her. Neither Tiffany-Dawn, who true name was Clarissa, or Wilhelmina, ever fully forgave their brother for associating with Boot. For the most part Boot, if affectionate, ignored her and Wilhelmina, which was fine with them.

Tiff as she was called by her family, wanted to go to Hollywood, become a star, and marry a rich man, and escape from the west Redemption. In fact, soon after leaving Sunrise High School, she became a Cocktail waitress at the Prancing Stallion Bar and Grill. Eventually, for a few years, she became a titty bar dancer at Tata's, the back part of the Prancing Stallion.

This grieved Wilhelmina.

All three learned how to fend for themselves, but they also learned to value family loyalty. They took care of each other. Tiffany-Dawn was the designated holder of the all important food stamp card, which she took it upon herself to get. Honey Buns paid no attention to a bare cupboard, since she rarely stayed with them. It was Tiffany-Dawn and Angus that got her up on time, fed her fried eggs and over cooked beacon, milk and oatmeal, and got her to school. Tiffany-Dawn washed her clothes; Angus helped her do her homework. He also kept bullies away. Tiffany-Dawn cooked all meals, mostly canned vegetables and tuna or hamburger helper. She kept both Wilhelmina and her brother out of trouble, and was more of a mother to them than Honey Buns.

Angus bought Wilhelmina a girl's Bowie knife and taught his kid sister how to fight with a knife, his favorite weapon besides a hand gun. Thereafter he stopped giving her shooting lessons. However, she continued target practicing on her own. It was a pleasant discovery for Wilhelmina that she could shoot pretty well when she wore glasses.
Later, it was he who did a term in the Marines. She never did.

Is there something wrong with my eyes? She asked the School nurse, near tears one day. Others frequently by mocked her for squinting.

The kindly nurse, a tall, slender African woman called Mbwoka Martinez smiled and looked at her with large sad hazel eyes.

First, tell me whom I'm talking to dear!

Wilhelmina Cromwell Smith.

Well, Miss Smith, why don't we test your eyes and see?

After test, Mrs. Martinez smiled, and gave her a cookie and small container of milk.

Is it hard for you to read?

Not if I hold the book close to my face! Said Wilhelmina.

Does your mother or father see you reading?

My father's dead, ma'am.

What about your mother?

She doesn't have much time!

Well, come back here first thing in the morning. I'll give you a note for your teacher.

Nurse Mbwoka Martinez had a surprise for her in the morning.

Miss Smith, can you try these on?

She handed her a pair of brown frame glasses.

It turned out that she was near sighted. She knew that Wilhelmina's family was neglectful, if not poor, so Mbwoka Martinez paid for the glasses herself, and did not tell her. As a result, she got what she felt were big clunky glasses.

She looked at them with distaste.

Mbowka a smiled at her.

You'll like them better if you try them on. She adjusted them for her, and put them on her. The world snapped into focus for Wilhelmina. The dour, unhappy little girl smiled. She looked into the face of Mbwoka and grinned. The Nurse was so kind looking, and pretty. The class, the clouds, the trees, the grass, the other children---it was all so entrancing. How beautiful North Redemption, North Texas suddenly seemed! What she saw entranced her.

The excitement turned her into an amateur photographer.

Tiffany-Dawn was as excited as her younger sister when she got home. Yet she had to make dinner. She seized her mother's old 35 mm Canon SLR, gave it to Wilhelmina.

Go take some pictures out in the yard, but don't go anywhere, or Mama will kill me!

From that day on that Camera became hers. Honey Buns, who rarely used it, shrugged indifferently about forfeiting her camera.

I probably woulda pawned it, she said with a devilish smirk. Willy, these pictures are great! I think we have a professional photographer here!

Then she went out carousing with Boot, and did not return for a week.

Thereafter she became a photography geek. She documented her world in black and white pictures. Her big Sister was one of her favorite subjects. At first Tiffany-Dawn played the fashion model, but soon grew indifferent, and allowed her to capture her images at times when she was unaware. Tiffany-Dawn emerged in those pictures as a thoughtful, contemplative girl.

Wilhelmina practiced her shooting. With glasses on, she rarely missed.

Wilhelmina did any work available to a precocious little girl to buy film. She babysat, washed dishes, mowed lawns. Everywhere the shutterbug went she snapped pictures, often in black and white.

She went to work at Toot and Tote'm during her Senior year at Sunrise High School and went to work full time there upon graduation.

It was Wilhelmina that many of the stick up boys ended up confronting when they went to do the deed at Toot 'n Tote'm.

To Angus's surprise, while still in her teens she became a local legend after gunning down at least fifteen stick up artists over the length of a few years, who tried to rob the Toot 'n Tote'm, killing eleven and leaving the rest crippled. All efforts by her family to get her to quit proved fruitless.

The body count was not higher because some got away wounded, but most died soon after.

It was rumored that if she could help it she left none alive, and even tracked down some of those who got away secretly on her own time, and finished the job, for the sake of mercy. After all, it was cruel to let a wounded beast escape to die a suffering death.

One evening a tall, muscular young black guy walked in to Toot n Tote'm. He had an easy, charming manner, and the sexiest lips she ever saw on a man. He was lean, and handsome enough to die for.

She was convinced he was a stick up artist, casing the store.

He simply stared at her with a confused smile. After he came in a few more times she found out he was called Troll.

The Police loved her and protected her. It did not hurt that she comped them free donuts and coffee whenever they came by. Though she claimed that it was a store policy, she secretly paid for it out of pocket.

After each gunfight, when the press came calling, she deliberately made herself scarce and never spoke to reporters out of shyness. She was friendless, graceless, flat chested, mostly flat assed, and was battling a raging case of the zits. She briefly had a gangly, be-pimpled boyfriend with greasy, stringy hair, and an immense Adams apple, who came by her home occasionally, wearing an oversized T shirt and droopy jeans.

When he came by, he stood about the porch, chain smoking, saying nothing and would finally relieve her by leaving. She was relieved when he finally announced that he was gay and stopped coming around her. Tiffany-Dawn was her best friend. Black Angus didn't count because he was her big brother.

Other than that, her only friends were Dusty and Rusty, cowardly German Shepherds, and an irascible, scrawny, flea bitten one eyed grey tabby, who she called Bubba. Bubba too hated the world. He viciously bullied Dusty and Rusty. He grudgingly adored her, and she adored Bubba in return, and that was enough. Fame did not fascinate her.

She considered herself ugly. Her mouth and eyes seemed too big, her chest was too small, her butt lacked curviness, and she was too skinny and wiry. She had no idea that she was quite beautiful in a quirky way.

She disguised herself with floppy sunhats and oversized sunglasses stolen from her mother when the press tried to take her picture. To everyone's surprise, Tiffany-Dawn , as much as she craved fame, stepped up, along with Angus, and did everything to protect her shy younger sister from the unwanted attention.

So the press relied on hyperbole to describe her, calling her a throw back, a modern day, blood thirsty Girl Gunslinger-gunfighter, which enraged her.

The Redemption Morning News' Crime reporter, Elkin Wyeth, a vicious, closeted Sodomite, renamed the store Toot-Shoot 'n Tote'm, and called her Willy Earp, thus earning her eternal hatred.

Both names stuck.

It rankled her because she only allowed her family and friends to call her Willy. To everyone else se was Wilhelmina.

It surprised Wilhelmina that after each of the engagements, as she liked to call gun battles, as her dead father called them in the treasured letters that he once would send home along with pics of the Nam, after each engagement, she felt nothing. No anxiety, no guilt, no fear. Nothing. The only thing was she would feel a small amount of thirst for a cold can of Diet Pepsi. Then she usually chewed a piece of sugar free Juicy fruit. Afterwards she would go home and play with Bubba, if he wasn't in a bad mood, or read one of her mother's trashy paperback romances.

Or she would look through family albums and read her daddy's letters. She visualized the jungles of the Nam as she read his letters and daydreamed about him.

Concluding that all the stories of sleepless nights and troubled consciences were hype, she cleaned her guns and hoped not to be caught without them. She received a letter of commendation from the City, and a raise of a quarter an hour after the third engagement.

Several second Amendment groups made her an unwilling poster child for their causes, and sent her Commendations and checks to aid her through the traumatic moments following such a harrowing ordeal. She had no idea what they meant. She wondered why they sent her the checks, and politely returned them, over the loud objections of her sister, but the guns and bullet-proof vest that she was sent she kept.

The store Manager, in light of the apparent danger, and in light of the publicity that his store was getting for failing to provide adequate security, bought her a used bullet proof vest and allowed her to keep her two cowardly German Shepherds, Dusty and Rusty, with her in the store, in lieu of hiring a security guard. They shyly hid beneath the counter.
He also paid for her pistol permit, and gave her a five percent discount on any personal purchase. Upon reading about her Isaiah was intrigued.

Immediately, even before they met, she knew that she and Wilhelmina were kindred spirits.

Mingo became worried.

Killers respect killers, she told him frankly, to relieve Mingo's concerns that she was returning to Lesbianism.

She and Mingo sought her out at the
Toot and Tote'm, introduced themselves, and
became fast friends with her, even if they came
from different sides of the track. Wilhelmina
knew who Isaiah was and felt over-awed by her.
To Isaiah's surprise, she discovered that both of
them grew up in the same SDA Temple, and that
Willy as she liked to be called by friends, was a
Westia Fellowship member, though she was not a
Member of the Westia Queendom.
Always on the look-out for such talent, Isaiah
talked her into leaving the dangerous store. She
quickly befriended and hired her as a special
assistant. They became fast friends, and She and
Mingo quickly adopted her and Troll.

Isaiah felt a strange kinship with the
Troll, and found it eerie how much he looked and
acted like her and her big brother, Romero. It
surprised her to discover that he was raised by
one of the Kenyan cousins of her mother.
Kenyans families tended to be very tightly knit,
so it surprised Isaiah that she did not know Troll
at all.
She wondered if Troll was a relations, but
it seemed she never got a chance to make
inquiries.

It was even more remarkable how Isaiah's mother reacted to Troll. When she entered his room in the recovery facility, for the first time, she froze upon looking at him, stammered something, and hastily fled. She avoided any further contact with Troll. She and her husband Lupe sank into a well-concealed depression.

The nurses tell me your doing great, big man, said Isaiah, kissing his forehead. Troll looked at her dryly.

I don't feel great, Prophet, he whispered.

I can't live with this, said Mingo.

Aw, listen at you! Said Troll.

You're family! Said Mingo, nobody does this to our own!

Lookit...Jus' tell us who did it, ok? said Isaiah. It'll be handled, I promise.

Like you handled that situation at temple for your brother and Mouse? Asked Wilhelmina.

Tiffany-Dawn came ad stood behind her sister and rubbed her shoulders.

Willy---

My name is *Wilhelmina.*

Isaiah raised an eye brow and sighed.

Wow. Are you saying----

It was a major disaster, Queen. I'll handle my own probs.

Isaiah sighed.

I've always called you Willy---

Yeah, that's what my *friends* call me!

Isaiah stared at her.

Lookit, said Mingo. We feel your pain, Troll is family, but be careful what you say, ok?

Isaiah made a gesture, asking him to hold on.

You saying we're not friends now?

I don't know what I'm saying! Said Wilhelmina.

So *Wilhelmina* are you holding me personally responsible for this?

No, said Wilhelmina.

Are we to blame? Why?

Wilhelmina raised an eyebrow and looked away with her eerie eyes.

Well, said Isaiah, whatever you think, this will be handled---

No! said the Troll in a broken voice. No revenge, no paybacks, no get evens, ok? So I got my ass kicked…Big deal! Let it go.

Bullshit, Teddy-Bear! Said Wilhelmina.

Red, you better mind me! He said.

No, screw you, Poppy.

Poppy? Or Papi? Asked Isaiah with a smile. That's what Julio calls my brother…

Poppy, the flower, said Wilhelmina. Chryssie named him Willow and Poppy.

Little Red head gurl, you *listen to* me, and watch that mouth. Enough with bad words too!

I said *bullshit*, ok? said Wilhelmina, and wiped her eyes.

Red, don't *make* me take you over my knees! I'm not as hurt as you think! You hear me gurl?

Wilhelmina laughed, and kissed his forehead, then his lips.

Isaiah's hackles rose. She looked at Mingo and he too felt the eeriness. Troll sounded almost exactly like Romero making threats to Julio or Mouse, like Ralph Cramdon to his wife in the Honeymooners; threat that were never kept.

I may have to give you a spanking, even though you kissed me.

Promises, promises! Said Wilhelmina, sticking her tongue out at him.

Alright now, he said, chuckling, then he winced.

She put her face against his and rubbed nose with him.

She and Troll looked at each other and he tried to laugh.

I'ma take care of this---- Wilhelmina whispered.

We're gonna take care of this! Said Safflower.

Why not let the Police handle this? Asked Ivy.

In West Redemption? Asked Isaiah. Really? I'm as close to Police as West Redemption gets.

Y'all don't get it, said Tiffany-Dawn. It's a family deal, and the only ones that can handle it are me or Willy. Now Willy, stay here! I'll---

No! you're pregnant Tiff! Said Wilhelmina.

Last time I checked, so are you and Chryssie, said Ivy. We really need to turn this over to the----

No! said Wilhelmina. It ain't how it works.

We gotta draw a line, said Chrysanthemum. This is *our* husband, Ivy. King Willow, *we CANNOT allow* this! We're honest people, we bother no one, but we aren't going to play victims. Queen Hibiscus, Tiff? This is a *we* deal.

No! Said Isaiah. You're part of the Westia Fellowship! It's protected by my crew. Troll, was it the Steel Wheel Confederates?

The Steel Wheel Conf-idiots, mumbled Wilhelmina darkly.

Was it your brother in Law who did this? Did Big Black Angus do you like this?

He didn't answer.

Queen, you're not backing some of us, he finally said. We can't help it if we believe as we believe.

Teddy-Bear, hush! Said Wilhelmina. This is personal, Queen.

Can you explain that? Why would Big Black Angus do this to you? I thought you two were buddies….

Stay out of it, ok? said Wilhelmina. If Angus or his boys did this it's a family blood feud….red neck stuff. Either he dies---- or I do.

Every one turned and stared at her.

You can't do your own brother, said Mingo.
Wilhelmina snorted.

Y'all ain't the boss of me! She answered coolly. I'm not one of your cholas, or gang bangers.

Little Red? Said Troll. I done told you, ok?

Don't you be acting mad with me, ragamuffin!
Please hush up that mess! Please?

Let me be, ragamuffin!

I won't have it, darling!

I said what I said!

I'ma take you over my knees in a minute! Said Troll. Anyway, Angus wouldn't do this.

She smiled and kissed his forehead.

Baby, this is a family thing, said Wilhelmina.
I *am* your family! Said Troll.

She said nothing for a moment. She began to stroke his dreadlocks gently.

I know you are sweetheart. Which is why I'll handle it!

I need you to chill out, muffin!

Chill me out then!

How?

Laughing, she kissed him.

Are you chilled out?

A little you'll have to do a little more.

I'm injured.

The relevant area seems unharmed.

You still can if-----

Ok, ok, there are other people in here, said Ivy.

Elder? Queen? Said Wilhelmina. You got nothing to do with it *now*...

Baby I'm parched, said Troll wearily.

If you quit *drooling* when that skanky yellow bone nurse comes in---

Oh G, are you starting that again?

I don't want her in here! Neither do Chryssie, Tiff, Saff or Vy.

I can't control that, and I have *not drooled*! Troll laughed, then started to cough.

Can you go get me a Zippy Juice, muffin? He said. Please?

Wilhelmina gave him an icy look.

You're avoiding the subject!

Quit being jealous! You know where I sleep! Next to you!

Teddy-Bear, I *mean* it! Quit *eyeballing* that skank!

I have not eyeballed any one!

Yeah, right!

Too much meat on her...I like my meat close to the bone, said Troll.

She poked out her tongue at him.

Zippy Drink? Apple? I said please, ok?

Fine! But don't make me beat her down!

Why would you? You know you're the only crazy girl I love!

Wilhelmina grinned. You're not counting Safflower?

Wild and crazy ain't the same thing, he said.

They all laughed.

I *better* be your only crazy girl, you Teddy-Bear!

You won't be if I die of thirst....will you ladies go with?

Ragamuffin!

Tell the nurse I need water too.

She huffed but got up all the same.

Ok! Just quit being bossy!

When Wilhelmina left the room with the other women he said to Isaiah, Don't let my Little Crazy

Willy do nothing reckless, ok? She might kill Angus for sure. Stop 'er.

Was it Black Angus ?

Big Red? Black Angus, he said carefully, Black Angus is a dumb-ass. A buddy. Big ole Orc...

That's what I hear he calls you, said Mingo.

Calls you an elf, said Troll. Romero says you're a vampire, I hear...

Mingo grinned.

Beats being an Orc, *retard*, he answered.

Troll smiled.

He's a buddy, said Troll. I don't know if it was him behind it or not, but I seriously doubt it…..he's pretty much turned his back on Lil Red and me….

Why?

If it's all the same, Queen, I'd rather not discuss it.

Aw come on Troll! Said Mingo. What about MaGoo?

Troll laughed.

MaGoo? My pocket size buddy? I doubt it.

Are you sure?

MaGoo's my brother. That little crook is too busy scamming people… he's confused.

Isaiah nodded.

Would you like to tell me about that? Is that why this happened?

I can't discuss it. This is not on Goo.

Troll, we need to understand what's going on here, said Isaiah. This might be about us.

Nah...MaGoo? He said. He's just confused---both of them--- by how me and my lady are changing....

Right! Some would say you are both hippy flakes, said Mingo trying not to laugh. Vegans, Freegans, naturist, nudist, barefoot, top-free lifestyle, simple living flakes!

Troll laughed and winced.

Ain't that a description of you two? Asked Troll.

Isaiah looked genuine confused.

The say the same about you both, Elder, said Troll. You told me that you two are Adamites and domestic Nudist!

We never said that! Said Isaiah.

Do you wear clothes when you're alone in private?

No, said Mingo.

See? You claim you like sleeping under a tarp or under the stars....

We do! Said Mingo.

My favorite flakes!

They all laughed.

We don't really do the nudist thing, unless we're alone, said Mingo, but we do live simply.

You and him act just like he does with my big bro, Romey, said Isaiah to Troll, bemused.

Troll smiled and said, He can't stand me!

You two jus' need to get to know each other, said Mingo. He's into simple living too!

We're ahead of our time, said Troll. They laughed harder.

He was as tall as Isaiah's brother, Romero and equally as dark and brawny. At times Isaiah thought that they were family. Like Romero, he wore thick dreadlocks and a beard, as well as glasses, but there a gentleness to Troll that truly made him seem more like a Teddy-Bear than anything else. Both Isaiah and Mingo felt protective of him. Notwithstanding the occasional half serious threat to take Wilhelmina over his knees, he was a playful, kindly man. And what no one knew was that she liked being spanked by him, and loved making love after he did it. It was part of their foreplay for him to scold her then spank her.

The slender Wilhelmina adored him, though when she first saw him naked, saw the size and girth of his member, she was convinced that it was physically impossible for her to make love to him. She was gripped with despair. Even so, she adored him, and stalled him for any intimacy beyond what they could give each other with their hands and mouths. But he was too in love with her to be driven away. He was also patient.

It was Isaiah who urged her to marry Troll. She told her friend to mind her own business. Wilhelmina had a mind of her own. Yet she loved and trusted Isaiah. Finally she confessed her fears to Isaiah, who offered her some simple advise.

I'm scared.

Of what?

I'd rather not discuss it! What's it to you?

You're both good, sweet people, and you deserve the best, said Isaiah.

Awwww! Said Wilhelmina, spontaneously hugging Isaiah.

So tell me..what are you scared of?

You know…intimacy---with *him*, nosy!

Why?

Maybe…maybe he'll tear me open.

Isaiah patted her hand.

I never have heard of that kinda thing, said Isaiah. One day ten pound babies may come out of down there. What he has can't be worse than that. We're indestructible down there.

Queen, Troll is…my Troll is a *monster*! Down there…great to look at, but a thing is scary *big*!

Count yourself lucky!

Queen! I'm *serious*!

Ok. I have a suggestion to make.

What?

Spit or KY Jelly, and plenty of it. Tightness makes for happy couples.

They both laughed until they cried.

How would *you* know what I should do?

Well… Elder Mingo, silly goose.

Are you *serious*?

He's a regular dragon!

Get out….

Big things come in small packages.

Elder Mingo? He's----*big*?

Gurl, let me tell you! Said Isaiah. An ancient Oak tree.

Nah-uh! Not that I would notice!

Big man, big tool, little man, all tool, said Isaiah. You need to hang out with me and my sisters in law…the things you would learn!

No wonder you're so happy! Said Wilhelmina.

They giggled.

Actually he was helped by Mingo and Romero. Surprisingly, though he helped, Romero did not seem to care for Troll. He mostly helped for the sake of learning. Just as he once viewed Mingo with distrust and dislike, viewing him as an interloper, he viewed Troll with the same spirit. That he and Troll looked so much alike made it worst.

All of Isaiah's and Mingo's effort to bring the two closer met with iciness from Romero, and shy embarrassment from Troll. As for Wilhelmina, she developed a deep, unshakable detestation for Romero, compounded by loathing inspired by her realization that Romero disliked her and Troll. When she met Mouse and realized how much she looked like her, she felt a sense or revulsion when she realize that she might be one of Romero's type.

Eeeew! She said to herself.

She and Mouse, however, became great friends, as did she with Romero's other wives and Pilegeshim.

I don't like the guy, Squirt. I can't tell y'all who to be friends with, but I don't intend to associate with him.

Great Romey, that's just great.

Sorry sis. Something about him freaks Mommy and Papa out…I don't want him around, ok?

When Mingo approached him, Romero was open and honest.

He weirded out my ma, said Romero.

Why?

It's weird how we look alike! I don't need the confusion for Mami!

Even so Romero agreed to help Mingo and
Troll when he heard that Troll was building
a Tiny house on wheels. Actually Troll
didn't need help. He was a good carpenter,
and was perfectly capable. He simply
wanted to know Romero, so he readily
agreed when he heard Romero wanted to
help. Selfishness was Romero's motivation.
He too wanted to learn how to build one.
They barely spoke as they worked around
each other, as friendly as Troll was. Both did
a great job of studying each other without
being noticed. Troll, who had no family to
speak of, felt a deep sense of fascination,
and wondered what it would be like if he
and them were family.
Then the Tiny house was finished.
Relieved, Romero took to avoiding any
contact with Troll.
The little house was like a jewelry box. It
was sparsely furnished with foldable Shaker
furniture, refinished or made by Troll.
Wilhelmina was ecstatic. It mattered not to
her that people thought they were crazy for
living in such a small home.
They moved into the tiny clutter free little
home on the day they married.

Then they rode off on his lovingly restored Harley, originally purchased from a junkyard, for their highway honeymoon into New Mexico. Camping at times, staying in bed and breakfasts at others, they were gone for weeks.

They came back solidly bonded. Troll, occasionally given to silent brooding, was joyous and deeply at peace. The murderous, quiet Wilhelmina came back a new woman. Centered and self assured, master and conqueror of the mighty python and its adorable owner, she knew she was married for life.

In the morning until early afternoon she managed the gift shop in the vast Westia Fellowship Hall for Isaiah. Thereafter she worked with her husband repairing and refinishing furniture, and building twig furniture from boughs taken from tree trimmings.

He purchased an old abandoned store front with some acreage for a few thousand dollars a few years before because it was near Toot 'n Tote'm, where she then worked. He had no idea that he existed at the time.

He was raised by Rose, a Kenyan nurse who
he called Auntie, though she was his cousin.
He knew nothing about his family or
personal history. When he asked, his kindly
Auntie told him that he was an orphan.
They lived in a modest bungalow in the
West Redemption, near Methodist Hospital,
where he thought she worked. He
practically raised himself, since she worked
very hard, and worked all hours.
He had food, shelter, and clothes, but little
else. The small, ramshackle little bungalow
had no radio or television. He was friendly
to the other children around him, but he
mostly kept to himself. Even though he was
never told so directly, he was given the
strong impression that he was living in
hiding, and that he should keep to himself.
He made no close friends. In his early teens
he met his best friend, a diminutive boy
who others called MaGoo, because he wore
strong glasses.
MaGoo's family seemed to be desperately
poor, and so to an extent both of them were
outcasts, though no one picked on Troll
because of his size. Part of what drew
MaGoo to Troll was that no one bothered
him when he was with the bigger, quiet boy.

The two became close friends. They shared a love of the woods, and began to hang out in the woods together. They had no camping equipment, but the learned in the Library to build temporary shelters, and how to make fires, by watching survival videos. They also learned about edible wild plants of North Texas.

He grew so fast, that it seemed that he outgrew his clothes every few months. His clothes always seemed ragged, and ill fitting, and he was always in need of a haircut, so he was teased and called Troll. Yet where he dressed that way out of need, other kids from the prosperous suburbs, wore distressed jeans and ragged t shirts out of a sense of youthful disaffection, and he was popular with them. They dressed that way out of choice, he out of poverty. But among those kids, to be called a Troll was considered cool, not a put down. At any rate, he was so likeable, and had a good sense of humor, and took no offense, so others called him Troll with affection, and maybe a small measure of pity. His hair was worn in a thick Afro.

A young Janitor at the school, a young Jamaican black man called Hiram, took pity on him and taught him to twist his hair into dreadlocks. He also taught him about Ganja, as a sacred weed of wisdom, that altered consciousness, and brought one into a state of spiritual openness to the Heavens. So Troll learned that to smoke was something that was done as a part of worship. Since he was not any sort of worshipper, he avoided smoking it.

Hiram and his wife, who Hiram called his Queen, took him under their wing, and taught him to buy himself clothes at Goodwill, with the little money he earned cutting lawns and cleaning yards.

To save money on clothes, his aunt taught him to tie sheets into tunics and robes to wear around the bungalow, or at times just a towel around his waist. When he was home by himself, which was often, he became comfortable with wearing nothing at all.

He grew up haunting the libraries with MaGoo, and tramping through the woods in the Nature Center on Mountain View, not far from I-20, as well as any other woods that he could find near his home within biking distance. He was friendly and polite, but fought a sense of loneliness, born of having no family.

One day he found a book on the topic of Naturism, and was intrigued. He devoured it and any other book that he could find on the topic of Nudism. He began to haunt used book stores, hoping to find more books on the subject, and found magazines about nudism instead.

Like any growing boy, he was intrigued to see the pictures of women with no clothes, but was fascinated that men, women, children, some of them attractive, some not, seemed to be happily engaging in normal activities with no clothes on.

In his late teens he found his way to a nudist camp ground near Fort Worth, and was treated with polite friendliness, though with a measure of curiosity. He was the only black person there. A wiccan hippy, family, the Bells, took him under their wings. The wife, Ivy, openly admired the size of what she called his equipment and his physique, with the indulgent approval of her husband, Slope. They were hairies, as they called themselves, meaning that they did not shave or cut their hair. They wore their hair in long pony tails. They took pride in keeping their pubic hair well groomed.

She had straw brown hair, and piercing Violet eyes. What she called her big bush was a natural red. Quick to laugh, and smile, she was a muscular, thin woman, with a narrow waist, thick, strong runner's legs, and flawlessly tanned skin. She had tight little pear breasts with large red nipples that he couldn't stop looking at. She was amused by his callowness, but impressed by his endowment.

The women took charge of him. They bound his growing dreadlocks into a thick ponytail with a black ribbon, and he loved the result.

He became Ivy's pet. To his surprise she was an art teacher. She was not much older than Romero or her daughter, which he found curious. While in the woods on a hike, alone with Ivy, the wife, she spread a towel behind some bushes, and asked him to apply sun tan lotion to her, and to brush the bush. He laughed and followed her instructions. She explained that due to a medical condition her nipples were sore, and did he mind licking and sucking them to make her feel better. He smiled and did it as she masturbated, until he offered to assist there to. Then she gave him his first blow job, and spent the afternoon initiating him into lovemaking.

As they lay in each other's arms in the after grow, he chuckled.

What, cutie?

You talk so dirty! He said. Fuck me! Fuck my pussy! Let me suck your cock!

That isn't dirty! She said laughing. Does it turn you on? Come on, tell the truth!

Well, *yeah*!

See, she said. It's part of making love, talking raw. I tell you I wanna fuck you, eat my pussy, let me suck you big black cock----

He moaned.

-----because it turns me on too, but I mean I wanna make love to you.

What's the difference?

Oh baby! It's gonna be a joy to show you!

She openly discussed it with the husband and her only child, a teenage daughter, with delight. Periwinkle studied him, especially his penis. They congratulated Troll, and toasted both of them with a glass of wine.

He was confused.

Later that evening, Periwinkle, the daughter, took him into the woods with a beach towel and some candles, and a bottle of wine.

I'ma show you a few things that old hag can't! she said.

She's hardly older than us!

She's in her twenties, which makes her an old woman!

But for the fact that she had curly purple hair, and green pubic hair, she looked like a younger version of her mother. She explained that Slope and Ivy had an open marriage, and that Ivy was her step Mother.

Dude, you know as young as she is, she can't be my mother!

How old is your father?

Ancient! He's like forty!

Oh! Does he have a girl friend?

No.

No offense, but is he gay?

You scared he wants to suck your cock?

Periwinkle laughed. Don't worry! He's not gay!

Doesn't he mind that I screwed his wife?

No! He's grateful!

Why?

She needs dick, but you're the only dude that's turned her on! Slope was wondering if she was into me!

Ohh!

See? He doesn't wanna lose her.

Why would he?

Daddy's impotent. But he adores her!

Promise you won't try to take her away from him?

How could I?

She laughed.

You're so innocent! Promise?

Absolutely! Totally! Will it bother her if she knows me and you---

Are you kidding?

Does it bother you, Periwinkle?

Does what bother me?

That I fucked your step mother.

Who cares?

Can I do her and still do you?

Sure! Now quit worrying and come here
and fuck me!

She was his first girl friend. She never
complained if he gave her step Mother what
her father couldn't. Dour, intense,
passionate, she was his only love then, right
until the day she was found hanging in her
closet.

Slope Bell became the older brother and
father figure Troll had never had. They
argued about everything, especially politics,
which Troll knew little about. Slope was a
socialist, and gradually won Troll over. Yet
if he was a socialist, he also liked making
money. He bought and repaired old houses
in South redemption. He made Ceramics
and twig furniture. Everything he made he
sold. Troll became his sidekick and assistant.
Slope Bell rhapsodized about wine and beer
making, and about the making of cheeses at
home. Troll listened, taking it all in. He
assisted Slope as much as he could in all his
hobbies, and learned a great deal. He
developed a passion for brewing beer and
wine and cheese making.

Slope and Ivy talked endlessly about nature, simple living, small houses, camping, protecting the earth, Carbon foot print reduction, recycling, Naturism, Veganism, hairiness, and on and on. They played guitars, sang, drunk wine, argued, fought, made up and seemed crazy.

Wadaya expect? Said Ivy. We're hippies!

He was hooked. He spent more time in their home than he did in the old bungalow where he still lived. Their house became more a home to him than anywhere. Usually he slept with Periwinkle, or with Ivy in the guest room.

At the end of that first weekend Periwinkle gave him their phone number, and drove him to downtown Redemption, from where he caught a bus home.

Call us during the week! Said Slope. We're going out to a nudist camp near Tulsa!

You're coming with!

Great! Said Troll.

The next time he saw them later in the week, to his surprise, Ivy and Periwinkle wore their hair in dreadlocks.

The Bells became his surrogate family.
Except on Holy Days, which meant every
Friday and Saturday, there were no family
meals as such at the Bell house. They
nibbled throughout the day, and drank wine
or smoke weed in the evenings.
Bowls of fruit and vegetables were in every
room of the house. Everyone ate when they
felt like it. Ivy generally made them food
when they asked her to, otherwise they
raided the fridge and hoped for the best.
What they did together was drink wine with
cheese in the evenings, then they discussed
what they drank and tasted critically.
The Bells were Reformed Jews. In fact they
were disaffected Orthodox Jews. Yet nudism
was irreconcilable with their faith, so they
worshipped among the Reformed. They
taught him about Judaism, and he drank it
all in. Until then, he really didn't take the
idea of G-d seriously.
They treated Troll as one of the family,
including when it came to the High
Holidays and Sabbath. It little surprised
them when Troll decided to convert.

The Bells were High School teachers, and they viewed him as a favored student. He was in and out of their house, like a relative. Periwinkle and her Mother, Ivy, introduced him to body building. Ivy, an art teacher, saw his large muscular body as a piece of clay for her to shape. Under their tutelage, he became a body building buff, and regularly started jogging. His body transformed into a piece of living evolving sculpture. When he looked into the mirror, for the first time in his life he truly loved what he saw.

Ivy painted miniatures, and never any painting larger than a letter size sheet. Portraits were of no interest to her, but she painted images of his changing body. From her he learned and was taught him to love beauty wherever he found it. From her he learned to love culture, painting, music, poetry. In exchange, he gave her the pleasure that a younger man can give an older woman, even if he was her daughters lover.

Mister Bell was a Shop teacher. From him
Troll learned more than he could ever thank
him for. He taught him to work with his
hands, to fix engines, to ride motor cycles, to
make twig furniture, to weave baskets,
make cheeses, bake breads and to brew beer
and wine.
He also taught him to live with the pain of
loving without being loved back, and
knowing that your woman belongs to
another man, even when the man was one
who you viewed as a son. Troll was
determined to avoid living that lesson.
His other sidekick, MaGoo, was extremely
secretive, but he told him that he too was in
fact a Jew. Troll was endlessly curious, and
MaGoo taught him a great deal about his
faith, which he called Ancient Judaism.
Moved by his friends curiosity about
Judaism, MaGoo, who always wore a
beanie, he bought a large one for him, as
well as a Star of David. Thereafter, Troll
always wore one, if mostly under a base ball
cap worn backwards, like MaGoo.

MaGoo told him stories of a friend he had once had called Priest, though his real name was Romero. MaGoo swore that Romero looked identical to him and was probably a long lost twin. Troll took it half seriously, and laughed at him.

Dude, I'm serious!

Whatever, you little clot!

He was taught to work hard by his Auntie, who told him she barely had any money. So, he mowed lawns, cleaned yards, and waited tables to make money to help his Auntie. In fact, he loved waiting tables. He found a part time job waiting table at Cosmic Comida, a Mex-Tex hippie restaurant, which featured many Vegetarian and Vegan dishes. The Chef and owner, Safflower, took him under wing. He met her the first time that The Bells took him there. She was Slope's adopted sister, from a Sephardic Jewish Dominican family.

She was in a bitter tirade, cursing her waiter, who finally fled after she smacked him on the head with a stainless steel bowel before pulling her gun.

I wait tables, said Troll without thinking. They looked each other up and down. She was nude, but for an old truckers hat and a gun belt slackly worn.

Who the *FUCK* are you?

Troll.

What the *fuck* kinda name is that?

He said nothing.

Slope, where ja all find this big *fucking* animal?

For the first time he and Safflower looked at each other. They briefly stared into each other's eyes. His knees shook. Abruptly she looked away, and he felt as if he stumbled and was about to fall.

He's *hot!* Is he some sorta ass fucker? He's queer, isn't he?

Oh my G-d! said Periwinkle. *NO*! he is not *queer*!

It would be great if he really could wait tables!

No way, Saff! Said Slope.

G-d *dammit*, Slope! Help a bicth out!

I *forbid* you to work here, Troll, said Ivy to him.

Hey, you don't *own* him! Said Periwinkle. He's not your slave!

Neither do *you*! Said Ivy. Dammit, Peri, I saw him first, ok?

You still don't own him!

Save your attitude for somebody else!

I need a *waiter* Slope! Wailed Saff.

You shoulda thought of that before you hit Smitty on the head with that cast iron skillet! Said Slope.

Quit being an *asshole Slope*! All of you! He's here to *eat*, Saff, not to be brain fucked by my psychotic sister!

And I feel like sucking his *cock*, but things don't always work out the way we plan! *I NEED A FUCKING WAITER!*

Find someone else, Saff! Said Ivy furiously.

Fine, dammit! Just let him help me out today, if he wants!

Don't *do it!* Whispered Periwinkle in his ear. She'll eat you *alive*! My Aunt's a *psycho*!

Shut up Peri! She screamed then busted into tears. I *heard* you! You disrespectful little bitch! That's how you think of me? Who nursed you when you had Mono? Who got rid of your zits?

I'm sorry! Said Periwinkle.

Who makes you that lentil soup you like? As good as I am to you? After all I do for you! None of you give a *shit* about me!

Saff, stop it! Said Ivy. Shut up!

I expect cruelty out of Ivy, but you too, Peri? Periwinkle started crying.

Aunt Saff, I said I'm sorry!

Please don't argue! Said Troll. I'll do it! I'll do it!

Well, it's up to you, said Slope. You could at least let him eat!

It's ok, I'll eat later, said Troll.

Ok, said Safflower smiling, wiping her eyes.

Tips, and I'll give you pretty good dough.

Among *other* things, I bet, mumbled Ivy bitterly.

Not counting a *STD* or two, mumbled Periwinkle darkly.

Ignore them! Said safflower. Tips and 10 an hour!

Wow!

Cool?

Cool.

We're not high volume, but our stuff is high dollar, and my customers are big tippers.

You are a nudist, right?

Yeah.

Well? Nude up! Strip off the rags!

She studied him as he disrobed.

Body builder, huh?

Not really. Vy is trying to make me one.

Runner mostly.

Now let's get your pretty ass in my kitchen and apron you up!

Where is it?

Follow me.

She had honey colored skin, and chestnut colored hair. Her thick curly pubic hairs grew thinly to her belly button, and her forearms and calves were downy with little brown hairs. For reasons that he never understood, the hairiness of her muscular body gave him a crackling diamond cutter. Unlike many Dominican women, she had a perky, muscular rear and thighs. Curly brown pubic hair grew in between her legs, and to the inner edge of her rear. He began to fight a losing battle with a hard on. She walked so fast that her rear swung.

I feel you *watching* me butt, asshole!

I can't help it, you're right ahead of me.

Are you looking at my ass?

Ahhh----

It's ok to check out my ass. You like it?

He laughed.

Awesome!

Do you like to fuck?

Yes *ma'am*.

Well' no touching in the dining area. You want some pussy? Fine! Ask me! Just not in front of my diners!

Ahhhh—

If you're nice, I'll Cow girl straight and reverse later!

Peri----

Peri doesn't need some dick as bad as me,
asshole! And don't ask for a fuck when
we're busy! I'm trying to make a living here!
But I'm generous about fucking, ok?
Well----
You're going to need an apron. Social rules?
Be polite and gracious! Don't *fucking* curse
in front of these *motherfucking ass*holes, ok?
I never curse!
Learn to! Don't fuck my customers during
work hours! If you fuck'm after hours, wear
a rubber. Do you do guys?
No.
Why the fuck not? Fine. I don't do pussy.
No one handles that fat cock in this place
but me. I'ma give you a longer apron! I
don't want any skank or fag checking out
your dick! When you're here? Your cock is
mines!
What?

Look, sweety, I haven't got the time to cock hunt. I haven't gotten any cock in a while. I couldn't fuck Smitty---his balls smelled like his ass. And I can't fuck anybody I do business with, it's not professional. I got an oral fixation. I like to suck cock, but I think free love is bullshit. I means a bunch of over the hill assholes wanna get their dicks sucked, even though they can't get it up. I generally have one man only in my life and right now I'm looking. I own all the boners you get during working hours, ok? Like the one you got now!
Huh?
She got on her knees to tie on his apron from the front.
Cock-sucking and fucking calms me down, but I can only be with one man at a time.
From now on that's you.
You don't know me!
It's it a deal or not?
Me and Peri—and Ivy---I have---
I'm not talking about that, I'm talking here!
Ok.
You can share my bed when you work late!
Ok.

I'ma need you here 24-7 just about….now, I can't let you go out in front of my customers like this! This fat hard-on will scare the white people! You'll scare them.
The sacrifices you must make!
She chuckled and drew his manhood into her mouth.

There was a tiny dining room in the back that featured nude dining, and Troll was the favored waiter in that room, though he was in fact the only waiter for a long time. He waited on the nudist diners in the nude. In the main area he wore a wrap around apron. There were no chairs or table in the nude room. Many small group of diners dined while lounging on the floor with their bare hands, off their hands.
There were no spoons knives or forks in the restaurant. What surprised him was the neatness, and fastidious politeness of the bare hand eaters. He expected to be gross out at first, but he quickly came to see that there was nothing gross about eating from one plate with bare hands.

Slope's adopted sister, an exile from San Francisco, possibly on the run from a warrant, the tall, buxom Jewish-Dominican American, Safflower, was a hairy nudist. A rageaholic, she cursed like a sailor, and threw things around the outdoor, open air kitchen when mad, and played acid rock endlessly, to Trolls annoyance.

She also claimed to be a pacifist.

One of Troll's jobs became to keep her from getting into fist fights with anyone who annoyed her. A devout naturist, she worked barefoot and nude, but for aviator sunglasses, an apron and a Chefs pouf; the pouf was in fact an old, grubby, decrepit truckers cap. Ropes of dreadlocks always spilled down her back. She also wore shoulder holster with a Sig-Sauer 9 mm P229 hand gun, and a few clips of bullets, as well as a Bowie strapped to her hip. Every where she went she was trailed by a black German Shepherd guard dog.

She was the hardest working person he ever met. The Restaurant had no electricity, and the only fuel was firewood.

She prepared many raw Vegan dishes, even though she did cook meats, most of her customers were Vegetarians. A wiccan Jew, she spoke endlessly about vibes and crystal energy. She also smoked copious amounts of Marijuana, and usually ended the evening with him with a frisky tumble on the straw mattress on which she slept in a tiny house behind her restaurant. It was a small round Cottage with a conical thatched roof, and sat in the middle of a crazy, quilt work garden of edible flowers, vegetables and berries. Much of what she cooked she grew.

The cottage was covered in a colorful mural of a garden filled with nudist of all colors. It was painted by Safflower. Behind it, hand dug into the ground, there was a sweat lodge, and a steam room, as well as a hot tub. Only a privilege few were allowed to use any of that, and for a hefty fee.

She claimed that Troll's lean, hard body was her one addiction. She loved smoking weed and sucking Troll's dick, she claimed. Marijuana was medicine that soothed her temper. She loved to be sodomized by him, and insisted on anal sex at least for a while when they made love.

The Cosmic Comida was located on a dirt road in the middle of nowhere, far into the edge of the Trinity River Forest, East of downtown Redemption, far into the woods, behind a thick copse of Pecan trees. In the autumn it was a great place to harvest Paper shell Pecans. The small building where it was housed was the oddest he ever saw. It resembled a thatched Quonset hut, and it was built of bamboo.

It was an unlicensed restaurant.

Many of the dinners ate out among the trees in the nude, shielded by a bamboo grove. Several also paid Safflower a fee weekly to be permitted to set up a tent.

Both Periwinkle and Ivy mockingly called it the Cosmic Commune, but they loved going there. If it was not really a Commune, the Cosmic Comida was a hippy colony.

The only difference in between Cosmic and Comic is an S, said Ivy dryly, though she and Slope were frequent diners.

Slope supplied the Cosmic Comida with his home made beers, wines, and cheeses.

Ivy and Safflower bore each other a cordial, bitter detestation, partly because each wanted the other out of Troll's life.

Safflower was Slopes' half sister., so they tolerated each other.

His Auntie came around less and less after he became a teenager. She was in the country illegally, and he discovered that in fact she wasn't a nurse at all, but an illegal healthcare worker. He came to realize as he got older that she had another life, and that the little bungalow where he lived was not really her home. It was where she housed him.

Just at about that moment, she was arrested by Immigrations. He saw her at a detention facility in down town Redemption, and she told him that he had family in the city, but he could get no more out of her. She briskly told him of the bills that had to be paid, and when they had to be paid. Beyond that she would say no more.

She told him to make sure the bills got paid or he would be in the dark and cold without water.

It terrified him. Then something strange happened. At the end of the month he received a letter confirming that all of the bills were paid, along with a few hundred dollars in cash for food and his expenses. Soon afterwards a brand new television and a brand new boom box were delivered to the bungalow.

He lived with a profound fear of the poverty with which he lived.

Finding n abandoned store on loop twelve, he turned it into a squat.

He repaired the storefront and opened his "antique furniture store", selling scavenged furniture harvested from dumpsters and reconditioned by him. What he mostly sold was twig furniture, which he learned to make from Slope, and watching videos on YouTube. He made them with just about any flexible tree trimmings he could buy or scavenge. Originally he sold them on the side of the road on the far west edge of the West Redemption.

He began taking over old shacks then he refurbished them, for rent or resale. He also got an old shot gun shack at a tax sale across the street from Wilhelmina's home on the West edge of the Redemption.

It was there that they met one day soon after he moved in temporarily, while he made repairs. He preferred to live in the back room of his store.

He was wearing raggedy cargo shorts with
nothing else on as he mowed the front lawn.
She looked at him with utter loathing,
assuming it was Romero, who she detested.
But the thick mane of dread locks, and the -
bulky, rippling muscularity of his physique
told her otherwise. Later on she found out
that he was a Naturist, and practiced
nudism at home. Other than a modest matt
of hair on his chest, his body was hairless.
He did have a thick, well tended beard, and
a head covered by thick dread locks that fell
to the middle of his back.
What made her knees wobbled to where she
was afraid to move was his physique. With
powerful, muscles, a slender waist, and
broad brawny shoulders, full thighs and
calves, he looked like a Greek sculpture of
an athlete come to life.
She moaned involuntarily.
When he saw her he stopped dead in his
tracks. He looked the slender jogger up and
down. She was on the tall side of medium,
had a large red afro and adorable freckles.
But what mesmerized him where the
strange haunting eyes. He grinned but for a
moment neither could say nothing.

Her leg muscle shook badly. She frowned at him, unmoving.

She had been jogging, and stood sweating in black spandex shorts and a skimpy sports bra, breathing through her open mouth, almost panting. She did not care for blacks, and cared even less for the muscular, bearded, dread lock wearing man. He wore a choker of tiny black beads, she noted. He gave her a look through his gold rimmed spectacles, and gave her another brilliant grin.

Hey neighbor! He said. And something tugged at her heart. She felt a unspeakable thrill and a twinge of fear. Not for her safety either.

She nodded curtly.

Hay is for horses. You moving in here, mister?

He smiled and nodded.

Mister? He chuckled. Remember me?

No.

Call me Troll.

Why would I do that? I refuse.

Why?

You certainly ain't a Troll!

Folks call me that cause I'm hairy.

You're not that hairy. I can't say I approve.

Don'tcha work at the Toot n Tote'm?

Yes sir. Used to.

I thought I seen you there. Ain't you been
on the news?

She groaned.

I'm tell you now, don't call me *Willy Earp*.

He laughed, and said, I *hated* that name!

Why?

It's insulting.

Exactly.

That gets on your nerves too?

Yes sir. It's----

Insulting?

Yes! Like Troll.

Most folks agree! Want a beer, ma'am?

There's a cooler on the porch.

Sure.

Normally she rarely drank.

Are you through jogging?

I run, I don't jog.

K. Are you through though?

Yup.

Then keep me company while I mow this
lawn!

Ok….

The beauty of this mower is you can talk as
you use it cause it don't make no noise.

She went into the yard wordlessly, thinking that there was no harm in being a beer to the good.

She took a beer out of a ice filled stainless steel bucket. The floor of the porch was carefully painted grey, and the rails were painted white. A few well tended Geraniums hung from the ceiling.   The beer was in an ornate bottle, but had no label. She took a swig.

Great beer, sir! She said. You didn't get this at the Toot n Tote'm, I betcha!

He threw her a grin over the shoulder.

It was the best tasting beer she ever tasted. There were Adirondack chairs made of Willow twigs on the porch with a small twig table in between. Something told her he didn't have many friends. Not wanting to leave, she sat on one; it was incredibly comfortable. She settled back and watched him mowed the lawn wordlessly through half open eyes. She felt comfortable, though she only wore running shorts and a halter. He moved with a slow lion like grace. The workings of his limbs and the muscles took her mind into a state of dreaminess---

Abruptly she pulled her hand from between her thighs, and prayed he had not noticed her rubbing herself. Masturbation was her one vice that she indulged in, and she kept it as her own secret. She hadn't realized she was doing it. She wanted to flee, but her legs felt rubbery.

She took a deeply breathed in the calming perfume of newly mowed grassed and the scent of Wild Blossoming flowers. It was late spring. It was a warm, pleasant day of a kind that made her love to be outdoors. Fleecy clouds were lazily floating by in a pale blue sky. Redbirds were singing in the ancient pecan trees that lined the streets; cicadas were chirping, and sweet smelling marigolds, roses and mums were in bloom along the side fences of the yard. The breeze was gentling and rustling the leaves, and the branches swayed in slow dance.

The breeze mussed her hair. She wondered if she looked a fright, but understood that it was alright all the same.

He hummed as he mowed.

She noted that he was using a motor less mower.

What kinda lawn mower you got there, sir? she finally asked.

Amish hand powered mower, ma'am, he said.

Why not use a regular mower?

It's all about the Carbon foot print.

Do what?

I don't care to pollute the air, he said flashing her a grin that made her feel weak and giddy yet again. It began to annoy her, how casually he worked his charm on her. Across the street, her brother Angus came out of the house and saw her sitting on the porch. He took a long, luxurious yawn, scratched his flat, hairy abs. His coppery hair worn in pony tail, along with closely cropped beard, he too wore cargo shorts and nothing else.

He squinted and leisurely ambled across the street.

My big bro, Bow-bow, said Wilhelmina with dry, mocking affection.

He leaned on the white picket fence and watched Troll work curiously, saying nothing.

Hey neighbor, said Troll, giving him a heathenish grin too.

Hey yourself, said Angus, smiling uncertainly at his sister.

Romero, what are you up to?

Huh? Said Troll.

Bow-bow, this ain't him, said Wilhelmina
with a shudder of confusion.
Get out of here…
Would I be sitting here if it was? She asked.
Romero?
Troll smiled.
That ain't my name.
Really?
Yup.
Ain't you Romero?
Nah, my name is *Ramiro*---but people call
me Troll.
Troll laughed.
Ain't this weird? Said Wilhelmina.
Angus shrugged.
What kinda mower is that?
I ordered it from Amish country, said Troll.
It's old fashion.
Seems to do the job real good, said Angus.
You two related?
Angus chuckled.
How can you tell?
Matching red hair? Your eyes?
Angus laughed.
What about'm?
You two got them eyes…They're
remarkable! Especially hers.

Wilhelmina Angus looked at him closely, and laughed.

That's my kid sister Willy. I'm Angus.

Care for a cold one, Red?

Angus laughed.

Red is what his dumbass friends call him, said Wilhelmina.

Oh, said Troll. Grab a beer, Red.

Sure!

On the porch!

And just that simply Angus and Troll became friends. Unlike his sister, who had no conception of herself s black woman, he took quiet pride in his blackness, little of it though there was, though he lived among whites who assumed he was one of them. He simply didn't bother to clarify the matter. Contrary to Willy, Angus had nothing against other blacks and counted many his friend. Like Romero, who his sister hated. It astonished him how much like Romero Troll looked.

Ever heard of a doppelganger? Asked Angus.

Huh?

A double, a mirror image. A twin.

Do what?

You got one.

Never mind, said Wilhelmina.

I been told there's some kid around here
who looks like me, but I have no brothers.
 Angus took a beer out of the melting ice,
twisted it open, and took a swig. He moaned
and melted into the other chair.
Dang! Where ja get this *beer?*
Homebrewed!
You gotta be kiddin' me!
No, honestly!
I *love* this!
First one's free, second one'll cost you, said
Troll grinning.
Angus laughed. How much?
Understand, this is gourmet beer…
Gourmet beer? Whatever, said Angus.
Two bucks a bottle, but with a meeting the
neighbors discount? Nothing.
Angus laughed.
He studied Romero.
Can you make a lot of it?
Yup.
Make it. I'll sell for you.
Troll studied him.
Sure.
Deal, said Angus. How about them
Cowboys?
Oh *G-d*! Wailed Willy wearily. Can't men
talk about anything else?

Both men laughed. They started chattering enthusiastically about football.

She got up, strangely feeling very much at home, determined not to sit through another long discussion of the Redemption Cowboys, and casually wandered through the open door into the small adobe cottage to explore. Troll glanced up briefly and did not seem to mind, and she was feeling nosy. It smelled of new paint, varnish, and roasting chicken.

Her stomach growled.

With a floor of ancient polished Oak, dark with age, the lovely adobe cottage was immaculate, but for a few unpacked boxes. The cathedral ceilings seemed about 15 feet high. She looked up with fascination at the dark, rough hewn round beams and Vigas that made up the ceiling. The cottage was elegantly, sparsely furnished. She wandered leisurely from room to room, swigging beer, looking at the newly painted rooms, and his furniture. It was all very well-designed and pleasing to the eye. South West Rustic, it was called. She smiled.

In the center of the living room on a red
Navajo rug, sat a small, old fashioned
Victorian horsehair couch covered in wine
colored leather, with an anti-Makassar on its
back, a matching chair, and a delicate
looking side tea table sat next to it. A flat top
steamer trunk served as a coffee table.
Facing the Windows was a fireplace. An
Oak blade ceiling fan wafted lazily around.
Other than a small coffee table with a cut
glass vase full of wild flowers behind the
couch, and a wreath of dried grapevines on
the wall, there was nothing else in the room.
He had a roll top desk in the corner of the
dining room with a bookshelf on top that
almost rose to the ceiling. It was crammed
with books. Near it stood a break front
China cabinet, displaying a full set of hand
painted Mexican crockery. In the center sat a
rectangular Mission dining table with
matching chairs. It was covered by a beige
linen table cloth. Across the room he had a
side board with wine bottles and goblets on
top, as well as two tall pewter candle
holders at each end.

Other than a high bed, covered with a multi-colored quilt, a dresser and a chair, there was little else in the bedroom. She noted a door to an ensuite. Every room had an Oak blade ceiling fan with brass fittings. Throughout the house, the wall trim was glossy white, the ceiling trim was white, and the walls were adobe brown. The floorboards and waist scatting were varnished oak. She stopped to study the family photos hanging in neat rows on the walls in thin black frames. They were photos purchased at garage sales of other people's families.

That realization made her feel a sense of compassion and sympathy for him.

In the tidy eat in kitchen, a chicken surrounded by vegetables, was roasting in a Westinghouse stainless steel Crockpot, steaming away. Next to it steamed a Proctor Silas rice cooker. She smelled rich Basmati rice fragrance with delight.

Copper pots and pans hung over an island near a reconditioned restaurant stove. Next to it sat a medium sized stainless steel fridge.

On the round Mahogany table in the center of the room sat a half full Decanter of Pinot Noire with a few goblets next to a cutting board with a wedge of cheese sitting on it, besides a tray of gourmet crackers. She picked up the cheese knife, cut off a tiny piece, chucked it in her mouth and kept moving.

Later she discovered that all of it was rent house window dressing. He lived far simpler than that.

She went into the large back yard.

She was pleased to see that it was weeded, mowed, and the back half was plowed. Apparently a garden was to be planted. She noticed a weight bench and weights in the car port. She walked around to the front back to the porch down the driveway. Her brother was gone. Troll was raking up the trimmings. She leaned on a pillar.

Where's my brother?

Took off. Told me to look after you.

Older brothers…dumbasses.

He laughed.

I wouldn't know.

Why?

Never had one. Brother or sister.

Wow, she said.

He looked at her curiously.

Your mom must be a black Martha Stewart, she said.

He shrugged.

I adore Martha. I never had a mother.

Wadaya mean?

I'm on my lonesome. No kin.

 Are you like an orphan?

Kinda.

Can't say I ever met one before.

I was raised by a make believe Aunt and she me told I had no parents.

Awww…that's sad…How can that be?

She told me they were gone.

Gone like dead?

He stopped and stared her and scratched.

I take it for granted that's what Auntie meant.

Gone might jus' mean runoff.

Huh?

Maybe they're alive.

I seriously doubt it.

Why?

People jus' don't abandon their kids.

You really believe that?

He shrugged.

I wish I coulda met my mom, you know?

Who knows? Maybe you will. I was raised by my mom…

You know something? I never really
thought that I might have parents
somewhere.
Look into it.
I would love to meet my mom….
Be careful what you wish for.
Don't you like yours?
No comment.
You gotta Pop?
Died in the Nam right after I was born.
Oh no…sorry.
He was a Marine.
Awesome.
You did a great job here. This place was a
wreck, she said.
He chuckled. But it had good bones, so
rehabbing it was easy. So do you like it?
Your house looks great, mister, she said.
Aw, can't you call a brother anything else? I
got a lot more to do.
Need a trash bag? I got plenty, she said.
Nah, he said, I compost.
Compost?
Yup. I the creating pollution.
You're something.
Don't you care about the ecology?
I guess…I notice you got weights….

Soon as I'm finished, I'ma pumped some iron...wanna join me?

She took a swig of beer and said nothing. She gazed at the lawn and liked how it looked.

You look tight, you jog, so I figure you work out too, right?

She look at him wordlessly.

You could spot me, he said, you could work out too. You seem to be in shape, but you gotta bulk up those muscles.

She said nothing to that.

Cat got your tongue, huh? He said, flashing her another one of his grins. Her knees quivered; she had to sit down.

You got a lovely home, she said. You done real good with it so far.

I been fixin' it, before I moved in---but I'ma rent it out and keep living my little cottage on wheels---or at my shop.

Where is your shop?

Up the way from Toot n Tote'm. You don't like me, do you?

She swigged her beer.

You seem cool. Can't say I care for coloreds---as a group.

Why?

It ain't personal. That's how mama raised
us….which is weird, cause we're colored
too. But don't say that in front of Mama.
He laughed at her indifferently.
You got that lily white skin going on with
them freckles? But your hair…and that
pretty little nose? You look a bit like a sister.
Right. I got black in me, she said. Daddy. I
seen you coming and going….
He flashed her another grin, and it was all
she could do not to grin back and lose her
dignity. Did he know how his laughter and
grins affected her?
Abruptly she felt put upon.
Quit *grinning* so sweet at me, She snapped.
Huh?
You're affecting me.
How?
You're smile makes me weak…. You *devil!*
He broke into a rich deep laughter, and she
felt wounded.
Don't you *laugh* at me! You dread lock
wearing *ragamuffin!*
I'ma dread lock wearing *ragamuffin, huh?!*
He laughed harder and she found herself
grinning.
Ragamuffin? Where ja get that word?
My Mama.

He laughed again.

She sounds like character.

Oh, you think it's funny? Well, for me? You're a *ragamuffin!*

He smiled without answering, but raised beer as a toast and swigged. When he was through with his lawn, he went around the side of his house. She followed him as he took the mower to the car port without need of further invitation or any hesitation. They worked out together, speaking little. As he did bench presses and she spotted him, she realized that she was standing with her crotch practically in his face. An inexplicable urge to laugh over came her, but he beat her to it. He had a deep, rich laugh that tugged at her insides. She smacked his head gently and laughed along. And then he did something which should have freaked her out, but it seemed very natural and innocent. He kissed her crotch, then kept on lifting his weights.

Kingdom of The Willows
Book 1: Blessing of The Mother
© Antonio R. Belizario

It didn't trouble her. She understood he
meant it as a reassuring gesture. At that
very instant she realized that this was a
gentle child-man. She intuitively sensed that
he was lonely, as was she. Somewhere in
that afternoon, she ceased to think of him as
anything other than her neighbor and new
friend.
You jus' a regular sweet ole Teddy-Bear,
ain'tcha? she said, trying to sound sarcastic,
but actually sounding amused and moved.
She laughed uneasily, because she sensed
that they were going to be together.
Thereafter, unless she was upset, ragamuffin
or Teddy-Bear was all that she ever called
him.
Afterwards he announced that he was going
to take a shower. It was evening by then.
Ain't you're folks gonna wonder where you
are?
At my age? She snorted. They know I can
take good care of myself.
 She followed him into the house.

It seemed the most natural thing in the world for her to follow him into the bathroom. She was sweaty and wanted a shower too. She leaned on the sink and watched him casually undress. Somehow that he wore no underwear did not surprise her. He smelled of cinnamon. He put his shorts in a hamper. She seemed to be under an enchantment.

He turned on some soft, quiet jazz.

Then he turned and she saw his member and gasped.

Do you mind?

She shook her head.

Is that thing real?

Pardon?

Is it supposed to be so big?

He said nothing.

She studied his hairy body, especially his manhood, and he stood looking at her with hands on his hips. Standing a few feet from him, she realized how powerful, how physically imposing he seemed.

I ain't here for no sex, ok?

He said nothing.

I hate hoes and skanks. I ain't one, ok?

He took off his spectacles and just gazed into her eyes.

May I---may I touch your thing?

Again he said nothing. He closed his eyes.
She reached over and took his manhood in
one hand. He gave a single moan, and her
insides shivered. He grew massive, hard,
and erect.
She dropped it, like it was red hot.
He open his eyes and looked at her like a
lion, without anger, or threat. His eyes were
full of total confidence.
I ain't going to suck you or fuck you, she
stammered, I ain't gonna do no sex. Ok?
Again he said nothing. He smiled and
stepped into the shower.
Somehow she felt as if he had just won,
without knowing what it was that she felt
she lost. An urge to slap his face came over
her.
Without speaking, without being asked, she
found that she stripped off her clothes
angrily and followed him into the shower.
He turned on the water, and let it glide and
beat all over him with his back to her.
It's too cool, she said.
Without any surprise at her presence in the
tub, without even looking back, he adjusted
it.

For a moment he stood with his broad back to her, leaning his head on his folded arms again the wall, letting the water fall on his back and shoulders. Something about this man seemed sad to her. His Dread locks fell to the middle of his back.

She ran her hands from his shoulders along his sides to his waist.

Nudity don't mean sexual, he said.

I ain't a sexual person, she said.

He didn't respond.

She held her forehead to his back with her eyes closed. He turned to face he and leaned back against the wall. They stared into each others eyes. She felt like crying briefly, without knowing why. She pressed her forehead into his chest. He did and said nothing. Lifting her head gently by the chin, he looked into her eyes. She didn't know why she did it, but she bit him hard on the shoulder until he bled. He breathed deeply, and winced when her teeth pierced his skin, but he did not move or say anything.

She licked away the blood.

Tears were flowing down her face, diluted by the water, but he could tell she was crying.

Now it's your turn, she said.

What?

Mark me on the same spot.

No!

Mark me!

He hesitated, then he bit her shoulder.

Harder!

Why?

You need to make me bleed!

I don't understand.

Do it.

He did, and felt strange when she tasted the sweet coppery flavor of her blood.

He didn't understand why, but he started to cry.

Then they stood with their foreheads touching, shyly staring into each other's eyes as the warm water beat on them. Later all that she remembered was the joy of his hand gliding over her skin, washing her, and of her hands on his skin. Then they held each other.

They did not make love. He showered himself, and she did too. All the while she looked at him wordlessly, warily. Then they washed each other's backs.

When they came out he dried her carefully. Taking blow dryer, he dried her hair carefully. He also bandaged their bite marks.

Those bite marks became a bonding symbol in between them.

He wrapped a panel of Hawaiian silk fabric around his waist and knotted the two top corners, creating a skirt that fell below his knees, though it left part of his thigh and leg uncovered.

He turned those devilish black eyes on him after putting on his specs.

You shouldn't have to put on those sweaty clothes again, young lady.

She laughed. I guess…what do you suggest? I'ma through 'em in the washer.

He got an old twin size sheet of black silk. He measured it against her, swiftly tore a swath along the edge, tied two corners together, then tied it to the corresponding edge. How he did it she did not know, but he helped her put it on, and suddenly she was wearing a sleeveless, calf length tunic that hung from both of her shoulders.

He tore a ribbon from the remaining swath, and brushing back her hair, tied it around her forehead in the back.

Then he took up the swath and tied it as a sash in a graceful bow under her breasts.

She looked in the mirror.

Dang! How did you do that? In few minutes
you turned that sheet into a fancy dinner
dress by tying a few knots!
He laughed.
Elegant things are sometimes really simple.
It makes me look so graceful.
 Look, he said, do you mind if I stay naked?
With the gate shut and my privacy fence
nobody can see into my yard.
You're weird, she said.
I'll keep this on----
No! She said.
It's cool, he said, leaving the sarong around
his waist and legs.
I'm a nudist, he told her. At least when I'm
home alone, or with someone who's cool
with it.
Stay naked if you want….maybe I might've
if you told me all that.
Maybe next time, he said.
She stayed without having to be invited.

They had dinner by casndle light in the
back yard on a round redwood picnic table,
after he draped it with a white table cloth
and set it with her help. He put on a CD of
smooth Jazz as they ate. Mostly they looked
at each other as they ate, occasionally
smiling. They also shared a bottle of
Sauvignon Blanc.
Normally I'm a Vegetarian, he said, mostly
Vegan, but I been craving baked Rosemary
chicken.
So can I ask you something?
What? Asked Troll.
What's your real name?
Huh?
I'm sorry, mister, but I ain't going to call you
Troll.
Why not?
I can't call a friend troll.
It's ok, it doesn't bother me.
It does me.
Troll for me means someone who grows out
their hair and is cool.
I'm still not gonna call you that.
Cool. I'm your ragamuffin, right?
Are you a thug?
Why?
I don't associate with'm.
Oh.

Are you an outlaw? Are you on the Lam?

He laughed.

Why would you think that?

Why won't you tell me your name?

Oh! Sorry. My *real* name is Ramiro. Ramiro X.

She gave him a stare.

You know what's weird? Big Brother has a old buddy from High School. Looks exactly you. Guess his name?

I got no idea.

Romero. Which is why my bro called you that. Romero Martinez.

Troll broke into his deep sounding laugh.

What are you laughing at?

Oh snap! That's *my* last name too! I say X cause I have no family.

A sense of eeriness came over her. feeling scared for him, she felt chilled and shivered.

For what it's worth? She said. He's nothing like you. I despise him.

Why?

He's an arrogant rich kid son-ova-bicth who likes to claim he and his harem of women are poor.

He has a *harem*?

Hell yeah! Married his childhood sweet heart, who used to be a drag king, I hear, then broke up his sister in law and her lady, Mouse, by having a baby with Mouse, then he turns around and has a baby with his sister in law too! If I was his wife? I would shoot him! He has all three living with him!
Are you serious?
I'm telling you!
What's a drag King?
Chick that dresses like a boy.
I thought that was a stud, he said.
Studs are gay. Drag Kings might be straight. They say his own *cousin* and *her* girl friend are his women, even though they're a couple! Sleazy ass rich folk!
Sounds like a modern day Caligula, said Troll. I don't know anybody rich.
Who's Caligula, yo?
Roman emperor. A Total dick.
Well *he* is too! Born with a silver spoon up his ass to two yuppies. Always Jewing down my brother when he does work on his motorcycles. You know why?
Why?
Says he's poor. There oughta be a *law*. I say, Big bro, charge him the right price! Stand up for yourself! But he's like, no, no! That my old friend! And he's poor!

Is he?

Hell no! Lives in a big ole *hacienda, a mansion* up on Page Street on *five acres* of land with three wives and a gaggle of sons. Ten thousand square feet! Fulla antiques! Place looks like a Museum! You know how much that house cost him?

How much?

Zip! The son-ova-bitch got it as a wedding present! The place is worth millions! We live in a tiny shotgun shack. *We're* the ones is poor!

He sounds like a character! He said. How do you know so much about them?

I work for his sister now. I seen their house. Get this: he lives next door to where he grew up, right? His folks still live there right?

He married the girl next door, huh?

Yes sir! She grew up with her grandmother. She gave them the house as a wedding present. His father owns a big company, and they own a buncha rent houses. Turns out the house he grew up in is just as large? And he's gonna get it when his folks either die or retire!

Wow! So he's a scammer, huh? Asked Troll.

And he's taking food out of my brother's
mouth? Lord, I *despise* him! I was acting a
little cold before, cause you put me in the
mind of him, but you're so sweet---well,
forget I said that! I don't know how many
high dollar cars and motorcycles they got
and he thinks he's *poor* cause he waits tables
in one of his rich grandmother's restaurant
some of the time. You might even know the
place.
Where is it at?
I think it's called Miguelita's? Jefferson Blvd,
in Downtown Redemption?
I've seen it! I thought of seeing if they let me
wait tables, but I'm intimidated.
Why?
It's so upscale.
Fancy, over priced hole, ask me! Said
Wilhelmina. I hate the rich. My mama owns
a little take out? You can get a full meal for
under sev'n bucks. You go to Miguelita's?
You're lucky to get Quesadillas for under
twenty! And she has at least four more
locations!
What does he really do? Asked Troll. Does
he work?

Kingdom of The Willows
Book 1: Blessing of The Mother
© Antonio R. Belizario

What do all rich boys do? A whole lot of
nothing. Claims he goes to college, claims
he's an artist, and humps his wife and two
live in women. Then goes across the street
and humps his cousin and her lady. A total
piece a slime.
How do you know they're his women?
They don't try to hide it! They keep having
babies by him! The idiots never heard of
birth control!
Well, said Troll, I don't run in those circles,
but I hear tell some rich folks are doing that
kinda thing.
For real?
They call it the quiver full movement.
The what, yo?
You know, he said, a quiver full? They want
as many baby's as they can have.
Be *fruitful and multiply*, she said dryly. More
like, be irresponsible and have a buncha
brats you dumb asses. Who's gonna think
that way if they ain't rich?
I guess they're pretty loaded, he said.
His family owns most of that neighborhood.
I call it Yuppie-ville. His sister's good
people, but him? I *despise* him.
You know his sister?

I work for her. She's like…like a Monk. She and her husband sleep in their mother's yard, under a tarp, come rain or snow. They hardly own any clothes. Everything goes to him. She grew up in a rich family living poor.

Wow! Really?

She and her husband? They're Pastors, even though they're not much older than us. They run a big ole church---they call it a Fellowship, but some people think it's just a gang thing. They're kinda sorta gang leaders---but they're tryna end the gang problem from within.

Sounds crazy to me!

Maybe, maybe! I just left Toot n Tote'm. I hated leaving, and went to work for her. but I'm told it's not safe for me anymore.

She took a sip of wine unhappily.

Why?

I hated leaving. That's the only job I ever had. I wanted to buy the place one day…

They paid me chickenfeed, but I got to do a job I was good at, you know?

So why did you quit?

Isaiah talked me into leaving…

Who?

My boss…I shouldn't call her that, she's a buddy.

Any regrets?

I miss some of the people I knew
there…anyway, I make a lot more money,
and I work better hours.

Ever thought of being a cop?

Nah, she said, don't get me wrong, I respect
the Police, but you gotta be a bully to be a
Cop.

I agree.

Why da I leave? The Police say the friends of
some of those I shot might wanna catch up
with me. I say bring'm on.

You like a fight, huh?

No, but I don't like running from one either.

You aren't running. You are retreating.

I hate that! It's as bad as running. Are you
making fun of me?

He gave her a surprised look.

Sorry…I'm angry to be run off my job!

Maybe it's a blessing in disguise!

Maybe! Isaiah say's after six months? I will
be part owner of the Fellowship shop I'm
running. I'll bring it up in two months. I'm
trying to make it earn more money.

How?

Well, I want people from the neighborhood
to see it as a neighborhood store, not just a
Fellowship store..bring in more products…

What if the people who might be looking for you find you there?

She shrugged.

I pack my gun everywhere I go---besides? Most of the fellowship members are former or current gang members. No one's gonna bother me there!

They got up and began to clear the table.

It comes down to safety, she said.

Then I'm glad you left, he said. The leftovers were put in the fridge.

With a bowl of mixed fruit and a bottle of wine on the ground before them, they sat out on the patio on a garden bench listening to the sounds of the outdoors combining with the soft music. They held hands.

Look at the stars! He said. That's what I love about this neighborhood!

What?

At nights you can see the stars!

Spontaneously he got up and took an old army blanket and spread it on the lawn before the bench. Then he laid on his back.

Wacha doing?

Star gazing! Ever done it?

No sir, not as I recall.

Join me! He patted the space next to him. Come! Join me!

She hesitated then laid next to him.

I've never done anything like this, she
whispered.

Like what?

All of this! This whole afternoon, she said.
Being with you…we actually showered
together.

And washed each other's backs too! I seen
you nekkid! We seen each other nekkid!

And you held me! Now here I am laying
next to you stargazing!

Aw, it's all good!

It better be!

He smiled and said nothing.

I like to meet him one day, he said.

Who? Bubba?

You know? The dude?

Huh?

The one you were telling me about?

Why would you wanna? They're a buncha
snobs, with their fancy ways.

I'd still like to meet him. Maybe we can be
friends, you know?

I doubt it.

She raised herself on one elbow and stared
at him suspiciously.

So, can I ask you something? She said.

Hmm?

Do you wanna fuck me?

He looked at her gravely and said nothing for a moment.

Do we gotta go there?

You're too sweet to be true, she said.

I just want to enjoy the stars with you right now.

No, really. I wanna know.

He briefly raised up on his elbow and sipped his wine.

Do you know I made this wine? He asked kindly.

You also made the beer, right? She said. You are an ole *bootlegger*.

He laughed.

Am not!

So answer my question.

What question?

Quit dodging!

He sighed.

The problem with rushing into fucking? He said. You end up with a fuck buddy instead of a friend and lover. Been there, done that, hated it!

Meaning what? She asked.

Fucking is for dogs and cats and animals, he said. Can you be my friend?

She nodded gravely.

Ain't you a Naturist? Ain't that part of it?

I am a man, not an animal. I am wondrously made in the image of the Most High. There's a sublime part to nature that maybe only those who feel it know about.

You're talking G-d and heaven?

Maybe. I don't like to fuck. I don't even like the word.

I agree. Makes me feel cheap to say it.

Whyja bring it up then?

I wanna know where you want this to go…so you don't like to----f?

Not really.

Why? You're such a good house keeper, and so good looking….are you a gay-boy?

He broke out laughing.

No sweets, I'm not.

It's cool if you are. My sister isn't gay, but she's experimented.

That stunning looking chick?

Have you been checking out my sissy?

Heck, no!

My Boss Isaiah? She was a Lesbian for most of the time she was in high school, then she fell in love with Elder Mingo. You'll like him if you meet him. He's really cool.

Whatever. Honestly, I'm no gay boy.

Are you mad at me for wondering?

He shrugged.

Then what do you like?

You think I'm good looking, huh? He asked with a smile.

Dah!

Thank you…What do I like? I like to make love to one woman.

So…. you don't want to make love to me?

Not yet…not now…the time isn't right, he said. If it ever will be.

Good.

Don't get me wrong, ma'am, you take my breath away, you're so fine!

What-ever!

It's got to be Ying-yang. You're all that and a bag of chips, but we gotta get to know each other, and you gotta want me too. So right now? I don't wanna do anything but become your friend.

If you said you did wanna I woulda left.

Wow! I know.

I probably never will, she said. All I need is Bubba. I want you to know that up front.

Oh! Ok, he said softly.

Really?

Yeah, it's ok. How long have you been with Bubba?

Wadaya mean? I've owned him for years.

Oh. Where is he? Is he in the military or something?

He's missing an eye. The Military is out of the question. I can't tell you where he's at. he runs off and I don't see him for weeks. Then he comes home. Probably has outside interests.

He looked at her unhappily.

I see. I don't know that I like him.

He's cool. As to making love? I can't…That thing of yours? It's too *big*.

That's size discrimination, ma'am!

Sorry.

You're a nice lady, he said with an unhappy smile. We'll be buddies.

I hate that word too, she said, for man and women…Yeah… We're getting to know each other.

He kissed her forehead.

Enjoy the stars….he said. They laid silently, side by side star gazing.

This is such a sweet feeling evening out here, she said. How does it feel, not having a shirt on?

He smiled.

Great. It would be greater if I was nude.

It feels weird not to be at work…Ain't I told you I didn't really mind?

Huh?

About you being nude.

He looked at her.

Are you sure?

Just so long as it ain't sexual.

Huh?

Like I said, I ain't going to fuck you---make love to you.

Ok, I understand. I told you, I don't move that fast. And there's Bubba, right?

She said nothing.

He got up and took off the sarong and folded it neatly, then set it down to use as a pillow. She drank in his nudity with her eyes. As he laid on his back he swiftly became erect without noticing.

Like I said, he said softly, I wouldn't want to anyway.

No offense, but you sure you're not a queer boy?

He laughed.

This really does feel great out here!

So you don't wanna fuck? Then why do you have that boner?

That's just nature…if you're around nudist? Seeing a hard on, or erect nipples? Or if a lady leaves a wet spot when she gets up? It's no big deal.

You go to nudist camps?

Not really. I camp in places where nudist tend to camp sometimes, though. Nudist resorts are expensive for me. See, the evening feels so great, you're with a stunning woman, you get hard. But that doesn't mean you're ready to have sex with her.

Who's that stunning woman? You got a lady?

I meant I'm here with you, doofus.

Stunning? She said, laughing. Don't be a liar!

Who's lying? I try never to lie.

So I guess I should say thank you, but I ain't stunning.

You are to me, muffin!

She laughed.

Wacha call me?

Muffin...sorry.

Why? It's cool. I called you a ragamuffin earlier!

And a Teddy-Bear!

Anyway, I barely got boobs, and I got a small ass.

Beauty is in the eyes of the beholder, muffin, said Troll, taking a sip of his wine. I don't care for meaty ladies.

Alright…If you won't get it twisted? I wish I
didn't need to have nothing on either…
You don't need to. You can be naked if you
want.
She sipped some of her wine, considering.
This wine is fantastic! I really do wanna be
nude… I don't want you thinking it's a sex
thing…
Does Madame wish to undress? He said
with a Scot-British accent, getting up, and
standing straight.
Yes Mister Hudson!
Very well Madame! If you would stand,
please?
He offered her his hand and helped her rise.
She giggled.
Yes, Mister Hudson?
She giggled and got to her feet with a
flourish and a bow, and raised her arms
away from her body.
Hudson, undress me!
He undid the bow and carefully removed
the improvised dinner dress.
She stretched luxuriantly with her arms over
her head, and did a slow caper. Laying back
down, he studied her body and took a sip of
wine.
This feels so *cool*!

You're definitely your own girl, he said with
a smile as she sat next to him.
Why?
Nowadays? Just about most women shave
or trim their body hair.
Not me, she said. I ain't got no reason to.
Nobody ever sees me nekkid---until now.
Your legs hardly have any hair, but you
don't shave your arm pits, you don't shave
your pubes.
Should I?
No! I really am more a hairy Naturist, not
just a nudist. I think women should let their
body hair grow.
Why? She laughed. You want'm too look
like gorilla girls?
Personally? I'm into hair. I think shaving the
body is perverted. Body hair is a G-d given
badge of adulthood, or It's approach, you
feel me? The only people with no body hair
are children and porno actresses.
That's true, she said.
To me, it's sick to wanna make yourself look
like a child. You're hairy arm pits? That
glorious red bush you got? I ain't seen
anything as beautiful. I'd love to rub my
face in it. You're a natural woman.
They stared into each other's eyes.

For real? I could get my sister to give me a
trim or something…she trims and shaves
herself.
Tell her to accept her body for what it is.
Promise me you won't! I love your
hairiness!
She smiled.
Thank you!
Why?
Making me feel so---special.
You are!
Ok! I'll be a Troll Girl, Mister Hudson!
Look…I ain't tryna sexualize things ok?
Ok.
But…May I touch your hair?
Which a one?
He smiled politely.
Ok, so long as you don't mean any funny
business, Hudson!
He took a sip of wine, carefully put down
his goblet, and slowly, gently, stroke her
hair. She kissed the palm of his hand. Then
she closed her eyes and tilted back her head.
He tenderly stroke her pubes with the back
of his fingers. She purred.
With Madame's permission, I will kiss her
hand now!
Certainly not, Mister Hudson! You will peck
my lips first!

I prefer to kiss them, Madame!
She giggled.
Very well, Hudson! The wine is making us
act like this.
She laughed, and gave his lips several small
kisses.
Abruptly she pulled away.
What am I doing?
My fault! He said quickly pulling away.
Sorry!
No, no! I'ma confess something, your lips----
What about them?
They ain't safe! I wanna bite, chew them,
kiss'm, lick'm----
Stop gurl! I'll go crazy!
G-d! Maybe I'm drunk! She said.
It's ok! I been thinking that same about
those rosebuds you got for lips!
They stared into each other's eyes.
I need to behave, ma'am! We hardly know
each other like that!
It's ok!
I guess this wine is going to my head! She
said.
Do you not like wine?
It's not that! I normally drink very little.
Same here, he said.
But you like making wine and beer?

He shrugged.

So you're into Upstairs Down Stairs? He asked with a happy smile.

Oh, hell yeah!

Dude! He said, you know it's on Netflix, right?

You got Netflix?

Duh! Hell yeah!

They grinned at each other.

Would Madame care to allow me to make some pop corn?

Only if I can help, dear mister Hudson!

And then would the lady care to watch Upstairs Downstairs in my company?

Very well, Hudson! Lead the way!

He led her by the land into the house.

They plopped on the living room floor atop an old comforter before the television with some over sized cushions.

I feel cold, she said.

He got up and scrambled out then came back with a blanket for her.

You wanna cuddle under the blanket?

She gave him a careful look.

Can we? I'm not being a skank, ok? I ain't done this with anyone---

You don't need to say all that. I know.

Please ignore my thing, ok?

He spooned her, and wrapped her in his
arms.

G-d! She said shyly. That pipe you got
against my butt feels as hot as a stove.

Should I put on pants?

No, silly, it's all good! Tuck it between my
legs so it won't be poking my butt!

Raise up your leg a little? Ok.

Hmmm. They both said softly.

Let's not move, or do anything, cause this
could become something we both aren't
ready for.

You mean don't do this?

She tightened her buttocks, and grinded
back against him.

Hmmm! He said. I better get up!

No, she said laughing. I couldn't resist,
you're so civilized, Mister Hudson.

Now I gotta take care of my needs later!

She was thoughtfully silent.

You mean you wanna jerk off?

He laughed nervously.

I thought we weren't gonna get into any of
that?

Masturbation ain't sex, is it? I have never
seen anyone do that. Go on, do it!

 Are you sure?

You want me to help you?

What?

Sorry! I meant---

You mean you'll give me a hand job? He asked.

What's that?

He looked at her with a new awareness and kissed the side of her forehead.

Nothing darling, he said.

If you're gonna jerk off, wadaya need me to do?

Hold me? Maybe suck my nipples, if you don't mind?

I thought men had no feelings there. You like having them sucked?

Yes...Please don't rub your teeth on them or bite them!

Can I nibble them...and your ears? I wouldn't bite you!

He laughed.

You done this kinda thing?

No, she said, but I read novels.

Let me roll on my back, he whispered. Hold me as I do it? If you kissed me it would be sweet.

She slowly covered her face in soft kisses.

Like that?

Oh, *yeah* Muffin! Yeah, sweety!

Ummmm...Do whatever makes you comfortable...

Did I get anything on you? He whispered
when he finished, feeling mortified.
Yeah, a little. It feels so warm…You want
me to get you a towel out the bathroom,
ragamuffin?
Thank you, ma'am.
She came back with a steaming face towel
and a regular towel. She took hold of his
manhood with it and began to rub it.
Awww! He moaned.
What's wrong? I thought you were done!
I'm getting hard again! Squeeze me! That
feels awesome, muffin!
She looked at him with an innocent
earnestness.
I've watched videos with Tiff. Guys really
like it if you suck on it don't they?
I know I do, he said.
Look, if I sucked it, that ain't really sex is it?
He looked at her carefully.
You don't have to do that, darling.
Oh, sorry! I thought you might want me to!
Well, I do, but I don't want you to if you
don't really feel it!
It's only sex if you get inside my private, she
said. Right?
Are you sure you want to?
Smiling, she kept rubbing him.

I ain't ever done none of this!

Putting it in your mouth like in a video? It won't make you pregnant!

Are you sure? She asked.

I promise! And you suck on it hard but keep rubbing it.

Ok then! I'ma do this just one time for you!

He laid limply when she was thru.

I done died and been reborn!

You're stuff squirted up in my mouth, ragamuffin!

I'm so sorry---

It's ok! I just swallowed it!

Sorry, ma'am!

Why?

You didn't mind?

Should I have?

No, it's all good.

If anybody finds out? You're dead!

Don't worry! He said. Thank you? Do you ever?

Do I ever what, Teddy-Bear?

Do yourself?

She was laying next to him with her head on his chest. He had his arms around her.

Fair's fair, muffin. I'll help you just like you did me.

Ok, she said after a moment, but don't put your thing in me. Just your fingers and your mouth, right?

Ok.

They kept watching Netflix after they were done. Both were in a state of euphoria.

After gorging on buttery, salty popcorn, and watching two episodes she reluctantly got up.

Where are you going, Madame? The night is yet young!

It's past one in the morning, Mister Hudson! She smiled.

Awww!

This has been great! But it's getting late. I need to get home, she said.

Aww!

No, really.

Ok. I threw your work out stuff in my washer.

Thank you, Mister Hudson! she said, feeling touched.

They should be dry by now, Madame. I'll get them for you. She followed him into the small utility room. He looked away politely as she dressed.

Thank you for a very lovely evening, Hudson, she whispered.

Can I hold you?

She took him in her arms.

So what are we now, ragamuffin?

Two lonely people who came together? He whispered. We don't have to put a name to it. I wish it meant you're into me, cause I been into you since the first time I met you!

Really?

Absolutely, angel girl!

Awww! This---this is special....I need to go now.

I'll slip on some clothes and walk you across the street.

You don't have to do that!

It's not a problem, muffin!

Can I keep that dress you made me?

But of course, Madame! I certainly will not wear it!

She giggled.

Thank you Mister Hudson!

He kissed her lips and hand at the door, bowed, and walked away with the dignity of Mister Hudson. When she giggled, he turned and bowed slowly then blew her a kiss. She waved with a smile and went in. Her brother was asleep by the time she got home.

After that day, in a sense, they never left each other's side.

They worked out together every evening,
and had dinner a few nights a week. Other
nights they watched movies together. Then
one day they realized that they were
spending every minute they could together.
The elfin girl and the tall, muscular man
found that they were soul mates. He did
most of the talking, and never failed to listen
to her. After a few weeks they became lovers
regularly-----after a fashion.
After some months she introduced him to
the family when he came to take her to the
movies.
Hey y'all, I'd like to introduce you to my
friend Mister Hudson!
Troll chuckled.
Mister *Hudson*? Said Angus.
Ain't that the butler in Upstairs Downstairs?
Asked Tiffany-Dawn.
I thought his name was Troll.
Troll is a nickname she said airily.
I'm Miss Wilhelmina's butler Hudson! He
said with a smile.
Troll? Said Honey Bun. What the hell kinda
name is that, boy?
Mama! Said Angus. Well pleasure to meet
you *mister* Hudson!

Her older brother liked Troll and saw that he was good for her. He never objected to the relationship. He and Troll were fast friends.

Tiffany-Dawn nodded and shook his hand with a smirk and a flirty wink, though they already met.

Tiffany-Dawn looked at him, indifferently the first time they met, and greeted him coolly with a friendly smirk.

Oh my G-d! He's a *hunk, Willy!* She whispered into Wilhelmina ear later. Grade A beefcake!

Honey Buns looked at him with open dislike and barely said a word upon meeting him. She ignored his hand when he offered it. He pulled his hand back shyly.

Aw, the *bootlegger*! She said icily.

Ma'am, I'm not a *bootlegger*. I----

Never mind, buddy! Said Angus, Mama's being Mama.

Am I?

They all chuckled nervously.

Wilhelmina? Honey Buns called her daughter into the Master bedroom with a jerk of the head.

Who is this *boy*? Asked Honey Buns.

He's not a *boy*, he's a *man*!

How do you *define* man? Asked Honey
Buns.

Mama, *stop it!* He's my best friend!...Mama--
-this is special!

Wachu talkin' about gurl? Asked Honey
Buns. What he do? Mess with your little
twat?

I want your blessings on this!

She sneered.

Are you outcha natural mind, gurl?

I'ma be with him, Mama, and I want your
blessings!

How long have you known this...*troll*?
Asked Honey Buns.

Long enough!

Is he some sorta nigger pimp? Asked Honey
Buns. Or a drug dealer?

No Mama! If you weren't my mama...

What? Asked Honey Buns. *What're you
gonna do Willy?*

You need to watch your mouth Mama!

What do you know about this *boy*?

Will you *stop* calling him a boy? He's a
gentleman, and he's very kind!

He wears *dreadlocks*, said Honey Buns. like a
Rasta *drug dealer*, and they look *disgusting*!

I think they're *beautiful*!

They're *unsanitary*! said Honey Buns.

Oh *really*? I mean to get my hair into dreads *tomorrow*, she said, to her own surprise.

Don't be stupid! said Honey Buns. You got *good* hair!

I'ma get nice *thick* dread locks!

You certainly will *not*!

Don't tell *me* what to do, *mama*!

I will so long as your under *my* roof!

Who says this is your roof?!

Wilhelmina, I *forbid* you to see this man if you're going to live here!

You want me to leave?

Gurl, said Honey Buns. what's gotten into you?

I liked a fro, I like braids, but I'll like dreads better now!

That's out of the question! said Honey Buns. No childa mines is gonna do that. You *will not* get dreadlocks!

You're not the boss of me! Don't tell me what to do, mama!

He's *colored*! said Honey Buns.

So? I feel like a *fool* for parroting all that *crap* you say about coloreds. The fact is, I can't *stand* most white people! And *I'm* colored too, mama, and so are *you*!

Your half black! said Honey Buns. And you're considered white here!

Mama, *you* ain't *white!*

Now you listen to *me*! said Honey Buns. You
are *19* years old! You don't know *shit* from
shineola!
I just turned twenty, or have you forgotten?
Yeah, I'm street legal too!
That *Troll* is trouble!
He is not!
You're not old enough to know your mind,
child, said Honey Buns.
You're outta line Mama!
I don't approve, said Honey Buns, of his
kind being across the street from my home
anyway!
His *kind*?
He's a darkie! said Honey Buns. A *nigger*!
Mama---*SOME TIMERS I HATE YOU!*
He's a nigger Wilhelmina!
Mama! Mama let's walk *away* while we *can*,
ok?
She glared at her daughter, but said no
more.
Anyway, this isn't your home! Said
Wilhelmina. Uncle left it to us, you just get
to live here. You live with Boot!
Don't be foolish, gurl!
Wilhelmina folded her arms angrily and
glowered at her.
What are you *saying*, ma?

I don't approve! said Honey Buns.

And? I *want* your blessing.

Why? asked Honey Buns. Why?

I know how you deal, mama. I wanna know we'll be left alone!

I can't allow you to do this, said Honey Buns.

Then jus' leave us alone! ok, mama?

I'll *not* bless you! Do you understand? I *forbid* you to see him! Stay away from that *nigger* or face THE WRATH OF HELL!

Well, I guess this is good-bye, mama, said Wilhelmina carefully, cause *you* are *not* the *boss* of *ME*!

You better not *defy* me, said her mother with controlled fury, I won't be held *responsible*, Willy!

I'll take my stuff out of here tomorrow, said Wilhelmina. I'm not to be pushed around, mama. *Stay out of my way* or *THE WRATH OF HELL will seem like a picnic to you, lady!* She stormed out of the room near tears.

Are you ready, muffin? Asked Troll worriedly. Are you ok?

Yes, *dear* Mister *Hudson*! Let's get going please!

Tiff, Angus! He said, heading out. See y'all!

She took his hand and left, with a furious
challenging look over the shoulder look at
her mother in parting.
The two women were enemies thereafter.
This talk is *not* finished, young lady! Her
Mother called after her, not realizing the
gulf that was now between them.
Let's stay in and do Netflix, ok? she said, her
voice shaking, when they crossed the street.
I just wanna be alone with you.
Sure.
The minute they were inside she threw
herself into his arms and broke into sobs.
Muffin? Darling what's wrong?
Will you take me to get dreadlocks
tomorrow morning?
Are you sure darling? What----
Oh I'm *very* sure! She won't give us her
blessings!
Really? Well, don't worry---
Ragamuffin, Teddy-Bear, you don't
understand! My Mom is a *total* bitch!
Sweetie---
G-d I *hate* her!
Aw, darling don't say that! Your blessed to
have a Mama!

She's dangerous! Said Wilhelmina, She hurts
people or she has people hurt them for her!
We gotta be careful. I *mean* it, ragamuffin!
Look, if she's got a problem with me----
FUCK HER!
Muffin! Don't! That's your mother!
You know how many people she's cut?
She's a *total bicth! I hate* her!
Look, I don't wanna cause a problem! I
found a tenant...I'll be leaving at the end of
week...I meant to tell you.
She looked at him with utter despair.
So you're *leaving me?*
What? Absolutely *not!* I told you before I
was going to rent this...I lived in a tiny
house on wheel behind my store. And I got
my cabin on wheels. I don't need a house
this large for just me! *I'm* taking you out of
here!
What? Are you telling me what to do?
No darling! I'm asking! I mean---Will you
come with me----
Yes! *Yes!* She laughed and threw her arms
around his neck.
Angus watched his sister leave, shaking his
head. Then he opened a beer and took a
long swig.
We're gonna lose her, he said.

I carried her under my heart for nine
months, said her mother. She's part of me!
Willy's a good kid, mama.
I understand.
Never causes trouble, minds her own
business…she took a job in her junior year
in high school. And before that she was
always mowing lawns or babysitting.
What are you saying? Asked his mother.
She deserves respect.
You think I *disrespect* her? I don't see your
point.
I won't let you hassle her, you hear me?
Wadaya say to *me*?
Mama, you *leave* them *alone*!
Hush your *mouth*! Said Honey Buns.
I *mean* it, mama!
And I said *hush*! I'ma *protect* my children!
Protect *Willy*? Mama she don't need you
meddling!
This is my *house* and you're my *children*!
What's your problem?
He's *nobody*! He's *colored*!
Well Mama, what are *we*?
We're *accepted* as *white* here! That's all that
counts.
That's not what my driver's license says!

Don't be stupid, Angus! A *colored* boy gives
you a few fancy cold *beers* and *you* roll *over*
and let him *cozy* up to your *sister*!
Willy needs some one. Troll is good for her.
This ain't about *beer*, Ma!
No, it's about a *colored* tryna get *above*
himself with a *white girl!*
Willy isn't white, mama!
Hush, I said!
No! My father was black, and he was good
enough for *you*!
Your father was a *quadroon*!
Qua-who? he laughed. A *what*? Mama, your
making me good and *mad*!
He has no people, he has no family. How
did he come by the money to buy that old
house across yonder? Who is he? What kind
of *education* does he have?
Mama *please*! You got *nuthin'* but a *GED*!
Which I worked hard for! Boy, *Willy's* been
in the *papers*! She's met the *Mayor*! She's got
a chance to be *somebody*! She's *gonna* be
somebody! I want better for her than that---
that--*troll*!
Mama, I said *Leave them alone!*
Don't *dare* raise *your* voice to *me*! She's *my*
daughter!
Well *me* and *Tiff* raised her, not *you*! You
were too *busy* running the streets with *Boot*!

Y'all are gonna mind me! This is *my* house,
and y'all are *my* children!
Uncle left us the house, mama. He's *good* for
Willy and he's *good* people! Better than any
of those *psychos* in SWC!
So what?
Sometimes I can't *stand* you! You leave
them alone, you hea'?
He stormed out of the house and roared off
on his Harley.
Her mother sat at the kitchen table and
sipped some beer Troll had brought.
Excellent beer, she said mockingly as her
other daughter came into the kitchen.
Weathers about to change.
Hmmm.
Tiffany-Dawn sat with her head in her
hands, leaning on the table.
You battling another migraine, darling?
Yes ma'am, I am now!
Her mother smiled gloomily.
Willy was nervous about introducing him to
you, Mama. So concludes another visit!
Her mother chuckled forlornly.
I better get home and make dinner for Boot.
He's a sweet person mama.
Boot?
Boot is a *fool!*

Watch ya mout' na, gurl! Boot is good to y'all.

Boot is a buffoon, Ma! I was talking about Troll.

Her mother snorted.

Why don't you like him? Asked her oldest daughter. Can you jus' tell me? Woman to woman, ok?

Why don't I like that *darkie*?

Why do you wanna call him a *darkie*? You never did Answer Angie! What are we?

She started to cry.

Shut your mout', na, gurl!

Daddy was a *darkie*---

I said *hush, na*!

You're a *darkie*---

She slapped her daughters face.

Make that the last time you lay a hand on me, mama.

I've had enough lip from a you!

And the three of us, me, *Angus* and *Wilhelmina*, we're *darkies*! So slap me again for speaking the truth.

Gurl, I'm *warning* you, you need to watch ya mout'!

Don't put on an act for me! Quadroon my *ass*! I *seen* daddy's pictures. He was a dark *black* man and I'm proud of it. A long hard dick cover many sins, huh?

HOW DARE YOU?
Tiffany-Dawn laughed at her.
What has happen to you, Mama? Texas
made you into a bigot!
Hush!
The three of us? Said Tiffany-Dawn . We
consider ourselves *black* and we're proud of
it!
Since *when* do *I* need to explain *myself* to
you?
Mama, *please*!
Do *I* need a reason to dislike a darkie?
But you're *black*!
Am I?
Boot *loves* you *because* he loves *black* women!
Boot *likes* him!
Boot *likes* good *beer*!
Ma, if this is really a race thing…
Her Mother snorted.
Then Why? Willy's really upset! I told her
how you might act. She says she'll move out
if you got a problem.
Oh well!
Her mother drank more beer indifferently.
Ma, you know Willy, said Tiffany-Dawn.
You'll push her away if you cross her. Troll
is really good for her.
Who told y'all that?

Me and Angus think he's good for
her...Troll's good people, Mama. If you
really don't like him? If you interfere? Let's
face it, Willy can't stand you as it is. You'll
lose her!
I'll take the chance!
I happen to know the truth! She's your
favorite, isn't she? You'll only push them
closer.
Her mother smiled and sipped her beer and
chuckled.
Every time one of us meets somebody you
do this!
That's a lie!
Is it? I'm smart enough not to introduce you
to any one of my----
Girl friends? Said her mother with disgust.
That's *so* unfair! I dated *one* girl, for a while,
and have dated men ever since!
I wouldn't know, you never bring no one
here!
Should I? Look at you! Look at how you act!
When Angus met Minnie? You carried on
just the same!
She's Mexican *trash!*
And now you have a grandson who they
won't let you meet!
That's on them.

Mama if you push Willy out, I swear, so
help me, *I'll* leave!
You'll *What?*
Me and Angus won't be far behind if she
goes!
And what where will you go? A'whoring?
I won't be here is all!
Maybe this house isn't big enough for me
and you now!
Maybe not!
Well, you have a choice to make. If you
decide to leave, you know where the door is
and how to use it!
You never have cared for me, have you
mama?
Not since it turn out you have a taste for
pussy, Her mother sneered.
Well, hissed Tiffany-Dawn, I don't, damn
you!
If you decide to leave? Don't let the door hit
ya where the good Lawd done split ya, na,
and where a good dog shoulda bit ya!
I'll be across the street, mama.

Chapter 2

Because of Troll Wilhelmina discovered
nature. Weekends were frequently spent out
at the lake in their tiny cabin on wheels. He
and MaGoo owned a small sailboat which
they took turns using. They built it
themselves. At first it seemed to her a
glorified row boat, and it really was no
bigger. Yet it was well designed. She taught
her the joys of flying on the water, driven by
the wind. Sailing became a passion of hers.
An avid bird watcher, he regularly spent
time tramping and trampling through the
Trinity River Forest with her, snapping
pictures of birds and animals; and they
frequently canoed Trinity River.
Everywhere she went her camera went also.
There were also spots along the River where
they could hide their Tiny cabin on wheels
and stealth camp in his Trinity Forest. At
other times they simply sheltered under a
Tarp, and shared a double sleeping bag.
On one of the Forest camping she got to
know MaGoo, Moon, and Lil Bit, for whom
the Forest was like a home.
She met Moon and Lil Bit on the shore of the
Trinity River, around a bend west of the I-35
over pass.
I want you to meet some friends, said Troll.
Who are they?

Forest friends.

Did you meet them here?

Yup. But we hang out in the forest, and sometimes we visit in the world too.

What do they do?

Well, I don't ask them too much about what they do for a living, but they love the forest…maybe they earn money here in the forest, too.

Why do you always whisper in the forest?

He smiled.

The forest has ears!

They hid their canoe and hiked south into the forest, until they came to a small clearing in a large grove of Willows.

A meandering creek ran through it to the river. She took a deep breath with her eyes closed, and listened to the babbling water, running between rocks. Larks and redbirds were singing. She opened her eyes and gazed up through the gracefully swaying branches, and their leaves, rustling in the wind; she looked at the fleecy clouds slowly moving like a herd of sheep through the blue sky. She smiled.

She took a deep breath.

This is so gorgeous! She said. She laughed and threw her arms over her head. It's beautiful!
What I wouldn't do to be nude! He said.
She giggled.
Same here! Ragamuffin, I wanna take pics of you nekkid in the woods!
Sure! Can I take some of you too?
Only if they're for you!
Baby, I don't want any one seeing you nekkid but me! He said.
I wish we were already nekkid, daddy!
She wore a clunky pair of hiking boots, a thick grey pair of knee high wool socks, baggy cammo shorts, and a green tee shirt that came to her belly button, along with a floppy khaki hat. Troll was dressed in ratty green cargo shorts and an even rattier cammo T shirt. He was shod in Jesus boots.
I love it here too! Said Troll. This may private property, but I just love it here. There used to be a no trespassing sign, a way back, but I always sneak in here to be among these willows. We may be trespassing, but I love camping here!
Troll made a bird like whistle, waited a moment and did it again. A responding whistle came.
They're here, he said.

Who?
Moon and his lady Lil Bit!
Lil Bit? What kinda name is that?
He laughed.
She's a Lil Bit of a lady! Real small!
How do you know?
Wait and see.
In a moment Moon and Lil Bit emerged
from the woods, fastening their cammo
shorts. Both were tiny. Lil Bit was very dark,
and wore her hair in long dread locks, as
did Moon. She was extremely athletic
looking, and quite pretty. Her thighs and
rear were muscular. Moon was slight, wiry,
strong looking and fair skinned. Both wore
matching cammo boots. Both had their
heads covered with a Cammo scarf, worn in
the style of forest warriors. Their shorts and
the tee shirts they wore were also cammo,
but the sleeves on Lil Bits had been cut off at
the shoulders. The snug fitting shirt came
down to cover her stomach, where it had
been neatly trimmed. It was slit at the throat
down to the cleavage of her small, firm
breasts.
They flashed Troll and her welcoming
smiles.

Their slightly clammy faces, and their
languidness gave her the feeling that the
two had been disturbed while making love.
Hey, hey! you two! Said Troll.
What up, Big man!
They shook hands and did a half hug at the
same time.
Hey Troll man! Said Lil Bit, giving him a
quick hug and a peck on the cheek.
Lil Bit! How are you darling?
Y'all, this is my lady, Willy, Troll said shyly.
Wad-dup! Said Moon. This sweet lookin'
thing with you? Daaayum!
Wilhelmina laughed.
I'm Moon, Miss Willy, and this is my lady
and sister in law, Mrs. Lil Bit.
Wilhelmina seemed surprised.
I'm Willy. Pleasure to meet you.
Pleasure to meet you, Miss Willy! Said Lil
Bit.
They shook her hand.
Where's your husband? She asked Lil Bit, to
her own surprise. I meant do you have one?
A flash of pain passed over Lil Bit's face.
Baby---Troll began.
Nah, it's ok! said Lil Bit with a strained
smile. I'm a widder!
A widder? Asked Wilhelmina.

My husband Peanut suffered from a heart
ailment. Passed away two years ago---in my
arms.
Her eyes filled with tears.
She bowed her head. Moon took her in his
arms and she wrapped hers around his neck
then buried her head against his chest.
Shhh! Shhh! Shhhh, said Moon.
After a moment they came apart, but he
held her around the shoulders, and she held
him around the waist.
My condolences, said Wilhelmina. Sorry to
have made you cry.
Oh, it's all right, said Lil Bit, wiping her face.
I don't even know why I started crying.
Most of that's behind me now.
Since we gonna be friends? Said Moon. You
should know, this ain't nothing grimy.
You don't need to----Troll began.

No, I don't mind, said Moon. Me and my wife have a happy, open marriage. Me and my lady here, Lil Bit, are business partners and best friends. I'm partners with my wife, and she's my best friend too. The three of us are. A few months after Lil Bit husband, Peanut, died? She was staying with me and my wife? My wife suggested that I give her some comfort. She loves her sister, and she figured as close and we are, it be a good thing.

I misunderstood, and was offended, said Lil Bit, laughing. My sister is like, you know you too love each other! Always have. I thought she was sayin' I was tryna take her man, but she's like, nah, I mean, we got an open marriage, and you two get along and is best friends, why not be lovers? Keep it in the family. She goes, I mean I know I can trust you, and I don't want you to be alone. So, I tell her, Lil Bit, I be honored if you *was* my lady! Said Moon.

I'm his *other* wife now, said Lil Bit playfully. He kissed her.

You *are*! For *real* for real! I consider you my wife, jus' like your sister.

Love you, boy!

Love you too, gurl!

Thank you, Lil Poppa! Said Lil Bit, kissing him.

A diminutive couple, with a fearsome reputation as Redemption premiere stick up artist, a modern Bonnie and Clyde to hustlers, Troll and Lil Bit were even shorter than MaGoo.

Always heavily armed, they spent a great deal of time in the forest. They dressed in expensive cammo outfits, for reasons known only to them. That he was missing an eye, like her Tabby, Bubba, made her feel a kinship with the sad little man. Upon meeting her, she took a quick liking to her.

Ain't you that girl from Loop 12, yo? He asked.

She didn't answer.

They's always talk about you on the streets, said Moon. Personally? We robs drugs dealers and hustlers only. It's as grimy as hell to rob folks that's tryn' hard to earn them an honest living. I ain't never robbed a tax payer in my life.

Me neither, said Lil Bit.

I've never been involved in any of that, said Troll. I love to make and honest dollar. I love to recondition furniture, build twig furniture, and I make ceramics.

And you buy and fix old houses! Said
Wilhelmina proudly.
He smiled and kissed her.
That's right. I got some rent houses, and I
sell them too. I may not be getting rich, but I
make a pretty good living.
Well, we got money you can put to work for
us! Said lil Bit. Buy us some rent houses!
Her sister does a lots of that, said Moon, but
you don't ever put all your eggs in one
basket.
Lil Poppa, don't nobody carry eggs in a
basket any more! Said Lil Bit.
True, sweet thing! It's jus a saying!
I'm jus sayin'! she said.
Tell me something, Red, said Moon.
She laughed. My Family calls me Red.
Oh, really? Tell me something, said Moon,
you know you need to be careful, right?
Why is that? asked Troll carefully.
Some of these grimy cheese toes out here
talk, is all! Said Moon.
The Police tell me to watch my back, said
Wilhelmina.
I won't let anyone hurt you! Said Troll,
putting his arm around her protectively.
Thank you, ragamuffin!
Moon laughed. They used to call me
something like that!

Raggedy man! Said Lil Bit, laughing. They
still do. Mommas tell they kids when they
being bad, y'all better watch out or the
Raggedy Man goin' get you!
Why? She asked.
Cause with my help? He done robbed a
whole bunch of they men that out there
slanging! Said Lil Bit, laughing. And we put
led in some of they asses too---a buncha
them. I don't know why they call him
raggedy! Lil Poppa dresses fine!
They try to make me sound like a monster,
said Moon, unhappily. But I'm in semi-
retirement now anyway. We've moved on to
better things.
What do you do now?
We're urban micro farmers! He said. Lil Bit
looked at him and broke out laughing.
Not to mention urban herbal relief eco-forest
natural farmers! Said Lil Bit, laughing.
Ganjentrepreneurs!
Gurl, hush! Said Moon, playfully swatting
her rear. They tussled amicably, laughing
for a moment. Then he hugged her from
behind and kissed her neck.
Doesn't this create a conflict in between you
and your sister? Ask Wilhelmina.

Why would it? Asked Lil Bit. There are
sisters who can't stand each other and are
always competing, but I help raise my sister.
Everything we had when we were little we
shared.

That's like me an my sis, Tiffany-Dawn ,
said Wilhelmina.

If she loved Troll and was into him, what
would you do? Asked Lil Bit.

Woow! Said Troll. Can we cahnage the
subject?

No, hold up! Said Moon, see me and this girl
have been best friends right? Her husband
died? My wife knows me, and loves and
respects me. She figured she wanted the best
for her sister!

You are so modest! Said Wilhelmina.

Lil Bit laughed loudly. All that I'm saying?
All nothing wrong with sharing a man.
You'd be shocked how many men fall in
love with they sister in law. Why? Well, you
gotta figure the woman that's the most like
you is your sister, so if a man loves you it's a
no brainer that if he gets along with your
sister, he might come to love her too. So if it
happens? It means your blessed. Your sister
isn't gonna try to steal what's yours, you
feel me? Cause sharing ain't stealing.

Look, we got a camp set up, yonder ways in
the bushes! Said Moon, but as nice as it is
out here? This might be a good time to just
sleep under the stars.
Cool, said Troll. Muffin would you mind?
I've never done it before, said Wilhelmina.
Ok.
Well, Red, said Lil Bit, if you're Trolls lady?
Now that we know you? Won't nobody
come near you.
Why?
Cause we love the Troll. We'll put out the
word? They mess with you? They Mess with
us!
Well, thank you she said. Don't go to no
trouble….don't put yourself in danger.
Moon and Lil Bit laughed.
She don't really know who we are, said
Moon, smiling. Ask Isaiah about us.
I'ma take Red to the River and soak my feet
in the water! Lil Poppa, keep an eye on
dinner?
No problem, ma'am!
They walked at a leisurely pace to the River,
found an overhanging log that looked
sturdy, sat down, and dangled their feet in
the water.

How long have you and Troll known each
other?

A few weeks.

We'll, you lucked out girl, he's a good man!

Thank you!

You smoke? Asked Lil Bit, lighting a joint.

I drink a little wine.

Neither does Troll…Gurl this more natural
than wine!

No thanks all the same.

She took a deep puff, held her breath, and
coughed up the smoke.

Aw! If you don't cough, you don't get off!
Wilhelmina dandled her feet in the water,
feeling a sense of peace. Lil Bit reclined on
the fallen tree.

This takes the edge off, she said. You know,
some woman are afraid of men with a
package.

Excuse me?

Men with big dicks, sis. This here? She
waived the joint. This here takes the fear
away.

Am I that easy to read? She laughed.

I suppose Troll must be a little on the large
size. But I'll tell you something? A little man
can hurt you bad if he ain't kind. But large
men? Most of them are gentle. I'm not tryna
get in your biznez either.

That's ok.

Apropos of nothing Lil Bit said, Do you realize that there are sharks in this river? There Asian carps in here and catfish in here…some of those Grass Carps are huge. Fancy folk wanna call 'm White Amur, but they're Grass Carp. You can pan fry 'm, broil 'm, bake 'm…they're delicious.

Chinese folk LOVE 'm. Them bad boys can weigh up to forty pounds and be damn near four foot long.

You like it in the forest, huh? Asked Wilhelmina.

I love it here.

So it's not just being an…

Ganjentrepreneurs?

Lil Bit Laughed.

Sharks in the Trinity *River*? Said Wilhelmina.

Yeah, right! They're called Bull Sharks, said Lil Bit. Which is why the invasive carp stuff is a hoax. I think Sharks eat 'm.

Whatever you say! They're some sharks in the forest too… Ganjentrepreneurs!

Ouch! Lil Bit laughed. That's all about the dollars. Do y'all wanna get paid too?

Huh?

We trust y'all. Do y'all wanna make some bank?

We're ok.

Well, if y'all ever wanna..

We're good!

You know something? Sid Lil Bit. There all kind of animals in the woods here.

Alligators, Deer, Bob Cats, coyotes…

Why the nature channel stuff? Why you telling this?

I know about real danger. Troll ain't dangerous to you… Here in the Forest, or in the sack.

Ok.

Remember one thing? said Lil Bit.

What?

It all goes easier if your high, said Lil Bit. And you----

Get some KY Jelly, right? She laughed. That's what everybody says!

Lil Bit took a deep toke. She held her breath then released a plume of smoke slowly.

Personally? Said Lil Bit. I think KY is overrated. Get a little drunk first. I say let your man eat something really sour to make his mouth slobber, then you 69 until your coochy is good and slobbery, and he has a real ramrod diamond cutter. Right then? You say, give it to me baby boy! And even if you're fucking King Kong, that thing'll slide in easy as pie!

You're *disgusting!* Said Wilhelmina, laughing.

Disgusting? Said Lil Bit, laughing along. For a Lil Thing like me? *All* men are too big! But gurl, let me tell you, I *love* me some *dick*!

You *are* nasty! I'll remember what you said! So you and your sister? One man?

And?

What is it like? Sharing a man?

It ain't no thing if you love him, said Lil Bit. You know the damndest thing? If a man has more than one woman, and it's all out on the table? They stay true to their wives. Candy ain't as sweet if ain't nothing keeping you from it. And they respect a woman that don't treat 'm like property. Come on and let's get to the camp, get some cold root beer.

Did my Troll make the root beer too? She
asked innocently, as they got to the Camp.
They laughed.
Troll don't make everything folks drink,
gurl, said Lil Bit.
But I *do* make my own Soda and root beer
too! Said Troll, and they all laughed.
Come here, sweets, said Troll. Let me show
you how to make fire. It's an art. You got
your Magnesium rod, right? You take the
back of your knife, right? You got have
tinder and kindling, right.
Waja have in that baggie? Isn't that laundry
lint? She asked.
Yes it is! Said Moon. Best tinder in the
world!
You gotta have some kindling and different
size firewood, right? Said Troll. You strike
the magnesium to spark the tinder like
THIS! Presto!
Cool! Said Wilhelmina.
You gotta add kindling and more wood....Is
MaGoo here? Asked Troll. He was sitting in
the shade of an immense ancient Willow
tree.
Not yet, said Moon. He'll get here with the
wives a little later on.

By the power self invested in me, said Troll
gravely opening a beer, by the ancient
wisdom of the Great Willow, I declare this
fete, shindig, wing ding and jamboree in the
willows to be in *PEACEFULLY* in session!

Hmmm, said Lil Bit solemnly, then she
started to laugh.

Are you two still at war? Asked Moon with
a smile.

MaGoo and Troll, explained Lil Bit. I'm
hearing something in the woods Troll.

Do you mean y'all would have a paint gun
war in a beautiful old wood like this? Asked
Wilhelmina.

Of course not! Said Troll gravely. That
would be *beyond*, immature!

That's what I'm sayin', said Moon with a
barely straight face.

Lil Bit Chuckled.

Yeah, *yeah*! *I* think it's really *immature*! Said
Troll loudly, looking into the woods
nervously.

Hell, *yes* it's immature, said Lil Bit, enjoying
the silliness.

So *yeah*, I squirted him first, but come
on…enough is *enough*! If push comes to
shove? I'm *ready!*

The wives? She whispered into Troll's ear.

MaGoo's three ladies, he whispered back.
I'll explain it later.
So Red, said Moon, are you not Honey Buns
daughter?
Yes.
Your Mama is something else! Well, our
families ain't close, but she's my mama
cousin!
Really?
Yes Ma'am! Ain't Angus your big brother?
Yes!
So, you realize you my cousin, right?
Really? Asked Troll and Wilhelmina.
She my cousin! Troll, you know Mouse?
Yeah, but not really. She's that dude you say
looks a lot like me's lady, right?
Right! Mouse is kin to you too, Red!
Get out of here! She said, amused. I seen her
at the Fellowship…she's something else.
I been thinking on that since I reads about
you, he said. Troll, you gotta be good to my
coz!
You bet! Said Troll happily. This means
when she marries me----
When I marry you? She asked in good
spirits.
Ok! *IF* you marry me---
One day, she said.

One day *soon*, I hope, said Troll, smiling.
Moon? Lil Bit? You just won't be friends!
We'll be *family*! Squealed Lil Bit with
delight, hugging Wilhelmina and kissing
her cheek.
For real, do y'all figure MaGoo is still
waging war on me?
Moon laughed.
I just say look out for little snakes, said
Moon looking into the woods.
I'm tired of it! I mean, he knows I'm
bringing my lady, and you would think he'd
show a little *respect*!
Lil Bit laughed. He says War waits on no
man!
Normally, said Moon, we'd be home by
now, but my wife Sleep----
Your *other* wife! Said Lil Bit.
Right, baby! My other wife, he said, smiling,
my other wife is in Houston for a few days.
We figured, let's hang out with Troll!
A strong stream of water shot out of a
nearby bush, extinguishing the fire, just as it
was merrily burning, and a second blast
caught Troll on the face and knocked off his
glasses.
Wow! *Ambush!* Said Moon, diving for cover.
He and Lil Bit laughed.

Dang-it! Troll swore, and pulled a Super Soaker out of his back pack.

MaGoo! Called out Troll. Come here a minute! Let me holla atchu.

They heard laughter from the bushes.

Dude, called Troll. You put out my fire! You *broke* the *truce!*

More laughter.

I worked *hard* to build this fire. You've gone too *far, dude!*

He charged into the bushes with the massive water gun. The others ran after him. MaGoo was on the run ahead of him, laughing, dodging blasts of water.

What's going on? Asked Wilhelmina chasing after Lil Bit.

Troll's repelling an ambush!

What?

Water gun war! Said Lil Bit laughing.

What are you talking about?

MaGoo and Troll have been waging a water gun war for most of the summer. Puppy and me's neutral.

Who started it?

Troll! You get to fight til you're water gun's empty or you reach the willows and call for a truce. The Willows are a neutral zone.

He just attacked him IN the Willows.

MaGoo is tricky. It's all about ambushes!

What the…*get down*! Said Troll.

Abruptly a little woman rose from the side of the road and unsuccessfully blasted all of them with a super soaker, giving MaGoo a chance to make his escape.

Double dangit…We been led into *another* ambush! Be careful! Yelled Troll.

They tried to flee back to the Willows, but were attacked yet again from the bushes from both sides of the path.

Troll returned fire.

We're surrounded! Yelled Troll. Get down! Get Down!

He blasted the bushes with his Super Soaker.

The attackers fled into the bushes gleefully giggling.

Get down! Yelled Troll, second Ambush!

He blasted the wood with water, but the three little women were gone.

Wyja blast *us*? Yelled Lil Bit, laughing. We're not *in* this!

You're running with the enemy, they called.

They heard the delighted laughter of MaGoo's wives.

I'm in this now! Said Moon, pulling out a water gun of his own.

Puppy? Said Lil Bit laughing.

Why they do us too? Asked Moon. I'ma even this up.

Truce! *Truce!* Called MaGoo. We're in the Willows, so we got refuge!

They all laughed.

Shame on you ladies! Called Lil Bit. You ladies act so *dignified*, but here you are in the thick of this *foolishness!*

The women laughed from within the bushes.

Truce! Called MaGoo. We're in the Willows!

No deal! You ambushed *us* when *we* were in the Willows! Called back Troll.

Two wrongs don't make a right! Called MaGoo. I called for a Truce! Rules are Rules!

They flanked us and went back to the Willows, said Troll. Sneaky little *turd!*

I ain't hearing no *truce* until *MY* water gun is empty! Said Moon. I'm circling the Willows and ambush *them!*

All y'all are over grown kids! Said Lil Bit. Come on Red! Let's go back.

No. Give me a water gun! Said Wilhelmina.

No! Keep her safe Bit! I'm with *you* Moon, said Troll. Muffin? If they get me? Have a towel ready! *I'm going in!*

Look out for them little ladies! Called Lil Bit.

They ran into the woods.

Kingdom of The Willows
Book 1: Blessing of The Mother
© Antonio R. Belizario

You see the *bull corn* I have to deal with?
Said Lil Bit shaking her head, smiling. You
gotta love'm! This is what you get when the
Willow Kingdom Blood Brothers are together!
Who? asked Wilhelmina laughing.
One night the three had a little too much
wine for their own good! They poked their
fingers with a pin, held them together, and
declared themselves *Willow Kingdom Blood
Brothers!* blood brothers and family, and
vowed eternal friendship! You fight one,
you gotta fight them all!
That's deep! Said Wilhelmina.
I don't know how serious that all was. You
give certain men a water gun, and out
comes the little boy!
That's how Wilhelmina was introduced to
the water gun war.
So the four were friends with her brother,
and MaGoo was a nominal member of the
SWC.
And Moon was her cousin!

MaGoo and Moon were Troll's best friends. He was however closer to MaGoo. They were an odd threesome, The tiny, elfin brown men, and the tall, muscular dark man. They were bonded by a love for the outdoors, but it was more than that. In their own way all three were outsiders. Moon grew up in a neighborhood that hated him for being the product of a violent rape. MaGoo was a small, clever man, unjustly distrusted by those who were intimidated by his cunning. Troll grew up without a family, always wondering where he belonged. She noted something. At times Troll was possessed of a profound sadness that he would never discuss.

MaGoo was a practitioner of something he called Ancient Judaism, which permitted him to practice polygamy. Troll, who was mentored by a disaffected Orthodox Jew, who practiced Reformed Judaism, was a Reformed Jew, who practiced as an Orthodox Jew. Moon, a member of the Westia Fellowship, Messianic Jews, was convinced that it was no more than Christianity, which he despised, and was secretly in a conversion class that was organized by Chinita, along with several other Westia Fellowship members in an Orthodox Shul. It was one of many such classes Chinita secretly organized. It was understood that if Isaiah found it out, it could trigger an inter Fellowship war. Chinita was living out of a back, staying on the move.

Even so, when they were together, they rarely spoke about their faiths. Mostly they enjoyed acting like men who had never before had true friends.

Usually Lil Bit and Moon would leave before MaGoo arrived, on such camp out days. This was because MaGoo and his ladies arrived late in the afternoons. Moon and Lil Bit usually returned home by then. On some nights MaGoo and his ladies failed to appear at all and she and Troll spent the night camping out alone.

MaGoo knew and loved the river better than anyone. He knew the plants, the animals, the birds and the flowers. Moon's love and adoption to the forest was instinctual. He loved it for it's beauty, and because he felt at home in it. All three canoed the river often through the summer, even into autumn and on warm winter days. Sometimes together and sometimes alone. They knew every curve, every bend, every fallen tree. They knew where mushrooms, berries nd pecans were best found. They amicably quarreled about the best fishing and swimming holes. For they knew where all the trails and tributary in the Redemption led from the Trinity. It was a spiritual home to them, too.

Their personalities complemented each
other. Moon was a planner, and bold to the
point of recklessness. Troll was gentle and
even tempered, with a love of humor.
MaGoo was secretive, but a loyal friend. If
Troll was gentle, MaGoo had a mean streak,
and was very protective of his friends.
Strangely, he referred to the River as The
New Jordan.

They also spent a few days a week foraging
or fishing. Troll and MaGoo claimed that
fishing with a simple cane, harvested from
the woods, they caught more fish than
fishermen with expensive tackle.

Frequently MaGoo and his ladies would join
them when they camped. Sometimes Angus
and his lady Minnie went with them. Mister
MaGoo and Troll were fanatical about the
forest, sharing a love of the River and the
Forest. MaGoo regularly spent days far in
the forest with little more than a Tarp, a
bedroll, and a tramp cooking kit. He
frequently spoke about mysterious group
he called the forest people.

She never stopped to think to think about
what he meant.

She noted and discussed with Troll that MaGoo had several well hidden semi-permanent shelters and huts throughout the forest, as well as rustic tree houses. It fascinated her how hard they were to find. Apparently Moon and his sister in law, Lil Bit, were MaGoo's partners, because they knew were all the shelters were hidden. Isaiah knew that they were Ganja growers, Ganja-entrepreneurs.

Like MaGoo, both Moon and Lil Bit tended to be very friendly, but secretive at the same time.

She rediscovered her world when they went tramping and foraging for mushrooms and herbs in the woods.

Troll also knew of several lonesome swimming holes that he took her to. The secretive Mister MaGoo took to inviting them to his various haunts; hidden dells and meadows and ancient trees and boulders in the forest.

Frequently they camped in its more breathtaking spots. Usually they camped at such spots MaGoo brought a hand full of tiny girls who he referred to as the forest wives. At first, it surprised her that those tiny girls, were adults; but they were. These were young women, it was very clear.

Are they from a community of midgets?
Whispered Wilhelmina into Troll's ear the
first time she met them.
They aren't midgets, whispered Troll.
They're normally proportioned----they're
just really small!
They're *gorgeous*, ragamuffin! *Look* at them!
Miniature models! They got so much style!
And they're *tough* too! He said. They're
scared of nothing.
Ragamuffin, don't laugh ok? Are these---
hobbit women?
Troll stared at her.
They carry Khukuri knives, bow and
arrows, side arms…*Warrior* hobbit women?
Why not ragamuffin? Hobbits are fighters if
they have to be. But don't Hobbits have
hairy feet?
Only Hobbit males have hairy feet, said
Troll. MaGoo *does* have hairy feet.
Dude! They always wear hiking boots, she
said. Maybe that's why!
You are right.
Ragamuffin, I'm telling you, these are
hobbits! Maybe MaGoo is too!
They fell into each other's arms, laughing.

When the subject came up of who and what those women were, when they were alone with MaGoo, he politely changed the subject.

They---we—are the Thirteenth tribe, he said shortly one day, the other tribe had patriarchs, but we had our matriarch, Dinah. Then after that he would say no more.

Thirteenth Tribe? MaGoo what is that? Asked Troll. A political group? A faction? An Eco group?

Let's enjoy the camping, said MaGoo.

I've never seen grown women so small, Ragamuffin, she told him when they went to bed.

But MaGoo would say no more.

Although they did not wear cammo, the dark green combat fatigues that the miniature mystery women wore was just as effective. All had the names of growing things. There was Marigold, the oldest, probably in her mid twenties, Thyme, in her early twenties, and Sage, who was about Wilhelmina's age.

She noted how they acted the first time they
met. The three young women adored
MaGoo, and treated him like a King. They
usually greeted him joyously, and took
turns giving him passionate hugs and
kisses. MaGoo was always besides himself
when he saw them. He never failed to bring
them candies and wild flowers, or some
small presents. He could never bring them
enough books, it seemed. Always they seem
to emerge from out of nowhere in the forest,
and when the camping was over they
vanished into the forest nowhere.
Once they were in camp, they usually
disappeared briefly, to emerge in silken,
dark green caftans, with gold embroidery
around the collars, cuffs and hem. Though
they looked the same each outfit was
different. They also wore turbans of the
same color.
MaGoo would usually emerge with a
similar caftan, of dark rich blue silk, that
went slightly below the knees, and had
elaborate golden embroidery that covered
most of the chest, and went from the wrists
nearly to the elbows, with a matching pair
of billowy britches. He also would wear a
beanie with elaborate silver embroidery.

All including MaGoo wore richly, sumptuously embroidered black colored velvet slippers.

Marigold picked the large ancient shade tree that day in the heart of the Willow grove, near where they made their cooking fire. Then they she spread a few old Mexican blankets on the ground, on top of a cammo tarp, then unrolled a plush Persian rug on top. She found out that the rugs were very light. Thyme put a large, elaborate silken rug cushion in the middle, with three lesser pillows around it. Another lesser rug with simpler pillows was next alongside it for her and Troll.

MaGoo would sat there with his legs folded underneath, and his hands on his knees, looking like a Sultan, or Caliph. One of them, Thyme, would brought out an ornate brass basin and ewer, and carefully washed his hands, face and feet.

Sage brought her and Troll a simple basin and a bowl of warm water, and they washed their own hands.

Out came then polished brass trays and bowls, brought by the three, along with a brass decanter and brass goblets. Marigold filled a shiny brass decanter with rich smelling wine, and placed it before MaGoo with a bowl of mixed fruit. He poured each of them, Troll and her included, a goblet of wine. Marigold knelt before him and pour him a goblet of wine. MaGoo pronounced a prayer, and his women said Amen. Then MaGoo drained his goblet. All of them followed suit.

Beloved, the wine tastes wonderful! MaGoo said.

Thank you darling, I'm pleased that you enjoy it!

All of you look beautiful, my darlings!

It is wonderful to see you, my love, said Thyme.

Thank you beloved! Said Sage, smiling. We've begun to weave you a new Tallit!

I can't wait to see it! He said. Will you tell me how it looks?

Later, beloved, said Marigold, later! Permit us to make you dinner! Tonight we will make you a feast to remember.

Why? Asked MaGoo, smiling joyously.

She handed him a small scroll.

He opened it carefully and unfolded it.
Baruch Hashem! He said excitedly.
Little father, I as well! Said Marigold.
Finally, may the great name be praised!
But that's wonderful, my darling! Said
MaGoo. Should you be on your feet?
This early on? She said. The women
laughed. I'm fine darling!
Each of his women then received an
embrace and a kiss on the lips, beginning
with Marigold.
May you all be blessed, my beloved
darlings!
His ladies bowed, and responded in a
language that sounded like Spanish, bowed
again, and commence to making dinner,
whispering among happily themselves. She
noted that all three of the women, as well as
MaGoo, wore a small holstered gun, and a
long curved dagger, with jeweled hilts, in
beautiful, jeweled scabbards on their hips.
Usually that was how it was.

Feeling wretched, she sat, leaning against
Troll, with his arm around her shoulders
watching along with him. Sitting with her
legs were drawn up against her, with her
chin on her knees, and her arms around her
folded legs, she felt profoundly embarrassed
and upstage by how they treated MaGoo,
while she did so little for Troll. Her eyes
began to fill, so she quickly wiped them.
Darling? What's wrong, muffin? He
whispered in her ear.
I'm not much of a woman to you, am I,
ragamuffin?
Why do you say that?
I don't care for you right, I give you what
you really want in the bed----
Am I complaining?
It's not the point.
You're a good lover, Muffin.
I suck you off, like a gay boy!
In that case, you sure are one pretty red
head gay boy!
She punched his chest.
Ouch!
Meany!
Shhh! Sweetheart, stop! I'm happy.
I'm not giving you enough.

Women suck off their men, and men suck off their women.
A the same!
You like me eating you too. It's all good!
I want to be your woman totally, not just your cocksucker!
Shhh! It'll all be fine. Ok? Ok?
Ok. Is this for real? Wilhelmina whispered in Trolls ear, trying to smile.
What?
How they treat him!
That's their customs, he said, thirteenth Tribe, he whispered back. He's their king, and they're his Queens. They really love him.
I think it's sweet!
What're y'all mumbling about? MaGoo asked jovially. Me and my angels? I don't get to see them but a few times a week, ok?
Why is that? She asked.
They live in the Hidden City Of HaShem, was all that they could get out of him. Troll, why aren't you wearing your robe and clothes---
That's all right, I----
Ah, *come on*, big man! The wood is cut, water hauled, fire lit, and all the dirty work is done, even though me and you will have to do the dishes----

No, I will! Said Wilhelmina.
MaGoo smiled at her and shrugged.
Come on, big guy! We gotta dress right for
the ladies! You owe it to Miss Willy. It's time
to enjoy the splendor of being in the forest
on a wonderful day, big man.
Troll laughed. Well….
These are joyous times for us! Ain't it grand
out here?
It is, buddy!
We're not just bums grubbing in the forest!
We are in a very happy mood! I've had great
news!
What?
I'm be a daddy soon, maybe more than one!
Awesome Mags!
Please, buddy, go put on your robe, you'll
enjoy yourself more!
Why?
You'll be more comfortable, buddy! Then
drink wine and we'll play our Bamboo
flutes for our ladies as they cook.
MaGoo---
This way of dressing is very comfortable,
big man! My life is about to change. You too,
dear Willy! Marigold, my dear beloved, can
you not supply our friend's lady with some
more comfortable attire?

We're fine, little brother! Said Troll,
laughing.

Nahh, I won't have it! You'll be more
comfortable in this style of clothes! Lounge
wear has nothing on this. Miss Willy, simple
living and camping out doesn't have to
mean that your uncomfortable.

Mister MaGoo, we're ok, Willy told him.

Come on you two! Troll, let's play our flutes
together after you dress!

Ok! Ok buddy! said Troll, rising. For you
and your ladies.

Me? Said Wilhelmina, I'm ----

MaGoo took out a long bamboo and began
to play. That ended the discussion. He
played a slow, sinewy, gentle melody that
seemed to speak of the spirit of the willows.
It was a gentle, soothing air that made them
all feel at peace.

Chapter 3

Marigold and Thyme, got up and moved
away, and pulled her up and away,
giggling.

Kingdom of The Willows
Book 1: Blessing of The Mother
© Antonio R. Belizario

Marigold called out instructions with a
laugh to Sage over her shoulder, and left her
to tend the cooking. Sage made a remark in
their language, and the other two women
laughed.
She says that we prefer girl talk to cooking,
said Thyme, and they laughed again.

They took her into the bushes, into a skillfully built round shelter, which from the outside seemed like a vine overgrown mound, but inside turned out to be a very cozy, neat, windowless cottage, with smooth white adobe walls, and a high ceiling, built of arched boughs densely covered in vines. The vines were so dense that neither sun or rain could penetrate them. The flat, hard packed earth floor was covered with fragrant rushes, overlaid with sumptuous Persian rugs. She noted a very large well appointed futon covered with a quilted red silk comforter against the wall, and four round fluffy silken cushions. From the ceiling on a chain hung an old fashion brass oil lamp. She guessed that at night the futon served as a bed for them. Ceramic vases filled with wild flowers were spaced at equal intervals along the wall. Their back packs and supplies were neatly arranged into shelves built into the wall. Scented candles burned in little niches along the walls, but she noted that though the cottage was windowless, the inside, was as bright as the outdoors, even with the small round door through which they entered closed.

Do you see that water bottle in the ceiling?
Asked Thyme, sensing her curiosity. It is
filled with water and a little salt. Through it
the sunlight enters and is diffused! Do you
notice how well it lights this cottage?
Wow! Said Wilhelmina. What a great idea!
Thyme poured her a basin full of warm
water from a brass ewer, into an ornate
brass basin. Then she gave her plush towels,
and a small, highly wrought jar of soap that
smelled like honey.
We will leave you for a moment so you can
freshen yourself!
Thank you so much!
You must rub this oil on your skin, after
you've washed, said Thyme, handing her a
small vial of oil. It is Marigold oil, made of
the seed of the flower. It will protect you
from mosquito bites. Discard your bath
water in the bushes. We use soaps that
nourish the Earth.
They turned to give her privacy. She took a
towel bath gratefully, redressed and went
out and poured the bath water in the nearby
bushes.

Marigold, who was busily rummaging through her pack as she hummed, came to her holding clothing in her hands when she came back in.

You will not know how to wear this. Please, remove those clothes, and permit us to help dress you!

I better not...

Why not, my dear?

Well----

Aha! You were coming to spend time in the forest and wore no under things!

How shameless! Said Thyme playfully.

The two women laughed. She laughed shyly.

Who cares? Sais Marigold. In the woods? When we come for pleasure with our beloved? Neither do we! We are simple people! Please, dear child, we are all women in here!

With the profoundest embarrassment, she stripped and folded her clothes neatly, and stacked them. She thought of covering her breasts and privates, but felt foolish for thinking to do it.

They appraised her with measuring eyes, indifferent to her nudity.

This sheet and scarves will do, said
Marigold to herself. Please kneel, you are
much taller than us, my dear.
She knelt.
You do not shave you body? Asked Thyme.
No.
Nor do we, Thyme reassured her. Why
should we? Were we not made as women
with body hairs by the creator? Can one
improve on his handi-work?
To be honest, until I met Troll, I really
haven't had a man in my life.
Women who shave their bodies are whores!
Said Marigold.
I'm not usually naked in front of people, she
said shyly.
Sadly, that is not true of your sister, said
Thyme.
What?
Marigold scolded Thyme in their language.
I meant nothing, pardon me, said Thyme
quickly. You are young. You have the body
of a young woman, as do we. You are
troubled by the size of your breast, aren't?
Wilhelmina nodded.

Do not worry. If you are troubled by the size of your chest do not be. You are still quite young. When you have children that will change.

She was too mortified with embarrassment to speak.

With Thyme's help, Marigold took a dark green sheet that appeared to be the size of a twin size sheet, with a wide, golden paisley border. Holding it width wise, they passed a corner under her arm and tide it along the edge of the sheet over her opposite shoulder so that it fitted her snugly, but comfortably. Now the front of her body was covered. Please do not be discomfited by how we care for our dear MaGoo, said Marigold, determining precise how to fit the garment over the next shoulder in a comfortable but modest fashion. We understand that it is not your custom to treat your men with the same level of dignity, but we are taught to treat our men differently.

I wasn't raised to do it, she said, but I find your ways to be very moving. I want to learn. I would like to be like you.

Good, said Marigold. I noticed how you looked as we served our dear. She who is blessed with a good husband, must cherish him. A woman must expect certain things from her husband and he of her, or the marriage will be hard. First you must honor your husband.

Wilhelmina said nothing, wondering how MaGoo could be married too all three. Were they talking of someone else?

A woman should never use vulgar language, said Thyme, and never in the presence of her husband.

Men must be respected, said Marigold, especially ones husband.

Call your betrothed or husband, said Thyme, by terms of endearment to let him know how precious he is to you---it will also remind you that he is precious and to be honored.

Like what?

My darling! Said Thyme. My cherished one! My love!

Or My beloved! Said Marigold. My dearest! Sweet words to the loved ones are like a bouquet of flowers. Call him any sweet tender name that lets you know how much he means to you!

Troll is the first man I've been involved with, she said shyly.

Hmmm, said Marigold. I see. You are very young. You modern women need to treat your men with greater love and honor.

What about him? She asked. Shouldn't he call me sweet names too?

The two women laughed.

Dear Wilhelmina, said Marigold, men are as children! You teach them how to treat you by how you treat them! The more you honor and dignify them the more they will honor and dignify you.

The other corner of the sheet they brought under her other arm, then they brought the fabric snugly, but comfortably against her side and tied it on opposite shoulder to the edge of the sheet in the back, in the same fashion. It effectively covered her body from neck to ankles, leaving her arms and shoulders bare.

Why are you ashamed of your body? Asked Thyme.

I...I do not like the way I look. She stammered. Both my sister and mother are very beautiful. I'm...plain.

Hmmm, said Thyme. And who has told you that? Troll thinks you are very beautiful.

How can you tell? She asked, smiling uncertainly.

It's in his eyes.

You have nothing to be ashamed of, said Marigold briskly. You have an attractive body! Your hips are neither to wide nor too narrow. One day you will be a good wife to Troll and bare him healthy children. Your hips say that one day you will bear children with comfort. Will you marry Troll?

She rose from her knees.

If he wants me…if he loves me.

She looked at her appraisingly, and adjusted the fabrics.

Excellent! Marigold rolled a matching scarf expertly and tied it into an elaborate bow off center from the front of her body around her waist. Suddenly she was wearing very chic, if modest looking gown.

They smiled expectantly as she looked at herself.

Do you like how you look?

I love it!

There is beauty in simplicity! Said Thyme.

Troll made a gown like this for me! She said with a smile.

Really? Said Thyme. You see? He is one of us! But we are not through! This is how our women have dressed even since the days of Father Abraham. Please, sit on one these cushions, and let me turban your lovely red hair. Do you realize that in ancient days Israel's women wore their hair in these--- Dreadlocks?

Yes, dreadlocks.

Marigold tied an artful turban around her head.

This looks great! She said looking at herself in a small mirror of polished brass that Thyme gave her. I don't normally wear head coverings, but I love how I look in a turban.

A woman's hair, said Thyme, is her glory and the essence of her beauty! Only your husband should be allowed to see your body's hair, and your head's hair!

And my dear, said Marigold, if you don't cover your hair in the forest, insects and twigs will find themselves into your air along with leaves and dries grass…it can be very messy!

Wow! Thanks you for telling me!

The three of them laughed.

Finally Marigold draped a second scarf around her shoulders as a shawl.

And now you are a Princess fit for your King!

It'll be hard to serve Troll dressed this elegantly!

Do not worry! We will serve you! You will be our guests!

No! I'll help, she said. I want to serve him. I want to treat him like y'all treat MaGoo.

As you wish! Said Marigold with a smile.

Wilhelmina was surprised how much more comfortable she felt. Though fully clothed, she pleasantly as if she was naked.

Thank you so much!

Troll was deeply pleases when he saw her.

Muffin! You look incredible!

Wow, my dearest ragamuffin, you look incredible too!

Thank you---my beloved! He said with a surprised smile.

He was wearing a robe that fell to below his knees, and pantaloons like MaGoo's, only less elaborate. To her he looked like an ancient African king.

They feasted, drank wine, played flutes and small little harps, until a little after dark.

That night when they went to bed, they talked.

I know some Spanish, and a little Hebrew,
Troll told her, but I swear, I think they speak
in Hebrew and Spanish.
Dude! I think it's called *Ladino*, said
Wilhelmina.
What?
It's like a Spanish version of Yiddish!
You ever notice they wear stars of David?
Asked Troll.
And so does MaGoo! Said Troll. Those
outfits they arrive in? They look like *IDF
uniforms!*
You notice how they always have their hair
covered? Said Wilhelmina. Boo, I think
they're Israeli *Commandos*!
They stared at each other, and fell into each
other's arms, laughing.
Are we going crazy? Troll asked her.
Baby, pointed out Wilhelmina, the tallest
one is not even four feet tall!
She's about three and a half. I'm starting to
think you're right, muffin.
Really?
They *gotta* be hobbits!
Whatever they really are? I wished my
Mother talked to me like they do. They are
so wise and sweet! They teach me stuff. I
really like them. I want to get to know them.

They could be from a hidden village of
hobbits in this forest that nobody knows
about, ragamuffin!
Israeli hobbits in North Texas?
Mexican-Israeli ones! She said. Again they
started laughing.
She never forgot the first night that they
camped with MaGoo and his ladies. They
feasted, drank wines, and played their
bamboo flutes into the night. The women
got up and danced, then the men, and more
music and feasting.
Do you know something? Said MaGoo,
slightly in his cups. When I lived on Page
Street? My family lived in a small garage
apartment, May they be
blessed. I had a handful of really great
friends. The first time Moon introduced me
to Troll here? I thought he was a kid I knew
back then called Romero. We used to call
him Priest when he was little.
Priest? Asked Troll with a beam.
You've heard this before, said MaGoo.
No, keep talking! I never get tired of hearing
it.

Priest! Said MaGoo, sipping more wine. He was the peace maker, you see. One of the best friends I ever had, Troll. But then along comes this new boy, Julio. Mean as a rattle snake. Took over the neighborhood, killed more kids than you can imagine a child killing.

Killed? Asked Wilhelmina. Are you serious? Never been more serious. Yup, took over the neighbor. Took Romero away from us too. After a while? He had no use for old friends. Julio, Julio, Julio! Julio's grandmother really rich, right? We thought Romey tuned into half a fag.

Why? Asked Wilhelmina, in spite of herself. A couple of times? We caught them making out as they got older. Julio kicked our asses if we tried to talk about it. Me? I always thought Julio was a queer boy! We finally had it out with Romero! Romey? It's him or us!

MaGoo laughed.

I guessed it was him, huh? Asked Troll with a laugh.

Romero kicked my butt! Even as a child, Julio was a killer…no one could prove it, but we knew…wouldn't have done any good, anyway…besides, some said she killed them who needed killing… Knocked me down, broke the only glasses I had, which was pretty bad! I thought I'd be blind without em.

Shhh! Shhh! Said Marigold, caressing his back.

Oh, thank you darling! It was a strange time….we knew there was something off about Julio… Never have had good eyesight! Anyway, him and Julio gave me plenty of money for new ones---but pops took it from me…me and ma ended up going begging for glasses at the Lions Club….

Romero sounds like a real jerk! Said Wilhelmina.

Nahhh! He was crazy in love with Julio, and didn't even know it…I still loved Romero like if he was my older brother…Troll you remind me of him, except you would never hurt a friend….

You got it buddy, said Troll.

Guess what? Years later? It turned out Julio was actually a girl passing herself off as a boy…Romero found out? Guess what he did? Did he beat her up? Did he accuse her of lying to him? Nope! They got married and been married ever since! Two weird ducks! …. Seem to be very happy….Romey is something! Married her sister, and the sisters girl friend…

I've heard that about him, said Wilhelmina. Me? I could never share my husband!

She looked at Troll carefully. He took a sip of his wine and gazed shyly into the fire.

If you married me you'd never have to worry, he said softly. I'm a one woman man.

Ha! Said MaGoo. What do any of us know about the future?

Is it right to have more than one wife? Asked Troll.

Of course, said Marigold. Pagan infidels forbid it, not the creator.

We never did make peace, said MaGoo, draining his cup.

He looked at Marigold and smiled.

Will this be the last one of the night, o dearest? She asked filling his goblet.

Yes, darling girl, yes, said MaGoo. If we had only known who Julio really was…

He raised his goblet.

L'Chaim!
L'Chaim! They all said, and drained their goblet.
Dear friends, if you will excuse me? He got unsteadily to his feet and trundled off to his bed with the aid of his ladies.

When they left the grove of willows in the morning MaGoo then left alone and dejected. But thereafter he arrived and paddled back with them in their canoe.
She saw the forest women many more times, and they gradually warmed up to her. Troll they knew and liked.
At nights they retired to the round hut, the temporary shelter. They stayed in an identical shelter, previously built by Troll and MaGoo, that was equally hidden. MaGoo was a master of building such shelters, He and his ladies always built their shelter camps a short distance away behind a tree or bushes for privacy. According to Troll, they were nudist, but would not go nude before anyone but their man. From behind the bushes or trees, the moans, screams and giggles that they would hear made it clear that these were MaGoo's ladies, and that they serviced him together.

MaGoo and his ladies began and ended
their days with secretive chants and prayers
using prayer books that they would not
show her and Troll.

In the mornings of such camp outs, the girls
would emerge from the shelter MaGoo built
shyly with suppressed grins. During the day
they fully dressed in dark green, with hair
coverings. MaGoo would emerged in a
shapeless robe, wearing cargo shorts and a
leonine grin.

In a brass ewer, with a two handled cup,
both Troll and MaGoo doused their hands
alternative, starting with the right three
time, washed their faces noisily, then dried
off and said a prayer, to which the women
responded with an amen. Then they did the
same.

Then the two donned strange ponchos with
fringes a the end, and tassels at the corners,
along with an ornate beanie and said
another prayer. He tied a small black box
with leather straps to his arm and forehead,
and said another prayer. Finally, he would
took out a long, fringed scarf, wrap it
around his head, prayed softly. All four
prayed standing, facing East, rocking back
and forth.

Then for a moment they prayed silently occasionally bowing.

They made breakfast for MaGoo as well as her and Troll. She frequently helped. Then they whispered prayers over their food in their language.

They spoke very softly, with a strange accent. She was shocked at how bawdy they could be, as they taught her how to forage for nuts, berries, fruits, mushrooms tubers and greens to make meals. At times they found honey combs.

Are you Jews? She asked.

They looked at her nervously, and exchanged looks.

It's ok, we're friends.

Why do you ask that? Asked Marigold.

Those pendants you wear.

What you see here---it stays secret, yes? Asked Thyme.

Yes, said Wilhelmina. We're friends!

Very well! Said Sage. Friends…

Teach me your language!

Why? Asked Thyme.

I want to learn about Judaism!

And why is that? Asked Thyme.

I don't believe in Christianity. I worship at a place called the Westia Fellowship…we have all walked away from Christianity, but---
What faith do you practice now? Asked Sage.
For a while, we believed in Messianic Judaism----
Messianic Judaism! Said Marigold with contempt, and spat on the ground, as if the very name polluted her mouth. Messianic *missionaries*!
I agree, said Wilhelmina. Most of the Fellowship are now secretly studying Torah----
Very good, said Marigold.
And we want to become Jews, she finished.
And? Asked Thyme.
Maybe I want to be a Jew.
Are you not certain? Asked Thyme.
I'm certain.
They looked at her nervously.
This conversation is pointless---for now! Said Marigold. Let us forage for berries!
And the Dandelions are delicious this time of the year…we will also check our fishing line! The men like to fish, but if we want fish to eat, we must actually catch them!
They all laughed.

Troll and MaGoo did the fishing on those trips---or tried. It was a matter of pride to fish "old School" for them. Each had a long Bamboo pole harvested from a grove in the forest. That and some line and a hook was all they used, with whatever bait was at hand.

That afternoon they sat by the River in their shorts, with their fishing poles, wearing straw fishing hats. They spoke softly.

I can see it all now, said MaGoo softly, so as not to scare away the fish.

What?

You do nothing but talk about Tiffany-Dawn and Chrysanthemum.

They're *characters*, that's why. They're really out there hippies…I adore them.

I think you're in love with both.

Troll laughed.

MaGoo, I'm not like you.

How is that?

I can't have four wives like you. I belong to Willy.

How long do you think you're going to be around them in the nude with your wanger standing without something happening?

See, MaGoo, what people like you might not get is that nudity and sexuality don't go hand in hand.

MaGoo laughed.

You're kidding yourself! You're in love with both of those girls. Are they seeing any man?

No, we all just keep to ourselves.

So, said MaGoo, neither one has a boy friend?

No.

Do they date?

Nah. MaGooo---

And they're not dykes?

MaGoo, do you have to use that kind of language?

If they're not lesbians, and have no man in their lives, then they're into you, buddy. So how does it play out? Are you going to leave Willy for one or both?

NO!

Or just man up, and embrace both as sister wives to Willy?

I would *never* leave Willy!

Ok. Then tell them to git!

MaGoo that is not necessary----

Look they've saved up some money, they---

MaGoo, I'm *not* going to do that!

Why not? Why keep a ticking time bomb in your house?

Because *I love* them, ok?

MaGoo chuckled.

You're still not being honest, buddy!

What do you want from me, MaGoo?

I want you to quit sounding like a boy scout and admit the truth to yourself!

And what truth is that?

Troll, dear buddy, you're in love with your lady, Willy, and with the two of them too!

Where's it written you can't be?

Do what?

One man one woman is Pagan-Christian bullshit.

Troll said nothing, feeling furious, but not really knowing why.

Ok, alright?

Ok what, you lump?

Maybe your right, ok? Now let's just fish.

MaGoo chuckled and patted his friend on the back.

Yet it turned out that just as Marigold said, the women were the ones who caught the fish. Mostly they caught Asian carp, or grass, black, silver, and bighead carp, which turned out to be very tasty and plentiful.

They are considered an invasive species here in America, said Marigold, but they're delicious when properly prepared.
The secret is to marinade them in lemon juice for a time, said Thyme enthusiastically.
Dear Wilhelmina, you are in for a feast tonight! Said Sage. We dry them and eat them through the winter---
Or smoke them! Said Marigold. Oh, they're delicious when smoked with Mesquite wood!
They can be caught in the winter too! Said Sage. I get tired of preparing silver fin or Kentucky tuna, which has been dried.
The others laughed.
What's so funny? Asked Wilhelmina, laughing along.
Those names she used! Said Marigold. Fancy names for a simple fish! Carp is carp!
No winter fishing for me, said Thyme.
Winter fishing is too cold! Said Marigold. Better to eat the dry stock during the cold months.
They came back with several medium sized fish. MaGoo and Troll caught a few. The men cleaned the fish, and gathered firewood. Troll started a fire surrounded by stones. He also hung a cast Iron pot over the fire and fill it with peanut oil.

Wilhelmina and the women donned Aprons
that covered their entire fronts. Then
women dipped the fish in beaten eggs,
rolled them in spiced flower and fried them
in the bubbling hot oil. Soon the woods
were filled with the delicious scent.
MaGoo and Troll set out clean dishes and
played their flutes as the women cooked.
They drank wines, and waited with
watering mouths for dinner.
They also fried a mound of batter dipped
potato wedges. All were dressed in Kaftans,
but they wore simpler ones than they had
the night of the celebration.

They usually brought elegant leather bottles of wine, trail mix, and little flasks of freshly pressed extra virgin olive oil in their back packs. They also brought cheeses wrapped in leaves with them as well as cured meats and smoked fish. The cheeses and cured meats they brought were such as she had never seen before. Along with incredible tasting cheeses and sausages that she knew come from no store, they created incredible salads from wild Blossoms, berries and tender greens sprinkled with pecans and boiled Acorns. They also foraged wild rice, which she had no idea could be found in North Texas.

What she loved in particular was the delicious multi-grain flatbreads they made fresh on a cast iron griddle, along with buns and cookies.

Usually MaGoo or Troll brought a Cast iron griddle and a Dutch oven, even if they weighed a great deal. It was with those that the women did most of their cooking. The women also brought copper skillets, pots and tea kettles.

Is this your idea of simplicity? Asked Wilhelmina with a smile.

This is traditional! Said MaGoo, loftily, and would say little else on the subject.

Troll and MaGoo gathered wood and made a fire before each meal.

Before every dinner they all washed and dressed festively in clothes like they wore the first night. MaGoo happily allowed his ladies to trim his nails and buzz cut his head, except for his neat, well groomed beard and a wedge over his ears. He loved to paint their nails and toe nails. Following that, he regularly retired with the three into their shelter until late morning. After lunch they usually went out to hike and forage. MaGoo believed in Minimalist camping. When camping alone, he rarely carried more than a canteen, multi-tool, a homemade hunting knife, a magnesium rod, a Poncho which could also be used as a tarp and a bedroll. His ladies carried the same, along with backpacks. They also carried small, holstered guns. At times they carried ornate, double barrel shotguns, with brightly polished copper barrels of a kind that she had never seen before.

They were very secretive about their weapons, and allowed no one to touch or examine them. When Wilhelmina saw their camping knives, they were ornately made, obviously not store bought.

They were suspicious of her and Troll, but were friendly to them because of MaGoo. MaGoo knew how to live off the land, and taught her and Troll a great deal about the wilds foods of the forest. Yet if anything, MaGoo's three ladies were even more knowledgeable about the forest and the river. If any question arose about plant, animals or water, he deferred to them. They were master foragers, and even better fishermen. They rarely hunted, but they loved to trap. She loved the elaborate foods the forest girls would make using the wild foods of the forest, and fish from the river. It wasn't until after several such camping trips that Willy realized something. The women were always accompanied by enormous wolfhounds that kept themselves well out of sight. When she asked them about it, the three women exchanged a look. Marigold shrugged, them whistled sharply. Three dogs that stood almost five feet in height ambled out of the bushes.

Don't be afraid, they won't hurt you or troll, said Sage.

They know you now, said Thyme.

They're awesome! She said. May I pet them?

Of course! Said Marigold.

Hello! Hello! She whispered, petting them.
The three dogs drew near her and sniffed
her. She stroked their heads.
Are they wearing---are these saddles?
As small as we are? Said Sage. We ride
them.
She was stunned speechless.
This is another----began Thyme.
Thing that we must keep secret, said
Wilhelmina. I understand…trust me. Look,
no offense, ok? I gotta ask this. Are you all
MaGoo's wives.
Yes we are, said Marigold bluntly.
Is that legal here in Texas?
The three women looked indifferent.
Marigold shrugged.
Who cares? We live by our own rules in our
community. Among our people? It is lawful!
I don't know how it would be to share Troll.
Men are not capable of being true to only
one woman, said Thyme. Why ask them to
be hypocrites and to do in secret what is
allowed by Torah?
So you are Jews? Asked Wilhelmina.
The two younger women looked at
Marigold.
We are Jews, she said, as you have
concluded, quite correctly.

Thank you.

Why?

For being honest with me! Can you tell me about those strange looking knives y'all carry?

This one is full of questions! Said Marigold smiling.

I'm not trying to be nosy...

Dear Wilhelmina! Marigold looked at her carefully, then with a flourish, pulled out her Khukuri, and swung it in a figure eight pattern so swiftly, it whistled.

She struck a fighting stance, and Cried out *DINAH!*

Wilhelmina started.

Then grimly, with clenched teeth, Marigold simulated a Khukuri defense, as if she was fighting several opponents with it, as if she was surrounded. She hacked, parried, thrusted, slashed, and hacked at the air, dancing in a circle, leaping up and down, hopping at times, lunging forward, or leaping back. The other women stepped back, with ill concealed awe, pulling Wilhelmina with them. It made her little realize that the diminutive woman was a masterly fighter.

Enough, sister, enough! Said Thyme, worriedly.

Abruptly she stopped and laughed. She was sweating. She returned the Khukuri to its scabbard, and drank from her leather canteen. The other women applauded her. She stood with her fists on her hips, returning her mind to serenity.

This is a Khukuri, said Marigold calmly, as it is called today. It is razor sharp with a heavy blade. Beware of the 13th tribe and their knives, the saying goes! With one blow, it can cut off a head, or sever an arm, or cut through a young tree. It is the preferred weapon of our assassins.

In close quarters, said Thyme, it is one of the deadliest weapons in history. A skilled fighter of my size can fight off several people with just this knife, if they attack us with bladed weapons, and even with guns.

It is an ancient knife made by our people, said Sage. It was taken by a group of apostates who married into the Ghurka tribe, and became Buddhists. They taught the mighty Gurkhas to fight with these knives, and they have become of the most famous fighting knives in history.

You can stab, said Marigold, hack or slash with one. In a desperate situation they can be used as a throwing knife. You can also strike with the hilt if it is not your intention to draw blood. It is also a tool that can be used for various tasks here in the wilderness. In close quarters I prefer it to the gun. Would you like to learn how to use it?
Oh, absolutely! Yes! I want to own one!
Very well! The use of a Khukuri is a Martial Arts discipline unto itself. It is not mastered quickly. I have used one for years and have yet much to learn.
How much would one cost?
Bah! Marigold waved a hand dismissively. Wilhelmina my dear, not everything has a price, but all things have a value. A well made Khukuri is priceless. Do you realize who is one of the best makers of these knives?
Who?
You call him MaGoo. I will order one for you and Troll!
Wilhelmina, what do you really want of us? Asked Thyme.
She studied them carefully.
Your wisdom.
Ahhh, sighed Marigold. You truly wish to be of the 13th Tribe.

Teach me Hebrew…teach me Judaism!
The three looked at her carefully.
I expected this, Marigold said strangely.
You are of the awakened ones---possibly a
returning exile!
What? She asked.
Sage chided Marigold in their language
hastily.
Marigold was the shortest, She was slightly
more than three feet tall, but the others
deferred to her. She radiated strength and
wisdom. Thyme and Sage were close to four
feet tall. Yet they looked at Marigold
questioningly. Marigold said something
curtly to them.
Are you truly a friend to us, and to our
MaGoo? Asked Marigold.
I'd like to be…
Either you are, or you are not!
Yeah, I guess.
That is not an answer!
Yes! I'm your friend! No doubt!
So, you wish to be one of us? Asked
Marigold.
She nodded.
I want to be a Jew!
Why? Thyme asked.
Judaism is truth, Torah is Truth, she said.

What of Troll? Asked Sage.

I think so. Troll is a Reformed Jew.

Speak with him, said Marigold, we do not think highly of reform Judaism, but we think highly of Troll. If he agrees we will teach you both---if our husband consent.

Your husband?

Rav Moshe.

Who is that?

You call him Mister MaGoo. As we have said, he is our husband.

Wilhelmina looked at her carefully.

Who are y'all? Please tell me.

What we tell you---if we tell you---goes no further than here!

I understand, she said, but I keep no secrets from my Troll---but we don't discuss our secrets with anybody.

Very well, said Marigold. We are Jews among Jews.

You're confusing me!

We are the descendant of Dinah.

Who?

Jacob's *only* daughter. No matter what you are taught, Israel had thirteen tribes---her descendants are the secret tribe and the thirteenth tribe of Israel.

I was taught that there was a daughter, she said, but not much else.

Yes, said Marigold, She married a servant of
Jacob, a small man -----I believe you call
them in your language *pygmies*? Nobel races.
He was of the Nobel races of Asia. I will
briefly quote for your edification, from a
historic book of wisdom: "Pygmy is a term
used for various ethnic groups worldwide
whose average height is unusually short, by
the standards of the Nephilim; so called
anthropologists, who are in fact busy body
grave robbers, define "pygmy", who as I
have told you, are truly called the noble
race, as any group whose adult men grow
to less than 150 cm (59 inches) in average
height A member of a slightly taller group
is termed "pygmoid." Pygmoid includes
much of Japan, China, and South East Asian
people. The best known pygmies are the
Aka, Efé and Mbuti of central Africa. There
are also pygmies in Australia, Thailand,
Malaysia, the Andaman Islands Indonesia,
the Philippines, Papua New Guinea, and
Brazil, and of course, the Thirteenth Tribe of
Israel, descendants of Ya-el and Our Great
Matriarch, Dinah. The term also includes the
Negritos of Southeast Asia.

There are communities of our people throughout Europe, the Americas, and of course, throughout the middle East and North Africa.

That means that Moon, Lil Bit, said Wilhelmina with growing enthusiasm, Chinita and Mingo are probably either Pygmy or pygmoid!

Of course, said Marigold. Many so called Mexicans are descendants of the noble race! Most of your friends are descendants of our people. They are a more sustainable, noble type of people. They don't eat the vast quantities of foods that Nephilims Eat, they know how to exist without despoiling nature.

There are many people in the Americas that are of our ancestry and do not know it, said Thyme, this is indicated by their size, their superior intelligence and beauty.

I see, said Wilhelmina.

There is not one city in this world in which our people are not represented, said Marigold.

Many were trapped and sent here as slave in slave ships, said Sage.

The term "pygmy", If I may continue, said
Marigold a little testily, is sometimes
considered pejorative. I certainly see it as
pejorative. We are the Noble race! An
ancient and mighty people! However, there
is no single term to replace it. I of course
prefer the Nobel ones! Many so-called
pygmies prefer instead to be referred to by
the name of their various ethnic groups, or
names for various interrelated groups such
as the Aka (Mbenga), Baka, Mbuti, and Twa.
The term Bayaka, the plural form of the
Aka/Yaka, is sometimes used in the Central
African Republic to refer to all local
Pygmies. Likewise, the Kongo word
Bambenga is used in Congo."
Are many of these people descendants of
the 13th Tribe?
Of course, said Marigold, they are Anusim!
I hope not to offend you, but are you
quoting from Wikipedia? Asked
Wilhelmina.

Of course! Said Marigold impatiently, with a scowl. It contains a plagiarized distillation of our historic ancient writings. We migrate through the Sahara into North Africa and into the middle East, and from there throughout Asia and Europe. During the Exilic period in Egypt our people inter mixed with the Israelite further. The latter day pygmies are race degraded by the abuses and uses of the Nephilim. Nephilim corrupted our blood lines. In the Golden days, the Nobel ones were a truly noble race, feared and renowned for their valor and craft. They were also wealthy Merchants. Dinah and her Mother, you see, were blacks. Leah's mother, Ya'el, was a Princess of the Pygmies, given to Laban in marriage. Leah was the first wife of Jacob and the mother of many of his sons, who through her were of black lineage, and of the Little Jews. This is were the term Jewel comes from, of course. She gave birth to Reuben, Simeon, Levi, and Judah, Issachar, Zebulun, and Dinah. Six of the twelve tribes of Israel had not only pygmy blood, but the blood of Africa in their veins. Why think you that the true Jews tend to be short men of color? Joel was a cousin of Leah. And To Jacob he was as a son, and he was named

Joel. He was circumcised and was taught the
faith of Israel, and Jacob gave him many
sheep for services rendered. You see, he was
a great spymaster. His size made it possible
for him to enter places and conceal himself,
which larger clumsy men could not do.
Much of Jacob's wealth came with the aid of
Joel Ben Israel, as he was known. As Jacob
grew rich, so did Joel. He was a great
merchant. Spying and the craft of the
merchant go hand in hand, you see.
In effect, he was a bridge? Asked
Wilhelmina.

Precisely! He loved Dinah, and even after her rape, he loved her. Many assumed that she was not truly raped, but she was. He slew and killed like a ravening beast those who were responsible, with the aid of her brothers. It was he who snuck into the city where they dwelled, and drugged the city water, to render the men of the city helpless, even though they had been circumcised. It was he who open the gates to allow Jacobs son in. And he and they slaughtered the men of the city where she was raped. It was he who personally slew the rapist after first castrating him with a dull knife. He begged Jacob afterwards not to slay her, but to give her to him as a wife. Jacob held him blameless for the slaughter, for she was his betrothed. So, Joel was given our Matriarch, Dinah as a wife. He received a dowry of several heads of cattle, sheep and goat, not to mention several tents and an army of servants skilled in warfare. Leah was Jacobs only son, you see. Through the joining of their bloodline we became the unknown and unsung thirteenth tribe of Israel, descendants of the only Princess of Israel, Dinah, and an adopted Prince of Israel, her convert husband.

They dwelled in the caves near Huron and took to concealment. Why? It is obvious. In the caves they created Cavernton, the Great, a city of fabled beauty and elegance that surpassed that of Jerusalem itself, some say. It's scholars and merchant were re-known, but the location of the city t9o this day is a secret.

Does it still exist? Asked Wilhelmina.

I will neither confirm or deny, said Marigold. Prophets and even King David himself took refuge there when he was pursued by King Saul. Of course he took an oath of secrecy. Yet it was a secret city, and thus it remains unknown by Nephilim-ic history. Yet when ever reference is made of a Prophet or Patriarch dwelling in a Cave, they Speak of Cavernton, the beautiful. It is a city that was kept secret to this day, but in the caves they created yet another hidden city. And her children married among the children of the twelve princes of Israel. And yet her descendants became isolated unto ourselves, because for reasons unknown, possibly because our forefathers was small, as was Dinah, they were all quite small. Smaller even than the descendants of the children of Leah born through her sons, who in turn were small. Yes, yes, history does not tell this, but our oral tribal history teaches us that both Dinah and her mother were of the small people. And so even among the Jews, we became isolated, forming hidden communities of our own close to the Jews, although we have always dwelled close to the descendants of Reuben, Simeon, Levi, and Judah, Issachar, Zebulun, and Dinah. Rabbinical Judaism teaches not these truths,

for much of it is unknown to them. They are
not of the little people. Even so, through
their Patriarch, Judah, all Jews have the
blood of the proud, great people, the so
called pygmies.

It is partly of us, said Thyme, that Holy Writ
speaks when it says that a mixed multitude
left Egypt with the children of Israel. Our
ability, our gift, to hide allowed us to avoid
enslavement in Egypt. Where our fellow
Jews have gone, we have followed, but we
secret ourselves even from them.

Why?

There are practical things, said Marigold,
that we can only obtain from our fellow
Jews. Holy books, for example. Access to
Sofers…we lack Rabbis that are formally
trained. Among us there have always been--

--bridges?

What do you mean? She asked.

People---said Marigold, impatiently. People
who are large enough to obtain those things
by mixing with giants, yet small enough to
be of us!

Pygmoids? Asked Wilhelmina.

Precisely.

And so that is what MaGoo is? Asked
Wilhelmina.

Precisely, said Sage. Rather, MaGoo is one of us.

And Moon, and Lil Bit?

They are converts, said Thyme. But perfect bridges due to their Pygmoid size. Without doubt, they are descended of the small folk.

They are indispensible to us, said Sage, and we have made them rich!

Perhaps you are telling too much, said Marigold.

No, sister wife, said Sage, this one? This one? This one we can tell her.

A red heifer, said Thyme.

The three women laughed, but Wilhelmina glowered at them.

A mere jest, said Thyme, forgive me.

She and Troll may be Nephilim, said Sage, but they are of the Forest---they will not betray us.

What are Nephilim? Asked Wilhelmina.

Take no offense, my dear! Said Marigold uneasily. Giants.

She started to laugh, then noticed that they spoke in earnest.

We are not *giants*, and I promise, If you do not call we a Nephilim, I won't call you hobbits.

They in turn glowered at her, then broke into laughter along with her.

She will not betray us, said Marigold. We
will study with you.
We, said Marigold, will make you and him
wealthy with the blessings of this forest.
There are many things that are priceless
which are only found here. Truffles,
Mushrooms, fruits, teas, herbs, berries, tree
nectars---
Aren't Truffles only found in Europe?
No dear one, they are found in forests
throughout the world, and the ones found
here are excellent!
And Marijuana? Asked Wilhelmina
carefully.
Of the highest organic quality! Said
Marigold boldly. Wisdom weed. They
looked at her carefully. We grow it…no one
but us knows where we grow it. There are
thousands of acres and thousands of us! In
one growing season, hundreds of millions of
dollars are grown. We have networks of
distributors around the world.
She stared back at them.
I am not a drug dealer, and I don't want to
be one, she said.

My dear, you will not have to be, said Marigold. We will assign you an allotment of our crop, and it is sold through our agents. Moon and Little Bit are among our top distributors and brokers. Our beloved Moshe is possibly the Most important Agent for the distribution of this extremely costly product. You will receive payment through the business that you and your husband own.

Is this why y'all befriended us? She asked sadly.

No, said Thyme, but this is a proposal only made to friends.

Troll is a wonderful friend to our husband, said Sage, but you truly love us for who we are, not just because we are wives of MaGoo, yes?

Yes, said Wilhelmina.

We wish for a favor, however, said Marigold,---if our husband allows us to teach you, and we have no doubt he will.

What is that?

The days of Rav Moshe as a Bridge are drawing to an end...please do not tell him we have told you this, yes? But he is a man with four wives, and among our people, a father cannot be a bridge.

How does he have four wives?

We are his Wife! There is another, Iris! Why
is that important?
I'd like to know, said Wilhelmina. Help me
to understand you better.
Our people still live by the traditions of
ancient Israel, said Sage. Our men are
permitted to have more than one wife, in
accordance to their ability to win them, be it
by wealth, wisdom or winsomeness.
We share husbands, said Thyme, as did
Jacob's wives----and so we are sister wives.
You would do well to learn that from us.
Why do you say that?
You have a sister who needs a good
husband…she is on a path, which might
prove very bad….can there be one better for
her than Troll?

Chapter 4

It was not that long after sun down. The affluent late summer aroma of Marigolds, just before they begin to wither, perfumed the air with a sad haunting scent. It was one of those North Texas evenings when the dog days of summer are over, but the air still smells of heat, with a hint of change, when a hint of leaves beginning to fade is in the air. A warm restless breeze was playing in the dying tree leaves and the wilting grass. Troll felt an indefinable expectation, not knowing what it was for.

It was in an evening, soon after Wilhelmina moved in with Troll, that Tiffany-Dawn showed up at the door of his shop with an arm draped around the shoulder of a strange little young lady friend, and a 64 ounce bottle of Troll's beer in the other hand. She was in the company a striking, small, pixie like, dark brown girl with a thick mane of dreadlocks. Each wore a stuffed backpack. She had an arm around Tiffany's waist, and Tiffany-Dawn had one around her shoulder. Whether they did it out of affection or to help each other walk steadily was not readily apparent. The two girls took turns drinking from the 64 ounce bottle of Troll Beer.
Outside was parked a disreputable looking green colored Chrysler Minivan, plastered with a loony-tunes assortment of colorful stickers, advocating every conceivable oddball left wing feminist, and environmental issue, not to mention some about, Naturism, Vegetarianism, Vega-free-gan-ism, animals rights, and the Sierra Club.

Tiffany-Dawn was half drunk, and her friend seemed very high. Both were barefoot, and wore dark blue, lose fitting, homemade, madly, wildly colored tie- dyed muumuus, made of recycled diaphanous, almost transparent, twin sized bed sheets that fell almost to their ankles. Seemingly they wore nothing underneath, as their erect nipples indicated. Also Tiffany-Dawn s breasts were a little larger than that of her friends firm breasts. It was obvious that neither wore a bra. They were an quite an arresting pair, worthy of arrest. Their eccentric dresses were seemingly worn with nothing underneath, their erect nipples indicated. Also the two wore thin, beaded leather straps tied around their heads to hold their locks in place, and several homemade bracelets and colorful bead necklaces. What amused Troll was the leather ankle bracelets and toe rings each wore. Each women hair was worn in thick, ropy dreadlocks. An Ankh pendant of old ivory colored bone hung around each of their necks on a black string. They smelled of musky, of patchouli, and Marijuana.

It surprised Wilhelmina to see that her sister, like her, was now wearing her fiery red hair in dreadlocks, decorated with a hand full of cowry shell, as was that of her friend. But for the gold rimmed granny glasses Wilhelmina now wore, and a slight difference in height, with Wilhelmina being slightly taller, they looked a great deal alike.

The little young woman with her sister was a very strange species of bird: she was a black hippy. Not that it mattered. Wilhelmina wore a sleeveless, tie dyed t shirt dress that fell to her ankles, and she too wore nothing underneath. She found it a very comfortable way to dress. Troll wore baggy cargo shorts and tie dyed T shirt with the sleeves ripped off. Then a realization hit her. How and when it happened she didn't know, but in a short time after she left home, Wilhelmina out of the blue realized, she and her sister independently of each other, became hippies. And then she at last understood something else: Troll was no wannabe Rasta, he too was a black hippy. Knowing not why, she felt an irresistible urge to giggle. Without warning, to his surprise and enchantment, she turned his head and kissed his lips.

Tiff! squealed Wilhelmina, with genuine delight. Hey, hey, hey!

Hey little gurl! Said her sister. She fell into her arms in tears for a moment. Did you miss your big sissy?

Yes! I sure did, sissy!

Troll and the friend sized each other up warily, then she gave him a roguish look, along with a big loopy grin that he found unsettling. What drew his allure was the large, brown buccaneer eyes, and the full, sensual lips, glistening with lip gloss, that seemed to always leave a slight triangular opening in the middle which revealed enchanting milky white buck teeth. It was a mouth that invited kisses. A pretty little Brownie of a girl, a pocket sized pirate, her eyes twinkled with tomfoolery and mischief. For no reason he could think of, he felt a little taken aback. He knew immediately she was a rascal and more than likely a playful, meddlesome nuisance, who might prove to be a delight or the bane of ones existence.

He nodded curtly. She ignored his nod, and studied him inquisitively with amusement. Then un-self-consciously, she poke the slightest tip of her tongue to the corner of her mouth and licked it, and he found he had to immediately look away.

What's wrong Tiff? said Troll anxiously. I'm loving the dreads, baby gurl!

You know he's got a weakness for red heads with locks! Said Wilhelmina. How do you think I ended up with him?

You bowled me over with your beauty, said Troll. And you didn't have locks when I first fell under your spell.

These old things? Said Tiffany-Dawn . It was my way of saying kiss my ass to our miserable Mama! But now I love 'm too!

Wachu up to, sissy? Asked Wilhelmina. You gonna hang out? I haven't seen you since I left home! And you haven't returned my calls!

I been ashamed!

Why?

Things haven't been going as well as they could.

Really?

I walked off my job not that long ago!

Do what?

I've joined the ranks of the unemployed, kiddo! I quit, Willy!

Great! Woohoo! May the Tatas AND the Prancing Stallion burn to the ground and be damned! I hated you working there! What happened gurl?

Wilhelmina looked at the friend suspiciously.

I couldn't take it anymore, Willy! I won't ALLOW them to abuse ole Chryssie! This here is my best friend in the whole wide world, Chrysanthemum D. Keys! My Besty!

I thought I was your besty, said Wilhelmina with not too playful resentment.

Sisters are a special kind of best friends. Your part of me. Me and Chryssie? We're all we GOT!

How y'all doin'? Said Chrysanthemum regally, her head weaving ever so slightly. She gave them all her goofy, loopy grin. Call me Chrysanthemum, Chryssie or Mums, jus don't call me late for dinner. Mums are my favorite flowers but I love me some Hibiscus too---

Chryssie just started waitressing tonight---- started Tiffany-Dawn , her voice shaking. And--- And I got my pretty ass GROPED by a drunk ass redneck! Said Chrysanthemum, laughing without enthusiasm. Not once, but TWICE! I guess they figured I gotta be a skank if I'm waiting tables, right? It ain't no-thing, sweets, please don't cry, you know I can't stand to see you cry!

He groped you? Said Troll, oh no! Let's find him! I'll beat him up for you!

Hey, calm down big guy! Said Wilhelmina.

No, really, I'll beat him up if he's still up there when he comes out! I won't let him disrespect Tiffs friend!

Troll, you get yourself arrested! Said Tiffany-Dawn , with amusement, not knowing if he was being playful or serious.

I don't care! Said Troll.

Don't bother boss! Said Chrysanthemum, strangely moved. It's the Euro-male dominance mindset, thinking all women are just hoes there to amuse them! Men need re-wilding, civilization makes'm unnatural beasts. Re-wilding? Asked Troll. The freeing mankind of de-humanizing, unnatural domestication. Their sexuality becomes distorted by this uptight, Judeo-Christian Paganistic culture. Like Catholic Priests? The Creator never told them to give up sex! It's a self imposed, dehumanized form of life. They do it and become hypocritical perverts. In the same way? We cover ourselves with clothes and we too become hypocrites with distorted sexual urges. They're so out of touch with the true sight of a female body, or even a male body, that the drink brings out the animal in them at the sight of a woman. Anyway, first time I go, sir! Please be nice! Second time? I dumped a pitcher of cold beer on his head to cool him off---- Wooohoo! Tiffany-Dawn laughed, and kissed the side of Chrysanthemum's face, then gave her a hug. I'm soo proud of you, sweets! I have never seen anything funnier---

I was told to git! Said Chrysanthemum, laughing along. On principal, there's nothing wrong with getting a grope --- by your lover--- which I don't have. Don't get me wrong, I'm strictly dickly, if I say lover I mean an hombre, but see, I'm celibate, and if you don't have a relationship with me, and you ain't my lover, what makes you think you can touch me, right?

Why did you take a job in that pit anyway? Said Wilhelmina.

I had some foolish ideas about being a waitress in a titty bar…I'm a nudist, right? Don't hide your body, and your body won't hide you, right? I'm like, hey! It's all good! I was so disgusted by how they treat those poor ladies, I knew it wouldn't last.

And like, I said, I've had it! Said Tiffany-Dawn , breaking into tears again, and hugging Chrysanthemum around the shoulder. I'm like, I won't let y'all treat my best like that! You want her to git, I'ma git too! She's my best friend, dammit! And I'm sick of feeling like a piece of meat! All y'all treat us like meat, I said! So Merle---the manager---he calls me a bulldagga, and says me and Chryssie have a hankering for each other's fur burgers, which is a damn lie, and so I kicked him and the nuts!

Woohoo! Said Chrysanthemum, laughing uproariously and hugging then kissing Tiffany-Dawn cheek.

Oh Tiff! Darling, you never shoulda started dancing, said Chrysanthemum seriously, with a quaver in her voice. I hated to see you doing it!

We needed the money, Hun!

I know, sweets, but dancing? Most of them gurls are low down skanks! You? You're not! You're a fine person!

Aww! Said Tiffany-Dawn . Thanks buddy! I never wanted to! I got pressured into it, but I preferred waiting tables. And the money was good.

Well if there's a good night to get fired this was it! Said Chrysanthemum, I made us some really good tips! Tons of moolah, baby gurl!

Yeah but how long will it last? We're gonna have to pay rent, and we gotta eat!

Sweets, why are you stressing? It'll be ok!

We been sharing a motel room, said Tiffany-Dawn , sniffling. We may end up sleeping in her van, we're practically homeless now---

Darling gurl, said Chrysanthemum, I'm telling you we'll live in the woods in a tent, so don't worry, Bluebelle!

My sister living in a tent? Said Wilhelmina smiling. Are you kidding? Are you crazy? Anyway, who is Bluebelle?

Bluebelle's my name for sweetie here, said Chrysanthemum, with a radiant smile. Bell spelled with an e at the end, the French word for beautiful! I love me some Bluebelle! Anyway, Queen Hibiscus, all the Patriarchs of Israel dwelled in Tents! If it was good enough for them---

Who is Queen Hibiscus? Asked Wilhelmina, fighting a losing battle with a case of the giggles. Why, you are, of course!

ME? Since when?

So you renaming my gurl? Asked Troll dryly. Are you a Patriarch of Israel?

What's that supposed to mean? Asked Tiffany-Dawn . Why're you using that tone?

You know, boss, you don't have to be mean to me! Said Chrysanthemum. Fine and handsome as you are, I'm not scared of you.

Troll, do-not you talk to her like that! Tiffany-Dawn busted into tears again.

Shhh! Shhh! Said Troll taking her in his arms. I din't mean anything.

Sorry, Miss Chrysanthemum! said Troll. No offense meant. Queen Bluebelle! I like that.

You? Said Chrysanthemum to Troll gravely. You're not no troll or a Troll. There oughta be a law requiring you to cover your lips---they're so fine they could cause a traffic accident from women looking at them and not watching where they're going!

*Chryssie quit being a flirt! Said Tiffany-Dawn .
No disrespect to Queen Hibiscus, said
Chrysanthemum. You're not no troll or Troll.
Really? He asked smiling.
You're a secret King. You have yet to come into
your Kingship, your secret patrimony. Your
name? Your name is… Poppy if you behave, but
your true name is King Willow of Wild Forest
Willows.
Poppy? King Willow? Wilhelmina, laughed,
and clapped with delight.
A Poppy is a wonderful flower, said
Chrysanthemum, not to be confused with Papi,
Spanish for Daddy.
He's my Papi! Said Wilhelmina.
Come here! Come here! Said Troll, and he gave
her a lingering kiss.
Get a room, said Tiffany-Dawn dryly.
You know something funny? Asked Wilhelmina.
There's a grove of willows that we love camping
in out in the forest! There's a big ole willow tree
in the center. Biggest willow I've ever seen. We
think it's part of a ranch. And you know what
we call it?
Willow's Kingdom? Asked Tiffany-Dawn .
Almost! Said Wilhelmina. Kingdom of the
Willows! Chryssie, how did you know about it
Chryssie?*

Chrysanthemum looked at her modestly with perfect seriousness.

I didn't, she said softly. It's written all over him.

A sense of spookiness touched all of them briefly.

Chryssie is, like, you know? Said Tiffany-Dawn , A Psychic? I prefer to call her a Seer!

I don't know about all that, said Chrysanthemum with amusement.

King Willow? Said Troll, laughing. No, it's Ramiro, but they call me Troll.

Who ever called you that don't know a thing! Said Chrysanthemum. Look at you, boss! You're noble, my handsome Nubian King! Look at your majestic, stately height! You're CLEARLY royalty!

They all laughed.

Oooh! Chryssie has a crush on you, Troll – King Willow!

King Willow! Said Wilhelmina, with enjoyment. She started to laugh. He's the sweet King of my heart! I like that! Anyway, how you gonna come in here creating chaos? Who do you think YOU are?

You? She said to Wilhelmina, looking at her gravely, You're Queen Hibiscus, the Valiant!

Wilhelmina and Troll laughed.

Isn't she a hoot? Asked Tiffany-Dawn . She always reading thick ole books! Ole Willy's as valiant and brave as a tiger! Hibiscus are Willy's favorite flowers too!

I didn't know that, said Chrysanthemum, with a modest surprise.

And what about me? Said Tiffany-Dawn , getting into the fun. You've never given me my nature name!

I have, but not completely!

Why?

That's because it was not truly clear until now! Bluebelles are gorgeous flowers, but now I see, Bluebelle! You're true name is Sister Queen Bluebelle, of course!

You? Said Wilhelmina. You're a drunk and high little pixie! You are Queen Chrysanthemum! I like her, Tiff! No wait! You are a wandering Queen, returned from a journey of self discovery to claim your throne, in the wild woods! And to find yourself a Prince or King to take as a Consort or your King!

Chrysanthemum made a funny face at Wilhelmina, and grinned, and then she bowed regally.

My Lord and Ladies! She said ceremoniously. I will be your Seer and court Jester!

Somehow, her solemnity lacked the humor she intended. They laughed uneasily.

We're clowning around, but we have nowhere to go! Said Tiffany-Dawn, glumly. It won't all seem so funny when we're dodging trolls and bums in the woods!

Stop CRYING, dear Lady Bluebelle! Said
Chrysanthemum. It's all good, baby gurl! I'll
keep you safe! First, I'll set up my tarp, I'll take
out my trusty Magnesium rod, then I'll build a
fire, we'll make camp, and we'll be fine!
Did you leave home? Asked Wilhelmina of
Tiffany-Dawn , feeling surprised.
You BETCHUM, little gurl!
When?
After you had it out with Mama?
Oh, sissy! Why?
I REFUSE to tolerate her behavior!
Oh, sis! sis! Said Wilhelmina.
Did I do the wrong thing?
Absolutely not, Tiffany-Dawn !
She slapped me Willy! I warned her to make it
the last time. I warned Mama! If you left? I'd
leave! I warned her, Willy!
Thank you for standing up for me, big sis!
I wasn't gonna let her treat y'all like that! The
house wasn't BIG enough for me and mama
anymore! She hates Troll for being dark,
Chryssie! I mean, like, look at him! He's like, a
gorgeous hunk! Yeah, he might be a little on the
slow side, but---
Says who? said Troll, laughing. Why do you
think I'm dumb?

---Boot was ripping mad at her, said Tiffany-Dawn , and so was Angus! Boot likes Troll! I'd rather go live in a flea bag motel, then stay under the same roof as that woman, the way she talked to you!

She wiped her eyes, as did both Wilhelmina and Chrysanthemum. Wilhelmina squeezed her sisters shoulder fondly.

Why didn't you come here to us? Asked Troll. You know mi casa es tu casa.

So what happened to trusting family? Asked Wilhelmina. Why didn't you tell us you had nowhere to go?

I ain't tryin' to be no charity case, Wilhelmina! I pay my own way!

That's with strangers! Said Wilhelmina. You're a part of me.

The same day? We hooked up at a coffee shop when I just got in Town, said Chrysanthemum, platonically, you feel me? I walked up to her and I says, Bluebelle, what up? It's gonna get better! Instant friends! This ain't a Lesbo thing! Say, what the hell kinda name is Redemption? We moved into a so called room together further up loop 12, near thirty five, to save on money, neither of us being flushed with foldable ducats, and we been best friends ever since! She my gurl! I love me some Bluebelle!

That's it! Said Troll. Look, you're family, Tiff, you'll stay with us! I won't allow you to stay in the forest with a crazy stoner! We live in a small space, but we got the room for you!

Are you sure?

Willy? Asked Troll. Queen Hibiscus, wadaya say?

Wilhelmina squealed with delight and threw her arms around her sister.

Great Papi!

I'll work to earn my bread and board, ok guys? Said Tiffany-Dawn . Now, y'all, me and Chryssie are a package deal----

Who he calling a crazy stoner, boss? Chrysanthemum asked peevishly, smiling loopily, with a tinge of hurt. I ain't either, King Willow! Maybe my feelings are hurt. Being handsome don't mean you get to be mean! Be nice to those you meet on your way up, boss! Sorry! Said Troll.

You diss me? Said Chrysanthemum, I'll sic my DOG on you!

Troll please you might want to stand back, said Tiffany-Dawn anxiously. Her dog Ripper has survived HUNDREDS of dog fights! Step BACK, for your own safety!

Troll and Wilhelmina exchanged a frightened look.

Chrysanthemum took out a small bedraggled looking black Teddy-Bear from her back pack and held it out toward Troll and growled.
You might wanna stay back, King Willow! Said Chrysanthemum.
This is a part pit bull part Rottweiler! Said Tiffany-Dawn seemingly seriously.
Troll smiled and laughed. Wilhelmina laughed along and spontaneously hugged Chrysanthemum.
My King is ALWAYS taking in strays, said Wilhelmina. We got a double fence section off so the dogs don't get in the garden? It surrounds the yard, right? We have a few pits and every other kind of dog. They serve as our guard dogs.
Cool, said Chrysanthemum.
Your dog? That dog don't hunt, said Wilhelmina wryly.
You think this is funny? Asked Chrysanthemum gravely. Don't come too close to him, King Willow!
He laughed.
No sudden moves please!
Why?
He might take your arm off, boss! Easy, Ripper, easy!
Please don't sic him on me! Said Troll gravely. That ain't even necessary!

I see your sacred now, huh? Asked Chrysanthemum. Grrrrr! Alright then! Easy Ripper! Grrrrr!

It seems, said Troll, I can't help but stick my foot in my mouth with you!

Jus' keep Ripper in mind and behave, boss! I won't let him hurt you!

Thank you so much, said Wilhelmina dryly.

What about my Chryssie, here? Asked Tiffany-Dawn . She burst into tears again, and hugged Chrysanthemum around the neck. We're a package deal! If you take me in, you gotta take her too! I'm all she's got! I can't leave her in the cold! She's un poco loco en el coco under the best of circumstances!

Hey! Said Chrysanthemum. That's a dang lie, Queen Bluebelle!

They'll eat her alive! Said Tiffany-Dawn .

Will you be ok, Chryssie? Asked Wilhelmina.

Of COURSE I will! Said Chrysanthemum.

No she won't, said Troll. You will if you stays here.

I been on my lonesome most of my life! Ripper will rip anyone to SHREDS who bothers me!

Where ja grow up? Asked Wilhelmina.

Bouncing around from foster home to foster home without kith, kin or kine!

Don't you have kin? Asked Troll.

I have Ripper and some other family.

A Teddy-Bear and a rag doll don't count as family! Said Tiffany-Dawn , despondently.

Ok, said Chrysanthemum, then not that I'm aware of, but for my dead Grand mama, who I never knew.

Well neither do I, said Troll. It's hell to have no family.

They looked at each other sympathetically.

Ripper and the others are good to me!

I mean people! Said Troll. I love my dogs, but they're not people family.

You make those that are yer friends your family, boss, said Chrysanthemum softly.

What if you don't have any? Asked Troll.

I got Gripper and Raggedy Anne. Until a few months ago? Didn't even know I had a Grand mama!

Well, you got me now! Said Tiffany-Dawn . Where you go? I go!

Aww, listen atcha, said Chrysanthemum, clearly moved.

Troll – King Willow? Asked Wilhelmina, tearing up. If she's Tiff's besty, she's a friend of the family, right? What are you going to do?

Look, said Troll, you'll stay with us!

You ain't the boss of me, boss! Said Chrysanthemum friskily. Me and the Ripper---

Don't be ridiculous! You're staying!

Chrysanthemum laughed.

Oh, don't worry about me! Queen Hibiscus?
King Willow? Point ole Chrysanthemum at a
forest! Me and the Ripper will be fine! My
Grand mama Cherry Blossom left me a piece of
land near the forest here about, which I'ma get
when they probate her estate. I can bum in the
woods until then. My last foster mother,
Morning Glory, taught me about the woods. She
taught me everything I know and love! She was
a hoot! I live outta my back pack anyway! I'll set
up my tarp in the woods and----
Do you not have anywhere to go? Asked
Wilhelmina wearily. That Teddy-Bear is not a
killer dog, and your stuffed animals are not your
family. Quit kidding around with us!
I love then as family!
All that's fine---said Wilhelmina.

As I said, I got the woods! Y'all jus look after my little lady-bug for me, and it's all good. Tiff, I'll come get you when I get my land! My Maw-Maw left me some land round about here, which is why I'm back in Tex-ass — Tex-ass, get it? Hahaha! Tex-ass full a exes who tex us as asses do! But I love the woods, which is why I'm happy, cause the land she owned abuts the Trinity River Forest — which I have never been in---it is actually forest land — my land---so I'll be living in the forest, you feel me?...I can't afford the room without a job, and neither can Tiff, but I hear the forest around here is pretty cool, and---

You have nowhere to go right now, do you? Do you? Asked Troll. You shut up about staying in the woods! I won't ALLOW it! I have no time to look for you if you get lost! You ain't staying in the woods alone!

Well, I'll like to see you stop me, boss!

She'll get raped and murdered in the woods! Said Tiffany-Dawn angrily. I'm warning you, Chrysanthemum, I'm not gonna let you go stay in the woods like a wild woman!

Nature is my home! I stayed in the Redwoods by myself for months---not really by myself, I was staying with this crazy ass chick called Moonbeam and her puppy dog Renaldo, for a time, but she met this tree and started communing with it, and I didn't wanna come between them---

Communing with a tree? Asked Wilhelmina, fighting an urge to laugh.

Oh yeah! She fell in love with this old redwood tree and they became lovers, she'd sit and hug on it, whispering sweet nothings, and would spend most of the day around it naked, making love to it---

A tree? Asked Wilhelmina, biting her lips, fighting a losing battle with the giggles, as she heard more of Chrysanthemum.

Yeah, yeah! Now, she did smoke an awful lot of primo weed! Some people called us and our buddies black hippies, but we were into living holistically. Nude Yoga, raw Vega-free-gans, nudist and natural in nature, you get it? Do y'all do Yoga? Nude Yoga is beyond spiritual! Did I mention that I'm a Negro nudist-naturist? See the alliteration? I can't say I care for calling myself a negro! I'm a New African! Why did I do it then? Alliteration! Negro nudist natural naturist! We we're practicing naturistic nudism as circumstances allowed. We were barefoot and naked all the time, mostly, and we went topless when we had no choice, because we preferred total nudity, and we went bare assed if there were nudist around we didn't know. You understand the idea of going bare assed? You wear a loin cloth, without anything else. I won't wear a thong! Thongs are nasty! The other option is to wear shorts or a wrap and go topless. Top less Freedom! You feel me? If boss can go bare chest why can't we be topless? I mean, man do it, why can't women? Discrimination! Why do they treat a woman's tits as evil? They want you think they go into hooter frenzy if they see free swinging gazungas, and gotta rape a woman for daring to bare her boobies. Why can't nursing mothers go shirtless and nurse their babies publicly? The Culture of rape! Bare the

tatas, get forcibly raped, right? It's one of the
way that women are denied their right to live
nude and natural, with the threat of rape.
Nudity exposes the power of sensuality to the
carnal minded, but it reveals truth of the heart
too! We could eliminate pornography if we all
stopped the clothe game! Think about it, y'all!
Hey---said Wilhelmina. Can you---
Imagine all people leaving themselves open to
communing with nature, without anything man
made to block the cosmic vitality of the air, sun,
the moon, the stars!
Hey! Listen----said Wilhelmina.
Wood, water, weather, wigglers, widow makers,
and two legged wolves Is all I worry about in a
forest! Me myself, I'll wear a muumuu if I'm
around cloth wearing dummies, like boss here---
muumuus are a nudist woman's best friend---I
love wearing muumuus---when I have to! Said
Tiffany-Dawn, you're totally clothed but totally
naked at the time---if you wanna be! I hate
wearing bras and panties!
I need to ask you---started Wilhelmina.
----those that don't believe in being sky clad,
continued Chrysanthemum. You see the
meaning of sky Clad? If you nude up? The sky,
the air, the sun, are your clothes! Oh, to be just
covered by the sky, but---

Hey! Hey! Said Wilhelmina. Pipe-down, lady!
As funny as you are? Be quiet a minute, please?
We're tryna figure out what to do, and you're
not helping!
Did you hear her? said Troll, laughing. She
called me a clothe dummy!
I'm jus' sayin', King willow!
Well, living nude is liberating, right Chryssie?
Tiffany-Dawn laughed. Chryssie is a talker!
I really need to say, Chrysanthemum said
gravely, If I'm giving y'all offense? I am a user
of the strongest grade of medical marijuana, and
I might've over indulged tonight...
Why? asked Wilhelmina.
Why not?
Are you sick?
In what sense?
Tiffany-Dawn laughed. She's sick of bull corn!
Now, now, Bluebelle! said Chrysanthemum, I'm
hyperactive, hyper mental, hyper vocal, hyper
literate, hyper creative, hyper-hyper, really, and
I'm a singer song writer, and I'm a poet, and I
suffer from a sense of spiritual malaise, a
paralysis due to excessive analysis, at times that
can only be eliminated with a inner cleansing
with weed of wisdom smoke. You might call it
getting high. See, humans----
Hey! Said Wilhelmina. You're giving me a head
ache! Can you please slow down?

Do-you-have-a-place-to-stay? Asked Troll, smiling. No! You can't go stay in the woods by yourself, ma'am! I won't let you!
How you gonna stop me, boss?
You need to be reasonable!
I might sic The Ripper on you in a minute! You're staying here, quit goofing around!
You are sucha male chauvinist---
Can you be sensible, please? Said Wilhelmina.
Why not? I got a 357 Magnum, and I know how to use it! I'm an Eden-ist.
Well, maybe I am too, said Troll, but the forest here? It's wild wood, urban forest, not some California State Park.
How should that concern me? I'm on a Mission! We gotta return to the Garden! Man went wrong when we first began to wear clothes. Why did we have to wear clothes? Because we fell out of harmony with the eternal one! How do get back into harmony? Get rid of all the deceit, concealments, cove ring---stand naked before the Creator! Cast clothing aside and stand nekkid and as free of pretense a Jaybird, I say! Reclaim Eden! Reclaim Eden! We're made in his image, right, so how can being naked in his presence be---
Hey! Said Wilhelmina, please slow down? Are you under the influence of something other than grass?
Pardon?

Why are you so manic? Are you high?
Yes. I mean----- just grass. We mighta smoked a
spliff or two on the way here.
A spliff? Said Troll.
A big ole joint made by hollowing out a cigar
and stuffing it with weed. Though I cut my
Mary J with a liberal dose of oregano and clove
sticks.
Wilhelmina laughed. Oh, my G-d!
Well, a little beer, too, said Tiffany-Dawn.
Chryssie stays high…You know what? I'm
sobering up. I ain't drunk no more!
To begin with, you were never really drunk
anyhow, sugar pie, said Chrysanthemum with a
mischievous grin.
Huh?
We're drinking near beer, darling!
What? Said Tiffany-Dawn . This is Troll Beer!
We drank the last of the Troll Beer last night! I
loved the bottles, so I saved them! I filled this
bottle with near beer at the bar!
Troll beer came in a brown ceramic bottle
without label that looked like a hairy Troll
wearing a crude leather tunic.
Well--- you owe me for my share for the beer,
gurl!
I paid for it, you didn't, sweets! Said
Chrysanthemum.

The two looked at each other. Abruptly they broke into laughter.

What am I gonna do with you?

Hold up! Troll, did you say? Is that this here hunk? Is this hairy Simian hybrid specimen the self-same TROLL of Troll Beer? Asked Chrysanthemum.

The one and only! Said Tiffany-Dawn , cackling.

So King Willow, said Chrysanthemum thoughtfully, studying him carefully, this is mighty good beer, boss! Tasty! Mighty tasty. Yes indeed… Are you aware that this beer is being widely, illegally distributed by a buncha redneck bikers called the SWC?

Troll just looked at her indifferently.

Are you aware that this enterprise---criminal enterprise, I might point out---is apparently quite profitable?

He smiled.

Am I to take it that you are the mastermind behind bootleggery?

Look---started Wilhelmina.

Now, now! Said Chrysanthemum austerely, holding up a finger, do not impede the course of the law! Let your client answer for himself, please! Well sir?

We all gotta make a living! Said Troll indifferently.

Have you got a license to make beer or wine?
Chrysanthemum asked sternly. I take it you
don't? You know that bootlegging is a
prosecutable offense in this jurisdiction. Correct?
Troll laughed.
He and Wilhelmina looked at her curiously.
Look, said Chrysanthemum frowning,
prosecution discussions might be premature, and
ain't even necessary, if you could see your way
to making another two cold 64 ounce available to
us…
Tiffany-Dawn snorted, and all three women and
broke into loud laughter.
I could, but you two are flying high enough,
said Troll shaking his head, chuckling along.
Whatever happened to southern hospitality?
Asked Chrysanthemum.
Why are you high all the time? Asked
Wilhelmina.
I love the mystical magical effects of the weed of
wisdom! said Chrysanthemum. And so I sought
for it, and I sought hard!
In other words? said Tiffany-Dawn . We toked
up on the way here.
I find that it helps to reverse the inner withering
tide caused by the materialistic culture that we
live in, not to mention that it expands the
consciousness, and----
Why else?

Chrysanthemum took in a quavery breath.
Why? I'm feeling a little---rattled.
Awww! Tiffany-Dawn embracing her. Come
here, you poor little thing!
Why are you rattled?
My thought don't ever stop racing unless I'm
doing something or singing!
But are you normally this squirrelly if you're not
high?
Squirrelly?
You talk so fast and you're saying so much.
Do I? No…maybe…I'm hyperactive, you know?
Why do you say that?
I been diagnosed as hyperactive…and I'm
experiencing Un-comfort-ability.
There's no such word! Said Wilhelmina with a
kindly smile. You mean discomfort, right?
Dan-git Willy! Said Tiffany-Dawn . Quit being
a cruel school marm!
I don't know the woods around here, confessed
Chrysanthemum, and I'ma have ta stay in them.
Maybe---
Maybe you're a little scared? Asked Wilhelmina.
Maybe.
Well, don't even think about it! Said Troll. It's
not safe! I can't and won't allow you to do that,
ma'am!
She looked nervous.
So you gonna be my protector, huh? My Knight
in hairy armor?

Someone has to be, said Troll bluntly. You're to high to do it yourself!

I may have no choice, boss, said Chrysanthemum.

You can't go in the woods around here by yourself before you know them, said Tiffany-Dawn . It's an urban forest. All kinds of bums and riff raff and trolls, like him here, skulk, creep, prowl around, lie in wait and hide out in there. Troll and Wilhelmina laughed.

Even these two rogues have been known to lurk around in them!

Troll and Wilhelmina laughed.

Chryssie, don't make me have to fight you!

Maybe you're a little scared? Said Troll.

In nature you worry about the double U-s, said Chrysanthemum. Wood, water, weather, widow makers, wigglies, wild life, including two legged wolves. Yeah, I'm scared.

You should be, said Troll. The woods here can be cool if you know what you're doing. The bad people hang out in the outskirts---but not even that many of them do.

You know why? Asked Wilhelmina.

Why?

The woods around here are haunted, said Troll.

Naw-uh! Said Tiffany-Dawn , and they snickered. Don't say that! I'm scared of ghosts!

Well, I won't argue, boss man, said Chrysanthemum, trying to sound mocking, but sounding grateful instead. You insist on protecting me and taking the charge of me? Fine, hombre! Be my knight in hairy armor, King Willow, with the leave of Queen Hibiscus? I believe in ying and yang, and if you got too much ying and not enough yang, or you're ying but wanna act like yang, then you got yang yang or ying ying, and the flow of energy is unbalanced, because the Ying without the yang may seem like completeness, but the Creator didn't make Adam and Steve, or Ada and Eve, he made Adam and Eve because one is Ying and other the yang, and when you have ying and the yang you got----

Dang! Said Wilhelmina, barely able to avoid laughing.

--- Man might be the ying, and woman might be the yang, or the opposite, man the yang, and women the ying, but they both can't be ying or yang at the same time or---

You mess up the cosmic balance? Said Wilhelmina and she began to laugh. Do you talk this much if you're not high?

Definitely not! Well, maybe more…

She's feeling a little rattled, said Tiffany-Dawn . She's a darling! But she makes a lot of sense--- and she's a hard worker!

Ladies, for the sake of mutual understanding, ok? Asked Troll. Are you a couple?

They looked at him solicitously.

Do what?

You two seem to be lovers! Said Troll. Are you two a Lesbian couple?

If it was anybody else, said Tiffany-Dawn with controlled fury, I'd ask them to step outside with me, dude!

Woe! Woe! Said Wilhelmina.

Did you put him up to asking that? she asked Wilhelmina furiously.

No! Calm down!

For the record? Said Tiffany-Dawn , near tears. Yes, Chrysanthemum, I briefly experimented with that lifestyle, but it didn't suit me! I hope you won't think I been laying in wait and setting you up!

Shhh! Said Chrysanthemum. He didn't mean anything, he was jus asking! These days you never know!

Why do people assume if you're close to another woman you got a predilection for fur burgers? Asked Tiffany-Dawn . Me? I want a man! I want a good man!

Fur burger? Chrysanthemum laughed so hard that she collapsed against Tiffany-Dawn . Oh my G-d, I'ma pee myself in a minute!

Oh, no, no, kind sir! said Chrysanthemum. Just buddies. BFF! We shared a bed, we slept naked, and well, yeah sometimes we cuddle platonically, but it wasn't a gay thing, we never played tickle the kitty, or suck the tatas, it was strictly platonic; see? we're both strictly dickly. I don't do yang on yang or ying on ying! Not that there's anything wrong with yang on yang or ying on ying, if that's your thing, but I'm---

Strictly dickly? Asked Wilhelmina, laughing. We need to figure out where you are gonna stay! Do you have some place to go or not?

If you wanna define a place as a house, condo, shed, shack, shanty, cabin or room---or if you define a place as a state of being in consciousness, or nature or----

That settles it! You're staying here! Said Troll.

If I can find a safe place in the woods and set up my tarp, and---

Other than the woods, do you have a place to go? Not really, she said meekly, at long last. Lookit, I can't go to a shelter. Been there, done that! I hate shelters.

Well, said Troll compassionately, I wouldn't wanna end up in a shelter. Like I said, you stay here with us until.

Until what?

Until never mind, said Wilhelmina.

We got a tiny cabin on wheels----began Troll.

DUDE! Yelled Chrysanthemum, Do y'all believe
in the concept of tiny houses? Do you live it?
That's how to end homelessness! Why would
anyone assume you're just a dumb hunk?
Who assumes I'm just a dumb hunk? Asked
Troll with a grin, looking at Tiffany-Dawn, who
studiously avoided his eyes.
He poked her playfully in the ribs. She snorted
and started to giggle.
I'ma get you, Tiffany-Dawn!
That's what you get for assuming I'm a muff
diver!
I just asked! Said Troll, you two are so sweet to
each other!
Tiff is very affectionate, said Wilhelmina.
Did I say that some one assumes you're dumb?
asked Chrysanthemum. Hmmm…why did I say
that? I believe in Tiny homes too!
We live in one, said Troll, right around the back.
Cool! Outstanding! Though I love sleeping
under a tarp on a hammock. Show it to me!
We'll take you camping, said Wilhelmina. We go
a few times a week! And we spend a buncha
weekends in the woods. We'll try tarp camping!
Can't we try it, ragamuffin?

Ok, Muffin! Great! said Troll. We got a little cabin on wheels we go out to the lake in, too, said Wilhelmina. When we take it to the lake you two can stay in the regular little house---unless you come with. Look, you should know? We're hairies, and domestic Nudist.

Fairies? Asked Tiffany-Dawn , chuckling.

Tiffany-Dawn , hush! Said Wilhelmina.

No, not fairies! said Troll laughing. You nit! We don't cut or shave any of our body hair. To me, like, it's an extension of the nervous system.

What is? Asked Tiffany-Dawn .

Hair, said Chrysanthemum, they're like exteriorized nerves. They're like antennas on an insect. Highly evolved 'feelers' or 'antennae'. They transmit tons amounts of important info to the brain stem.

Yeah, said Troll, the limbic system, and the neo-cortex.

Oh my G-d! Chrysanthemum said clapping with delight. Hairies? Are you serious? Bluebelle said y'all are nudies, but I thought nah, she was kidding!

We are simple living Vegans, said Troll.

Unless someone else buys the meat, said Tiffany-Dawn dryly.

Vegans wannabes, said Wilhelmina, laughing. We try to be fruitarians too! Anyway, shut up Tiff! Quit picking at us!

Sometimes we're raw Vegan too! Said Troll, But we do relapse and eat fish or chicken occasionally. We also do yogurt and cheeses.
Oh King Willow! Queen Hibiscus! Said Chrysanthemum. I'm loving this, boss! I'm a raw Vega-free-gan! Do y'all do Yoga? You gotta do yoga!
She's take me dumpster diving behind Safeway Supermarket! Said Tiffany-Dawn . What a hoot! American stores throw out tons of perfectly good food! Said Chrysanthemum.
We got pounds of perfectly good fruit! Said Tiffany-Dawn . Saw a rat bigger than a cat too! Ain't that right, Chryssie?
We don't go nude while we're in the shop up front here, said Troll. In the workshop I go topless, or I lock the door to the workshop and go nude or bare-ass. We both mostly go barefoot, or if we have to we wear Jesus boots. Willy wears clothes up front, around clothe dummies, but when she hangs in the workshop, she's like me. We got a pretty large enclosed yard with a ten foot fence, so when we're home out back or in our garden, we go totally nude. Our yard is an organic edible garden.
So the garden is really your home? DUDE! You're EDEN-ISTS!

Definitely. Look, said Troll, we're closed! Let's turn out the lights, set the alarm, and go OUT there! I'm starving, muffin!

Look? Chrysanthemum, said Wilhelmina, you're butt is staying here! Shut up and don't argue! Personally? I love the Forest! I don't want a nut with a 357 roaming loose in it! There are enough nuts in the woods around here!

They all laughed.

Hey! Said Chrysanthemum, laughing along. Thank you Miss Queen Hibiscus! And Mister King Willow!

Were you thinking MaGoo, Muffin? Said Troll. I'ma tell him you said that! said Wilhelmina. Come on y'all!

Excellent! DUDE! You two make twig furniture? AWESOME! I LOVE to make twig furniture! I can help you! Me and Moonbeam used to make Twig furniture from tree trimmings or bush trimmings, I loved working with Bamboo, and we'd sell them by the side of the road until she fell in love with a redwood tree, and like I said, I decided that three is a crowd, there wasn't a whole lot of room in her life for a human, and she had jealousy issues about the redwood, and----

Great! Said Tiffany-Dawn , smiling. Calm down hun!

I'm feeling headachy! Said Troll dryly.

Can I go nude too? Asked Tiffany-Dawn . I'd love to try it!

Sure! Said Wilhelmina, if my Ragamuffin doesn't mind. Sweetheart?

Sure, he said hesitantly. We stay nude in the yard or in our little house, ladies.

Great! Said Tiffany. I'ma love this!

Look, is this like family only nudity?

Huh?

You did say domestic nudity?

Yes? Said Wilhelmina.

Which implies that only those who are of the domicile are welcome to do it, as opposed to visitors, I mean like, the ying and yang thing, with a person from outside the family for domestic nudist, or even for a female relatives----

If you stay with us, you get treated like family, said Wilhelmina with weary friendliness. Right, ragamuffin?

Absolutely!

Chrysanthemum and Tiffany-Dawn followed suit as if they did it every day.

Right, muffin! Welcome to our kitchen and dining room! We do all our cooking and dining out here on that redwood picnic table!

I guess, said Chrysanthemum, I'm talking the big S thing.

Sex? Said Wilhelmina.

Kinda sorta.

Sexuality and nudity have nothing to do with each other, said Troll calmly. Nudism is not sexual, but we accept that there is a connection between sexuality and nudity.

It's the last thing that happens before you make love, said Tiffany-Dawn .

Which is? Asked Willy.

Taking it off! Shedding the clothes! Ain't that part of sexing?

But being naked does not mean you're going to have sex! Said Troll. If I get a hard on? Or you get wet and your nipples get hard? That's part of our instinctual animal nature. It's no big deal. It's all about accepting the re-wilding that comes with nudity.

The unity of nudity, said Chrysanthemum sagely, the unification of the---

It doesn't mean it's sexual even if you're aroused, said Wilhelmina. Is that what you're saying Ragamuffin?

Yes. It's only sexual if you decide to let it be. Naturism is about existing in a state non-sexual nudity, without excluding sexuality; unless there's a mutual attraction in between consenting adults and they decide it's going to be sexual. And for me, sex without love is "fucking"----

And "fucking" is for animals, said Chrysanthemum with relief. I choose to be celibate---

No wonder! Mumbled Wilhelmina.
---Celibacy allows a clarification of the senses
and the emotions, said Chrysanthemum, relieved
to be outdoors. Personally? I have no sexual
urges. I'm celibate because one day when the
right man comes, I'll be all his, and as a naturist
I don't believe in birth control!
I don't either, said Tiffany-Dawn .
I do, said Wilhelmina. What about you
ragamuffin?
He pretended not to hear.
The others disrobed. Chrysanthemum took of her
flip flops joyously and took off her muumuu. She
was nude, and it seemed that neither her or
Tiffany-Dawn had on anything else. She raised
her arms, took in a deep breath and stretched,
exultantly. Her arm pits were very hairy.
She took a deep, soothing breathe.
Muumuus are a nude girl's best friend, around
clothe dummies! This yard is a paradise!
We compost everything we can, and we dilute
the waters body in a five to one ratio, said Troll,
and we water with it, and look at how beautiful
it all grows!
Do you use a composting toilet? Asked
Chrysanthemum.
Can we not talk out that? asked Wilhelmina.
Y'all compost your poop? Asked Tiffany-Dawn ?
Eeew!

It's all good, said Troll. We don't wast water, and we're just doing exactly what they do at a water treatment facility.

Without wasting any water or contaminating the soil! Said Chrysanthemum. King Willow, I love it! I feel sooo much better already! The outdoors calm me. Oh, wait----Is it ok for me to nude up too?

She had a lean, athletic body, a curvy rear, smooth, dark, glossy skin, and her breasts were small and firm with perky nipples that were quite large. Her nipples were erect. She had a thick well maintained bush of pubic hair fluffed and glossy with Organic Olive oil, with a wispy trail that rose to her round little belly button.

I don't look bad for an over the hill gymnast, do I? Said Chrysanthemum, shyly.

Oh, you look great, sweetie! Said Tiffany-Dawn . She runs five miles a day and does her nude yoga deal! I can't do more than three!

Just keep running, you'll do five too! Said Chrysanthemum.

Tiffany-Dawn had red body hair, much like her sister, but where Wilhelmina was very lean with small breasts, she had fuller breast and slightly wider hips. Her arm pits were shaved, and her pubic hair were buzz trimmed.

I'm tryna get Bluebell to go hairy, said Chrysanthemum. I have gotten her to do yoga, now I'm tryna get her to eat hands only!

Let me get some basins and warm water, said
Troll, so we can all freshen up!
Let me help, sweety! Said Wilhelmina.
They were out in the yard. She and Troll pulled
off the clothes that they wore and folded them
neatly. He went to check the three cock pots in
which their dinner was cooking, before he got the
water.
She produced four PVC basins. They were
actually cut off pvc buckets. He brought a black,
five gallon PVC bucket full of warm water.
This is our solar water heater! He said grinning.
He and Wilhelmina chuckled. Do y'all mind
public washing? If you do? Or you gotta whiz?
Feel free to go in the bushes, or use the bucket
labeled urinal behind a tree. Don't worry, it has
baking soda and water in it---no odor.
Speaking of which, said Chrysanthemum.
Oh G-d! groaned Tiffany-Dawn, Please don't get
into that---
When y'all poo, plowed on Chrysanthemum,
undaunted, do y'all use water or paper?
Wilhelmina shrugged.
He's taught me not to use paper. We water wash
then we wash our hand with baking soda and
lemon water. We'll show you where we keep it.
I'm embarrassed to discuss it, but I now prefer
water too, said Tiffany-Dawn . It's a lot cleaner.
Water is more hygienic than paper, said Troll.

Yup! Said Chrysanthemum. Wash instead of
wipe, I say!
He filled up each of their basins, using a gallon
water bottle recycled for use as a ewer.
Wilhelmina brought each a neatly folded towel,
and a face clothe and a loofah pads. She and Troll
moistened the face towels, and liberally sprinkled
it with baking soda from a large plastic box on
the loofah pads. They stood on the side of the
strip of lawn that served as a patio. Both placed
their basins on a round twig table. They
carefully doused themselves, taking water from
the basin with tin cans turned into water bowls,
then they scrubbed themselves with the baking
soda covered loofah pads. Each washed then
scrubbed others back. Then they rinsed off the
face towels, and used it to rinse wipe themselves.
You get a good cleaning this way, using very
little water, said Wilhelmina.
I'll try anything once! Said Tiffany-Dawn.
Lately I been bathing with hot water ad no soap.
And the baking soda water doesn't hurt the soil,
said Troll, as they toweled off. It's bio-
degradable.
He and Wilhelmina dried each other's backs.
So y'all eat only with your hands? Asked Troll.
Hey, said Chrysanthemum, if you wash your
hands before you eat, why not?

It's something that the majority of the word still does, said Troll. Take India. Indians eat mainly with their bare hands.

Exactly! Said Chrysanthemum. The only other country with more people is China. They got billions of people! They eat with chop sticks which I think is a waste of good wood. And just about all Indians eat with bare hands. Same with a buncha Asian and African countries!

So what is that called? Asked Tiffany-Dawn.

They're bare hands eaters, said Wilhelmina.

All of us eat something with our hands, said Troll. Right Muffin?

DUDE! Said Chrysanthemum. It's part of living natural! There were no utensils in Eden!

It get's worst! Said Tiffany-Dawn , giggling. She's all about group eating.

What do you mean? Asked Wilhelmina.

Everyone eats off one communal platter!

No way! Said Wilhelmina.

Yup! Said Chrysanthemum, smiling happily.

Oh, my gosh! Said Wilhelmina. What is that?

Why dirty up more than one plate and use water unnecessarily? Said Chrysanthemum. Save on water. Smartest thing? Eat off lettuce or cabbage leaves then eat the leaves too.

Mexicans and some other societies use flat breads in the same way, said Troll.

Are you saying you two gurls eat off the same plate with your hands at the same time? Asked Wilhelmina.

If you wash your hands carefully in warm water, said Chrysanthemum, it's neater than eating with utensils, and it's more hygienic.

It may not look as pretty, but who cares? Said Tiffany-Dawn .

In a lot of parts of the world, said Troll, the entire family eats from one plate or pot.

Y'all wanna try it? Said Tiffany-Dawn , giggling.

Not tonight, said Wilhelmina dryly. To be honest? Me and Troll do that too as a couple.

It's a very efficient process if you eat with three fingers only! Said Chrysanthemum. It really bonds a family!

I don't know, said Wilhelmina.

You eat sandwiches and fruit, chicken and fries and burgers with your hands, right? Said Chrysanthemum. Ever eaten fries off someone else plate with your fingers?

Yeah, said Wilhelmina, with a growing interest. She always claims she doesn't want fries when I make'm then she eats all of mine off my plate, said Troll. Wilhelmina poked him on the shoulder, and poked her tongue out at him.

Well, you're into eating with your hands! Said Chrysanthemum. Some of us just take it further. We eat everything with our hands.

A different form of barefoot, right?

They all laughed.

Kinda sorta! Said Troll.

What about soups and drinks?

What about them?

How you gonna eat liquid with your hands?

You don't eat liquids. You drink them. You can drink using your hands, you know. But no, I don't believe in a group sharing one bottle.

People do it all the time with booze, said Troll.

Ok, look, I'll share a bottle with Chryssie, said Tiffany-Dawn , but I wouldn't with a crowd!

Eden is reclaimed a little atta time, said Chrysanthemum, anyway, I believe in cleansing the hands frequently, and especially before you eat!

Yeah, we've done the hand eating, and the one plate stuff, said Tiffany-Dawn , scratching her belly.

Sounds gay to me, said Wilhelmina.

It is not! Not a big deal! Willy, you eat Pizza with your hands!

Yeah, yeah! Cookies too! Said Wilhelmina.

You should try it, said Chrysanthemum. Group eating is very intimate.

I don't know, said Wilhelmina. I might eat with my hands from one plate with my ragamuffin, but you grubs better not put your paws on my food. This is something I'll need a little growing time about.

As the two women, washed and rinsed their skin, Tiffany-Dawn toweled herself, but Chrysanthemum folded her towel, sat on it, facing East, and meditated in the Lotus position. She believes in air drying, whispered Tiffany-Dawn . She meditates as her skin dries!

After a moment Chrysanthemum rejoined them. After looking at both of them in the nude casually, as did Wilhelmina, Troll politely looked away, but he got an erection.

DUDE! Said Chrysanthemum, Look at the SIZE of that giant baby maker! DAYUM, boss, you're a HOSS!

The women giggled.

Dah-yung! that sucker looks HARD too! Look at his nipples! You probably make Miss Willy walk bow legged all the time!

He realized then that he disliked Chrysanthemum profoundly.

The women tittered uncomfortably. Troll prayed that the ground might open and swallow him. To his complete horror Chrysanthemum squeezed his nipple, then casually took hold his penis and examined it.

Circumcised! Healthy, but barbaric… Please don't hurt us, Massa Troll----King Willow!

Troll looked mortified.

Stop it! He said, and pushed her hand away, but the others all laughed. To his utter humiliation, his nipple became erect, and his manhood grew harder and pointed upwards. Immediately he began to hate Chrysanthemum deeply.

Look, try ta respect boundaries, ok? said Wilhelmina, feeling sorry for Troll. You didn't like your ass getting groped, right?

She didn't grope him, she examined it! She meant no harm, said Tiffany-Dawn defensively. Chryssie's a hoot!

It's cool, said Troll. I didn't mind.

Sorry, King Willow! Didn't mean to violate your boundary! I feel like if I known you two all my life!

It's Troll, he said frostily.

I REFUSE to call you that, King Willow!

Whatever!

What kinda name is TROLL anyway, King Willow? It's a put down! It's like the N word. Would you let people call you N? It means you're a homeless bum!

Not to my old buddies, said Troll.

I know how to bum and I've lived on the bum, and it's no fun! Why do you call yourself that? Why do you as a nature loving natural hairy nudist allow yourself to be called-----
Wilhelmina tuned her out. She seemed so lonely to Wilhelmina. It seemed to Wilhelmina that Chrysanthemum spoke like someone who normally had no one to talk to or no one who listened.
I hate this crazy chick! Whispered Troll into Wilhelmina's ear, the first chance he got. You keep her away from me! You hear me muffin? Please?
She laughed loudly.
Oh, wait! You practice DOMESTIC natural nudity and I nuded in your domicile without asking for permission, so did y'all give me permission to nude too?
Sure. Look, said Wilhelmina briskly, if at some point in the future my husband and either of you want to be intimate---
WHAT? Asked Troll. How dare you Wilhelmina?
She waived aside his objections.

---- *at some point in the future, I just don't want it to be something that goes on in secret, so long as you remember he's mines, and he sleeps with me at nights. And don't do it publicly. I wouldn't wanna see it. Some of my best friends have sister wives, and I think it's no big deal if a man has more than one wife. Don't touch him till you get tested and show us the result, and don't touch him if he doesn't want it, please.*

Troll was stunned.

I – I'm humiliated –

Don't be, Daddy! You're a man, whispered Wilhelmina, You been around that little goat MaGoo and I been around the three wives too long. None of this freaks me out. I want to keep harmony in between us. I don't wanna ask you to do something you can't do.

You saying I can't be trusted? He whispered back, wounded. You saying I can't be faithful? She kissed him.

You know I'm not saying that, ragamuffin! Just don't be scared if something happens. I might not like it, but look at how happy it works for MaGoo and his wives.

What about kissing? Asked Chrysanthemum. I love kissing my friends.

What kind? Asked Wilhelmina. Like face or lips?

Either, said Chrysanthemum.

*You're just lusting for Troll's pretty ole lips!
Said Tiffany-Dawn .
He does have some fine looking lips! Said
Chrysanthemum.
So long as he doesn't mind, said Wilhelmina, I
am not jealous if he's kissed---
What if he kisses back? Asked Chrysanthemum.
Wilhelmina shrugged.
Well, in that case? Said Tiffany-Dawn , We
regularly take a test every month at the club---
not that I was screwing anybody, but they
require it---it's a topless club. I got my results
right here from Monday!
Me Too! Trilled Chrysanthemum.
Why did they make you take one? Asked
Chrysanthemum.
Because those sleazes see every cocktail waitress
as a potential dancer, said Chrysanthemum.
Can I sleep with y'all tonight? Asked Tiffany-
Dawn . I'm talking non-sexual, I got no interest
in my own big ole hairy dumb brother in law.
He's not dumb, Bluebelle! Said Chrysanthemum.
I think he's the smartest man I've met so far!
Troll looked at her, and felt some what touched.
He turned to thank her just as she leaned in to
peck his cheek, and their lips met. She kissed him
anyway, and acted casually about it.
Sorry if I got on your nerves, boss, she said.
It's all good, he said, as his heart pounded.*

*So can I sleep in y'alls bed? Asked Tiffany-Dawn
. I'm not feeling settled in here, and being in that
little cabin, even with Chryssie, has me a little
nervous.*

If it's ok with Troll, said Wilhelmina easily.

Troll looked frightened.

If it's ok with Willy!

Sure. Daddy, you are ok with it, right?

Yes darling.

*How large is your bed? Asked Chrysanthemum,
becoming much calmer.*

Troll looked scared.

Wilhelmina fought the urge to laugh.

*King size? Said Troll unhappily. We don't do as
lot of talking in bed---*

*You got any room for me? Said
Chrysanthemum. I'll sleep at the foot of the bed.*

*Of course, ma'am! He said. You can sleep next to
us, you don't have to sleep by our smelly toes.*

*My toes aren't smelly, said Tiffany-Dawn ,
speak for yourself!*

*So! Can we do a group sleep? Asked
Chrysanthemum. It's not sexual! In ancient days
communal sleeping, group sleeping, was the way
that humans kept warm and felt secure before
they discovered fire---think of being in a dark
cave---even after they discovered fire was to....*

He and Wilhelmina stared at her.

Don't worry, she said. I won't talk in bed. I'm feeling really a little scared too, you know?
Sure, said Wilhelmina. The more the merrier.
Really, said Troll. We'd love to have you.
Outstanding!
We try to follow the cycle of the day, said Troll. We don't stay up very long after sun down.
We eat a light dinner, said Wilhelmina. We eat leftovers for breakfast.
All I eat for dinner is a piece of fruit and a glass of water! said Chrysanthemum.
Not to be rude, y'all, said Tiffany-Dawn, but she's got me in the habit of doing the same! We usually split a big apple!
No, that's cool, said Wilhelmina. If you wanna grab a little off our plate---
Yeah, sure! I'd love to taste a little, said Tiffany-Dawn.
When they finished eating. Troll and Wilhelmina shared a small bowl of stewed lentils, a little bit of fruit and a little salad. Both Chrysanthemum and Tiffany-Dawn dipped a piece of carrot in the lentils and ate it out of politeness, but were surprised at how good it tasted, and ate a little more of the salad and lentils.
Tiffany-Dawn and Chrysanthemum split a large golden delicious apple with them. Each had a goblet of white wine.
They ate mostly in silence.

After they finished, they briefly laid on their back on a wool blanket next to each other in the middle of the garden, listened to some Teena Marie love ballads on a boom box, and star gazed. Troll stopped feeling annoyed. As they grew sleepy, they finished off the bottle of white wine, then they all brushed their teeth, washed their hands and faces, and prepared for bed. When they went to sleep, they climbed into the sleeping loft of their little house. Wilhelmina lay next to her husband, with her sister besides her. Tiffany-Dawn, who could sleep anywhere, swiftly went to sleep.

Chrysanthemum laid next to him, as near the edge of the futon as possible. She no longer seemed as confident or cocky as she was earlier before they went to bed. At first he was nervous, but when her body touched his back, she felt that she was shaking. Then a sense of compassion and sympathy for her filled him, and his annoyance earlier was quickly forgotten.

Miss Chrysanthemum? Are you alright? He whispered kindly.

Panic attack. She said anxiously. What am I doing here in bed next to a man I don't even know?

Awww!

Just a little scared. You know? New people, new place?

Wilhelmina nudged him. He turned on his back.
Come here ma'am, he said.
N-n-no I'm alright!
Come on, ma'am, I mean you no harm.
Oh, I'm ok! she whispered.
Ma'am, your shaking!
Just a little nervous! Panicky.
You got nothing to be scared of dear. I'd lay
down my life before I'd let anything bad happen
to you. And I ain't gonna harm you little sister!
I got my wife right here, and she's awake, so you
don't have to worry. Nobody's trying anything.
He gently drew Chrysanthemum to his side, and
put on arm around her. He patted her back,
reassuringly, as if she was a scared child.
Thank you, King Willow, she whispered.
You're safe, Queen Chrysanthemum. I'm a look
out for you. Your safe.
Thank you, kind sir!
She put her head on his chest. For a brief moment
she cried. He patted her back, and didn't think of
having a beautiful young woman in his arms.
She was just another kid without family and
without a home, and he quickly forgot any dislike
he felt earlier. He gently patted and rubbed her
back. Soon her shaking subsided and quickly fell
asleep. It surprised him to find that he was
crying too.

In the morning he woke up in their little sleeping
loft to find that his wife had gone to start
breakfast, and left them alone with him in bed.
The two lay on either side of him soundly asleep,
huddled against him. Tiffany-Dawn had her back
firmly pressed against him, and was lightly
snoring with her mouth slightly opened. He
smiled.
Chrysanthemum laid with her head pillowed on
his chest, with an arm draped over his belly.
Even as she slept, Chrysanthemum's hand glided
down from his belly into his pubic hairs, and
took hold of him and squeezed, though she was
asleep. He was mortified to see that he had his
arms wrapped around her. He also had a
morning diamond cutter. He pulled her hand off
gently, got up gingerly and fled, grateful that
neither one woke up.

Chapter 5

Wilhelmina was in the yard, finishing
preparation of a pot of oatmeal. Espresso was
brewing. He picked her up in his arms, kissed
her, without saying anything, took her into the
little empty cabin. She knew what he needed, and
so she got on her knees and fallated him for a
moment. They necked avidly for a moment, then
sixty nined. He made love to her with an ardor
that left both sodden and sweaty.
My Lawd, ragamuffin! She panted. I ain't mad
atcha!
Are you ok?
I ain't mad atcha! That was beyond awesome!
You gonna get some more in a minute! He said. I
been needing this since last night.
Did they work you up like this?
They're ok looking.
Are you mad at me?

No, mommy! But why did you leave me alone
like that with them?
Sorry, boo!
That was very cruel, muffin!
She smiled at him. What, daddy?
Leaving me alone with them!
Did they scare you? Sorry, daddy!
They were pressed and cuddled up asleep on me!
Daddy, I'm so sorry!
Scared me to death! And Chrysanthemum had
the baby maker in her hand!
So now you calling Mister Python the baby
maker too, King Willow? She laughed loudly,
almost rolling out of bed.
Muffin, it's not funny!
Are you sure she was asleep?
Yeah, but it's still scared the stuff out of me!
She's harmless.
I don't want to give a wrong idea.
I know. It's ok if being around them makes you
hard. The more for me.
Ok, look, I'm scared, alright?
Don't be. Part of why I married you is because I
trust you!
Why ja say that's stuff last night, muffin? Don't
I please you?
Yes.
Don't you want me anymore?

Shhh! Don't even ask that! My views about being a sister wife are changing! Can't nobody take my ragamuffin from me.
Can you please hold me, muffin? Can you say that again?
I adore you, baby boy!

Wilhelmina? Said Marigold. You are miles away.

Oh! Pardon! I was just thinking of the last months! My sister and a friend of hers moved in with us. Everything has changed.

Really? asked Marigold.

We want to bring them into the forest. How do you know about Tiffany-Dawn dancing---

We have *studied* you, ahavti! Said Marigold. She quit dancing, she said. She and her buddy now live with us. They work with us.

Perhaps these are going to be your sister wives? Asked Thyme.

Wilhelmina looked at her, surprised by the thought.

I don't know that I'm able to do that right now, she said. But I am willing to let him have more wives. And these two women are very close to me now.

Of course you can, said Thyme. It may not
be easy at first, no more so than it is for us.
But you have the advantage of us.
What do you mean?
Tiffany-Dawn is your sister, and you
already love her. Chrysanthemum has
become your sister. We had to learn to love
each other as sister wives.
You and he…you and he have a----problem?
said Marigold, but it is far more small than
you think.
What do you mean?
The forest have ears, said Thyme.
I still don't understand!
You are afraid to give yourself to him
completely, said Marigold, possibly because
of…how can one put this?
He is as large as a stallion, said Thyme.
Abruptly she broke into laughter. They
joined in.
Please tell me the truth, has Troll ever had a
girl friend or woman from the forest?
No, said Sage, he has no such interest
because of our smallness.
Chrysanthemum is small!
Not to us, said Marigold. Poor Troll is alone,
but for you. That is why we are overjoyed
that he found you.

Tears rolled down Wilhelmina's face.

I was afraid…I was afraid to give myself completely to him. But we went out to the lake some weeks ago, and we did everything. I'm still a little afraid, but not really.

We each had that same fear about our husband once! Said Sage. He too is very----

My *Dear* Sage, *please*! Scolded Marigold.

I'm sorry, whispered Sage.

We will supply you with a wondrous unguent, said Marigold loftily, that will serve to alleviate any issues that you might have about becoming one with him, once properly applied to the areas of concern.

Really, it's ok now, said Wilhelmina.

All the same! She ceremoniously handed Wilhelmina jar wrapped in parchment, covered in Hebrew words. She took it, and removing the square of leather that was tied to the top of it with a string, she looked at them carefully, studied it briefly, then smelled it.

It smells, hmmmm, it smells like…..KY Jelly and oil of cloves?

Cut with some denatured Olive oil, yes, said Marigold solemnly. It is a wondrous anointment that will make all things flow easier, as it were. I suggest one other thing.

And what's that?

Before you give yourself to him? Said
Marigold. Take an elixir that will soothe
and calm you. There is such an elixir that
from ancient days has been known to aid
nervous brides at the moment of betroth-
ment.

And what is that?

Fortified wine, lacking that, a few shots of
good whiskey, said Marigold solemnly.

Have you ever heard of Ripple?

Ripple? Asked Wilhelmina, fighting not to
laugh. Ripple is drunk by Winos.

Well? There you are! Beer will do, if nothing
else is available.

Hmmmm. Really, I'm no longer scared.

We pray, said Sage, that you and Troll will
become friends to our City across the new
Jordan!

What are you talking about?

Have you never wondered where we come
from? Said Marigold impatiently.

Well---yes…

There is a ---city? A Village? Call it a
Community of our people.

Oh My G-d! Do you mean Hobbits?

HOBBITS? Said Marigold. How *DARE YOU*
refer to us that way?

Well, you called me a *Nephilim! Sorry---*
Do not *insult* us with that name! snapped
Sage, suddenly enraged.
Calmly, calmly, said Thyme worriedly.
I'm *so* sorry! Said Wilhelmina. Even though
you *did* call me a Nephilim. I didn't mean----
No, I *cannot* help it, dear Wilhelmina, Sage
said. My anger is not directed at you.
Hobbits! *Hobbits*! Ahhh! Said Marigold
furiously. This is the *curse* of those *accursed*
books by that deceitful devil Tolkien! I read
them---in secrecy, and let me tell you: they
are complete and utter rot---no, Rubbish!
Rubbish! Beware of the *English*!
Why? Asked Wilhelmina.
They are a race of devilish *deceivers*, said
Marigold. Vow breakers!
Once *Tolkien* was injured in a bicycle trip,
and lost in the moors, near death, said Sage.
A Community of our people mercifully took
him in, said Thyme, knowing not the
serpent they had taken to their bosom, they
nursed him, cared for him and saved him!
Wait! Are you saying there are pygmies---I
mean Noble Ones---in England? Asked
Wilhelmina.
Of course! Said Marigold. The ignorant
boiled-beef eaters call them leprechauns or
elves!

I thought that was the Irish?
Ahhh, yes! Thyme. The drunken Catholic
potatoes eaters also call our people those
vile names! But this was in England, in
Oxfordshire. A poor, hungry university
student, he was! He was allowed to live
among them as he recovered, and
ingratiated himself. He deceived them as to
his intentions.
Like the evil, deceitful, loathsome *Nephilim*
that he was, said Marigold, how do you
think he repaid our kindness? He wrote
those *accursed* novels! He named us *Hobbits*!
But you should be grateful! She said. He
protected your secrets!
My dear, Tolkien was a *fool*! Said Marigold.
He protected *nothing!* What he *should* have
done was to keep silent! He *vowed* not to
speak of us! *Vowed*, I say! Instead he *libeled*
us! *Hobbits* indeed! What exactly is a *Hobbit*,
please? *Little tobacco smoking gluttons! They
live in holes with round doors. Laughing stocks*
with hairy feet! Look! *Look!*
She took off her velvet slippers and silk
stockings. Our feet are no *hairier* than yours!
We are *Jews* who happen to be *smaller* than
you giants! Not *wretched* little *hobbits!*

Hey! Hey! I'm not a *giant*! Said Wilhelmina, finally losing her patience. A person can shave their feet!

Please, sisters! Said Thyme to her two fellow wives, Gently! Mos mos, polle polle!

Very well, said Sage, very well!

You must excuse me, my dear....He came in contact with our

people, said Marigold,   and made a *mockery* of us with those foolish

books! May his name be *erased* and *forgotten*!

Can you please *not* call me a *Nephilim*? Said Wilhelmina, wanting to laugh because of nervousness. Friends do not call each other names. I'm not even that tall!

You are almost as tall as Troll! Said Sage.

True, she said, not wanting to argue. Why do you hide?

How can you ask that? asked Marigold, wiping tears from her eyes. Look at what happens to the dear little pygmies of Africa! A sweet, child like people of the forest. Who do they bother? No one! Consider how they are treated! Look at all that *Hobbit* nonsense!

Recently, according to NPR, said Wilhelmina, a ancient community of little people of your size was found in south Africa.

And their graves and burial places were desecrated, said Marigold sadly. We are made *curiosities* and *laughingstocks*, when we are not murdered! Look at how the poor benighted midgets are treated!

Are midgets noble ones? Asked Wilhelmina.

Many are, said Marigold. We are a *proud* people. If they *dared* treat us like that we would be forced to slaughter Nephilim! As did king David! We are not *murderous*. We prefer not to do so.

Are you saying King *David* was a ---little Jew? Asked Wilhelmina.

Was he not a descendant of Judah? Asked Thyme a little testily.

I guess, said Wilhelmina.

He had our blood, said Sage blandly. Holy writ teaches that he was the *smallest* of his family. Jesse was a descendant of Joel, as was his wife. You read between the lines…you follow? He may have been one of us, undoubtedly….

Yes.

We hide because we are small, said Sage, sadly. And even among our people it was not safe. Many thought we were ---how do you say? Goblins?

They are fools, many of them, said
Marigold, But we are just small people, yet
devout Jews, none the less.
You are very Militant, Marigold, she said.
The four women laughed.
Militant Marigold! Said Sage, and they
laughed harder.
Alright, enough! Said Thyme finally.
Help us, said Marigold. Rav Moshe is about
to become a father. One of his wives is too
far along to come spend time with him.
We have a very dear friend, who is teaching
us much of Judaism, said Wilhelmina. We
call her Diloris, but she is also called
Chinita. Then there's Elder Mingo…but he
does everything with his wife.
How does he feel about our faith?
He is the descendant of the Sephardic Jews
of the Dominican Republic—Just like his
wife, she said. He studies with us and
Chinita, but is afraid to tell his wife.
Hmmm. Bring them to us, said Marigold.
The wife is as tall as Troll, she said.
We know of Isaiah, said Thyme. Soon she
will face a great ordeal.
Time is of the essence, said Sage.
Why?

Before the birth of the child, said Marigold,
our husband will be recalled to our city,
New Cavernton the Beautiful.
To Israel?
No, said Thyme, across the New Jordan.
Suddenly Wilhelmina understood.
The Trinity River? Is that the New Jordan?
Yes.
Ohhhh…. Your city is close by!
Yes, said Marigold, near indeed.
Will we continue to do camp outs once he is
recalled?
Yes, of course, said Marigold, though if we
are too far along in our pregnancy some of
us will not come. Yet we will see each other
again, and you will see our babies.

Understand, though we live in Cavernton, said Sage, this forest supplies us with all of our food needs. This forest is perma-culture at it's best! Our herd animals are pastured here secretly. They fertilize the soil and eat weeds. Goats, sheep, and even miniature cattle and horses. The cattle are actually a cattle and Yak hybrid. There are thousands of free range chickens that we keep here, as well as many other kinds of fowls. There are vineyards and various orchards in this forest growing every kind of grape and fruit. We are experts at eco-forestry, and Natural farming. We seed the ground with seed impregnated clay balls and do no plowing or fertilizing. After, who is a greater farmer than the creator? The plants do their own plowing. The edges of the forest we sadly leave to the Nephilim, but in here? We frighten them away. Our wolfhounds chase them out if they try to enter, and we convince them that this place is the realm of haunt-lings, and ghosts.

We fell all intrusive trees that do not belong
here. We use them for implement making
and for firewood. We also remove invasive
plants and shrubs, and what is left? This
beautiful, bounteous forest. We have
mastered the art of allowing a forest to exist
as a wild place, while we grow our food in
it, and harvest the bounteous wild foods
that are there to be found. This forest is a
preserve of our green city, and though you
do not see it, many of us live here in the
trees and under the ground in berms and
other forms of sustainable housing, in a
chain of small eco-villages.
How? This is a flood plain!
We know how to cope with floods, said
Marigold with a smile. We prepare for the
cycles, and are homes in the floodplain
beneath the earth are built as semi-
permanent shelters. Many of us have
permanent homes in Cavernton.
I don't see any houses!

That is as it should be! Our forest houses are built as temporary sustainable dwellings built of living plants when possible to conceal them from the eyes of outsiders. They are built to be unobtrusive to nature. There are many small prosperous eco-villages built all around you and under the earth here. The River and the larger streams and creeks are our roads and highways.

Why is it I've never seen any of this?

Remember the cottage where we dressed you? Said Marigold.

She smiled. I get it!

If our houses are not noticeable, it is because, said Marigold, dear Wilhelmina, we know how to conceal ourselves.

Will I ever see any of this?

In time, said Thyme. You will see more. Soon.

Dear Marigold is also expecting, said Thyme. Perhaps so is Sage.

May the great One be praised! Said Marigold. Soon, so will you, dear Thyme! We need small people, dear Wilhelmina, who are believers, and who can be trusted.

So, said Wilhelmina resentfully, you'll have your babies and I'll not see them until they are older!

The three women smiled sympathetically.

Or maybe not, said Marigold. Maybe you
will come to our home as a guest to see our
newborns.
I would really like that!
We need *bridges*. Recruit them for us…we
love you and our friend Troll! We will help
you become rich, but you must use the
wealth wisely!
I will help you, said Wilhelmina. You
mustn't tell my husband we have made this
agreement.
Why?
Money for him is not as important as it
should be. Rearing children, if we have any,
will be expensive. If he marries me…if I
don't lose him!
You won't! said Thyme. And I'm certain
that you will marry you sooner that you
think!
And perhaps we will throw you a wondrous
wedding feast! Said Sage.
I would love that! I would love it if all of
you came if we get married!
You will! Said Marigold.
He would refuse to accept anything, but I
know he will help.

We will also extend you two our protection!
Said Marigold. You like the Wolfhounds,
yes?
Oh, yeah! They're awesome!
To begin, said Marigold, in a few weeks we
will give you wolfhound puppies of this
breed we used as protectors and steeds.
They will be brought to your home. We will
give you of the kind that grow almost as
large as you! They are expensive to feed,
and their diet is quite unique, but we will
teach you the caring and feeding of them.
That is very kind! She said. Thank you.
It will be our pleasure, my dear, said
Marigold.
If Moshe approves, said Sage, and grants
permission, we will start to teach you of our
faith and Hebrew in the morning, if
HaShem so wills it!
One day? I wish to see your hidden city,
said Wilhelmina.
They were stunned into silence.
As much as we would like that---that---that
is impossible! Said Marigold.
I vow here and now to never reveal any of
this! She said.
They eyed her carefully and conferred in
whispers.

We will consider this, said Marigold. It would please us greatly to show you our home and give welcome to you. Yet the decision cannot be ours. In time we will tell you. First you and Troll must convert completely. With approval of our husband, if your husband is willing, we will give lessons and materials to study before we depart.

Chapter 6

A few days after the first camping trip they took into the forest everything changed. This was weeks before Tiffany-Dawn and Chrysanthemum moved in. Still, she did not give herself to a man who she felt she could not live without. She finally decided to spend one last night with him, explain why she could not be with him, then let him go. She then planned to go home and take a bottle of 500 milligram Doxipins. She couldn't fulfill his needs fully, so she knew she had to let him go, yet she could not go on without him, for he was her life and without him there would be no more life.

They loved going to the lake on nights when the weather was so raw that no one else was there even if the moon was out.

Such was the night on which Wilhelmina chose to end her relationship and her life. The full moon blazed. The wind howled. It seemed all the leaves were gone. It was one chilly, windy autumn night. They were listening to The Quiet Storm, in his cabin. Tiny, cozy, the rustic cabin was built on a flatbed trailer on wheels. It was parked by a stormy Joe Poole Lake. They were staying on the wide plank floor on his thin futon, atop a antique Navajo rug. Snugly covered with a handmade quilt of hers, they were in a mellow mood. They were in front of a brisk, fragrant, crackling mesquite wood fire. Vanilla scented candles burned, as the wind moaned seductively. Her life changed that night. It happened after they drank most of a bottle of his delicious homemade Pinot Noire. After a candle light, grilled fish dinner, after eating homemade cheese cake with a velvety peach reduction, they were just basking in the warmth. She forgot her fears of his hugeness. She reasoned that she owed this wonderful man at least one night of total pleasure. If he tore her up, she would soon be dead, so what did it matter? So she set her fears aside.

She gave herself to him in every way. No lubricant were needed, as it turned out.

69? He asked.

Please! She whispered.

To her amazement, soaking wet as she got, she squirted! He gasped with pleasure. And she did not scream, she howled.

Without discussion or planning, he mounted her. Slowly, gently, he entered her, and pulled out then pushed further in. There was a sharp sting of pain, as her hymen ruptured, but it was quickly forgotten. She came again and again, gasping with pleasure. Thrusting her hips against him, the intensity rose until he was practically pounding into her. Suddenly she howled, again and again. Then he roared like a lion, and she felt an explosion of his burning essence squirt into her. Her insides clenched and a waves of spasmodic electric pleasure seized her and didn't seem to end.

Both were astonished by how well it went. It went on through the night. He was so gentle! She suffered no harm, the pain she briefly felt was the rupturing of her hymen.

After she caught her breath she laughed with delight.

What, muffin?

Marigold and Lil Bit were right!

Huh?

That was AWESOME! You didn't tear me up! What was I afraid of?

He kissed her lips, and it was the sweetest kiss of her life.

They fell into a deep sleep. When she awoke by late morning she could barely speak. She felt ecstatic. She lay in his arms, as he slept, wondering if it was all a dream. Then abruptly she wondered if he had, or wanted to have another woman. After all she'd ben through! He might be planning to dump her…She became furious.

Hey! Hey!

She slugged him on the shoulder. She hit him on the chest with her pillow.

He awoke groggily.

What the….Little girl…why ja hit me for, muffin? He asked sleepily, giving her a kiss.

You won't get away with it, you hear? I'm unto you!

He blinked.

Huh?

You got another woman behind my back?

No!

Liar!

Gurl, I said no!

If you have another girl---

Quit tripping!

Ok…No other women, buster!

I don't want no one but you!

You told me about Mrs. Bell.

She's like family.

You can only be with me, ok?

Fine with me! You're the one who always says it
would be cool to have sister wives!
That's different! I'm talking about you
SNEAKING around with skanks!
He smiled reassuringly.
Well, I don't!
She threatened to clip off what she called the
python if he ever saw anyone else.
That kind of talk is unnecessary!
He was hurt.
I mean it!
That's not funny!
Well…maybe I've shouldn't have said
it….sorry…
Ok…you're so crazy!
Am not! I hope Bubba approves of you!
Oh, yeah, Bubba! Listen to me, muffin: I won't
share you, ok? You gotta chose!
Why? He'll probably like you.
What if he doesn't?
All this time I'm with you? I ain't with him and
he misses me and I miss him. It ain't sexual
between me and him.
Yeah? How old is he?
I don't know.
When did you have him?
Huh?
Bubba. Who is he? Your little son?
No! My secret sweety!

*Now you listen and listen good, gurl! I said I
won't SHARE you!*

Really? What wrong with you?

*If he's not your son, or your man, he's a former
lover, right?*

Bubba's my Tabby Cat!

WHAT?

He started to laugh.

A tabby? For real?

*Yes! I want him to be a part of your life too,
Teddy-Bear! Same with my dogs, Rusty and
Dusty! They're big great German shepherds and
I'ma breed them and sell puppies.*

So---you really care for me, muffin?

I gave you my virginity! She whispered.

Oh my G-d! Really?

You're my first man!

I'm going to be your only man if you let me.

I want you to be!

So you're my baby gurl?

Yes!

*Until now, you hardly seem to want me! He
drew her into his arms.*

I was scared!

Of what, darling?

Of ripping open!

He started to cry.

*Muffin, don't ever be scared of me! You think I'd
hurt you?*

Not you---it!
If you keep squeezing it like that we won't be having this talk!
Why?
We'll be doing something else!
That's what I was hoping!
In a minute. We need this talk. It is me!
I know that!
Well, I wouldn't hurt you! Don't you love me?
I adore you, Teddy-Bear!
Please learn to trust me like I do you.
Ok.
As long as you denied me? I'm wasn't feeling loved!
They sat in each other's arms crying.
I ain't experienced like you…I been scared…look at the sheets!
Wow! Oh my G-d…I didn't know.
I was a virgin, you know?
He looked at the blood stains on the sheets with awe.
My sheets! He said.
She slugged his chest.
Ouch! I'm messing with you!
Ragamuffin!
Oh, my sweet little muffin! I had no idea! Did it hurt?
A little…but it doesn't now….you were so gentle!
Well, these sheets are a precious treasure to me.

Why?
These are a bond between us…I'ma fold them
just like this, and I'll sew them in a special gold
velvet bag with gold thread.
Why?
Cause I'll treasure them for the rest of my life,
my sweet virgin girl….one day, when I'm
buried? I want them buried with me.
She felt something strange running down her
face. She touched it and looked at her finger tips.
She looked at her tears with surprise.
She tried to speak but a knot in her throat kept
her from saying anything.
I been crying?
Shhhh! He said, kissing away her tears. You're
my beautiful virgin girl!
I ain't cried since my daddy died, she whispered.
I didn't mean to make you cry, muffin! I never
knew my Daddy.
Aww! Really?
One day? I wanna be a Daddy, he said.
He looked her in the eyes.
A man should be his girls daddy, she said. You
wanna be my daddy?
Aw, listen at you!
No really, you my honey …you gonna be my
sweet daddy?
Yes…but I don't have a mama…you gotta be my
mommy!

She grin a brilliant smile. Ok daddy!
First time I seen you smile like that,
Muffin…I'm sorry I made you cry baby.
Why? These are sweet tears….
After happy, tearful discussion, they made love
again.
They had a light breakfast of croissants, cheese,
chilled fruits, and espresso.
Spontaneously they went out and got a marriage
license. The next day they were married by Isaiah
and Mingo at the Westia Fellowship Hall.
Thereafter she and Troll were inseparable. She
and Troll worked together in what Wilhelmina
called an antique store, but what Isaiah saw as a
jumble shop before the marriage. They also
managed the Fellowship gift shop for Isaiah and
Mingo.
He immediately fulfilled one of her dreams right
after the marriage.
Wilhelmina loved Victorian Houses, with their
beautiful multi colored paint jobs, and their
ganger bread trimmings, but she was obsessed by
the environment, and wanted to live in a home
with a small Carbon foot print. In a word, she
wanted a Tiny House on Wheels.
On the day of their marriage he presented her
with a surprise: the keys to a miniature
Victorian mansion built on a dual axel flat bed
trailer. It was parked in front of the fellowship
Hall with a red ribbon tied around it.

Thereafter they lived together in their tiny 200 square foot home. They kept it in the enclosed backyard behind his shop. It had brass fixtures, stainless glass windows, a sky light, a ceiling fan, a tiny ship galley kitchen with cast iron appliances, and miniature bathroom, a cozy loft, and a small wood burning stove. Built with recycled fixtures and oak trim, lumber from old houses and recycled pallets, carefully painted with milk paint, it was also powered by solar panels, and had a backup propane heating system.
Troll built it himself in secrecy, in hopeful anticipation of his marriage.

Chapter 7

In the autumn, with Chrysanthemum and Tiffany-Dawn in tow, for the first time, with MaGoo and his wives, as well as Moon and Lil Bit, in addition to harvesting the garden they grew together, they harvested pecans, mushrooms, berries, wild teas, and several bushels of wild Mustang grapes. They turned the grapes into wine and jelly. They frequently fished through the autumn and winter sans any fishing license. Furthermore, they hiked extensively, and biked to every corner of the Trinity River Forest, where they could go that way. They took long Canoe trips up and down the Trinity, camping in the forest. Often they invited Chinita, as many still called her. They began to regularly take her on the camp outs. So came she and the other two to know MaGoo's wives.

Chrysanthemum quickly came to love the Trinity Forest, and became fast friends with Chinita and MaGoo's wives, as did Tiffany-Dawn. By then there was no longer any talk of Chrysanthemum living alone in the Forest under a tarp.

It was agreed that she would work with Troll, since she loved building Twig furniture. Tiffany-Dawn worked up front with her sister, but mostly she spelled her at the Westia Fellowship Book Shop.

She proved to be a dynamo when it came to building twig furniture. Her sense of design was remarkable.

When she worked, she worked in silence, almost. She loved to hum softly. At first she and Troll found it very easy to work together. He was convinced that he misjudged his feelings about her, because the person who he came to know through work was focused, and very earnest. He loved her work ethics, and quickly concluded that she had a great flair for creating such furniture. She was also quite adapt at making Wreaths and other Rustic curios.

One day after they had lunch with
Wilhelmina, after the three drank a few
goblets of wine, he was working with her,
and asked her to bring him a rasp. She
handed it to him, and stood behind him
watching him work. He turned and thanked
her absentmindedly, and peck her on the
lips, having had no intention to do so; their
lips lingered together and the kiss
deepened.
When she realized what they were doing
she pulled away and returned to her work.
She told him that she was not feeling well,
and needed air. It was late in the afternoon,
by then, so she knocked off a little earlier
than she usually would have and spent the
rest of the afternoon working in the garden.
But for sun glasses she wore a large floppy
straw hat festooned and emblazoned with
dried flowers. She wore nothing else.
He found her out there and tried to
apologize.
What the *hell* was that, boss?
I'm sorry---
Please, I don't wanna discuss it, boss! Look,
should I leave?
No! Come on, chill out! I jus wanted to say I
was sorry, it musta been, the wine---

It can't happened again, ok? Sorry. We
shouldn't have done that!
I know, I---
Your wife and sister in law are the best
friends I have, she said
furiously. They're my only friends. Please
don't do it again!
After that she kept away from him and had
little to say to him if it
did not concern work.
Something strange happened. The less she
had to do with him the more he thought of
her.
When she took brakes, covered from head
to foot in an artfully tied dyed muumuu and
a turban made of a recycled bed sheet,
barefoot, she normally sat in front of the
store on the ground or on a stump, playing
her old, scuffed up guitar. She sang simple
songs about nature, rivers, trees, flowers
and the forest.
She was a talented Singer song writer. She
had a sweet raspy voice that people found
moving and charming. Customer took to
dropping money in her decrepit guitar case.
She had a box of CD that she made herself,
and with their permission she sold many to
customers.

She turned over a share of what she made to Wilhelmina, as an "investment" in what she called the Commune expenses.

This isn't a commune, were just a family, Troll explained, but Chrysanthemum did not seem to agree.

The customers loved her. She talked them into displaying the twig furniture outdoors before the store.

She occasionally vanished to see a lawyer about the land which she was supposes to inherit from her dead grandmother. She came back one day with a flyer announcing an evening of music with Chrysanthemum. The flyers were passed out to customers, and many of them were posted.

She disappeared one day, and came back late in the afternoon with a CD case, containing one thousand gross. She explained that she meant to sell them at the concert. It was held in the field next to Troll's store. The audience brought their own picnic chairs, and she used the bed of Troll's pick up as a stage. They rigged up a sound system, cobbled from borrowed speakers and mikes.

They roped off the field and the audience
had to purchase tickets and did. Tiffany-
Dawn and Wilhelmina sat at a display table
fronted with a vinyl sign, where her CD was
available. Most of them were sold. Troll
played his African drums, tambala's, along
with her.
She announced that the proceed were to be
used for the Commune.
What Commune? Asked Troll.
We're a family, not a commune, said
Wilhelmina.
It's for the cause, she said.
Cause?
What's your vision, King Willow? What are
you all about? Nudism? Naturism? Simple
living? It's all a cause! We're on a mission.
When she was outside, she proved to be a
natural sales woman. She was patient and
funny with the customers, and remained so
whether or not she sold them anything. She
never pressed. Customers loved her. They
also loved her singing.

Thereafter she usually joined Troll in the back, locked the door, and strip off everything but her turban, and she worked. And worked. She accepted no pay, insisting that her "share" be reinvested in the Communal fund. Troll and Wilhelmina explained again and again that they were not a commune, but just a family. She would nod absently and keep working.

When they worked together Troll could not keep his eyes off her. Frequently she worked in a tattered pair of old, ripped, frayed daisy dukes, made from a pair of old faded hip hugger denims. She wore it more as a tool belt than clothing. She had a remarkable derriere. It was neither too large or too little. It was rounds, firm and shapely. Hip huggers, the daisy dukes left a large part of her rear cleavage exposed, and at times he couldn't stop looking at it. What made it worst was it had holes and tears in all the wrongs spots it frequently unbuttoned itself, and the zipper opened exposing her fluffy pubic growth. Yet if she was totally nude his urge was worse. He suffered from a case of the raging hard-ons around her.

But it wasn't her full, firm, gymnast thighs, her flat abs, and the lovely breasts that looked like perfect twin mangos that enchanted him alone. She enthralled him with her zaniness, her loopy humor, and her harangue not mention her tirades. And then there was her humor. She could make him laugh until he cried. She could melt him with a single glance.

His obsession for her was paralleled by that that he had for Tiffany-Dawn. When sober she was calm and serene. Customer loved her even temper, and no one ever question that she began selling items at a bigger mark up. She was determined to earn as much as she could for them. She made little effort to hide that she was attracted to him, without objection from Wilhelmina. She flirted with him endlessly, and he was delighted. She inherited her mother's derriere, and he loved to embraced her from behind and to nuzzle her neck when they were nude. Her usual response was to chuckle, make a half hearted objection, and press her buttocks back against him.

Almost effortlessly, he and Tiffany-Dawn
became lovers, with Wilhelmina's approval.
She had a gentle, soothing spirit, and they
kept exchanging looks. It became obvious
without much fanfare that he and Tiffany-
Dawn were in love.

How they became lovers was that one
afternoon, when business was slow, and
Tiffany-Dawn was bored, she said that she
wanted to sun bathe. Chrysanthemum was
too caught up in the work she was doing to
join her, and Wilhelmina was in a cranky
mood. Almost as an afterthought she invited
Troll to keep her company. He was feeling
distracted, so he agreed. She brought out a
Mexican blanket, a bottle of wine, some
fruit, in picnic basket and some sun tan
lotion as well as some baby oil. She asked
him to lotion her, and he soon blossomed a
diamond cutter.

She flicked it playfully and laughed at him.
They laid down behind the rose bushes, in a
very sunny spot.

I'ma want a massage in a minute, he said,
trying to sound stern.

She giggled.

Slow down, big bro.

They laid nude on an old blanket and used
his tummy as a pillow, after giving it a quick
kiss. They did not speak.
Why do dudes have nipples, Troll?
Huh?
Y'all don't feed babies, so why do you
need'm?
He didn't answer.
Would you turn you on if I sucked your
nipples?
You and Chrysanthemum and your
questions! Why would you?
I jus wanna see the results.
Fine, jus don't blame me!
She sucked and licked his nipples for a
moment. He laid perfectly still.
She looked at his manhood.
DAYUM!
Sorry! He said.
Why?
I ain't tryna sexualize this.
Shut up, boy!
He chuckled nervously.
Wanna full massage, Poppy?
When she was finished, he said, my turn.

Ok, but take your time, she purred. And you gotta do my front too…work on my titties and nipples, and don't be shy about my coochy either!

Tiff!

Oh, quit acting like a *Virg*!

First he gave her a massage, then her wiped off the oil and applied sun tan lotion to her again.

Troll? She purred.

What, pretty gurl?

Could I ask you something nasty?

He laughed.

Ok?

Would you consider eating my ass?

You want me to?

You know I mean my asshole, right?

No, I didn't, but I would if you want me to.

I dunno…maybe IF! She giggled.

IF what?

If you eat my pussy…but first you gotta do something.

What?

Play with my pubic hairs, and…

And what?

Suck my titties?

Willy…

Willy don't mind, she purred. AIDS is out
there…women who trust each other are
sharing healthy men.
Sure boo, he barely whispered.
Wait----
What?
Troll, if you do this, there ain't gonna be
much looking back!
Why?
Cause I'll need you like that at least once a
day.
Are you sure Willy won't mind?
No, droned Tiffany-Dawn purring, I cleared
it with her.
They wiled away the afternoon behind the
rose bushes, and took a long nap afterwards.
After Wilhelmina closed the Shop, she
persuaded Chrysanthemum to knock off.
The two took a bucket shower, and while air
drying, prepared a salad for dinner.
Chrysanthemum went looking for them
sipping from an icy glass of water and
found them entwined in each other's arms
asleep.
She poked him with her foot, and they
awoke with a start, and jumped apart.

Giving him a look of raw animal hatred, she simply said, y'all need to clean off and get ready for dinner. Please do not embarrass Queen Hibiscus!

She threw the water in his face.

Boss, I ought-a kill you!

Oh, *Chryssie*, stop! that's *unnecessary!* said Tiffany-Dawn. We----

Hush, lady bug! You don't owe me an explanation.

What the---said Troll.

I jus don't want you taking advantage of my besty.

Your being silly! Said Troll.

You wanna knuckle sandwich?

Huh?

How about it *boss*? You wanna *fight* me for dousing you? Let's *do it!*

Chryssie, *stop it!* Said Tiffany-Dawn breaking into tears. You're embarrassing me!

Don't be silly, Chryssie! said Troll.

Shame, boss!

Look----

I don't want y'all hurting lady Hibiscus!

We won't! said Tiffany-Dawn. It ain't like you think----

Ok...Sorry boss, Bluebell. None of my biz, right? Well, Bluebelle? Boss? Y'all need me to git?

Why you humiliating me? Asked Tiffany-Dawn.

I guess I may not belong here!

Chryssie, can't you please stop? Please?

How can you do this to Willy, Tiff?

What if I'm in love with him? Even if he is a little slow---

He's *married*!

Why can't I be his wife too? Seems to me, as much as your all over him, kissing on him----

Stop! Don't go there if we're gonna stay friends!

Ok, ok! But I'm not a skank, Chryssie.

Did I call you that? It breaks my heart to see you doing this, Queen Bluebelle!

Ever heard of *polygamy, Chryssie? I* wanna be another *wife to him, if he'll have me, ok?*

Is *that* what you're out here doing? There's a name for that: BYGAMY!

Look, Chryssie, pleaded Tiffany-Dawn,
there are millions of people who have room
mates. Who's business is it if the woman
roommate is a second wife to the man of the
house, if the wife agrees? It's ok for gay
people to marry, but consenting hetero
sexual adults can't have multiple wives?
Why not?
Are you sure that's what's going on here?
Said Chrysanthemum. How many
vulnerable women is he going to set up like
this?
Set up? *I SEDUCED HIM, CHRYSSIE!*
Where does it end, Tiff?
Where we want it to, said Tiffany-Dawn.
Look, Chryssie, me and you? We're besties,
right? Why can't you do this along with me?
You know you----
Shut up, ok?
Chryssie, you can't keep your hands off
him! And you know you're always going on
about his mouth---
 Tiffany-Dawn, what is wrong with you?
I'm in love with him, even if he's a bit dim! I'm
TIRED of feeling lonely, CHRYSSIE! I adore
him, and so do you ----
I'm warning you, keep quiet if we're going to
stay friends, Tiffany-Dawn! You hear?

Ok! I'm not a slut! And I *been* in love with him! Unlike some people I'm not scared to---
-
What about Queen Hibiscus?
Willy knows, Chryssie, and she approves. Troll started with surprise.
May I say something? Said Troll. I had too much wine, but I-am-*NOT* slow or dim!
Stay out of this, Teddy-Bear, said Tiffany-Dawn .
Ok, said Chrysanthemum, Then I'm outta line here.
Let's jus' drop it, ok? said Troll. Chris, one day you need to tell me why you hate me.
Look, you wanna fire me, boss? Said Chrysanthemum. Go on and *do it!* I won't discuss it with Queen Hibiscus! Y'all need me to clear out tonight?
Oh God, stop it Chryssie! Said Tiffany-Dawn. *Teddy-Bear, do something!*
Will you please chill out, Queen Chrysanthemum? Said Troll. Why're hating me? I mean, you do hate me, right?
Maybe, boss. Maybe! Said Chrysanthemum. Apropos of nothing she swung a punch at his nose but Troll ducked back.
Hey! Stop it! Said Troll, fighting the urge to laugh.

Get up and fight like a man!

Chryssie, I'm not going to fight you!

Chryssie, can you please *stop it?* Said Tiffany-Dawn, crying. Why are you *hurting me?*

Troll dried his face despondently.

Forget it, Chryssie, he said. We're friends, and you know it! I really don't get why you're doing me like this. I'm sorry I pissed you off, ok? Let's just chill out, ok?

Do you love her, boss? Asked Chrysanthemum sternly, on the verge of tears, or are you jus'----

Troll was totally surprised by the question. Yeah, he said slowly, with -Dawning awareness, I *am* in love with Tiff, ok? Even if she thinks I'm slow.

You hurt my girl? I'll kill you.

Chryssie, please stop, pleaded Tiffany Dawn.

We didn't *plan* this today, said Troll, but I'm glad it happened. *I am in love with Tiff!* I wouldn't be doing this otherwise. I'ma tell Willy too. My lady understands. I would *NEVER* hurt my wife!

Chrysanthemum stormed off and for days avoided both of them.

I may have just lost my besty! Wailed Tiffany-Dawn.

What's a Besty?
See, dear, I'm not saying your slow, but a
besty is like a BFF---
A BFF?
Best female friend!
So what is a male best friend?
BMF.
Chryssie will be ok---I hope!
 I'm to blame!
Nahh.
I love my crazy Chryssie, you know?
Shhh! He whispered, holding a weeping
Tiffany-Dawn. She's always hated me!
No! I think she's *in love* with you too,
Teddy-Bear!
Get out, gurl!
Nahh, really!
Well, said Troll slowly, she sure has a weird
way of showing it!
What if she is?
 Not! She tried to punch my nose, Tiffy!
Tiffany-Dawn laughed.
Wow…so me and you? Said Troll. I jus
thought we were out here for the
sun…then…I didn't know I'm in love with
you until I said it…Now we know exactly
what happened here…

From then on Chrysanthemum seem to have little use for him besides work. After a few days she and Tiffany-Dawn reconciled, but Troll she kept at arms distance. During work she was unfailingly polite to him, but impersonal. She was the usual cut up that they knew with the two young women, but Troll was coldly ignored. She refused to let him open up the subject of him and Tiffany-Dawn with her.

Even so, thereafter on a daily basis, he made love wildly to both his wife and Tiffany-Dawn, but more and more he fantasized about Chrysanthemum, and reviled, detested and loathed her for her aloofness. He wanted so badly to bring her down a notch, but he also wanted her affection. Yet he was always polite.

Chrysanthemum was seemingly totally indifferent to him and sex, happily insisting on the concept of non-sexual nudity.

Chapter 8

Kingdom of The Willows

Book 1: Blessing of The Mother

© Antonio R. Belizario

Chinita took to the wilderness. She found a
solace in the woods and on the River that
she never found anywhere else. She spent
many days tramping through the woods,
tagging along with Troll and Wilhelmina,
finding places to meditate in silence with
her Chumash and Siddur.

Marigold and the others silently appraised
her, Chrysanthemum, and Tiffany-Dawn. At
the end of the harvesting she gave
Wilhelmina a nod of approval, looking
towards the three young women.

She smiled in response.

Chinita was surprisingly knowledgeable
about Judaism, to the delight of Marigold,
and quickly made it known that she was a
Jew. Tiffany-Dawn studied with a growing
sense of enthusiasm.

Chrysanthemum reacted politely to the way she was expected to dress when they were around MaGoo and his wives, or Moon and Lil Bit. But the minute that they were in their own encampment, she as well as the others stripped of their clothes and shoes, folded them and put them away, and proceeded to enjoy the woods in the nude. She proved to be an indifferent student, until Marigold taught them about celebrating the New Moon. She listened in rapt attention, asking nothing. Thereafter she devoured every book that Troll and Wilhelmina had on the subject of Judaism. Chinita was marked as a bridge, and without knowing it, began to receive training. She was a willing, if unwitting student. She listened to Marigold, and MaGoo's other wives, listen silently with down cast eyes, doing as they did, dressing as they dressed. Unbeknownst to them, she quietly converted to Orthodox Judaism. This was long before they asked her to serve as a bridge.

She had a conflict then. She did not know whether or not to walk away from all of her friends in the Westia Fellowship. The problem was her quirky love for Isaiah and Mingo. She never revealed her conversion to Mingo and Isaiah, although she drew many followers to her views concerning Judaism. She very quietly guided several of her friend to convert, demanding, plus pleading that they keep their conversion secret, as well as help lead those who were like minded to her new found faith.

They succeeded beyond their wildest dreams.

The Westia Fellowship was full of cranks along with critical thinkers. Several had walked away from Christianity, furthermore had either turned into Hebrew Israelite, or Messianic, as had Chinita.

She softly taught, and quietly guided many into her new found faith provided that they sought her out. A day came when to her astonishment, in a very secretive, clandestine meeting, even Mingo himself sought her out and revealed his doubts and concerns.

Not that long afterwards, a lone figure in a black hoody showed up for a class which she paid a young Rabbi to conduct in secret. She asked no questions, said nothing, and left a few minutes before everyone else. She over took him, and was astonished when she saw it was Mingo. He fled into the night. Thereafter he avoided her, but kept coming again and again to the class.

In short order he secretly embraced Orthodox Judaism, yet he continued to officiate at the Westia Fellowship services. He became brittle and anxious. He was too terrified to reveal his true feelings to his wife.

He visited a probate firm and had a will drawn up leaving half of what he owned to his wife, and the other half to his favorite nephew, Pruny.

Upon doing that he stopped wearing a bullet proof vest.

Chapter 9

Things came to a head in between Troll and Chrysanthemum one afternoon, when Wilhelmina, and Tiffany-Dawn , it being a slow, rainy afternoon, hung a back in four hours sign on the door and went to pay bills and run errands. The fact was that they meant to goof off. A leisurely cup of sweet coco and cookies at their favorite coffee house, Beanie's, then an afternoon of window shopping and rummaging at some small, seedy thrift-stores came to mind.

If at first Chrysanthemum mercilessly teased and played with Troll, abruptly after the two incidents she ceased to notice if he existed at all. To say she ignored him was a kind understatement. She ceased speaking to him or even to look at him.

At first, before she caught Troll with Tiffany-Dawn, she played and tussled with him frequently, until she discovered that every time they did, he ended up with a boner, and she ended up wet. And too out of a misguided sense of camaraderie she and Tiffany-Dawn took to greeting and thanking Troll with a peck on the lips.

Had it not been for Troll and Chrysanthemum's mutual obsession with lips, which bordered on a engrossment, a fetish, all might have worked out differently. Both were obsessed by full, shapely, sensual lips. For Troll such lips rubbed with lip gloss were particularly obsessing. She had full, moist, chocolate-ty looking lips, and she always wore colorless lip gloss that smelled like strawberries. Her milky white teeth and the buck tooth which showed just enough to drive him mad became an addictive obsession. Every time she smiled or licked her lips he fought the urge to moan. It was a moment by moment struggle not to look at them. To his disgust, the fantasies became so overwhelming that he occasionally locked himself in a small stock room and masturbated. When he came out it only seemed to be worse.

It was worse because she took to following him around his workshop, at Wilhelmina's suggestion, hanging out there, to assist him with his twig furniture making. To his surprise, she prove to be a big help. She was quite skilled. It turned out that she was very gifted at it. The workshop became very productive. What should have proven a bond in between them became instead a further reason to obsess about each other. They worked in the nude, wearing tool aprons and goggles. On more than one occasion when something went particularly well, they kissed instead of high fiving, or touching fists. One afternoon an innocent peck turned into an incendiary kiss that swiftly had them in a clinch, tonguing each other's mouths and nibbling each other's lips.

Let's stop, he pleaded, pushing away. I got a thing about lips.

You too? She stammered.

Don't ask what I call lips like yours, gurl.

What?

DSL.

Dick sucking lips?

I'm not the kinda man who disses women----

She moaned.

I call lips like yours on a man pussy coolers.

You're lips drive me crazy, boss!

Let's not talk about this, ok?

For sure, she stammered, please let's not let it happen again, ok?

Maybe it's worse if we fight it!

You mean like, just---just---

We could do what we jus did and it would lose it's magic!

Or get worse! Maybe I should keep away, boss!

I really need your help in here, he said.

Ok, but let's not do that again, ok?

Right! No more kissing---on the lips!

She tried to only kiss him only on the cheek. It was hell for him. The more he saw her, the more she obsessed him. He found himself staring at her more and more. When she was engrossed in something she screwed up her face a little and poked the tip of her tongue out of the corner of her mouth. He found that precious and adorable. He so wanted to be included in her rants and loopy monologues, but she studiously addressed her cracker barrel zaniness to Wilhelmina and Tiffany-Dawn .

Then she caught him with Tiffany-Dawn . Nothing seemed to alter her affection for her best friend. If she was caught in a tryst with the mangy, low down Troll, it was clearly his fault to her.

He tried to include himself in talks involving her, almost to the point of seeming pathetic. At times she glanced at him with open annoyance. Each time she did, he felt as if his heart was pierced by her contemptuous eyes. At the same time he wanted to tell her this is my home, how dare you ostracize me in it!

It was a cold afternoon, so Troll started a fire in the wood burning stove that sat in the middle of the work shop, so it felt warm, and cozy.

Really, they'd all been working too hard, and the afternoon was so slow because of the weather that they all decided by unspoken agreement to spend the afternoon goofing off. All except Chrysanthemum, who considered hard work a pass time, if she wasn't endearingly, maddeningly, ranting and raving about any one of her quirky beliefs and practices.

The other thing she liked besides work and singing was dancing. She had a boom box, and not an evening passed when she didn't cajole them into line dancing, or free forming oldies from the sixties and seventies, or loud rap music. They insisted that he dance with them, and he had to act as if dancing nude with a diamond cutter as the three totally nude, sweaty young women cavorted around him, bumping and grinding, with titties jiggling, and asses shaking, to the music was no big deal. Wilhelmina and Tiffany-Dawn didn't have the obsessive energy for long term dancing like Chrysanthemum, but somehow, it soothed Wilhelmina to dance until she was sweaty and exhausted, a lit joint in the corner of her mouth. As a result he began to regularly take his wife or Tiffany-Dawn into the cabin on wheels alone for an hour or more before they all went to sleep, where they would go at each other gruelingly. Then he'd limp off to bed.

Chrysanthemum noted it all with growing anger, knowing not why she felt so upset.

On that afternoon, she was engrossed in completely a flamboyant looking twig settee. It was full of curves, twirls and swirls. He was secretly determined to not sell it when it was completed. It was too precious.

*The problem was her incredible energy.
Mornings for her began with calisthenics,
followed by a six mile jog through the woods in
flimsy jogging clothes, and for safety he usually
jogged with her. It was a challenge to keep up
with her. Half way thru her jog, she usually
smoked a joint to 'mellow out,' and he usually
toke a few tokes. Finally it became a group
activity, and to his chagrin, Wilhelmina and
Tiffany-Dawn loved the early morning jogs.
Their idea of breakfast became a glass of
Vegetable and fruit juice and some yogurt.
No amount of effort could persuade
Chrysanthemum to stop working that afternoon.
She lived to work and worked to live. When she
had nothing to do, her relaxation was to go out
and weed, and putter around the garden and
smoke a joint. Or she went out in front of the
shop and played her guitar and sang. Enjoying
what she was doing, needing no company, she
urged the two other to go on without her, and
take "boss" with them. He felt insulted,
affronted, and challenged by her attitude. He
would show her who really worked hard!*

They left and said they'd call on the way back.
They locked the front door, and the shop door.
Maybe she did not realize that he was there, but
with a grateful sigh of relief, she took off the
wrap that she worked in at times, and went back
to work, totally nude, a lit joint in the corner of
her mouth.
She didn't notice him, greedily drinking in
everything she was doing with his eyes.
He was topless, wearing a leather tool apron and
nothing else. He took off. Once again he was
bedeviled by a stiffy. He tried to work, but
couldn't take his eyes off her. Her skin glistened
with sweat. He muscles tightened and relaxed as
she worked. He adored her buttocks and the back
of her thighs---all of her back. A trickle of sweat
ran down her spine and it was all he could do not
to go over and trace the path it followed with his
tongue. He desperately wanted to bury his face
in her bush. An irrational, shameful desire to
smell her hairy arm pits, and to bury his nose in
her kinky bush, along with a yearning to bury
his nose in her rear cleavage seized him. Maybe
he would lick her----
At that point a cold dread crept over him. He
feared he knew not how his obsession might end.
How? He was concerned that it would end very
badly for him, if it all went wrong.
He clearly understood then that he either was on
the verge of madness or already was mad.

She wore a head phone mp3 and seemed to have no idea that he even existed. She nodded her head in rhythm to whatever oldies she was listening too. When she started gyrating, whipping, bumping and grinding her butt in rhythm to the music she was hearing, he lost the last of his self control.

He went to her and stood close behind her, dancing along, smelling the mild fragrance of her sweatiness with closed eyes, not knowing what to say. He fought the urge to grab her, and make love to her.

Chryssie? Excuse me, Miss Chrysanthemum?

She didn't seem to hear him.

Could I have a minute, please? Chryssie?

She looked at him with surprise, with ill-concealed annoyance, and partly took off her head phones.

Waddup, boss? Why you standing up on me like this?

He took the joint from her lips, toked, and returned it.

Could we clear the air?

There's nothing to clear. I'm kinda busy here.

Could we jus talk for a bit? Please?

Can it keep?

Aww come on Chrissie!

Can we get your wife in on it?

I rather just say this to you!

And what is might that be?

I'm so in love with you, Queen Chrysanthemum.

She stared briefly, snorted, and shook her head with disgust.

I'ma pretend I didn't hear that mess---

Sweetheart---

Get the f away from me, ok?

Look, I'm gonna lose my mind---

What are you talking about? What?

He felt near tears.

I think you're so...I'm STONE in LOVE with you, crazy gurl!

You won't feel so in love if I smack you on the mouth!

Gurl, I adore you! I'd kiss your asshole if you let me!

Would you be saying all that if your wife was here?

Gurl, please love me! Be nice to me! I need you!

I'm not hearing this!

I'm feel like if I don't get relief, I feel like if I'm a lose my mind...

Relief? Are you outcha your damn mind?! Get lost!

Have a little mercy, Chryssie!

Dammit, boss! Don't CHRYSSIE me! I'm BUSY!

Can't you please take a break?

Get away from me! Quit goofing off!

You wanna take a break? Please?

NO! Ain't you got something to do?
I can't focus for thinking of you,
Chrysanthemum!
That's ENOUGH!
Chryssie----
Don't even go there!
I'm sorry!
I can't BELIEVE you! Don't try to kiss me
again, either!
You been kissing me too!
Did not!
You know I'm right!
If I did, it was a mistake!
I can't stop thinking about you, gurl!
Boss, cool OFF!
Please be mines!
You need to stop!
Could I at least----can I stand near you?
WHAT?
Can I help you?
DANG! Whateva! Here! Here! Help me hold the
wood, and I'll nail. Just don't talk to me no more,
ok?
Sure! He said, feeling humiliated, but grateful.
Thank you ma'am!

She was working on a twig settee. She put on her head phone and goggles. They worked in close proximity, brushing against each other, and he accidentally touched her as much as he could. Surreptitiously he smelled her hair and his heart danced. His manhood brushed her buttocks and he grew lightheaded.

She took off the head phone.

Come on now, Boss! You heard of sexual harassment?

You THREATENING me? Really?

DAMN RIGHT!

Ruin me then! Sue me! I don't care!

Boss, you NEED to stop!

I gotta talk to you! He pleaded.

Talk, huh? What the f you gotta say?

You know what I wanna say!

Quit being pitiable!

Ever since we been kissing...

DON'T! That should never have happened!

It was not done intentionally!

But it did happen!

I'm in LOVE with you, gurl!

Are you out of your mind?

I NEED you!

You're really annoying me!

I can't think of anything but you!

Dammit boss! I said don't go there!

Look---

Doncha see I'm BUSY?

I'm losing my mind!
What part of I'm busy doncha get?
I've been good to you!
Send me a bill!
Do you have to be so cruel to me?
Alright boss, here it is. I got no time for YOU!
EVER!
Do you like hurting me? Huh?
Why did I ever think you was so adorable, boss?
You are really hateful!
So you wanna talk?
Yes ma'am! Please!
Let's talk! I hate hoes and skanks.
I ain't either!
Get this in your head: you and me? Not NOW,
not EVER, ok?
Aw, come on, darling!
DARLING? She laughed. REALLY? I love
everything about working here, except one thing!
What?
You! I can-NOT-stand-YOU!
Ok. Ok. I jus' wanna be friends then!
No! You wanna FUCK me like you're
FUCKING my best friend!
Awww, gurl, it ain't like all that…
Oh, really?
What if I love her? What if she loves me?
Do you, boss?

No! I adore her! I'M in love with her…we're
lovers…
What do you want from ME then?
I want all of you!
So you want a harem, huh?
Call it what you want, but yeah, I want you!
Can you please LEAVE ME THE FUCK
ALONE, niggah?
How can you talk to me like that? You're
murdering my heart!
DAYUM! I can't STAND you!
He nearly wept.
Don't! Do-not start crying either, my niggah, so
help me!
I might start crying!
Why?
It wasn't that long ago we were friends…Listen
to how you're talking to me!
Why can't you leave me be?
Don't you think I've tried? I adore you! I love
your dirty drawers.
DANG, I can't stand you!
Why? Why? I barely say a thing to you!
You're ALWAYS, always communicating
inappropriately with me, all the same!
Liar! How can you say that?
With your EYES! Let that be the last time you
call me liar!
Chryssie---

You keep SEXUALIZING me! You're always
DRILLING holes in the back of my head! You
keep EYEBALLING me! You walk around with
that big fat DICK standing, and just looking gets
me wet! I'm sick of it!
Yeah, humiliate me for being human, you
destroyed my pride!
If you're hot, go take a cold shower!
The kinda hot you make me feel, gurl, he said,
you the one who's gotta cool me!
I should slap your face, boss!
Do it! Do it!
Boss----
Please cool me off!
You're wife is my FRIEND! You hear me?
Don't you think I know that? he pleaded, How
do you think it makes me feel?
All you want is to get some!
Is that what you think?
That's what I KNOW! You want some so bad I
feel it!
I'm beyond sorry, I can't help it!
Well, man up, niggah!
How can you call me that? I hate myself enough
as it is!
Say what you really want!
Everything! All of you! I want our spirits to
merge! I want to hold, you, lick you, love you---
Listen atcha!

You want me to show how much I love you? I'll lick your asshole!
You DISGUST me!
Come on, now! Love making is spiritual. Everything about you is precious to me. Even when you smell sweaty from working. Gurl, I adore you! Have some mercy Chrysanthemum!
No!
Just let me hold you for a second!
I'ma find a lawyer and file a sexual harassment suit against you, niggah! How you like me now?
Fine! I'll confess! Take everything you want! Do I need to beg?
Boss, please, get a hold of yourself! I ain't nobody!
Don't say that! You're my Sorceress, my darling Queen Chrysanthemum, my Seer and Jester!
Her eyes filled with tears.
It ain't like that no more, ok? I hate you now, ok? You need to stop!
Yeah, go on! Hurt me for being under your spell!
You think I wanna hurt you? She said. Don't you see I wanna save us? Boss, you just need to stop!
I can't no more! You cast a spell on me! I feel possessed! I can't help it!
Well, she hissed, deal with this: not now, not ever! Understand, ho?

*Oh G-d, don't call me that! He fought the urge
to sob. I don't deserve it! It hurts to hear you call
me that! Just kill me instead!*

What is WRONG with you?

A DEMON got a hold of me! YOU!

Have some self respect!

*I've lost my pride and self respect! I can't stop
thinking about you!*

That's YOUR problem.

*I'm losing my mind! Why you gotta be sucha —
sucha---*

*Disrespect me! I'll slap y our face! I will-not
betray Willy, boss!*

Be mines OPENLY and it won't be a betrayal!

I don't LIKE you, ok?

Liar! You're a liar!

I can't STAND to look at you!

*You got a heart of stone. You liked me at first,
didn't you, Chryssie?*

*Yes, G-d help me! More than I care to let you
know!*

What did I do?

*You know dang well! Why ja kiss me that way
that day? You bastard! Whyju INFECT me?
Huh?*

*Whyja go and seduce-kiss me? Why ja have to go
around with that big fat dick standing so
temptingly all the time? Now I'm half crazy,
thinking about---never mind!*

Aww, darling!

Shut up! Don't DARLING me! You got a wife, you big muscle head skank!

Stop it! I'm not a skank!

Anyway, why you banging Tiff for, if this is for real?

I'm so in love with her!

You disgusting ho!

Don't say that! I've come to love her as much as she's come to love me, Chryssie. We need each other like that!

You're own SISTER in law?

It's BOTH of you two! You both BEWITCHED me!

BEWITCHED you? Bewitched you? Deceiver!

Why you calling me that?

I thought you didn't confuse nudity and sexuality!

I don't! I thought you said you were celibate!

I am!

Then why you feeling on my dick at nights?!

She gasped.

I do not! She stammered, flustered.

Yup. Right.

You knew I done that?

I can't sleep til I feel you touching me there!

You EVIL bastard!

Who's being a fraud?

If I do, I'm asleep when I do it!

Yeah! Really? Celibacy allows a clarification of the senses and the emotions? Remember saying that?

Shut up, ok? she pleaded. SHUT UP!

Personally? I have no sexual urges. Remember saying that?

Leave me alone, niggah! she said.

I'm celibate because one day when the right man comes, I'll be all his. I'll give myself completely, to him only, cause I don't believe in birth control! Remember saying that?

Now I SEE! She said. You were jus' WAITING to use my own words against me! You're so CRUEL and CALCULATING, to throw my own words at me!

What if it's me? Why can't I be that man?

Nudity isn't sexual, she said sarcastically, remember saying that?

If you were dressed in a BHURKA, I would still love you, darling! It ain't about our nudity!

DON'T CALL ME THAT! Why won't you let it be?

I can't!

I thought you were a man of values!

I am!

You have a WIFE!

My wife understands! Be my wife too.

Go find you a ho if you want some extra coochy!

I don't just want extra coochy!

Wachu want then?

You! Be another wife to me! You and Bluebelle!
You musta lost your natural frigging DAYUM
mind, you know that? That's BYGAMY! We
ALL go to prison!

Then be my civil partner! My Queen Hibiscus---
Willy understands!

I don't agree! Queen Hibiscus is a saint! If it
was me? I might cut your throat!

CUT IT! At least I won't feel this hurt no more!
How can you do this to Queen Hibiscus?
ANIMAL!

She wants sister wives!

You still shouldn't do it! Now, if you don't
mind? I really ain't got time to chit chat with
you! I got work to do, if it's all the same to you!

FINE! He said, turning and storming off. Just
ignore me and let me suffer! You're dead to me,
ok? You heartless BITCH!

Oh, HELL no! she said, pursuing him. Now you
fucked up! Waja say? Wad-da fuck you say to
me, my niggah?

She grabbed him by the shoulder and spun him
around.

He stood glaring at her with his hands on his
hips. She slapped one side of his face and then
back handed the other.

He laughed. You're adorable!

She did it again.

Is that all you got, he mocked, huh, you devil?
Slap me some more! You hit like a gurl!
You will NOT disrespect me!
You've been disrespecting me, Miss
Chrysanthemum! You don't deserve to be my
Queen.
You big hairy ANIMAL! Beast!
Chrysanthemum, he said carefully, I-hate-you!
You hear me?
She swallowed and bit her lips.
So? You ain't nobody---you ain't nothing to me,
she falters.
I hate your gorgeous ass, your sweet mouth,
your smooth skin! I hate how you make feel, I
hate your wisdom, I hate your originality, I hate
how you make me laugh, I hate how sweet you
smell, even when you sweat, I hate how you
chew so dainty-like, I hate watching you bathe! I
hate washing your back. I hate how the sun
seems brighter when your around. I hate the day
you walked into my life.
Don't nobody care! Said Chrysanthemum faintly
with growing sadness.
I hate your goofy grins! I hate your hair, your
fluffy bush, and most of all, the goofy way you
smile at me!
Oh, well! She said with a tremor in her voice.
back atcha!
I hate how you laugh and talk! You hear me?

*Back atcha, fool! Said Chrysanthemum she
barely whispered, a lump having formed in her
throat.*

Witch! Devil! You're EVIL!

*Sorcerer! Said Chrysanthemum with
diminishing conviction. Con man! Deceiver!
You're the one who cast a spell on ME! You're a
HOODOO man!*

*I been hating you since the minute I saw you,
gurl!*

*I hate you, too, boss, said Chrysanthemum with
a quaver in her voice. You jus a big, dumb hunk!
You think Tiffy AND me are stone in love with
you? WRONG!*

*Good, he half wept, you'll never get a hug outta
me IF you sleep next to me again!*

*I can't STAND YOU! She said, stifling a sob.
Who said I like sleeping next to you? You think I
jus live to be near you? Right — I mean,
WRONG! Don't nobody wants to sleep in your
arms! Don't nobody care to rest their head on
your hairy ass chest! Don't nobody love hearing
your heart beating!*

*Oh G-d! I'ma die in a minute! He said with a
sob. I'ma go hang myself if I can't have you love
me!*

*The things you just said really hurt me, Willow!
She whimpered. I been trying to act all hard but
two wrongs don't make a right! You're supposed
to be my kind King! First you make me all crazy
with kisses, then you bang my besty---like if I
never meant anything to you! I never knew you
were so cruel.
His lip quivered.
I'm so sorry, ma'am! He said. I have never
wanted to do anything to hurt you. You been
destroying my heart, too, but I don't … I
don't…really feel anything negative about you
darling! I adore YOU….
She wiped the tears out her eyes.
You think I could shape my mouth to say all that
and mean it, King Willow? I'm dying as we
speak. I been crying inside for days for ignoring
you! Can't you understand I'm ripping my own
heart out to say those things?
Then why say that? huh, Chrysanthemum?
Trying to SAVE you! Better I suffer than you
and Queen Hibiscus! I don't want Bluebelle
being hurt! I don't want to hurt the Queen, Lady
Hibiscus, that's why!
You built me up to destroy me!
No sir, King Willow! Don't nobody have to build
you up, my King! You're so frigging awesome!*

You don't need to lie! I was happy jus' being a troll. Why ja call me Poppy? King Willow? Why ja have to make feel…special? Magical? Why Chrysanthemum?

You just pretty much murdered me, King Willow!

What are you saying, darling? He said. Please don't say that!

If you meant all those hateful things you said…

Did you mean any of those evil things you just said, King Willow? If you do, jus kill me now, ok? Cause I wouldn't wanna live if you feel that way about me!

Darling! Darling gurl! I don't mean a word of it! I adore you, Queen Chrysanthemum!

He stood glaring at her with hopeless adoration. At long last he broke down and began to cry.

Hey! Hey! Stop it! Do not! None of that, ok? I'm sorry! Dang, I'm so in love with you!

I can't take that! Please, do-not cry, boss!

I can't help it!

Don't do that---boss? Please stop, alright?

You're gonna ruin me for loving you? I don't care! I'm in love with you, gurl!

You think I'd really sue you? Come on! Stop! Boss---boss? Please?

I'm so sorry, ma'am!

Don't cry, She said. darling – I mean boss! Aw, stop, King Willow---I'm sorry! Ok? I'm sorry, baby boy!

You don't really mean that!

I do! I was acting, ok? Ok? My beautiful darling, we can't be a couple! We can-not be lovers, but that don't mean I ain't feeling you! Ok? You know I love me some King Willow! I didn't mean none of what I just said, he said tearfully. I got no family but y'all!

Same here, She whispered.

Y'all are all I got!

Nah, darling, that ain't true! You got Queen Hibiscus, and Bluebelle!

But not you!

You can't really say that, King Willow!

I'm sucha crazy man! He smiled, trying to stop his own tears. Look, I'll never bother you again---

Hush, King Willow! Please don't say a thing you ain't gonna be able to do, sweets! She took his face in her hands, and wiped his tears off with her thumbs tenderly.

Come here! Come hear you beautiful fool! She threw her arms open to him. They briefly held each other, then she pulled away.

Please stop crying, King Willow! She said,
braking into tears, You know Chryssie loves her
some King Willow! You my protector, my knight
in hairy armor! You kept me safe that night,
remember? I was scared to stay in the woods I
don't know alone, but I ain't had nowhere to go!
And sleeping in a van can be dangerous. You
took care of me, took me into your home, into
your bed with your family! And I don't feel
lonely no more! I work hard to help y'all prosper
in return. Yeah, I want love! But I ain't selfish!
You think I'm so cruel, but I love me some King
Willow. and Queen Hibiscus? She's my blood
sister! I don't wanna spoil it for y'all!
You ain't gotta lie, dear! I understand. I won't
bother you again---
I'm being a b cause I don't wanna ruin things! I
don't even know what I'm saying---damn you,
King Willow!
Abruptly they grabbed each other and kissed
with a mad abandon and ardor, that stunned
both. Their hands were all over each other as they
became as if possessed.
Darling King Willow! My darling! Oh G-d, oh
G-d! I need you!
You want me? He pleaded, You want me? Am I
dreaming?!

No! No! King Willow! I can't take it anymore! I NEED it! I need YOU! Right here! She demanded. Hairy beast! Animal! Right NOW! She pleaded. On the floor! On the floor, baby boy!

They made love in a frenzy, biting, licking, sucking away at anything and everything on each other's body, moaning and sobbing.

She took his penis and sucked it with a vengeance, making a moaning, wailing sound. Bend over darling! Bend over gurl!

He licked her sweaty rear, he licked her woman hood, licked her armpits, and her anus. He splayed her buttocks and stuck his tongue into her anus, again and again, and sucked her clitoris. She thrashed and screamed as she began to come.

Let's 69! He pleaded.

No, I need that big fat DICK! Oh my G-d I NEED IT, niggah! Quit playing with me, boy! FUCK ME! BEAT MY COOCHY UP!

Aright, angel! Arrrrgh!

Niggah, do-not-make-love-to-me! FUCK ME LIKE AN ANIMAL! FUCK ME! YES! YES! DO IT! OH MY G-D DO IT!

I love you, darling Chrysanthemum! My witch! My angel! I adore you!

I love you too, darling beast! She screamed. I love, my animal!

They held each other with a mad joyfulness.
Sobbing he swept the worktable clean with one
mighty swipe of his arm, mounted her on it
roughly. She splayed her legs.
NOW, NOW! MOTHERFUCKER! I CAN'T
TAKE IT NO MORE!
He thrusted into her roughly.
AHHH! PUMP! PUMP! AHHH! OH MY G-
D! AHHHH!
You beautiful darling crazy gurl! He screamed
and half sobbed. I LOVE YOU! I LOVE YOU!
SHUT THE FUCK UP AND FUCK ME
HARD! HARD, my darling NIGGAH!
AHHHHH! AHHHH! She screamed as he
thrusted into her. OH MY G-D! OH MY G-D!
G-D, I CAN'T STOP COMING AHHHH!
AHHHH!
AHHH! AHHH! He screamed, I'M COMING
so hard I'MA BUST'N DIE! JESUS! JESUS!
ARRRRRGH! They both screamed. Aaaaaargh!
They Collapsed on the table, totally depleted, yet
quivering in each other's arms. They were in a
state of euphoria; their head were swimming. She
wrapped her arms and legs around him, then
tenderly stroke his dreadlocks.
Oh Lord! Lord! Darling! Darling King Willow!
I just ruined everything!
No, darling, it's all good!
Please forgive me! She said, sobbing. Oh Lord!
I'm sucha slut!

*No! No! Shhh! Shhh! He said, I been wanting
you! Shhh!*
*I can't ever face Willy again! I hate me! I
GOTTA LEAVE! I'll leave, ok? I'm so sorry!*
No, no! gurl!
I'll leave! I'll leave!
Shhh! Shhh!
*They finally got up, with wobbly knees, kissing
even as they struggled to part. They went and
showered together in the garden, feeling weak
and dream like. Then they cleaned the work shop.*
*I need sleep she whispered. Other than touching
myself, I ain't had no sex in years. Really? I ain't
ever had.*
How old are you?
Twenty. And you?
Twenty two. You're beautiful, chrysanthemum!
*Thank you, my King and Knight! I can barely
stand! I need sleep, King Willow! I'm bone
weary. I feel so tired!*
Let's go!
No! Let me sleep in the cabin by myself! Ok?
*Ok for now! He said. He picked her up in his
arms, and went into the cabin put her in the
bed. She was shaking. He covered her with
tender carefulness, and tucked her in.*
I'm so in love with you!
*Go, baby boy! Please! Miss Willy will be back
soon! I don't wanna hurt her!*

Shhh! Don't worry! He whispered. My Chrysanthemum! Get some sleep, darling, and thank you!
They parted with regret. She took two aspirins and two Melatonins and drank a glass of water. Oh, my King willow! I've ruined everything for us! She said to herself, and fell into a deep dreamless sleep, weeping.

Chapter Ten

She woke up to pee a few times, and gulped more water, then collapsed, and went back to sleep. She had no idea how long she slept after she woke up. She felt incredibly hungry, but renewed. A profound sense of relief suffused her. A great knot was gone from her insides. She also felt profoundly was sore, and groggy. It was possibly the next day in the evening. The tight, cold knot that celibacy created in her guts, the tightness in her body which only weed could loosen, all of it was gone.
All the same, she was also shaken.
Even so, she felt a lightness of spirit.

*She reviewed the incident, and wept with shame.
Then she made up her mind. She took a good
sponge bath and packed, crying as she did it. She
put on her turban and her wrap dress, which
Willy showed her how to make. It was made of
the softest green silk, and had a silk belt woven
out of the same type of silk. The fact was, Willy
made it for her, along with a matching turban.
I love, you Miss Willy! She had said, hugging
Wilhelmina around the neck. Friend girls
forever!
Wilhelmina patted her back.
Then Tiffany-Dawn insisted that Wilhelmina
and Chrysanthemum prick a finger along with
her, and she made them hold them together with
hers.
Life, spirit and soul are in the blood, said
Tiffany-Dawn , so by doing this we are become
true sisters.
This is just like what Troll and his buddies did!
Said Wilhelmina.
Natural blood sisters, forever? Said
Chrysanthemum.
Forever! Said Wilhelmina and Tiffany-Dawn ,
moved by the silliness of the gesture.
Now you're our sister in every way, said
Tiffany-Dawn .
For real for real! Chrysanthemum said. Love
you, sisters!*

Love you too, Chryssie!
She sought out Willy, praying not to see him.
Well good evening, Sleepy head!
Queen Hibiscus!
You been working like a Hebrew slave, and you hit the wall, huh? Didn't I tell you to slow down on the espressos? You been sleeping for nearly two days! Ragamuffin was really concerned. What's up?
Hey, Queen Hibiscus!
Why are you playing a clothe dummy? We're home! You should nude up!
She tried to say something, but for once in her life found herself unable to speak.
She knelt in front of Wilhelmina, and clasped and kissed her hands.
What the heck sis? Said Wilhelmina. Get off your knees!
No, sis! I'm here to abase myself, she said, and she sobbed. She tried to kiss her feet.
Gurl, stop! Get up!
She tried to help her up.
No, ma'am, I don't deserve your kindness! I played the ho, but I didn't mean to! I lost control.
Gurl---
Please let me be, and listen! I need to abase myself.
Oh, stop!

No Ma'am, I wanna ask---beg for your forgiveness…I wronged you and your husband ….I'll be leaving y'all now I guess…

Why?

I betrayed your trust and kindness! She wailed and broke into wrenching sobs. As kind as y'all have been, I betrayed you!

How?

She couldn't bring herself to say it.

Are you saying you got with Troll?

I'm so sorry! She wailed. Yes ma'am!

Well, don't worry, said Wilhelmina. Real men can't be stolen.

Aww, Lawd, Queen Hibiscus, do you think I'd steal from you?

No, but if a woman steals your man? He was never really yours, and never really a man, and she was not a real friend!

I wouldn't take anything from you, she pleaded. He adores you Queen! He wouldn't even think of leaving you!

And if a woman does steal him? Said Wilhelmina, she was never really your friend and he really wasn't your man! The best revenge would be to let her have him!

I ain't tryna steal him!

I know, sweet heart. I know! Am I a fool?

No.

We're blood sisters, right, Chryssie?

Chrysanthemum nodded, and covered her
mouth, sobbing silently. She was unable to speak
for a moment.

Then you just made love to him, but you didn't
betray me, did you?

Yes ma'am, but I feel bad just on account of that!
I am so sorry, I don't even get how it happened! I
just couldn't fight the urge anymore!

She sobbed again for a moment, hugging
Wilhelmina around the knees.

He told me about it, said Wilhelmina, patting her
shoulder, and he apologized, but we agreed that if
it happened it was ok, so long as y'all didn't hide
it. God blesses a man with a boundless capacity
for love. I'm not going to demand my husband
only love me. I don't care if he made love to you.

I'm sucha slut for doing it!

Or are you just lonesome for a man? Asked
Wilhelmina.

I don't even know what got into me!

I don't own him, She said, and pulled her to her
feet and gave her a hug. We don't own ourselves.

Who does?

G-d owns us. Go wash your face and come have
dinner, ok? And relax.

I don't deserve no friends!

Chrysanthemum, stop it!

I felt like I found a family here.

You have, goofy!

I deserve to keep living lonely!

Oh, shut up! We chose you.
Chose me?
A very wise woman, Marigold told me that a
smart woman selects her sister wives.
Sister wives?
You're good people. You get us. You're family
now. I trust you.
Really?
We knew this might happen, didn't we? Even a
good man will develop feelings for a woman he's
meant to be with, whether or not he sees her
nude. He never saw me nude, but he fell in love
with me. He loves you for you, not your body.
And it might happen again, ok? I'll expect you
two are at the start.
Of what?
The start of a relationship.
That will be the only way, cause me? I got
principles. Maybe I can't keep my hands off him
if I stay, but I don't do casual sex.
Or casual anything! Said Wilhelmina, smiling
unhappily. You work so hard! In between the
shop work and working out here in the garden,
you're working yourself to death.
It's the only thing other than wed that keeps my
mind from racing. You notice I don't talk when I
work?
We like to hear you talk. Slow down!
The two women embraced for a moment.

I don't think I can keep my hands off him, ma'am.

I didn't say you have to, if you're not using us, and you love him. Just don't lie, and don't use us. You call him King willow? Well, treat him like he's a King. You and Tiffany-Dawn ! He's my King. Be a part of. Build a family with us. Respect us so we can respect you.

Ok, if he wants me like that. If y'all will accept me into his life like that.

He does. We do, goofy.

I'll never disrespect you or your home, ma'am! Don't be ashamed!

She went back into the cabin and disrobed. The day felt wonderful. It was a warm, sunny autumn day. She purred as a soft warm breeze caressed her skin and ruffled her dreadlocks and pubes.

When she saw Troll she began to cry again. He looked so handsome in his nudity. She noticed with affection and a little amusement that he was becoming upright.

I guess you're happy to see me, or you must be feeling chilly! She said.

Shhh! Shhh! He said, taking her in the arms kissing her lips, and kissing away her tears.

He took her by the hand and walked her to the far back of the yard, behind one of the ancient apple trees that stood near the fence.

They sat at the foot of the tree, holding hands.

Look up at the clouds! Aren't they fantastic,
Queen Chrysanthemum?
She smiled.
You should see the apple Blossoms in the spring,
Chrysanthemum! You just wait!
I bet they're gorgeous, she said.
Trust me, they are!
Oh, boss----King Willow – I meant---Mister
Troll---
Poppy, King Willow, to you, Queen
Chrysanthemum!
I'm so sorry, boss!
Why?
I shoulda been stronger for you!
You are!
The Devil got in me, boss!
Then I must be the Devil!
I ain't calling you a Devil.
He smiled at her.
But---hey! Se said. Are you being funny?
Well, I did get into you, ma'am!
And how! I'm still sore, but in a good way.
They both chuckled.
It's not funny, King Willow! I'm saying I tried
real hard to do right---boss – I worked hard---
I know, darling! He gave her a kiss to the lips.
Then she returned it.
I did not plan our encounter!
Duh!

I am begging your forgiveness.
Same here, ma'am! You aren't responsible for it,
though!
I'll leave if you want me too, sir!
Why, ma'am? We were fated to be together!
From the first evening when you walked in, high
as a kite!
She laughed.
Really?
Yes ma'am! Don't talk about leaving!
It might be for the best.
Why you calling me sir?
Why you calling me ma'am?
Same reason, I guess. I was real rude to you. It'll
never happen again!
Same here!
Chrysanthemum…darling! Stay. I'll be like
MaGoo with you three.
What do you mean?
You and Tiff will be my wives too, if you'll have
me.
The law doesn't recognize that, King Willow.
Maybe the laws of man in this country doesn't,
but the Laws of the most high does. And in the
Kingdom of the Willows the law allows it! You
can't have too much family. You understand,
you've been alone.
I do.
I wanna have a family.
Maybe I should just leave, darling.

Please don't leave the Kingdom of the Willows, beloved Queen Chrysanthemum! You wanna make me beg again?

I ain't never made you beg at all, King Willow! Neither of us has anyone! But we got them! And we got each other now! I love being with you--- working with you---We love having you, and we all live so well together and-----

What?

I got profound feelings for you…really strong ones…

I do too---for you. Just what kinds of feelings you got for me?

I'm in love with you, no matter what I said. He looked away, ashamed.

All that mean talk? It was crazy making love talk. I wish I could take it all back.

And Miss Willy, dear King?

I'm as in love with her as ever. I adore my wife.

I'm so happy to hear that! That'll have to be part of our covenant, she said.

What?

You'll always love and honor Queen Hibiscus, and Queen Bluebelle---

And Queen Chrysanthemum? He asked.

Yes!

She wants this for us too. She wants sister wives. I'm in love with all three of you. Deeply. Y'all are my family, my world. I live and breathe for ya'll.

I fought loving you, King Willow! I fought as hard as I could. But you stole my heart that first evening! You're so sweet, and silly! When the others are asleep? I touch your dreads, and I touch your lips, and I love you so much it hurts inside!

They stood up. They gazed into each other's eyes, saying a great deal without speaking.

Have we known each other long enough, King Willow?

You've been here months!

Ok. How do we do the marriage thing? She whispered.

I'll check with MaGoo. But we can make a vow to each other.

For real for real? I'm not a slut! This was not planned!

I know!

Did I violate your trust?

No you did not.

Are you sure?

Yes ma'am, you don't have to leave! Miss Willy say's so long as we're not doing it on the sneak, and so long as she's number one---

She is! She is! She said.

Please, let's not be guilty. It was awesome! Next time---

Next time?

Next time, let's not let it build up like that! If we did it once a day----

Oh my G-d, that would be sweet! But you got to court us---me and Tiff.

Ok. Don't get me wrong, I adore my Willy! And Tiff? She's my star! But I love having you here too! I love having you near me! We have the freedom to make love anytime we want if you want! If you want we can be a...you know?

Ok, she whispered. Yes! Yes! But if you want to marry me, you have to do a traditional proposal to me in front of the others. And you might want to do the same with Tiff.

Ok.

I heard from my Grand mama Cherry Blossom's lawyer. I'm now the proud owner of a farm! A farm on the edge of the Trinity Forest! Less than twenty minutes from the river! Is that cool?

Wow! He said. Awesome!

So now all of us will have two homes! Or you can sell the stuf you make on the net an we can move over to the farm and sell this place if you want! The farm is not far from here anyway! We're gonna do some organic farming!

They took each other in the arms and kissed.

Hey! Hey! Called Tiffany-Dawn! Where are you guys? Dinner ain't gonna cook itself, and I only got two hands!

No sweat, Bluebelle! Called out Chrysanthemum.

Well, hurry up! Sleeping beauty! Unless you're still on vacation?

As all four sat to a dinner of salad and lentil stew, Tiffany-Dawn studied Chrysanthemum.

You hardly been talking all evening, she said. How's celibacy thing working for you?

Why you goin' do me like that Bluebell? She said, clearly embarrassed.

Tiff, enough, ok? let her be, said Troll.

Right, right! She said. How's that nudity without sexuality working for you, King Willow?

She laughed.

Big, sis? Said Wilhelmina.

What?

Quit being a tit!

Jus sayin'! Let's put it out on the table.

Chrysanthemum's lip quivered and she looked at her lentil porridge.

Tiff, said Troll, please let her be.

Come no now! I been telling her she needs a man, and I been telling her that man is you! Said Tiffany-Dawn. All that celibacy stuuf is fine, but not after you met a man your in love with!

I ain't said I was! Said Chrysanthemum.

Oh, really? Asked Tiffany-Dawn . Do you ever hear yourself?

I ain't said I wasn't baby gurl, but I ain't ever said!

He's all you ever talk about!

He's all you ever talk about, Bluebelle !

So let's talk about this! Chryssie, why are you looking so hound dog for? Are we going to be sister wives or not?

They all looked at Troll.

Wow! He said. I thought there was going to be a different way of doing this, but----first, Willy? Do I have your permission to have these two crazy gurls as my wives?

Wilhelmina looked at them.

Have y'all thought about it? Tiff? Chryssie?

Personally? Said Tiffany-Dawn with a smile. I think it would be awesome!

Why? Asked Wilhelmina.

I get a wonderful husband, and I created a life with my sister and my best friend all together! I think it's awesome!

Chryssie?

Wilhelmina, said Chrysanthemum, are you sure this is what you want? Are we taking something or part of something out of this that should only be yours?

I'm sure.

She turned to Troll.

Well Ragamuffin? Are you up to loving the three of us, and honoring the three of us? Are you up to being a friend, a lover, and a soul mate, and a provider to three women?

I'm not rich, he said. I can't tell none of you that I can do it all if y'all don't want to, or can't do your share. But I would love to! Willy, darling, there's a joy that's come into our lives, there's a joy that's come into you since they been with us.

Ladies, will you marry me?

Do you love them like a man should love wives? Asked Wilhelmina. Can you love all three without putting anyone on the back burner or to the side? We all gotta be special and important to you.

Yes ma'am, I can.

Sisters, asked Wilhelmina, can you both treat each other with love, and love me without jealousy, or resentment?

Yes ma'am, said Tiffany-Dawn .

Of course, darling Wilhelmina, said Chrysanthemum.

We'll have to look out for each other. There are those who ain't happy about me and Poppy Willow being together, much less him and both of you. We got to protect our family ourselves.

What do you mean? Asked Tiffany-Dawn .

Don't put it pass Mama to put someone up to doing something to Troll.

Especially if they find out what we are doing.

Wilhelmina looked around at all of them carefully.

A chill passed over them.

You know me. You know what I've done in the past. I'm not scared of using a gun to protect myself or y'all, but there might come a time when y'all might need to think of doing the same thing for the family. All of you. It ain't just a one person job.

Definitely, said Troll. The others nodded.

In the eyes of the state, said Wilhelmina, I gonna be the only real wife, but you got to know that in the eyes of the most high, y'all are his wife too!

We understand, said Tiffany-Dawn. Ain't that right, Chrysanthemum? I wasn't tryna rag you! I just want you to admit you love ole Troll, and ain't claiming you're celibate any more. And Chryssie, don't get mad at me for asking, but are you going to keep on doing the weed of wisdom thing….

Ain't y'all noticed? Said Chrysanthemum. I don't get High as much no more, but I do like some wine and beer with our meals.

Cool.

She patted her friends hand.

I'll say this to anybody! Said Tiffany-Dawn. I always thought Poppy, King Willow was a hunk, but now I also know I love him as a man too. I don't care who says he's a dim bulb! I'd be honored to be his wife and to bear his children.

King Willow, said Chrysanthemum, we can't let you off this easy.

Who says I'm a dim bulb----

They all laughed.

Focus, Teddy-bear! Said Tiffany-Dawn.

I'm serious! Said Chrysanthemum. We should court for at least a month, and we gotta get word to MaGoo, and to Moon and Lil Bit, and to Isaiah and Mingo. You need to get up offa your wallet and buy some engagement rings, and give us a chance to crow and be happy about our coming marriage, cause I know Tiff and I know myself enough to know that I am with you for life! Let's make some beautiful memories!

And you know what? Said Chrysanthemum. Can we please get married at that grove of Willows?

Tiffany-Dawn smile and clapped. That would be beyond awesome!

Anyway, ladies, said Troll. You know me and Wilhelmina are practicing traditional Judaism, and are going through a conversion. The Bell family introduced me to it, and I been practicing it for years, but what MaGoo and wives practice is an ancient form of traditional Judaism. I mean, y'all have been learning and studying, right? Are you prepared to embrace it?

Definitely, King Willow! Said Chrysanthemum. We already have.

Yes, darling, said Tiffany-Dawn . Remember that first night we got here?

They all laughed.

Who would have ever thought! Said Chrysanthemum. My darling King Willow! It will be an honor to give you my hand in marriage.

Then Trolls cell phone rang.

Chapter Eleven

He spoke into it briefly, then he dropped it and started crying.

The three women stared.

Ragamuffin? Darling? What's wrong?

You remember the Bell family? He asked.

Yes?

First Periwinkle died, and now less than a few years later her father? Slope? He just passed away from a heart attack.

Aww! Sweety! So what will you do?

I'll go down to Cedar Hills and help Ivy out if she needs me.

Well, said Chrysanthemum, you own a home on wheels…

I'll be gone a few days, it's not worth the bother. They own a sweet tiny home on wheels. Maybe Ivy will drive it here and spend some time with us. It'll make no sense for her to rattle around in that big house. I'll bet you she'll rent it out and live in her little house.

*Boss, not to be the boss of you? said
Chrysanthemum.*
Yeah?
We need to come with.
I agree, said Tiffany-Dawn .
He turned to Wilhelmina.
*Daddy, you and this woman has a history with
you, said Wilhelmina. We need to be with you.
We need to be there to support you, because she
needs to see what you've become and deal with
who you are now, not the teenager she broke into
manhood.*
His phone rang.
*Chryssie can you get it? Said Troll. I'm not up
to any more than y'all.*
Chrysanthemum answered it.
*Hello?... Who is this please?... Safflower?... Let
me check and see if he's here!*
*She looked at him and gave him a huge
mischievous grin.*
*He shook his head furiously silently mouthing:
I'm not here!*
*Ma'am, he's not available at the moment! No, I
have no idea when he'll be available!...Do
what?....I wouldn't advise you to do that….well
I don't advise you to come…. he may not be
available…Ok! Bye.*
What did she say? He asked, in a panic.

*She says tell that asshole I'm on my way! Said
Chrysanthemum laughing.*
Oh no! How did she sound?
Pissed. Look, boss, I CAN get my 357---
*No! No! Look, it's still not too late...I'ma go
camp out tonight..I'ma...*
Who is she?
*Slope's sister! An Ex! Used to be my boss. I used
to work for her! She has anger issues and-----*
*They heard a loud knocking at the gate that led
into the yard.*
*TROLL! called Safflower, I heard you in there,
mother FUCKER! So don't give me that SHIT
about being UNAVAILABLE, you lying son of a
BICTH!*
*Safflower? He said miserably, I'll be right there,
sweets! Chill out!*
He looked at them.
*Whatever happens, he whispered, just PLEASE
stay out of it! She's borderline psychotic on a
good day! Please! I'll handle her!*
*She kicked the gate open when he unlocked it,
and stormed in.*
*Fool ya didn't I, ASSHOLE? So THIS is where
you've been hiding? This is the hide out, HUH?
You DECEITFUL son of a BICTH!*
How are you Saff?
*FUCK how are you! Give me a kiss, asshole, or
so help me, I'll slap the shit
Outcha!*

He kissed her quickly.
Tone it down darling!
She was leanly well-built, with beefy arms and thighs, and as tall as he. She was beautiful, and seem to not care about it, which made her all the more alluring and annoying to the three women.
He stood nude before her.
Slope is DEAD! She shouted, inches from his face. You asshole! And WHERE were YOU?
I had no idea —
FUCK I had no idea! You who-son son-a-va BICTH! Slope is dead Troll.
She grabbed him by the shoulders and shook him.
Slope if DEAD!
I'm so sorry! How, Saff?
How the FUCK would I know? He had a FUCKING HEART ATTACK, you fucking dumb-ass!
He drew her into his arms and she cried on his shoulders.
She wore a decrepit straw cowboy hat that was not getting any younger, with a red bandana tied around it, and a distressed, torn up denim jacket with the sleeves hacked off, over a holey sleeveless t shirt, cut off at her stomach, as well as scuffed old cowboy boots, and worn, frayed, snug fitting daisy dukes covered in holes and tears, which left a slice of her back cheeks exposed. She wore nothing under them.

Get the FUCK offa me! She screamed abruptly
pushing him away. Quit FEELING up my ASS,
you whore son-son ova bicth!
I didn't feel up your----
Shut the fuck up and quit debating me! I'm
grieving, you dumbass!
Saff---
I ain't used to being dressed! I gotta get these
mother FUCKIN' rags offa me!
Nude up sweetheart! Said Troll. Nude up! She's
mostly naked---
HEY! Shouted Safflower, Don't FUCKING talk
like I AIN'T in the FUCKING room, asshole!
Saff, chill out!
FUCK chill out!
She undressed, furiously flinging off her clothes.
She flung the t shirt in his face. He pulled it off
and shook his head, smiling in spite of himself.
I don't have any idea when the last time was I
wore ANY fucking clothes! Said Safflower, to the
ladies. I FUCKIN' HATE CLOTHES!
She started kicking and stomping her clothes and
boots, screaming down at them, MOTHER
FUCKS! MOTHER FUCKS!
They just stared at her for a brief instance.
Hey! She said looking at the women. Who the
FUCK are YOU SLUTS? What the FUCK y'all
doing here? SPYING on me?
The three looked at her balefully.
Saff----Said Troll.

SHUT THE FUCK UP! Who the FUCK are you three little GASHES any-FUCKING-way? HUH? Are ya little freaks BULL DAGGAS? WHAT the FUCK are you FUCKING gashes LOOKING at?

Yelled Chrysanthemum jumped to her feet and slapped her face. Then hell erupted.

Oh, Hell no! BITCH.

Did you just SLAP ME, YOU LITTLE NIGGER GASH!

SHUT THE FUCK UP! Yelled Chrysanthemum. WHAT? WHAT? I'ma slap the SHIT outta ya AGAIN in a minute if you don't watch your mouth, you foul mouth slut!

Safflower stared at her with an open mouth, utterly amazed, rubbing her face.

AHHH! She screamed lunging at Chrysanthemum, but Troll grabbed her around the waist and pulled her back. Let me go! I'll rip that little GASH to shreds!

Enough! He yelled. That's ENOUGH!

No let that bitch go! Said Chrysanthemum. I'll KICK her ass!

No Chryssie! Troll got in between them.

You wanna do that again? Asked Safflower.

Come ON, you little BITCH!

SHUT UP!

Wada FUCK you say to me?

Chryssie---said Troll.

Get the hell out my way, boss!

Y'all chill----

NO, ragamuffin! ENOUGH of this! Said Wilhelmina. We LIVE here! I'LL slap your FACE TOO, big gurl!

You don't know us like that! Said Chrysanthemum. If you CAN'T control your MOUTH talking to us? GET THE HELL OUT or I'MA whoop your tall ASS and THROW your ass OUT!

Yeah! YOU TELL HER, Chryssie! Said Tiffany-Dawn, standing right next to Chrysanthemum. We can give an ass kicking or take one too!

Y'all won't do it alone! said Wilhelmina. She and Tiffany-Dawn , flanked Chrysanthemum. Sorry for your loss! But that's no excuse! You being DRUNK is no excuse for this EITHER!

Oh you bitches wanna jump me three to one? COME ON THEN!

NO! STOP THIS! Yelled Troll.

You talk to Teddy-Bear like that? said Tiffany-Dawn, we should whoop your ass for that! but he told us to let you make it! But YOU WILL NOT TAALK LIKE THAT TO US!

The little woman stood with her feet apart and fists on her hips glaring up at Safflower. Safflower seemed intimidated. Wilhelmina fought the urge to laugh.

Safflower stared down at Chrysanthemum with
her hands on her hips too. Abruptly she threw
her head back and laughed.
Wow! Oh SHIT! Wooooo! Safflower laughed.
DAYUM! What a FUCKING rush! You got a
big HEART little lady! ALL y'all!
We don't like being pushed around, SISTER,
said Tiffany-Dawn. We're not ASS-rags for you
to kick around.
Safflower laughed and shook her head.
Ok! My bad! I could kill all three of you, but I
won't! I'ma let you make it! I like you, short
stack! Sorry ladies!
Alright then! Said Chrysanthemum. This here is
the QUEEN Hibiscus, and this is her sister,
Queen Bluebelle. RESPECT!
Saff, said Troll, deeply embarrassed to the point
of mortification by all of it, these are my three
Queens. This is my awesome wife, Willy, and
my fantastic live-in fiancées, my ladies Tiff and
Chryssie.
Oh! What's up? She said apathetically, quickly
losing interest in them, barely paying them any
attention any longer. Y'all are in the life, right?
Do you mind me nuding?
She stripped off everything left without waiting
for an answer. Her ropey dread locks fell to the
middle of her back.

It did not pass unnoticed that he swiftly got an erection.

Why are you so angry at me, Saff?

DON'T FUCKING get me started again!

Babe---

Peri died and we NEEDED you, ASSHOLE!
She said, poking him in the chest at each point for emphasis. Slope NEEDED you!

Poke.

WE were all GOOD to YOU!

Poke.

VY and I NEEDED you!

Poke.

And what did you DO?

Saff---

You FUCKING BAILED on us!

Poke! Poke!

ASS hole!

Poke.

You FUCK-ing BAILED!

Poke!

I couldn't go around y'all! And quit POKING me, gurl!

Whyja bail? WHY?

I couldn't go in that house anymore, ok?!
Everywhere I went around y'all I saw her!

We NEEDED you!

Saff, I'M THE ONE WHO FOUND HER HANGING IN THE FRIGGING CLOSET!
ME! I can't get it out of my mind. CHILL OUT!

He broke into tears.

Troll, darling---

What did you expect? Did you want me to hang myself too? That's what woulda happen!

Who the FUCK told you to grieve alone? Huh, asshole?

I know, I know, ok? I couldn't HANDLE anymore after the funeral!

So you FUCKING stay away? Safflower demanded. Huh? You FUCKING avoided ME?

I LOVED HER! Said Troll.

So FUCKING what? She started to cry with him. I FUCKING loved her too! She was the ONLY FUCKING NEICE I HAD! Didn't you love US too?

Yes! You KNOW I do!

Well you have a FUCKING great way of SHOWING it, whoreson, son-ova-bitchin' ASSHOLE!

I was there as long as I could be!

She closed her eyes and sang quite movingly, HEY HEY MY MY! ROCK AND ROLL WLL NEVER DE! THERE'S MORE TO THE PICTURE THAN MEETS THE EYE! ROCK N ROLL WLL NEVER DIE! Remember that Troll?

He smiled, tears streaming down his face.

Dang, gurl! Why you doing me like that? Slopes favorite song…

*How the FUCK did HE know Rock n Roll will
never die? She screamed. He was rock n roll!
Now HE'S dead. FUCK Slope!
Saff, he said, I'm here ok?
She looked at him dully.
Vy and I NEED you now Troll! What are going
to do now?
You know what I'll do!
What? WHAT?
I'ma be there, ok?
Ok! But you don't FUCKING grieve on your
own! You don't FUCKING bail! And you don't
FUCKING stay away from PEOPLE who
FUCKING love you, ASSHOLE!
Ok, you wanna just keep YELLING at me?
HUMILIATING me in front of my family?
Sorry ladies! You wanna keep calling me
ASSHOLE? Fine!
When I call you asshole, she said loftily, it's a
term of endearment.
They all laughed.
IT IS! FUCK ALL Y'ALL!
Fine! SAID Troll quickly, hoping to avoid
another brawl. But I was there as long as I could
be! Sweety, I woulda lost my mind if I didn't get
away!*

You FUCKING ruined my LIFE, you whore-son son-ova BITCH! I don't fuck NOBODY anymore, and you KNOW I love me some cock, FUCKING ASS hole! You FUCKING get me ADDICTED to your FUCKING OVER SIZED COCK and then you FUCKING bail on me you FUCKING mother-FUCK whore-ass son-ova-BITCH!

Are you high? He asked. Are you drunk?

Combo..What if I am, ASS hole? I'M fucking PISSED at that DUPLICITOUS SON-OVA-WHORE-ASS BITCH slope FOR UP AND DYING ON ME! FUCK YOU SLOPE!

And you rode a hog here? ASKED Troll.

So fucking what? Yelled Saff. FUCK YOU AND THE HORSE YOU RODE IN ON, BUDDY BOY!

She glared into his eyes, and finally, her anger spent, took him gently by the back of the neck, collapsed into his arms, and sobbed on his shoulder.

Slope is DEAD, ese! My big brother, Troll! My only family! Wada I do now? Slope is DEAD, Troll! Oh G-D oh G-d! Slope is dead. I got nobody left now!

We got Vy, we got each other!

I NEED you Troll! She wailed. I NEED you, NIGGER!

I'm here! He said.

You'll just BAIL, baby! You'll just BAIL…
I won't sweet heart! He whispered. I won't!
We're all going to miss him, but we're going to
be ok!
Well, asshole, she said pulling away, WHEN you
return to the scene of the crime? YOU got two
VERY BIG surprises coming buddy BOY!
What are you talking about?
FUCK YOU! she said laughing, wiping her eyes.
That's what you get! I ain't telling you SHIT.
You're gonna find out the hard way! They pretty
much moved out of the house and they stayed in
the tiny house. I wanna see your face when you
see!
What surprises are you talking about, Saff?
Maybe if it wasn't so dark you'd see and figure it
out. You'll find out, dude!
We're going out there in the morning! Said
Troll.
See? She said. SEE?
What? he said.
Why not now? You're FIXING to BAIL! You're
                    SUCH an ASSHOLE!
No, I'm not!
Why THE FUCK not TONIGHT?
Saff----
You're BAILING again. AREN'T you?
No! We gotta take care of a few things before we
leave, but we're going first thing in the morning.
We? Who the FUCK is we?

Me and my ladies!
Yeah, right what-EVER!
Look it's starting to rain, Saff! I'm getting' cold
and so are my ladies. How did you get here?
I rode Slope's hog! She said. I left Silas with Ivy
and Elias!
Who's Silas and Elias? Y'all got another dog?
DOGS? She started laughing. You're in big
trouble, boy! You got two BIG surprises coming,
buddy boy! Do you remember Brutus?
How is ole Brutus?
He's misses you taking him for walks.
You can't get on the road in the state you're in
kid.
I gotta get back before morning.
Why?
I don't wanna drive in the daylight.
Saff, you're staying the night. In the morning
you'll come with, ok?
There at least thirty ticket warrants out for me!
Don't worry he said.
Can I stash the hog here and ride with you?
Won't Slope want it home----
Aww! Honey, honey! Slope is GONE! Slope is
gone, baby…
He stared at her dully and nodded slowly.
Yup! Yup! I didn't see him for a year,
Saff…Sure! Stash it here…Damn, Slope! Why
he have to die, Saff?

He held his head down.

Shhh! Shhh! She whispered, patting his shoulder and embracing him. Aww, baby, we're all gonna miss him!

She studied him quietly.

Damn him! He died like this to punish me!

Shhh! Shhh! He knew you were in a bad space.

Really?

Hell yeah! Me? I just assumed you're a sorry son of a bitch!

You're so comforting!

Ok, asshole. Where can I crash?

He showed her to the cabin, then he went into the tiny house.

When he climbed into the loft of Willy's tiny house, she sat up.

Where are you going? She asked.

I'm coming to sleep---

Are you? Asked Wilhelmina.

The other two women sat up and eyed him coldly.

I never said I hadn't been with any one before, he said.

Is that crazy chick your woman?

I used to be involved with her.

I was involved with some people…I told you about the Bells….it was complicated, ok? I was involved with this girl called Periwinkle, and with her step mom, Saff was her aunt, ok?

Who was Slope?

Slope was married to Ivy, Peri's step mom. Slope was injured in the groin and couldn't….take care of his wife's needs? He was like a mentor to me. He taught me so much! He wanted me to be with them because he knew the kind of person I was, you know?

So you were their stud?

No! It wasn't like that! It was open relationship, but Peri suffered from depression.

Because she didn't want it like that?

She suffered from depression before I came along. I used to spend a lot of time with them. One night I was over there, and she left her room in the middle of the night. I found her hanging in the guest room closet.

Did she leave a note?

Yeah. It sad she was sick and tired of being sick and tired. She always talked that way, you know?

People with depression sometimes commit suicide. It's not your fault.

I stayed with them till after the funeral, but I was scared I was going crazy. I kept going back, but I kept going less and less. Finally about a year and a half ago? I stopped going around them. I couldn't stay there anymore….Y'all are who I'm with.

Did you love them?

*Yes, he said. Slope was like a Father to me. He
taught me how to repair hoses, how to build
things. He taught me Judaism. I learned about
making twig furniture from him. He taught me
how to build Tiny houses. Ivy taught me ho to
body build and about sustainability.*

Do you still love them? Asked Tiffany-Dawn.

*I felt sorry for Slope. It musta been awful to
know that a kid who was like a son was servicing
your wife.*

Did he want you to do it?

*Even if he did…I wasn't cut out for open
relationships.*

So why did you do it?

I was young and stupid.

*So what's the difference in between that and
this?*

You're my wives---

We ain't married yet, said Wilhelmina.

*We will be, he said. That whole thing? It was all
about insecurity. I never knew where I stood. I
know where we stand.*

Where is that?

*We're a family. We're going to be married.
Willy is my wife and Queen.*

Were you in love with the three women?

*I was with Peri…I kinda sorta was with
Ivy…but she was Slope's wife! Saff? How
would I know? She's so over the top! You don't
have a chance to figure out what you feel!*

You're in love with her, said Tiffany-Dawn.

I'm with you three. Y'all are my life.

They simply stared at him.

Are you mad at me?

Shouldn't we be?

I haven't been untrue.

Why did you not tell us all this before?

Because I thought they were out of my life.

So if something bad happens are you gonna walk away from us?

It was worse than something bad. I found her hanging.

I guess I'm asking how committed you are.

I'm committed. Look…So y'all don't want me up here?

I'm not that wishy washy. Come on! Said Wilhelmina. I'ma need answers. You don't have to right now, ok?

Look, I been honest! I told you everything!

Are there any other secrets we don't know?

Honest, I've told you everything.

You got a whole lot of explaining to do.

Like what?

So what do you mean you're going to be there for them?

They need me now!

Well, we're not going to let you go through this alone, said Wilhelmina.

Thank you!

We're not gonna let HER eat you alive.
Please don't smack her again! She's harmless.
You need to tell her to watch her mouth.
What do you think those two surprises she was
talking about are?
He looked scared.
I honestly don't know.

The next day when they all drove out to the Bell
home. Troll picked up egg and cheese biscuits
and home fries for everyone, and a Toot n Tote'm
quart of orange juice, which they shared.
Safflower, hiding being dark sunglasses, was
hung over and had too strong a headache to be a
headache. She took several Aspirin. She rode in
the back of Chrysanthemums van with a big cup
of Toot n Tote'm Coffee. She groaned when Troll
tried to get her to eat and waved it away. She
threw up once by the side of the road as Troll
held her.
The first thing that he noted was that there was a
for Sale and For Rent sign in front of the ranch
style house.
He took out his Cell phone.
Vy?...Troll, dear...My condolences, ma'am....
How are you sweety?... I'm out here with
Safflower and my Queens....Can we come in?
Yeah, they're my three hairy fairies! We're all
nudies, so it's cool.

Look Y'all, he said to Wilhelmina and the others,
When we enter the yard? You don't have to nude
up if you don't want.
Are you going to? Ask Wilhelmina.
Yeah, but he's comfortable doing it, and so am I,
croaked Safflower, cause we been here before.
Used to be a second home to asshole hear.
Are there any men in there? Asked
Chrysanthemum. The only man who see me
nekkid is you, Teddy-Bear.
No, sis! No men! Said Safflower, who was a
great deal more tractable when sober and hung
over. The man of the house is gone!
Play it by ear, said Troll. Troll and Safflower
disrobed at the inside of the gate, once it was
locked. They folded their clothes and placed it on
a shelf.
Wilhelmina, Tiffany-Dawn and Chrysanthemum
looked at each other; Wilhelmina shrugged. They
undressed and folded their clothes and left them
on garden shelves near the gate.

According to Safflower the house was empty.
Like Trolls' yard, it was surrounded by a tall
privacy fence and gate, permitting nudity with
privacy. When they entered the yard,
Wilhelmina noted that the yard was taken up by
a large rustic garden. In the corner
perpendicularly sat a tiny house on wheels. Two
nude toddlers the color of dark honey, came out
on the small porch. They each had pacifiers in
their mouths. They stared at the newcomers
curiously.
They look kinda sorta familiar, mumbled
Chrysanthemum.
Oh my G-d! Said Tiffany-Dawn , do you think
they're------
Hey guys! Said Troll, picking up one of the
toddlers. Whatsya name, big man?
Wilhelmina was delighted by them. She picked
up the other and dandled him, cooing to him.
Safflower grinned with malicious delight for
reasons unknown kissed both of the little boys.
Aw come on buddy, what's you're name?
The little boy stared at him curiously.
Elias!
Hi Elias! And who are you?
Silas!
Who are you? Asked Elias?
Troll.

Ivy came out on the porch, naked. She grinned wearily. She had dark circles around her red eyes and looked exhausted, depleted.

The blond white woman wore her hair in dreads.

The three women looked at the lean, muscular woman and exchanged looks.

Troll! Thank G-d, baby!

Vy!

Come 'ere darling! She said holding open her arms.

He set down the child and took her in his arm.

I'm so sorry, sweety!

She held her head on his shoulder with closed eyes.

So good to see you, you big lug!

Vy! Vy!

They cried in each others arms.

Don't let it bother you, Troll. He's in a better place.

That sounds good, but…

Slope was really broken by Periwinkle's death, she said. That really crushed him. I just hope he's at peace now.

I'm sorry I've stayed away…it wasn't easy for me either.

Troll have you met the boys? Asked Ivy, pulling away, needing to change the subject.

She noted his awakening erection hungrily.

Sure! He said. This are my buddy Elias and
Silas!
Ivy and Safflower smiled at each other.
Who are your ladies?
He quickly introduced them.
I hope you ladies understand something, said
Safflower. My niece? Ivy's step daughter? She
was his lady.
And so were we! Said Ivy, boldly enough to let
them know that it shamed her a little to admit
that they had such an arrangement. That was as
far as our idea about free love went.
Me and Ivy had a lot of static about Troll, said
Safflower. But after Peri died, we decided life is
to short. Anyway, he bailed---
Saff, said Ivy. Please leave him alone!
Ok, ok! You're really kind to be so
understanding ladies. We have a history with
Troll. He may not see it, but he's part of this
family.
Well darling, said Ivy to Troll, let me formally
introduce you to these two little gentlemen! Elias
is my son, and Silas is safflowers son.
Oh really? Said Troll. Who's the Daddy?
We're hard core naturist! Neither of us used
birth control, said Ivy.
I wish I had known that, said Troll wryly. Who's
the Daddy?
Which is why we don't just fuck around, said
Safflower.

Would you mind not using that kind of language around the boys? Said Ivy.

Ok! Ok! Get off my back, Vy! I'm dying of a hangover!

Who's the Daddy? Asked Troll.

You'll get no pity from me! Snapped Ivy. I told you getting drunk and tooling off on the hog to Track this lug head down was bone headed!

Leave me alone! wailed Safflower.

So these are your sons? He asked.

Yeah, said Safflower.

HEY! He said. Who's the Daddy?

You, said Chrysanthemum. Right?

Ivy and Safflower exchanged a look.

Yes, said Ivy. Troll, you're their father!

The open relationship stuff doesn't mean you do a buncha men, said Ivy. You were my first lover after Slope---was injured. For me it mean that I didn't leave my husband just because he was impotent, but I could still love you!

Me? said Safflower. I told you I wasn't going to be with another guy, and I haven't found one yet! Maybe I'm not looking! Maybe---

Troll said nothing.

I'm not speaking to either of you! He snapped.

Troll! Said Ivy. Be fair!

So, little buddies, he stammered, trying to sound playful, I'm your daddy?

He knelt and played with the two boys.

Y'all are so wrong, he said.

So we're talking again? said Ivy.

Why are we wrong? Demanded Safflower. Don't even try to go there!

Please no arguing, you two, said Ivy. Come in and let me make y'all some tea, Let's talk about how we'll do Slope's funeral!

I need really strong coffee, Ivy! Whined Safflower, please! My HEAD!

In Texas you can Funeralize your own dead, said Safflower as they sat on the floor in a circle drinking tea in the little cottage.

Troll sipped his tea. Why are you telling me this?

Ivy put down her cup.

We're going to do it ourselves, she said. We're doing a natural burial!

Safflower nibbled an oatmeal cookie and sipped some of her milky, sweet tea.

How did you find me? He asked, mystified.

I googled you, you ass --- darling! Said Safflower.

Why didn't you do it before? Why didn't you tell me you two were pregnant?

We thought you wanted to be left alone after a time, said Ivy.

I shoulda been told!

Are you going to help with the funeral? She asked.

*Why didn't you two tell me about my boys?
How much longer were you going to keep it
secret?*
Don't be angry with us, baby! Said Safflower.
You're the one who left us!
I----
*Look, I tried calling you! Said Ivy. You didn't
return my calls!*
*I was about to lose my mind. I couldn't take
anymore, I'm sorry. After Periwinkle died I had
to stay away!*
*Well, we went by your home! Said Safflower. We
tried to find you.*
*I rented it out, and sold it off! He said. I moved
to where I'm at now!*
*We left notes! Said Ivy. I'm really sorry, hon, we
had no way of reaching you! You disconnected
your cell too!*
Ok, ok!
*Ivy watches the boy for me, but they need a
father, Troll! Said Safflower. Especially with
Slope gone. We know you seem to have moved
on, but we need you, and so do your sons!*
I'll help with the funeral.
What about after? Asked Ivy.
*Why don't y'all come hang out with us? Asked
Troll. If my ladies don't mind?*
Wilhelmina smiled at him.
I'd like to get to know my sons.

*Well, I can't take being here anymore, said Ivy,
and broke down. He put his arm around her
shoulder.*

Sweety, I'm so sorry!

*We'll come if you'll be there for us, said
Safflower sadly. The Cosmic Comida isn't that
far from you. All that time you were less than a
mile from me.*

*We need to family up right now, Troll, said Ivy.
Game times over! Slope is goes and now these
boys need their father.*

Troll looked at Wilhelmina. She nodded.

*Ok. We'll just tow your cottage down after the
funeral.*

What about me? Asked Safflower.

No one said anything.

*I'm perfectly happy to have guests, said
Wilhelmina. WE'RE happy to have guests, but
we don't want drama.*

*I'm really sorry, y'all, I was drunk last night!
Said Safflower. I'm hurting!*

Ok, said Wilhelmina. Ladies?

Tiffany-Dawn and Chrysanthemum nodded.

*Come stay with us, said Troll. We'll play it by
ear, ok?*

*Troll, you and Ivy are the last family I have!
Said Safflower.*

Willy? Said Troll.

*Some of us have issues with your rages, said
Wilhelmina.*

You've only known me for one night! She said.
And I'm coping with the death of my brother!
How does that excuse you behaviour last night?
Asked Tiffany-Dawn .
The other things is that we're about being a
family, said Chrysanthemum. We're not trying
to form a commune.
Neither are we! Said Ivy.
And there's gotta be trust! Said Tiffany-Dawn .
We're not trying to get Aids!
What does that mean? Said Safflower.
Neither are we! Said Ivy.
If you wanna do this, it's just about being
around Troll, said Wilhelmina. He's got wives
now.
Ok? said Safflower.
We're about having a peaceful harmonious
home! Said Chrysanthemum. We don't want
drama.
I never liked feeling that I was with two ladies
who were warring about me, said Troll. This is
about family, and the ladies gotta be at peace
with each other.
Ok, you know what? said Safflower. Fuck it!
Is that your attitude? Asked Ivy. Or do you
want a family for you and Silas?
I want a chance to be a part of my sons lives, said
Troll. Come on, Saff! You know you can stop the
rages!

*You can meditate with me, said
Chrysanthemum. We can do Yoga.
Are you into Yoga? Asked Ivy. I teach it!
Really?!
Yes! Said Ivy. Troll, I took a leave when Slope
got sick. I won't be going back to teaching...not
right now. I need out from here.
All we want is accountability, if you're going to
be a part of our family, said Wilhelmina. We
have one man around: my husband. We don't
wanna bring in any other man either.
To put it simply? Said Chrysanthemum, if
anybody wants to sleep around? Then don't be a
part of this. Can't nobody be into free love. Aids
is real.
I'm not into free love, said Safflower. Never
really have been.
And we're domestic family nudist, said Tiffany-
Dawn . We don't nude outside of the family.
I can live with all of that, said Safflower.
You know something? Said Ivy. We taught Troll
most of what he's into. The Nudism, the wine
and beer making, the Vegetarianism.
I was into nudism before I met you! He said and
laughed.
Naw-uh! Said Ivy.
Dude! I met you in a nudist camp! He said.
Yeah, but you had a lot to learn, she said.
They all laughed.*

*We're all each other's teachers, said
Chrysanthemum.
Well, I wanna be a part of, said Ivy.
Saff? Asked Troll.
She looked at all of them.
Ok. Absolutely.*

*Slope had a nude, outdoor viewing, and
Funeral. All of the guest were nudists. It was
conducted in the shade of the trees at the Cosmic
Comida. Then he was cremated.
He left Troll all of his Judaica. That included his
Tallits, Kippahs, and several stars of David. He
also left him the proceeds of one of several life
insurance policies.
Slope was cremated.
And so it happened that less than a week later a
rustic looking tiny house on wheels pulled by a
White Ford F-150 drove into their enclosed
Garden. It was parked paralleled next to their
tiny house and Cabin. Ivy, Safflower, Elias, and
Silas entered their lives.*

Chapter Twelve

One afternoon several weeks later as Troll was bussing tables after the noon lunch rush if you could call it that, Safflower stood in the door from the kitchen and leaned against the frame. She hitched her thumbs through her gun belt and studied him. She wore nothing but her truckers hat and aviator shades. A lit joint dangled from the corner of her mouth.

Hey, he said. What's up?

Thinking of Slope.

Aww baby!

Needing you.

He kept working.

Are you thinking of me like that? I thought ----

You thought what?

You're my little sister?

She snorted and laughed at him.

Troll, how the FUCK am I your little sister
when I'm older than you, asshole?
You're like a little sister now---
FUCK being a little sister.
I'm tired of your filthy mouth gurl.
Wachu gonna do? You're feeling strong? COME
ON!
He spun her around and gave her two sharp
swats.
She stared at him with an open mouth.
Are you crazy? See the gun I got?
Saff, fact is you like getting swats!
ONLY IF YOU'RE MY LOVER, ASSHOLE!
She broke out crying. I'ma tell Chryssie, Willy,
ALL OF THEM what you just did, asshole!
We can't keep doing it, ok?
SCREW YOU, I GOT NEEDS!
Things are so complicated right now, he said.
Sorry, baby.
She said nothing, but she licked her lips slowly.
Saff I'm begging, ok?
Begging? What're you talking about?
Can you please let me make it?
Let me make it? Make what?
You know what I'm saying.
Are you talking Ebonics again?
Will you stop with that Ebonics crap? It
infuriates me!
You gonna spank me? Let's see you do it again.

Get off my back, baby.
I don't know what the FUCK you're talking
about, Troll.
Why're you standing there looking at me?
Is there a law against that?
For the last time I got a family, Saff!
WE'RE part of your family too!
Things have changed, ok?
That hard on you got? Said Safflower. It's about
me! Has my name all over it!
Yeah, you know you're special to me like that.
It's pointed UP!
It's nature, ok?
You still want Vy and me.
I do! But----
You're fucking Vy on the sly! Don't lie to me!
Nah, baby---
You want some, asshole.
What if I do? Saff I'm married now!
Ok. Say I don't love you Saff.
He looked away.
Say it, say it!
Saff----
Go on! Say it, asshole!
You know I adore you, baby----
I adore the FUCK outta you, nigger!
Gurl…You crazy….
I want that DICK, asshole!
I'm married now!
And you got two live ins too, asshole!

The point is, it's not how it was, ok?
That's not what your DICK seems to think!
My dick doesn't think!
Seems so to me!
Kiss my ass, ok?
You want me to? Bring it over.
You're being impossible, Saff.
I'm tired of getting stealth fucked, ok?
What're you talking about?
Quit bull-shitting, ass-hole! If we're alone, or
we're in the kitchen, I can't bend! I get stealth
fucked, then it's like, baby I'm sorry, I lost
control!
Well, I'm sorry, you make me lose control!
I want stability, baby! I want a real relationship,
and I want it openly! No more stealth fucks!
Listen to me, gurl! We can't-----
You want my pussy don't you?
Can you please let me make it? Cool off, ok?
Cool me off.
Chill out, ok?
You know what? FUCK This!
She locked the door and turned the sign to close.
Troll, don't make me kick your ass, ok?
Yeah, you always have liked it rough, didn't you
Saff?
I NEED YOU, Motherfucker!

She grabbed him by the throat and pushed him against the wall. She kissed him and nibbled his lower lip, then nuzzled his neck.

Ok, asshole you know what I need.

He pushed her away, and she shoved him back.

Out in the world? You may be this hunky mother-FUCKER, who has a buncha chicks creaming their snatches, but here in my place? You belong to ME, NIGGER!

Darling, things have changed, ok?

Yeah, you got your wives, you got Vy, but you ALSO belong to ME! I told you, in this place? Your MINES!

She kissed him all over the face, and took his manhood in her hand and stroked it.

I'm saving your mouth for the fuck party me and you're gonna have right now.

Saff, please stop!

I'ma GET me some dick! Shut up!

No, we're not going to!

Troll, either you spank my ass or I kick your ass!

Kick my ass then! You think I'm scared of you?

Aren't you?

Sweetheart we can't!

Me and Vy OWN a piece of you too! I'm wife number five, asshole!

Baby----

And one way or the other I'ma get that dick!

Saff---

You got a house full of bitches---

Don't call them that!

---- all of who are getting theirs, but ole Saff
can't get any dick, right, asshole?

There you go again being psycho. I'm not doing
Vy, ok?

You need to be. That poor thing needs you.

Safflower! Darling, please-----

Either give it to me or I'ma take it!

He grabbed her face and kissed her lips almost
frantically.

I'm sorry---I ---I, He stammered.

She covered his mouth with a hand and went
down on her knees. She drew his manhood into
her mouth.

Chapter Thirteen

Isaiah became a power in the City of
Redemption, with a reputation that was
drawing widespread attention, but it
nothing to do with her underground free-
will nations involvement. She was earning a
reputation as a young urban leader and
Preacher. It was orchestrated by Mingo. She
was not his puppet, he simply believed in
his wife. Mingo adored her, and like his half
sister, Rosy, he thrived best in the shadows.
He worked very hard to remain in the
shadow of his wife. He was determined not
to do anything that threatened their love.
Chinita, Wilhelmina and Troll and his
ladies, all of whom converted by then,
introduced him to the Forest, and MaGoo
and his wives. By then MaGoo had several
children by his wives, and mostly lived in
the hidden City.
Mingo was quickly embraced by the forest
people.

Wilhelmina discovered the joys of wine
making. It intrigued her to tie plastic bags to
her feet, along with her two sister wives,
and smash tubs full of grapes, all nude with
him, then to see must fermenting into wine.
All four would sit, watching the bubbles rise
through his home made air locks with
fascination.
She and the other two learned how to make
cheese, and preserves, and how to can
vegetables from him.
One night, early in the relationship, when it
was just the two of them, after they finished
canning bushels of string beans, they went
to sleep, happy and tired, and she realized
that they were virtually living together.
That was before they married, before she
moved in with him.
They were also free-gans---or
Chrysanthemum turned them into one. A
few evenings a week they got cases of
perfectly good fruit and vegetables from the
dumpsters which they carefully washed and
preserved or canned.
From him they learned to love out of the
way Thrift Stores, junkyards and yard sales;
she truly to love them too.

They all delved into a minimalist life, and studied sacred writings with devotion. That was his obsession, to live simply and in harmony with nature.

Back at the beginning it didn't surprise her that he was a nudist. In the privacy of his one room home behind his shop, he never wore clothes. He never pressured her about anything, but spending a weekend at a nudist camping ground, during which she ceased to feel any self consciousness about nudity---since everyone around her was nude, and seemed perfectly comfortable--- she too, began to practice naturism when they were alone. Then she found herself being checked out by a man, and found it annoying. And then she saw a young woman checking him out.

They discussed it, and decided to restrict themselves to domestic naturism thereafter. Early on she, like him, gradually stopped trimming or shaving any of her body's hair. Not that she ever really had.

Long hair required care. It became even more so after she had her hair turned into dreadlocks. She stared at herself with a mirror in wonder after an old Rastafarian woman twisted her hair into locks in South Redemption. A slender, dreadlock wearing, freckled faced, fair skin black-girl stared back at her, and she was very beautiful.

Muffin! Said Troll delightedly when he came by in his Dodge Ram pick up to get her once it was finished.

Ragamuffin, be nice! She warned him nervously.

Darling, you're incredible! He said. You're so beautiful!

She threw her arms around his neck and laughed.

Great! I thought you might not like it!

And thus began one of her favorite daily rituals. Both at nights and in the mornings they groomed each other's hair, and with that came a great deal of petting and cuddling that was not really sexual. She loved brushing and combing his beard and his pubic hair once they showered.

At those moments he laid on his back, as she anointed his pubes with denatured olive oil, as she studied and played with his hardening manhood. A sense of pity for him filled her one evening. She felt at first that she was failing him. They were not yet regularly lovers. By way of apology, and out of true affection, she covered it in soft, gentle kisses. It thrilled her to hear him moan and whimper as she did. It aroused her to bring out his weakness with kisses. Without knowing that she meant to, one evening, as she groomed his pubic hair, she slowly took him into her mouth for one of those rare times.

He shivered and moaned, ohhh Muffin! She was hooked.

Something was loosed in her and she went
at him like a hungry lioness; perhaps she
became a little fey as it engorged and
thicken even more in her mouth. She went
faster, becoming more aroused as the tip
massaged her tongue, and when he
screamed and filled her mouth with his hot,
sweet tasting essence as faster than she
could swallow, her insides, of her
womanhood, clenched powerfully and
released again and again, filling her with an
electrifying sense of pleasure that made her
scream. As she felt herself going wild and
losing it, she lost sight of what she was
doing to him.
Stop Muffin! Please! He nearly wept, I ain't
got no more! I'm dry mama!
Out of breath, his essence dripping from her
lower lip, she drew away, with a wild
lioness like look in her eyes. She massaged
his abs soothingly, wanting to comfort him
more, but feeling to disoriented by passion
to gather her thought.
She laid her head on his stomach, and
continued to sooth his abs with gentle
strokes, as he shook with near weeping.
She wanted to comfort him, but all she
could do was to gently say, shhhh! Shhh!

Then she pressed her body to his side, and
her face into the crook of his neck, and
cuddled him against her with her arm like if
he was her baby. She closed her eyes and
pressed her face into the side of his. He
turned on his side and drew her into his
arms, as she found that she was shivering.
She fell asleep with her head pressed against
his chest.

Both had a deep dreamless nap, and woke
up feeling strangely renewed.

She noted a glimmer of fear in his eyes and
instantly felt remorseful.

I lost control, she said. I didn't mean to hurt
you.

Thank you, he whispered.

Why?

For love, for giving me relief, he said.

Darling, she said, ragamuffin, I know I'm
not giving you all you want….

Shhhh!

Daddy, I'm still a little scared, you know? I
don't know what I'm doing…I wasn't tryna
hurt you.

It was beautiful, all the same, he said softly.
When I'm drained and sated and you still
try to get more, it hurts, you know? I ain't
complaining, ok? Lovers need to listen to
each other, though.

Ok, daddy! But you *sexualize* me like that!
What if I lose control again?
We just gotta listen to each other, even if the
animal in us is awake and gone wild…
Then her turn would come. He rubbed
Lanolin or Brilliantine into her pubic hair,
and then he'd comb it with a wide tooth
comb. She fought the urge to draw his
mouth in between her legs. She felt a sense
of self-revulsion when she realized that she
wanted to forcibly rape his mouth. She
began to fantasize about making him go
down on her, and bruising his mouth,
busting it up, until he began to do it
without invitation. He licked and sucked
her gently, burying two finger deep inside
her and caressing her with them as he
sucked her gently. He brought her along
gently, building her intensity until she
started to buck against his mouth, thrusting
her hips rhythmically, arching her back. He
sucked her hard then, until she began to
scream, then he eased his intensity.
She rested his head on her belly, and he
hugged her with eyes shut. Her hair a snarl,
breathing thru her mouth, she felt a sweaty,
wet, sodden mess, and loved it.
Was it good, muffin?

Hmmmm! She responded. Daddy is was *great*!

But mostly the joys of physical affection, to be held, touched, cuddled and fondled, to have him play with her pubic hair as she played with his filled the day with a sense of love manifested as not just a word or sexual stimulation.

When they made love, thereafter, as they were able to in light of her fear, she was left drained, sated, ecstatic.

Even though she moved in with him, bringing very little, besides her guns, she still did not fully give herself to him at the beginning, until that special night at the lake.

Among the gifts he got from her was the joys of family, a sense of belonging and being loved unconditionally. Troll was a lone wolf, as friendly as he seemed. She drew him into her crazy family more and more. That included the SWC, though he had no interest in joining. Even if Honey Buns put on a good act of aloofness, her family and friends embraced Troll. He also got from Wilhelmina a new found sense of spirituality that was not just rooted in the love and beauty of nature. She loved to pray, meditate. If she had anything that could be called an obsession it was a spiritual search for truth in her faith life, which was one of the things that bonded her with Isaiah.

Chapter Fourteen

Troll and Wilhelmina studied Torah with
Isaiah and Mingo. The two couples
effortlessly became very close.
They all shared a fearlessness about
following the truth to where it led. They
delved into Hebrew Israelite-ism and
Messianic Judaism together, even though he
was a reformed Jew, they continued to
search and pray and study, almost
obsessively.
Isaiah, however, was very conservative and
sow to change her spiritual views.

It seemed almost inevitable that they befriended Chinita. She was the most radical member of the Westia fellowship, and was rumored to be going through a conversion to Orthodox Judaism. Isaiah did not believe it.

An almost imperceptible gulf began to open in between them an Isaiah as they got closer to Chinita. Or so thought Isaiah.

Chinita was no longer the lesbian stud with a shaved head, who went about braless in a wife beater and cargo shorts. She struggled with an addiction to steroids and anything else that she could swallow, drink, inject or smoke after the death of her sister, who died without ever coming to realize that they were sisters. Other than for body building, and the Westia Fellowship there was nothing left then.

Her love hate relationship with Isaiah lost its interest for her. All that Chinita wanted was oblivion. Oblivion from a drowning sense of emptiness, from the violence that branded her as worse than a monster, worse than a psychopath. As popular as she was, she knew that most of her circle feared her and did not really love her.

She lapsed into a type of homelessness. She went from the arms of one woman to another and to that of men, in a drug numbed blur, rarely if ever really knowing who she was in bed with, or caring. A time came when she surfed couches, or slept in doorways. She slept hidden behind the dumpster when the weather allowed, behind the small gym where she worked out.

The tiny gym was called Old School Hell. It was a place for old school body builders, with no new machines. Only free weights were used and summer and winter a wood burning furnace cranked out heat. It was not uncommon for newbies to be taken out by paramedics in a state of unconsciousness. Chinita pioneered what was called the suicide workout, which impressed many. She also found an ex con who was a martial artist, and persuaded her to hold classes at the gym.

The gym was her spiritual home, and if it was called Hell, it mattered not to her, for she saw herself as an unwitting demon. She'd pretty much raised herself on the streets, after Goldie, a convicted child-molester, lured her into a Lesbian relationship and into the Westinas. The Westinas were then a girl gang led by several of the most violent lesbian graduates of the Texas Youth Commission.

She became adept at fighting with a Bowie knife. She did a stint in TYC for attempted murder after one knifing, but was released on parole after a few years.

She came out as a body building fanatic with a shaved head, addicted to the martial arts movies, covered in colorful tats, and seriously addicted to roids. She was also hooked on the martial arts.

It was then that she found Hell's Inner Circle. Managed by lesbian body builder, Crow, it became the closest thing to a home she had. Crow, an ex convict, and a crusty old biker lesbian who ran Hell with an iron fist, took Chinita under her wings. In recovery from a serious Heroin habit, Crow was determined to help Chinita master her demons.

If the roids allowed her to turn her body into a monstrosity of oversized muscles, they also made her psychotically violent. She became ferocious as a martial artist. Because of her love for the martial arts, and because she looked slightly oriental, her street name became Chinita, or Chink for short. Chink was supposedly fearsome and vicious. Legend had it that Chink once knifed a man for a cigarette, but the legend was a lie. She knifed him for a piece of penny candy, as a matter of honor.

She never did smoke tobacco, although she smoked everything else.

She had what she called a code of honor, or the Code of the Chink, as she too came to call herself: give respect and expect respect, kill with a knife whenever possible, never stab anyone if you don't have to, but when you do stab someone, stab to kill, never lie if at all possible, but if you have to, lie like a poet, never kill for money, never kill a friend for money, never torture anyone, look those who you kill in the eyes if you get a chance, and kill mercifully if at all possible. For a time she made her living jacking cars and by robbing anyone who had money.

She was too much of a loose cannon to be allowed to live, leaders of various gangs decided. She was a ronin, an independent gang banger, who ran with the gangs but was a part of none. So although she had allies in the Westia Fellowship, and in the Black Girl Assassins, For years she lived with a several contracts on her head. So she lived her life constantly on the run. Yet by mutual consent, all the sets of the Redemption treated Hell as a place of refuge because of the R.I.P. Wall, and so it became a place of refuge for her. It was a wall of the gym covered with rows upon rows of the names and date of birth of gang members killed on the streets of the Redemption. Crow created it, but having discovered that Chinita was capable of remarkable penmanship, she named her the Keeper of the Wall.

More than anything that kept Chinita alive. The friends of the dead would seek her out in Hell after a murder had taken place, wait respectfully for her to finish working out, then approach her with a paper containing the name of the fallen soldier, date of birth and date of death of their friend, along with a cash donation. In tears they would ask her to make it pretty.

Chinita usually responded with tears and a hug.

We gotta stop the madness, she would say sincerely. May G-d have mercy on the dead and on us all!

And many would sit with her and talk to her and confess to her in tears the things that they had done, knowing that it would go no further, even when they confessed to murdering her friends. She would listen humbly and cry with them. Among her biggest supporters and protectors were Isaiah and Mingo. Strangely, many times they came to have a name added to the wall, though it was known that the person was killed at their behest.

So it was almost all the sets of the
Redemption came to view Chinita as a
strange kind of Saint. If she was never
murdered it was because no one could be
found among the gangs willing to kill her.
So those who sought to kill her were bounty
hunters from outside of the Redemption.
The gangs members of the Redemption, if
not their leaders, took care of them for her if
they knew who they were hunting for.
She refused to accept money for herself,
though she lived in poverty. She was not
much of a hustler, and was no longer
willing to rob anyone. Crow kept a jar for
her where mourners would stuff fistfuls of
money for the purchase of paints and
candles. But the paints and candles were
often donated by the self same people who
made donations, so she felt free to spend the
money on her needs, which was what the
donors intended.
Once a week she lit a row of candles before
the wall and sat in quiet prayer in the floor
before it for an hour. She rose each time to
find several people sitting or kneeling along
with her in prayer.

Yet nothing seemed to alleviate the pain that gnawed at her insides after the death of Clown, her sister. The Clown was also on the wall. Every time she saw her sisters name a stabbing pain filled her. Impulsively one day she slit both of her wrists. Crow found her behind the dumpster before she bled out completely. The paramedics, seeing who it was, the notorious gang banger, took their sweet time in taking her to the hospital; she was just another gangbanger to them. After she left the ICU they took her straight to Green Oaks, where she remained for months. At first she was more alive than dead, and spoke to no one. In the hospital she permanently borrowed without consent, some say, or allegedly stole a copy of the Transliterated Tanakh and a transliterated Siddur. In fact she traded it for a box of cigarettes. She quickly taught herself Hebrew, and plied a lapsed Orthodox Jewish patient who was receiving treatment for depression after Yom Kippur with questions upon question, which the Yeshiva boker answered grudgingly.

She came out of the hospital with a new sense of clarity and vision. She adopted modest dress and allowed her hair to grow out. She continued to work out and to do martial arts training, but she stayed off the roids.

She refused to answer to Chinita or to Chink, and insisted on being called by her birth name, Diloris. All of her friends-enemies, Isaiah and Mingo included, were relieved to see the change in her. None of her childhood friends, like Isaiah and her husband, ever really liked calling her Chinita or Chink. She renamed herself Diloris Bhat X.

Not that long after her return Crow died
unexpectedly in her sleep. It turned out that
she left Diloris Hell and the building where
it was contained, along with the hefty
proceeds of a life insurance policy, a sizeable
amount of cash in a savings/checking
account, and two pristine conditioned
Harleys as well as a Ford Aerostar van. The
building also contained three apartments,
one of which had been Crow's home. Diloris
had all the antiques with which it was
furnished auctioned off, banked the money,
and rented out the apartment. She turned
the tiny little office of Hell into her home, by
installing a military cot. It already had a
small bathroom, a small hot plate, a toaster
oven and a microwave. It was all that she
needed. The clothing that she owned she
kept in a private locker in the shower room.
Her clothes she washed in the bathroom
sink.
She lived with the austerity of a nun, and
like a nun, lived with none, and lived
celibately.
Her old lovers came around, amused at
rumors of her celibacy, but found that it was
all too true.

Then one day someone asked her for her prayer and blessings, and she did it with a profound sense of humility. And more and more people asked her for prayers and blessings, even though she told them who she was and how she lived not that long before. Chinita lived with her new found image, knowing that it was undeserved, not because she deemed herself a saint, but because she came to understand that her role in life was to be a servant.

She quickly drew a following, among them the Troll and Wilhelmina. Upon meeting Troll she assumed that Romero had acquired yet another red head, and was confused when he was introduced as Troll. She drew him aside and not to playfully scolded him for taking on yet another woman. She told him of how bleak a life she once lived going from woman to woman to men----

Dude! Troll said, and laughed. I'm not Romero, yo!

But, but----

You wanna hear something weird? Asked Wilhelmina, having over heard the scolding, Tell her your real name, ragamuffin.

Ramiro Martinez! Said Troll with a bright smile. But we're not related! I never even met the guy. Isaiah tried to introduce us once, but he wouldn't give me the time of day. But he did try to help me and Goo build a tiny house.

Chinita blanched, and felt queasy.

She and they spoke on the phone, having met her at the Shop of the Westia Fellowship. They invited her to hang out. She met them at their Troll's Store, renamed Willow Groves' Antiques and Collectibles by Chrysanthemum. Recently, through the auspices of their forest friends, she and Troll began selling wreaths, potpourri, a variety of hand dipped candles, and dried flowers and wild grown teas that proved quite popular. He asked Wilhelmina put her skills as a Convenience store manager to work, and reorganized the store. She also took care of the book keeping. The oddball store was not only paying for itself, it was generating prosperity. Even so, they lived modestly.

The small building that housed the store
was a medium sized Adobe cottage on Loop
12, with a great deal of charm, and
Wilhelmina set about capitalizing on it. By
agreement, Troll did his refinishing and
furniture restoration in the back room shop.
She ran the store. At Chrysanthemums
suggestion, they took to displaying the
Willow twig furniture made by Troll in front
of the store, and hung decorative stings of
dried chili peppers in the windows. The
store also received a new paint job, and very
bright fluorescent lights were installed,
along with a sound system. They began to
play music conducive to shopping. She also
talked him into selling gourmet candies, and
cookies, along with packaged tea and
gourmet coffees. The result was a
remarkable upsurge in business.
Are you ok? asked Troll, taking her by the
elbow. She looked t him and in a flash
realized the truth.
I hate the Redemption sometimes! Said
Diloris.
Why do you say that? asked Wilhelmina.
The more that things change, the more they
stay the same, she said.
Wadaya mean? Asked Troll.

The Redemption is full of sorry little secrets.
She shrugged.
How does it make you feel? She asked.
Having a doppelganger?
A what, yo? Asked Wilhelmina.
A double.
Weird. Curious, said Troll, not certain he
wanted to talk about it with her.
I grew up with a fraternal twin who I never
knew, she said. By the time I found out who
she was, we were enemies and she wanted
to kill me. She died without ever knowing
me as her sister.
How did she die? Asked Wilhelmina.
Chinita browsed the store.
The demons took her, she finally said.
Sorry for your loss, said Troll.
We hated each other, said Chinita. By the
time I found out the truth, it was too late.
Please dude, don't make the same mistake.
Well he hates me, said Troll.
Romero has a red headed wife, right? Said
Wilhelmina.
The Mouse. She lives with him and his
family, said Diloris. He calls her a wife, but
he's married to Julio. Plus Cat lives with
them, and rumor has it---
We know, said Troll, surprised by his own
impatience. He sounds like a major perv.

This was before the other women moved in
with him and Wilhelmina, and before he
became an accidental Polygamist.
Why? Asked Chinita.
All the women!
MaGoo does the same thing! Said
Wilhelmina.
That's part of his culture!
I see it as a beautiful thing! said Deloris.
Anyway, said Wilhelmina. I met her cousin?
They call him Puppy, but he calls himself
Moon.
Moon is his birth name, said Chinita. His
street name is Raggedy-man. That little
dude is the most feared stickup boy in the
Redemption---maybe in the Communion.
His family and my family are cousins, said
Wilhelmina, Him and Mouse are my third
cousins.
That's the Redemption for you, said Chinita.
We been hearing a lot about you, said Troll.
You're really down with Judaism, yo?
I guess.
Look, we're closing up, said Troll. We live in
a little house behind the shop. It's little, but
it's all the home we need right now.
Actually, said Wilhelmina, my husband
built me a Tiny House on wheel---

A What? Asked Diloris.

A small little house on a flatbed trailer! Said Troll with a warm smile.

During the day we use the back, she said but home is in our little house. We don't have much, but we're always happy for company. Would you like to join us for tea? And supper is cooking...

She started to refuse, but felt strangely moved.

Aren't you two nudist?

Yeah, but we're domestic nudist, said Troll.

Which means we only nude around immediate family, said Wilhelmina, which means each other.

I'd be happy to join you for tea!

We love the Trinity River Forest, Troll continued as they sat on the floor with a pot of tea and an assortment of homemade cookies. A lot of us go out there a couple of times a week, clean it, hike and cook out.

Is that Norah Jones playing? Asked Chinita.

We love her! Said Troll.

Would you like to join us? Asked Wilhelmina.

Where?

Out in the forest, said Troll. We'd like to discuss the faith with you.

Sure, said Diloris.

And so began their friendship.
Paradoxically, she became close to Romero
and Julio simultaneously, and their circle.
She was also becoming closer to Isaiah and
Mingo. She thought of Troll, and stared at
Romero with curiosity. Romero and his
Tribe knew and loved her sister, and in
drawing closer to them, they brought each
other a sense of comfort and solace.
Somehow, that Isaiah had once been
Clown's lesbian common-law, made her
begin to forgive Isaiah for all the wrongs,
real and imagined, that fueled their love-
hate relationship. Isaiah too, found herself
growing emotionally closer to the new
Deloris. She had so much in common with
her fraternal twin, the Clown.
Isaiah started to notice a secretiveness about
what Troll and Wilhelmina were willing to
say about their true beliefs; they seemed to
share that with Mingo, who also became
close with Diloris.

She was far too busy to check it. To an extent her various Endeavour were consuming her time. She and Mingo turned the yard of her parents house, combined with much of the yard of Julio and Romero into a micro-urban farm. They posted countless videos about that. They were also exponents of simple, minimalist living, and both posted and blogged about that. Then there was the running of the Westia Fellowship, which was a job unto itself. Directly or indirectly she and Mingo controlled several small business through partners and associates. Furthermore, she and Mingo were full time students Southern Anglican University.

If they were making anything, no one but a few people knew. They lived like paupers. Though they had many vehicles at their disposal, they actually owned none of them openly. They generally slept under a tarp in the yard, even in the foulest weather. Rosy, their financial wizard, knew that Isaiah and Mingo were become increasingly wealthy, though they lived a penurious existence. Isaiah wore clothes scavenged from her family and friends. The diminutive Mingo dressed from clothes found at the lowliest thrift stores.

At any rate, Isaiah knew that there was
nothing that her husband would do without
her. After a while she dismissed her
concerns.
Then soon after Slope's death, after Tiffany
Dawn and Chrysanthemum, Iris and
Safflower were all installed in his home,
Troll was jumped. His women went into
war mode. So did Moon and his family.
Troll after all was a Willow Kingdom blood
brother, and so needed to be defended.
Isaiah shuddered to think of what was about
to happen.

Chapter Fifteen

Isaiah and Mingo wore full body armor.
They walked into the smoke rising from the
fire in the steel drum like wraiths congealing
from the very smoke. At the edge of road sat
a row of Harleys.

Flanked by four silent, brawny German-Sheppard wearing canine Kevlar vests, Isaiah and Mingo studied the Steel Wheels Confederates as they approached them through the dark and smoke. Under their clothes both wore thin, full body armor, capable of stopping most hand gun fire, yet both felt tense. They noted with contempt that there was no security, no guards, not even a watch dog. Amateurs, they thought. Ironically, *Losing My Edge* by LCD Soundsystem was playing over and over, and maddeningly, it was all Isaiah could do not to start dancing. It was one of her favorite dance tunes. She and Mingo danced to it obsessively in secret at home at times. Dancing was their secret addiction. Unwittingly, Isaiah bopped her head in rhythm to the music. It was so *danceable*! But she had to preserve a certain measure of dignity...

In the warm river side breeze of the darkening evening, a fey-ness came upon her; she knew her husband had to be feeling the same urge. They exchanged a look and they struggled not to grin. She desperately wanted to laugh. She desperately wanted to dance.

Abruptly Mingo grabbed her by the hand
started to dance. Stifling an objection, Isaiah
was a little ashamed, but gave herself over
to the music, whipping her hair, laughing,
drowning in her husbands' hypnotic eyes,
and in the joy that dancing made her feel.
And for a moment in time nothing existed
but the music and her husband and joy as
they danced.

Others looked on in surprise at first; they
looked at them with bemusement and at
Black Angus questioningly; Black Angus
shrugged. They all rose to their feet and line
danced along with the young couple.

And then they switched to Lump by Mutiny
at mid track, and they danced with even
greater vigor, until they were sweating.

Abruptly Isaiah and Mingo stopped;
laughing and smiling, they wiped their
foreheads.

Woooohooo! Said Mingo. He kissed his wife
wondrously, still awed by the fact that
Isaiah was now his wife. A wave of fear that
he would lose swept over him.

Looking at their host, Isaiah smelled their beer, their body odor, and Marijuana. They were a gentle group, as groups in the Redemption went. She felt pity for them, stoners and aging hippies. Whatever their reputations as knife fighters, they seemed pathetic. It made her sad to do what she had to.

The small crowd of people, dressed in leathers, the men with long beards and hair, surrounding the fire were too numb or drunk or both to react with surprise to anything. Many of the women wore skank dresses, or leather halters with cut offs or short shorts or daisy dukes that left some of their rears in the wind. Just about all the women wore Cowboy boot or high heels. All wore too much make up. Most of them were verging geriatric weed heads, over the hill hippies, Texas flower children and blitzed out stoners. The rest were slackers and hangers on, seeking free weed and beer. Not a full set of balls in the whole bunch, whispered Mingo to his wife. Isaiah grinned wolfishly. Mischief always had it's pleasures.

To Isaiah it seemed that their dancing was
dispirited and joyless. They were going
through the motions. Clearly this was more
in the nature of a wake than a party. Even
so, they danced. Finally, one by one, the
wheezing couples, coughing, or heavily
panting, began to sit. Some coughed in the
deep lunged cancerous hacking hoots of the
long term smokers, and spat black loogies.
Disgusting pigs, she thought. It was
obvious that arthritis had to be an issue for
many of them. Their mood was sad, quiet
and somber.
Senior citizen gang bangers, whispered
Mingo.
Without the bang, whispered Taliqq.
Isaiah chuckled quietly.
Well, well, well! Said Red Black Angus,
huffing after dancing, *we know how to party*!
Visitors, y'all! A squad or *mercenaries*, and
hired-killers, the Queen and her *husband King*,
the angel of *death*!
Big Red! Black Angus, the *bossman*! said
Mingo by way of greeting.
What's up, bossman? Said Isaiah.
This is an honor, Queen, king Mingo---
I ain't a *king*, boss man!

Don't be modest bro…Anyway, glad to
have you. We're jus' out here having some
brewskis, worryin' 'bout a friend…and we
ain't packing, ok?
Out here? Mingo shrugged. That might be a
mistake. Thank G-d The Troll at least had a
Khukuri.
I knew I'd be seeing *you*….Ain't y'all thirsty
after all that dancing? Please have a seat.
If it's all the same, we'll stand, said Isaiah.
Thanks all the same, said Mingo.
Bring 'm two chairs---all the same. Y'all
thirsty? Want an Asani? Beer? Ya'll hungry?
We got some killer kosher bbq…costs a
ton…try a plate, ok? How 'bout some a
Troll's homemade brewski, Queen, Elder
Mingo? Stuff's incredible. Come on, y'all,
why doncha sit? Get these folks a plate and
a drink, Sonia! Go on, baby! Thank you
darling!
No thanks, said Isaiah. We're not drinkers.
I'll settle for a cold Asani, though.
It's said y'all never eat, said Angus
wondrously. How's that possible?
Who has the time to eat? Asked Mingo.
Don't y'all get hungry?
Not that we'd notice, answered Isaiah
politely. We do like to nibble, though…We
drinks tons of ice water.

Angus felt a sense of fear and revulsion.
There's a religion in India? The Janes. Their
Holy men consider it an honor and act of
Holiness to starve to death.
We're not Janes, said Mingo. We're not
starving. Were busy.
Y'all should eat, said Angus with genuine
compassion.
Aw, we're fine, thank you, said Mingo.
Thank you kindly for your concern.
A smallish girl got her and Mingo each a
bottle of Asani ice water. Mingo tossed his
bottle to Taliqq. He and Isaiah took small
sips gratefully from the same bottle.
Black Angus, Big Red, sat on an PVC chair
the near the fire, nursing a frosty 64 bottle
ounce bottle of label-less beer. It was dark
and rich smelling. Around him sat or stood
his inner circle, about five people, including
Deacon Navarro.
Notably, neither Honey Buns, or Boot, the
true leaders of SWC were, there.
Isaiah and Mingo ignored the former
Deacon though he smiled at them
ingratiatingly.
Black Angus, said Isaiah formally, You
know why we're here, right, my brother?
No, Queen, I sure as *hell* don't!

Let's cut the crap, said Taliqq. And watch
your mouth, you feel me, big man?
Black Angus looked at Taliqq carefully, ill
concealing his loathing for the mercenary.
You know what? Said Taliqq. Get that bad
look off your face, before it gets knocked
off? Ok, big man?
Mos mos, polle polle, said Angus.
Hey! Hey! You! *Cut the damn music!* said
Taliqq, and waited until he was obeyed. Ok.
How this goes down is up to *y'all*, but the
Queen and the Messenger need a word with
Mister MaGoo. You know me? I'll anybody
anywhere but we ain't here for your money
or your lives, but my boys got y'all covered
and they won't think twice, you feel me? We
ain't going to insult you by taking you
knives, but I better not even *see* a butter
knife, you feel me? So no mistakes, ok?
Easy, ese, slow, slow, *slow*, said a smiling
Black Angus, you're talking to *friends*. Here,
have a beer…
Nah, thanks all the same, said Taliqq.
Willy ain't talkin' to me, said Black Angus,
so tell me…How is the Troll?
Taliqq laughed and shook his head.

You *sittin'* down out here, said Taliqq,
drinkin' the man's beer like real people, as if
you're some*body* to him anymore, actin'
innocent? Let's cut the crap, ok?
Chill out, little papa, said Black Angus, Slow
down pardner! Don'tcha lose your top!
Lose my *top*? You threatening me, yo?
Jus' tryna say! Last time I checked we was
allies! Least ways with the Queen and
Mingo… Anyway, I *h*ear tell Troll may 'ave
gone into a fatal coma….tears me up….
Isaiah looked surprised, stricken.
We are allies, said Mingo, equally stunned,
which is why we're gonna keep it simple.
Troll and Willy? They're family to me and
my Queen.
I understand, said Angus.
Someone *has* to answer for this, big Red. The
guilty gotta go down for this.
In his mid twenties, Black Angus, unlike his
sister, was big, slender and jovial looking
normally. Like her, He was a red head, he
wore a long pony tail, and a short beard.
Like his sister, he had a hazel eye and a blue
eye. Normally jovial, uncharacteristically, he
seemed gripped by despair.

It ain't on my set, y'all…We're just mechanics, he said wearily; we ain't no *gangsters*…ain't no killers either. Jus' a motorcycle Club---a family is all.

Well everything is saying it's on y'all, boss man, said Taliqq.

Everything's *wrong*! Ok, we run a few chop shops…deal a little meth…We get drunk, we brawl…but we don't *hurt our friends*…

You're too modest, said Taliqq. Word is, your crew is making millions slinging Meth and Oxy…which you couldn't do if the Queen didn't look the other way or demand a bigger cut.

Maybe so, but ain't no one making no millions, said Angus.

Some one's gotta answer for this, said Isaiah calmly. We owe it to Willy. Help us out, ok? Justice, that's all we want. We only want who's responsible for it.

You want to *put this on* some one? Said Black Angus, The buck stops with me…Ok….*I'm* you're Huckleberry…

McBragg, we aren't blaming anyone, said Mingo, we want the truth is all.

I know Willy's hanging this on *me*, like I would ever harm Troll, but she's *wrong*…I know my little sister is out hunting me----

No, said Isaiah. I won't *allow* it----we don't allow family to kill family. We'll see to this personally for her.

So you ready to kill her blood? You sayin' you ready to kill ole Angus?

Aw, we didn't say all that, said Mingo. Anyway, if Troll is still alive, taking a life wouldn't be just.

Ok…tell her it ain't how she thinks…and do me a favor? Please? Ya'll leave my coz Mister MaGoo alone, y'hear?

Why you asking that? asked Isaiah.

There's been talk. It ain't on him…Trust me on this…

It's always your friend that take you out, said Mingo.

Maybe in your world, said Angus. You know it's me y'all really want. If my crew did wrong---and we didn't.

With all due, said a deep, sonorous voice, screw all that, Big Ang.

It was surprising to see who the voice belonged too. Coming from the shadows, he stood protectively in front of Angus. As foolhardy as the gesture might have been, it inspired a grudging twinge of wonder in everyone there. Everyone thought that both Isaiah and Mingo were murderous psychos, so it took a measure of courage to stand between them and someone they might be targeting.

Skeletally skinny, he was a small, weak looking. A frail, scrawny little runt of a young man, with a large hairless head, with lump of a nose, and eyes hidden in folds of skin and eye bags at first he appeared pathetic. His head oscillated in a curiously calculating, reptilian fashion, which seemed menacing. He wore large thick round glasses, with thick black frames, and he squinted at everything.

His left hand rested casually on the ornate hilt of a large wicked looking Khukuri knife, tucked under his belt. Besides him, holding his other hand stood a short slender, flat chested, plain-faced girl with Semitic features and an Aquiline nose. She too had a large Bowie knife on her left hip, and another tucked in her right boot. She was called Leah.

Isaiah noticed that, chillingly, all of them
wore similar knives.

Leah looked at them with cunning, knowing
eyes. Long curly flaming golden hair
cascaded down her back. Taliqq looked at
her with ill concealed affection. He looked at
MaGoo with hate.

Leah, said Taliqq. Lookin' good, girl.

Tal, she said, with an uncertain smile, good
to see you, dude.

Taliqq and MaGoo looked at each other with
amusement and mutual loathing. MaGoo's
fingers tightened on the hilt of his knife.

Goo, said Taliqq.

I prefer *MaGoo*, Tal, said MaGoo. Only
friends and my women call me Goo.

Woman? Or women?

As you prefer, said Magoo.

What about the bevy of beauties you bend
to your will in the forest? Said Taliqq.

I hear tell, said MaGoo, you're practicing a
new faith… Should I be saying *Shalom
Aleichem, achi?*

You can say whatever you want, ese, said
Taliqq dryly. How you keeping, MaGoo?

MaGoo shrugged.

So so. Como ta, Tal? Asked MaGoo.

I prefer Tal*iqq*, please, Taliqq answered.
Only my woman calls me Tal.
Used to be friends called you that too.
The way I've been stabbed in the back? I
don't do friends no more.
MaGoo laughed dryly.
Say what you want to me, but mind how
you talk to Leah, ok? She's under my
protection.
Not that it's none ya business, said Taliqq,
but that has nothing to do with Leah.
Anyway, how I talk to her ain't your biz,
four eyes.
Really? Until you got some discounted
contacts, you were a four eyes too! But hold
up! You must got Leah confused with one of
your skanks---if you have one, Tal*iqq*. She's
kin to me.
You been smoking skank loco weed again,
ese? said Taliqq. Jus' cause she's slumming
with trash like you does not make her *yours*.
She's *my* woman, four eyes. You keeping
low company, Lee.
Leah laughed, and said, That's enough boys.
MaGoo frowned, bowed his head graciously
to Leah, and coughed politely, then nodded
a greeting at Isaiah.
Queen!
MaGoo.

The MaGoo don't *allow* his set to take harm
for 'im, Big Ang, said MaGoo, turning eyes
on Isaiah.
What harm? Asked Isaiah.
He waived a hand dismissively.
Get your gats, Hide your unmarried girls
and women and all your good liquor, smoke
up your mota, look to your moneys and
your honeys…Cause the Magic man is here.
I'm *here*! Y'all want MaGoo, Queen? The
MaGoo is *here*! Yeah, *I'm* here. *Beware if you
ain't a friend*!
His friends laughed affectionately.
How *do* Mis*ter* MaGoo, said Isaiah stifling a
yawn.
How's Romero, Queen?
Isaiah shrugged unresponsively.
So you want me? I won't run, it ain't no fun
and I won't *hide* to save my hide. That ain't
no *lie*. I ain't afraid a *nothin'*! I can *take* an ass
kickin', but I rather *give one*. *Yeah*! So what
can I do y'all for?
He looked at Mingo and Taliqq defiantly.
Mingo and Taliqq exchanged a look and
laughed. Taliqq applauded mockingly.
Ok, Mister MaGoo, said Mingo. You can
watch your attitude for starts.

I ain't watching *nothin'*, said MaGoo. An ass kicking comes with my words, too.

Whooo hooo! said Taliqq. Big words for a *little* half blind, *sawed off runt*, four eyes.

MaGoo laughed.

You oughta know, you're a *sawed off runt* too, *Taliqq! Or is it something else? Maybe Jew-boy?*

Blind *and* stupid, I *shoulda* said, said Taliqq smiling brightly.

I *might* be a *little* blind but I can see well enough to kick ass if need be.

Taliqq grinned.

You wanna throw down? said Taliqq getting in MaGoo's face.

MaGoo smile, looking into his eyes over his glasses.

You feeling froggy, Taliqq? Said MaGoo. Let's jump, little chump!

Grow up, ok?

Ok, Mister *murder for hire!* Mocked MaGoo. I'm just confused…I'm hearing you're a Jew now, but I assumed you were down with the *Nation of Islam,* akhi, said MaGoo with a cruel smirk. M-u-s-l-i-m, I'm so blessed to be Muslim…shouldn't you singing that?

Loser! Snarled Taliqq.

Wait a minute, *didn't* the *Fruit of Islam* kick
you out after whipping your ass? Had to
take you to Communion General, didn't I?
Them boys don't play!
Taliqq shot a stream of saliva to the ground
through his teeth.
MaGoo turned to Mingo.
And *his coz king* Mingo of The holy hidden
City of Elohim---king of the *height challenged!*
They all laughed, except Taliqq, Mingo,
Isaiah, and those with them.
I'm tryna be a gentleman, but don't diss my
coz ----unless you wanna die slow, said
Taliqq sweetly.
MaGoo ignored him.
How *does* working for your own *wife* feel,
king Ming the merciless? Must be hard.
Looking into MaGoo's eyes
expressionlessly, Mingo said nothing.
MaGoo felt terrified, but barreled forth
recklessly.
Am I calling you the wrong name? Don't
Romero call you *half pint?*
Woe-o-o-o! Said some who were listening,
laughing.
Mingo ignored him.
You wanna piece of *me, four eyes?* Asked
Taliqq smiling icily. Disrespect him *again*.

I'ma turn *you* into *pieces*, said MaGoo, if you don't mind your *pie hole*!

Keep styling and profiling, said Taliqq. Your big Crocodile mouth is gonna get your little canary ass into an alligator bite in a minute!

If you're man enough to face me, said MaGoo, *man to man*…skip to the loo my darling lad!

Come on then! *Bring it!* Said Taliqq. Let's *do it to it!* knife? Gun? You pick.

You pick. Step to and lose your pride, growled MaGoo. I'd *love* to kick *your* ass.

Taliqq stood nose to nose with MaGoo.

That's *enough*, said Mingo, pulling Taliqq back.

K, k, said Taliqq with controlled fury, pulling away his arm.

MaGoo, said Mingo calmly, *chill*. We're here on business, so watch your *mouth*. Make believe you're a gentleman instead of back alley scum from the Forest.

Jus' tell *Taliqq* to mind 'is mouth too, *king*, said MaGoo. And don't be *looking* at *my* Kin's-woman, *Taliqq*…yeah, *my* KIN'S woman…she's with *me* now! See, unlike you? I don't share…The MaGoo don't *play* that!

Taliqq moved toward him again but Mingo restrained him.

Taliqq grinned.

Some other *place*, Taliqq said, some other
time, you feel me, four eyes?

Count on it, *putico*! Said MaGoo.

Putico? Said Taliqq. *Stay ready, MaGoo! Stay
ready four eyes.*

The MaGoo was *born* ready, young'n, said
MaGoo smiling bleakly, For sure. I *live*
ready too!

Whateva.

Yeah? Sleep with one eye open, ok? *Taliqq!
Back atcha----*

MaGoo, are you *done*? Said Black Angus,
amused. Quit *sassing* our *guests*. We don't
fight our *friends*. Unlike some, we ain't
mercenary *scum*...

Sure boss man, said MaGoo, as he looked at
Taliqq, and spat on the ground
contemptuously. But I don't approve of
small time *killers* for *hire* or *mercenaries scum*
coming among the *righteous,* comin' on *our*
land *disrespectin'*!

Taliqq laughed. What are all y'all?
killers for hire? Said MaGoo, *Sicario?
Mercenaries?* Scum! They got no honor.

Taliqq laughed and shook his head.

You used to be my business partner, fool, said Taliqq coldly. Last time I checked you a merc too, *sicarito*!

Once, said MaGoo, then I found *Jesus*.

Well I guess Jesus is missing his wallet by now! Taliqq threw back his head and laughed.

I ain't *sicario* mercenary *scum no more…*

Now you burn candles to San Mal Verde, right? Asked Taliqq. Keep talkin'! I'm remembering *every word!*

Fine by *me!*

That's *enough*, Isaiah said softly. *Mister* MaGoo… you're a hard act to follow…you're the *action* man around here, am I right?

As much as a legally blind *sawed off runt* can be, said MaGoo, smiling at Taliqq with distaste. Yeah, a hobbit, *sawed off runt----* like your little *sicario-conditierri* here---only I'm *way* smarter.

Taliqq laughed.

Ass needs kicking, drawled Isaiah mockingly, *MaGoo* is the man to talk to right?

MaGoo nodded.

See, ass kickin' is a *science…* I jus' arrange things *scientifically*, I suppose…

Exactly, said Isaiah. *Exactly!* Black Angus
says *kick ass*, and you *kick ass*, right----or you
arrange it? Right?
Sure. Exactly.
You're a man to be reckoned with, said
Isaiah, and respected.
I suppose…I consider myself boss-man's
peacekeeper, said MaGoo. With all that goes
with it. But that does not put what
happened to the Troll on us.
So, Mister MaGoo, *action man*, said Isaiah.
Tell me about what *action* happened to the
Troll.
You askin'? Or *tellin'?*
I'm askin' *you*, ok?
Really?
Hey, lighten *up!* You're jus *spoilin'* for a
fight!
So are *y'all!*
Will you quit showing out? Quit *high siding!*
Why don't *y'all?*
Now *look---*
No, *you* look! You come in *our* house acting
like the Red Devil himself, mad dogging
and bad *assing,* with your pistoleros and
sicarios and those *billies* in your hands, and
I'm in the wrong here? In *our house?*…

Your *house*? said Isaiah ironically. This is a *public* park.

All the same….*our* territory, our *house*….you come with a head full of *conclusions* into *our house*?…tryna *shoehorn* reality into what you *want* the facts to be…

I was born at night but it wasn't last night, said Isaiah.

Why can't you give us the benefit of the doubt? Said Angus. The word *allies* used to mean something around here…

Look, said Isaiah, fact is, Troll is black y'all are mostly white…..

So? Said MaGoo. You gonna play the race card? Come On now! We ain't *racist*…Me? I'm half black *Latino*.

Half black *Latino and all pendejo*, mumbled Taliqq.

Angus who was also black, started to support MaGoo, but remained silent.

You don't lookit, said Isaiah.

Mingo grinned.

Neither do you! Said MaGoo.

So, said Mingo, he was *practically* one of you, huh?

He *is* one of us! said MaGoo.

No! said Isaiah firmly. *He* and *Willy* belong to *me*!

Now you *hold on, dammit!* Bellowed Black
Angus, You jus wait one West Texas cotton
pickin' *minute*! You can mosey on up in here
acting like warlords, but Willy is MY
SISTER. I'm being a gentleman here, but no
matter what you think? She's my kid *sister*,
Queen, and he's *my* brother in law! Troll is
my Magus and Moreh! *They're mines!*
But we're the ones looking into this, right?
said Mingo dryly.
So say *you*! Said MaGoo.
They are *MINES*! Said Black Angus
furiously. And for the record? This is an
internal SWC matter, it don't really concern
y'all!
Dream on, said Mingo. Willy is one of *us*! So
is Troll!
All the same, said Black Angus, I *will* get to
the bottom of this!
You're doing a piss poor job of it, said
Taliqq.
We're on it, believe me, said Black Angus .
Really? Said Mingo, The way I see it,
bossman? Other than the little half black
Latino hobbit gangster *comedian* here, Mister
wonder bread MaGoo? You're jus' *rednecks*
down with *rednecks* ...
Angus guffawed.

Rednecks? Wonder Bread MaGoo? Hobbit gangster? Asked Black Angus, smiling with a laugh, amused in spite of himself.

A hobbit, no less! Said MaGoo, angrily but amused. Sayin' I'm *brown and crusty* on the *outside*, but a *white and soft little* hobbit on the inside.

The Steel Wheels Confederacy Crew roared with laughter. MaGoo laughed along.

They'd lived through a few gun fights with Magoo in the lead and referred to him as the little demon.

I get *no* respect. Groused MaGoo. Fact is? Most of the so-called red-necks here are half-blacks, of yella-blacks passing! I guess my *feelings* should be hurt!

Isaiah raised an eye brow.

I see you got Jokes, king Mingo! Said MaGoo after the laughter died, Well, better an honest *hobbit* than *a little vampire! You don't know the 13th tribe when you see it!*

Mingo laughed.

Does Romero Still think you're a vampire? A blood sucker---or some other kinda sucker?

They all laughed heartily again.

My point is valid, said Mingo.

Really? Asked MaGoo. For the *record?*
MaGoo is straight up Latino Mandingo
Warrior, *Africano,* Queen, but there's only
one race: human. The MaGoo don't see
color----*Rednecks* get along with your
Fellowship ... a buncha your Westia family
are *rednecks,* but they love you! We ain't
different. You're so tight with *Wilhelmina,*
and what is she? Get over being *racist.*
Ok, lookit, said Isaiah, with growing
irritation. *Jus* answer our questions and
we'll be on our way.
We drank his *beer,* said MaGoo, and we
drank his *mead.* Ok?
Yeah, for sure, we *know all about that*! Said
Taliqq. Don't forget his *wine too.*
Hey! *Hey,* durn it! said Black Angus
angrily, waja *tryna* say? We ain't *moochers,
dude*! We *paid him* full price for our alki-hole!
He was our *Magus* and Moreh!
Oh, *really?* Said Taliqq wryly.
And, added Leah, we helped him get *rich*
selling 'is beer and wine, and that's a *fact,
Tal!*
We drank his *mead,* said MaGoo, we drank
his *beer 'n wine*!
Rich, huh? Taliqq snorted dismissively.

MaGoo looked at Taliqq with contempt. Yeah, we loved his wine too. We *broke his bread* together! You know he bakes damn good bread too, don't you? Makes'm family to us. We don't sell our *souls* for *money like some do*. *Mercs* and *killers-for-hire* and *bounty-*hunter *idiots* wouldn't understand that, *sicario!*

Taliqq bristled. Now I'm an *idiot too*, right? *You* said it, I didn't, said MaGoo, but if the shoe fits, step….

Who put the hurt on the *Troll*? Isaiah repeated impatiently. If you boys didn't you know who did. In a minute, I'ma assume you're wasting my time cause it was *you*, MaGoo.

Honestly? Why?

If it wasn't you, then w*ho*?

I have my suspicions about a lot of things, but can't say we know, for sure, but we *will*, then the *wrath* of *hell* and *heaven will* descend on the *head* the *wrong doers and* the *wicked and I WILL be My makers WRATH!! I WILL BE Heavens sword.* Troll's my *best friend!* MaGoo panted with abrupt rage, and was briefly out of breath. Leah looked on with concern. He took out an inhaler and sprayed into his mouth.

Almost everyone looked at him uneasily.

Isaiah's flesh crawled.

Taliqq applauded sarcastically.

So why all the rumors about you pulling guns on him?

I pulled guns on him several times! Water guns!

Do what? Asked Mingo.

The two of them were engaged in a water gun war for most of the summer! Said Angus.

It's not over! Said MaGoo chuckling.

Dude, your grown! Said Angus. Behaving like overgrown kids!

Spoken by the grand master of *paint gun wars*! Said MaGoo.

Everyone laughed.

The boy is the father of the man, said Magoo. There's nothing wrong with having a little bit of the kid in us!

So your *denying* it was you? Asked Mingo casually. You boys *loved* Troll, huh?

Do you *care*? Asked MaGoo, struggling to regain his breath. He wiped his forehead and shrugged. Fact is, you're here to take *me*, and beat *your* truth outta *me*, then maybe put two in the back of *my* head, right? But anyone who *thinks* they can take out *the* MaGoo like that? They ain't *really* thinking right! They don't *really* know the MaGoo! The MaGoo has been beaten and smacked around by the best. Many have tried to take out the MaGoo, but the MaGoo ain't easily killed!

We *jus* wanna know the truth, said Isaiah mildly but with little sincerity. When-ja you see 'im last?

Leah offered her water to him, and MaGoo took a swig of gratefully.

Thanks darling! Yesterday …. Yesterday evening. We was here fishing not too far away…down yonder…best fishing spot on the Trinity River. Been comin' 'ere since I was knee high to a *tadpole*…use to come 'ere with Romero and the boys….

Watcha catch? Asked Isaiah.

Do what?

Watcha catch…if you were really out here fishing?

Very little---

I hear tell, y'all were having *words*…
drawled Mingo.

Who from?

Mingo smiled. That's *our* business…

Waja say you caught, ese? Said Taliqq.

I didn't.

Maybe Troll caught something---a beat
down from you and your boys, Mister
MaGoo.

Why would ja think that?

You were having words, right? Asked
Mingo.

Hmmmm…What if we were? That *illegal*?

Were you *arguing*?

Yup, we were..so what? We always argue. I
still love the kid.

Tell us about it, said Mingo. One thing led to
another, huh? Were your boys here with
you?

Lookit, said MaGoo, we *always* argued. Skip
it ok?

Why were you arguing? Asked Taliqq. What
else happened?

Lookit, we use filas, knives, said MaGoo.

Were there any cuts on him? Think on it.

Troll cut those boys to ribbons, but were
there any cuts on him?

I hear tell y'all don't knife y'all's own, said
Taliqq. You jus beat'm down if need be.
MaGoo smiled. Y'all ever tasted 'is beer?
I'm sorry, we don't drink, said Mingo
politely.
There was a time when your little sicario,
Taliqq, drank like a fish, taunted MaGoo.
Once I did, said Taliqq indifferently. Jus'
like you.
Stayed as drunk as Scooter brown, till I
pulled him out the gutter, said MaGoo.
Cleaned him up.
That's funny, said Taliqq. You got it twisted.
I pulled *your* sorry ass out the gutter. Worse
mistake I ever made.
If you ain't ever tasted 'is *beer*? Said Black
Angus, You'd understand our feelings...It
was full of love...love of *excellence ... love of
class*....Jus' like The Magus and Moreh ...
MaGoo, nodded and said, Y'all don't really
know 'im...

Ole Troll's a *genius*...an *artist*...Angus continued. Our resident Magus and Moreh ...Taught us *class*...We become beer and wine connie-sewers on account-a ole Troll...Makes every kinda beer and makes'm real *good*...makes great wines, cheeses, breads, crackers, cookies...incredible Chardi-nay...and...Pini Noirs...

Redemption's Martha Stewart, huh? Said Taliqq. You sound like if you loved him.

I let him marry my kid sister, said Angus, now didn't I? Stood up for him, didn't I?

Whoja have to stand up for him against? Asked Mingo.

Angus looked away carefully and drank his beer.

What were y'all arguing about, Mister MaGoo? Asked Isaiah.

MaGoo stared at the ground unhappily.

Ain't it enough he's hurt? Please let it be, he said.

I can't do that, said Isaiah. Did you boys jump him?

No! No! MaGoo sighed wearily. Ain't *no* rest for the *wicked.* Let me make it, ok?

You're wasting my time, said Isaiah.

I don't like speakin' ill of a hurt man, said MaGoo, I prefer not to *discuss* it, with *y'all* of all people. Ain't *no* rest for the wicked----
And *money* don't grow on trees, mocked Taliqq sarcastically. I got *bills* to pay, I got *mouths* to feed, and ain't *nothing* in this world for *free*.
Time is *money*, sneered MaGoo, and money is *time*, and you're all *about* the *money*, huh?
So we *understand* each other? Said Taliqq furiously.
Pardon, but your *point*? Asked MaGoo.
We don't have *time* for any more of your bs, said Taliqq, Quit showing out, quit wasting our time, *four eyes! Answer our questions!*
Showing out? Said MaGoo. No more than *you*!
keep it up! Said Taliqq, Queen says a word?
You'll get a *bullet* in your *butt in a minute*! I won't think twice. It ain't gonna be real fun to bleed!
I'm almost out of patience, *Mister* MaGoo, said Isaiah.
I'm tryna be helpful…ok, lookit, you insist on knowing? *Fine*! We argued about this ridiculous *conversion* of his to Orthodox *Judaism*!
Do what? Asked Isaiah, taken aback. *What* conversion to *Judaism!?*

*Yea*h, *conversion to Judaism*! Said Black Angus
heatedly. Orthodox Judaism, no less! *Now*
y'all see what we are dealing with? Ain't I
tole you, MaGoo? She didn't *know*! *Didn't I
say*, MaGoo?
I guess you were right, boss man…
You out living out under a *tarp*, said Angus,
getting in *contact* with your inner self,
Queen, experiencing *nature*, I 'ear tell,
enjoying married life to king *Mingo*, but
maybe your Fellowship is crumbling from
the inside….
What are you talking about?
Maybe you and *king* Mingo are losing
touch…all kinda *heresy* is being taught up
there! It's right up in your *house*, in your
own *family*---*maybe* under your *nose*, and you
don't see it.
Angus looked at Mingo knowingly. Mingo
paled.
Look, said MaGoo unhappily, he denied
*Jesus! he denied Jesus Christ, ok? OUR Lord and
Savior, G-d in The Flesh! It broke my heart!*

His lips quivered with emotions, but he looked at Taliqq cunningly. For some reason, Leah looked to be on the verge of laughing. So *hell* to the *yes, we argued plenty lately!* He's my *best* friend! I love the guy! I'm worried about his *eternal* soul… he denied *Jesus, for Pete's sake.*
I don't *believe that!* Said Isaiah.
Please believe it!
Well, Queen, he embraced *Yahushua, right*? Said Mingo, is there a prob?
Isaiah nodded. No—we do too…
Troll? Embraced Yahu-who? asked Leah, and laughed. Troll was a reformed Jew until recently!
You don't know what you're talking about! Said Isaiah furiously.
Slope Bell, his make believe father, was a reformed Jew, and Troll converted years ago! Said Leah.
You're lying! Said Isaiah.
Well you *should* believe us, said MaGoo, I'm worried about his eternal soul…
It means *nothing*, calmly said Taliqq, we *know* he believes in Yahushua….anyway, even if he turned Jew? So what?

Yahushua, Jesus! Said MaGoo impatiently, with a hint of humor. The distinctions are a crock! Take away the fancy Hebrew names, and it's all the same!

So what if he rejected Yahushua too? Asked Taliqq. *Maybe* he is justified. There are legit questions about the NT and Yahushua….what if it's all a lie? Wasn't the real Yahushua a Jewish Rabbi? What if Yahushua was just…a fraud like Jesus?

They all briefly stared at him, stunned by his words.

Isaiah sputtered incoherently, then was speechlessly enraged. Mingo looked visibly nervous for Taliqq.

Que te pasa, loco? *Basta*, he whispered to his cousin furiously. Calla te la boca!

So you are one of them? Dirty nasty little Jew! said MaGoo with venom. Sicario *Christ killer! Dirty filthy Jew-----*

Now that's *enough*, MaGoo! Snapped Black Angus . I won't have that kinda talk…We ain't Nazis *or* klan! People have a right to believe what they wanna…lst time I checked you only et kosher.

Ok, yeah, said Isaiah desperately, giving Taliqq a murderous look, The Troll Believes in *Yahushua* as opposed to Jesus, like us— I think----so yeah, he doesn't believe in *Jesus*, but----

He renounced *all of it*, Queen, yelled Black Angus, wiping tears out of his eyes. I understand why y'all call him Yahushua…But it wasn't that simple. He rejected *Yahushua, the NT, Jesus, the Bible…he* converted to Orthodox *Judaism* along with my little sister.

That's a lie! They woulda discussed it with me!

No…said Black Angus . They're too *scared* of you to tell you!

Scared of me?

You can't believe it, right? His soul is *lost* now…and my kid sister too…Now my kid sister won't speak to me. Look at his *FB page,* for Christ sake…

Fb page? said Mingo dryly.

Burned his *Bible*! Said Angus. He said on FB, burn the Bible! *Open your eyes!*

And what does that prove? Asked Isaiah.

The *Judaizers* filled *our* Trolls head with foolishness, said MaGoo angrily.

What *Judaizers?* Asked Isaiah.

Black Angus and MaGoo looked at Mingo nervously.

Mingo stiffened.

We ain't gonna stick our nose into your internal Fellowship matters beyond this, said Black Angus carefully. Talk to the Chink if you want them kinda answers.

So, a black man can't think for himself, I suppose, said Taliqq, shaking, visibly nervous.

I never gave a *damn* about his skin color, answered Black Angus bitterly. I *loved* the guy---once---right now I'm confused. *Hell, he's married to my kid sister!*

Fact is, you hated him for that, said Mingo. *NO!* *I* treated him like *family*. He is *family*…But burning his *Bible*? Turning on *Jesus*? I *can't* accept him *doing* that…I can't *allow* it….family or *not*! I can't *allow* that…

Ok, said Mingo. So it was *you* not MaGoo who had *him beat down?*

No, *No*! said Black Angus . We tried to *protect* him!

I says, *dude*, said MaGoo with a shaking voice, *dude, please*, ain't I had your *back*? Ok, lookit, do what your heart *tells* you, but don't be *attacking Christianity* and *Jesus*! You'll get yourself murdered! You gotta start packing a gat! I can't keep you safe!

So he doesn't have freedom of speech? Asked Taliqq. What if he doesn't believe anymore?

Real Jews ain't even *suppose* to *proselytize, Taliqq!* Snarled MaGoo.

Says who? asked Mingo.

So, he loves you enough to s*h*are his experience and you *jumped* him? Asked Taliqq angrily. Ain't he your Magus and Moreh?

No, I tell you! Quit *twisting* things! Said MaGoo. Our set? We're fundamentalist *Christians mostly! We gotta respect that.* I says, call 'im *Yahushua* if you want, but don't be *attacking Christianity* and *Jesus!* All we *all* have out here is our *Jesus*…so you wanna attack Jesus? You're attacking *us!* And I ain't got the *man power* to keep you safe! Did he listen? Nahhhhhhh…MaGoo's jus' a crazy dumbass *Christian* redneck wannabe, not some fancy smancy Jew boy. Isaiah was speechless.

What if he *is* a Jew? Asked Taliqq defiantly.

You should know, close as you two are, said Angus to Taliqq.

Taliqq flinched.

Jews are *good people*, stammered Taliqq. Wasn't *Jesus-a-Jew*?

You just outed yourself, Jew! Liar! Yelled
MaGoo, *Liar*! Jesus wasn't a damn *Jew…*
And what was he then? Asked Isaiah.
Jesus *is* a *Christian!*
Leah whispered into MaGoo's ear.
Bull! Said Taliqq. What if Troll *is* a Jew?
What has a Jew ever done to you? This is
America---it's his *right*!
Spoken like a true *Jew-boy!* snarled MaGoo. I
always *suspected* you…*False flagger!* You
ain't been a Christian and you sure ain't no
Muslim, you sell out, you're a *filthy Jew*! You
need a new name, kike!
Taliqq laughed.
I'm *Taliqq!*
Well, remember, *Taliqq!* said MaGoo, this
ain't jus the USA----it's The *Redemption,*
Texas! *Christian* country! The *Gold buckle* of
the *Bible belt, dirty Jew boy!*
He spat on the ground.
Taliqq glared at him wordlessly and looked
away.
So you gave *MaGoo* an order to *deal with it?*
Asked Mingo carefully, with controlled
fury, looking at Black Angus. What gives
you the right to beat him *half to death, to beat
'im into a coma?*

No! said Big Black Angus, We argued, is all! He's still *kin!*

Jesus, big Ang, don't you see? Said MaGoo, awareness-dawning. Look't *king* Mingo! Look at all of them! Black *suits,* white *shirts,* zitzits and a black *fedoras, Jus like Taliqq! king Mingo* here ---all of them---they're in the *closet Jew converts! Jus like Taliqq! He's* an Orthodox *Jew* convert too----

Isaiah smacked him down with the butt of her 9mm Glock. Surprised, abruptly crashing on his back, MaGoo was dumfounded. She shot a bullet next to him took aim at his head.

Say it again! Call my husband a Jew again! Isaiah said calmly.

Ok – ok – I'm sorry---

She kicked him in the ribs and stomped his chest. MaGoo drew his knife weakly but she kicked it away and pistol whipped him. Mingo looked on queasily.

Say it again!

For a moment all looked on in horror.

Now that's enough! Screamed Leah. *Stop it! Stop it!*

Back up! Snarled Isaiah, pointing her gun at Leah. *Don't make me say it twice!*

Shut up Leah! Said Black Angus. Stop it Isaiah. Please, ok?

Shut up Black Angus! Snarled Isaiah. *Shut up! You wanna diss my family? Say it again! Call my husband a Jew again! I'll dead you too, Angus!*

Aw, don't! Don't murder him! Pleaded MaGoo. *I'm begging, ma'am! I-I-I went too far!* No! No! No! *Shhhhhhhh!* Said Mingo to his wife, rubbing her back. Ignore 'im!

No, he *has* gone *too far*, hissed Isaiah. They've gone too far! I'll dead *t*hem all! Be *still*, ya'll! Yelled Mingo as Black Angus and the others got up angrily. Sit *down*! *Sit*! Don't make a *fucking* move! Said Taliqq. I see a knife? Whoever draws it is *dead*! Swiftly he had his Ak47 trained on big Black Angus. In the dark they could hear guns of Isaiah's soldiers being cocked.

Get up! Said Isaiah to MaGoo. Go on, get up! *NOW*!

He tried, but couldn't.

Isaiah back handed him across the mouth and kicked him in the ribs.

Get up!

I can't! Please don't murder me!

Don't *beg*, Goo, said Leah with calmness, if they're *fixin'* to *murder* us, let's die with *dignity*. You kill 'im? You *better* kill me too, *bitch*.

Isaiah backhanded her across the mouth. She took the blow and look at Isaiah with contempt.

I will if I have to! Said Isaiah.

Is that all you got? Murdering cunt! Said Leah, and spat blood on the ground. You hit like the weak bitch that you are!

Isaiah laughed.

Maybe I'll kill your girl before I kill you MaGoo, right in front of you.

For G-d's sake! Said MaGoo. Don't! *Don't!* What's wrong with you?

I tried to be lady like, said Isaiah. *Keep running your mouth, why don't you!*

I'm sorry, ok? said MaGoo. Leave 'r alone!

Tears flowing, Leah looked at Isaiah with defiant hatred.

The kind and *merciful* Queen! You look like a big money fashion model, your husband looks like an angel, your *richer* than Midas, but you got a chunk of ice in your chest, *Prophet.* You're here protecting a friend? Who protect your friends from you?

Be quiet darling, said MaGoo.

Screw that, Goo, said Leah. I'ma only die once. Every one kisses this psychos ass and she's gotten to think she really is a Queen instead of a murdering----

Isaiah started to shoot her, but Taliqq pulled
her away and blocked Isaiah's gun with his
back.

Leah *chill out*, said Taliqq.

I ain't scared of this *devil-woman*. You shoot
me, Queen? Do it right between my eyes, or
right in my heart, cause if I live? I'ma find
you and kill you slow. Then I'll cut you in
pieces and feed you to my dogs.

Isaiah sniffed indifferently.

Leah crouched next to MaGoo and cradled
his head.

Isaiah studied them grimly.

MaGoo, said Isaiah, I'm tired of your sass,
I'm *sick* of your *shit*, you hear me, *boy*? You
know my rep? You know who you talking
to?

I know, I know!

I'm *Queen of the Westia Nation!* You
unner'stan'? We rule! *I run the streets a North
Texas! Screw with me? I-will-crush-you! All
y'all! Forget Troll for a minute! I'll kill you here
and now if you disrespect my husband again! All
of you!*

I'm *sorry* Queen!

I been *too* patient! I *should* kill *all* of you
any*way*!

The air was abruptly electric with Isaiah's blood lust.

Damn right, Queen! Yelled one of Isaiah's body guards. *Yeeeeeehaaw!*

Good for you, Queen! Yelled another.

Enough of their *disrespect*!

Let's *do* these drunk-ass ofays and *Okies*, Queen, snarled one of Taliqq's soldiers. Ain't no one out here but *them*!

Let's *do* this, Queen! *Do 'm all!*

Queen, let's do these turkeys in the *woods, yo!* Right there and leave 'em for the rats by the river, said another.

How about it, darling? Isaiah asked her husband.

No! said Mingo. This is wrong, sweetheart! Let's calm now!

Let's do them for the *Troll*! Someone else called out. Let soldiers do what soldiers do, Queen!

Shut up, all y'all, *Shut up NOW*! yelled Mingo.

That's *enough, cabrones*! Said Taliqq. Stand down!

But----

We're-not-gonna-do-*anybody!* Said Mingo. *Ain't that right Queen?* You *do* somebody, you answer to *me*! Queen *calm down*. We're better than this!

Mingo looked at his wife, and realized she
was blinded by rage.
She was looking at Angus and his crew like
a hungry wolf before a kill. Unwittingly, she
was ignoring him.
A massacre was in the offing.
Don't do it, Isaiah! said MaGoo desperately,
with a note of recklessness. *Ok! Ok! Lookit!
Lookit*, it was jus' *me* and him out here. I
swear I left him by the river. I *swear* I left 'im
safe and sound.
Your lying! Said Isaiah.
No! No! There's no reason to *massacre* our
crew! Ok? Listen to me! You're a *Prophet,
woman of G-d*! Right? Right? Don't *do* this! I
know, I know, you got a rep to protect!
Right? If you wanna *do* somebody? You
wanna do a murder? Go on! But do only me!
Ok? Ok?
I want the truth!
You-don't-want-*the-truth!* Yelled MaGoo.
Stand away from me y'all.
MaGoo, hush, said Angus.
*No! Move away Leah! Troll and Willy are you
and Mingo's best friends. Ain't I right Queen?
You wanna kill! You want closure. Ok. I'm* the
one you wants, I'm your-- *I'm* your
Huckleberry! Ok?

Goo stop! Said Leah, gently shaking him. A sweating, shaking MaGoo pushed her away politely.

Who better to kill than an ugly little man who don't nobody loves? Asked MaGoo, struggling to breath. Bring down the light on *me! Leave my kin-woman alone! Leave my crew alone!*

For G-d's sake, don't murder'im! pleaded Leah, we would *never* hurt *Troll! Please listen! Are you listening? Don't* hurt my kin's man no more! *Help us,* Taliqq!

Your man? Huh? Tell us the truth! Said Taliqq furiously.

Kin's man you dim idiot! Said Leah.

Make me believe you, MaGoo! said Isaiah, cocking her gun, taking aim at Leah.

I won't lie and say it was me…Let my set be. It *ain't on* 'em! Wasn't Boss man ---or nobody else---none of them was even *here* with me and Troll! We argued, I got mad and left 'im 'ere by the river, I *swear! Safe and sound!*

Don't lie to me, liar! Snarled Isaiah at him. I don't like the *lies* you two were sayin', Black Angus …calling my family closet *Jews?*

I ain't tryna insult nobody, said Angus. Is being called a Jew an insult?

You wanna insult my *husband*? You think I gotten *weak*? You think I can't do *all* y'all? *Lookit, I beg your forgiveness for my manners,* stammered MaGoo. We tried---*I* tried to say nothing, but you insisted. Don't nobody else needs to die *here*---ok? Please! It's about me, ok?

Now *for the last time*, said Isaiah, taking aim at his heart, What-happened to The Troll? I know it wasn't just you, MaGoo. Who put the hurt on him?

Answer her, four eyes! Snapped Taliqq, taking aim at MaGoo. *Or you're gonna die!*

Ok. Ok. In the end, does anything we say to you matter? Asked MaGoo sadly, wiping his mouth, looking at blood on his hand off his lip.

Leah helped him stand.

Now Leah, stand away, darling. Stand away. You're the best, baby. I love you, I love you, baby! Ya heah? All y'all, stand away. Don't worry, ok? Didn't mean to lose courage jus now... See you on the other side. Queen, I swear, w*e don't know either!* We have *no idea* who put the hurtin' on *our* Troll!... Maybe Cinco and NAN? I don't know!

Isaiah looked at Mingo.

The *New Aryan Nation*, Mingo explained
hurriedly. New people---they're down with
some of the Nazi MCs. Jew haters. *Cinco* is
some tow head kid pullin' them all
together...
Don't do it, Mingo whispered in her ear. I'll
do it if you really want to, but let's just
leave.
I have no proof, said MaGoo, carefully
looking at Mingo and Taliqq, I don't wanna
finger anyone as may be *innocent*...But
innocence don't matter to y'all, now does
it?...Fact is, your here to *murder* me! You
rattled MaGoo for a minute!
Short though he was, he stood frailly to his
full height.
Well? *Go on*, do what you *gotta do!* I'm ready
to see *Jesus*! Put it *on* me.
Bullshit! Snapped Taliqq, flustered by a
pang of pity, blocking MaGoo from Isaiah's
gun by stepping between them. *Answer all
her questions!*
MaGoo shook his head with frustration.
I already *did*. MaGoo smiled at Taliqq. Th*is
is on you, isn't it?*
What?
Maybe you set it all up. It's all about *me taking*
Leah from *you, isn't it? You hate me!*

Yes, I do. I do hate you, but I wouldn't do
you dirt like that. If I stab you it'll be in the
face!

Then do your own dirty work, sicario.

Ok! Said Taliqq. You're a *dead man*, four
eyes! You're *DEAD!*

Wait, Isaiah said and held up a hand to
Taliqq.

Well? Asked Isaiah. Have you come clean?

I done *tole* y'all, ok? Meekly said MaGoo. ---
I-don't-know! You can *torture* me, keep on
beating me *and* tryna *scare* me *again*, but *I-
don't-know!* Look, let's *do* this. I'm ready to
die, ok?…. so do what you gonna do!

Tal, so *help* me, I *swear!* Said Leah. You
better not hurt 'im.

Isaiah did nothing. MaGoo waited for the
deepening darkness.

Darling don't! Don't! Pleaded Mingo, he's
being truthful.

You believe me, don't you, *Mingo?* Queen?
MaGoo asked. *I-just-don't-know!* But y'all
mean to murder me anyway, don't you?
Make an example of me…Go on, do your *rep*
murder, but *I-don't-know!* I *swear* I'ma *find
out* ----and get some payback fo' this, *Taliqq--
---* or die for *tryin'!*

Abruptly, frail though he looked, he bolted in a crouch like a startled jack rabbit with amazing swiftness into the darkness, and made for the safety of the river, followed by several blasts and volley of bean bags from the shotguns. He howled one time in the dark as if struck.

Hold your fire! Yelled Isaiah, coming to her senses; she found that she was crying. *Hold your fire*!

In a moment of clarity she realized MaGoo was no liar---probably---she hoped. The blood lust abruptly lifted. Instinctively she knew they'd just may have made a terrible mistake.

MaGoo! MaGoo! She called, Come back, ok? We won't harm you. We meant you no harm!

They heard a big splash. Then silence.

Aw *shit*! Said Black Angus springing to his feet. Aw *shit*!

Pandemonium broke out as some ran to get him out of the water.

They're shooting bean bags, said Isaiah uncertainly, it'll hurt, but it won't really do anything!

Get 'im out boys! hollered Black Angus, He might be doing himself *in*! After 'im ya'll! The River runs real fierce here! *Get 'im out!*

Why would He's *do himself in?* asked Isaiah
with nausea.
Guilt? To save us?…Blames h*imself*! Feels he
failed Troll and me. I been *scared* he would
do *this shit*.
We didn't come to kill him, said Isaiah
flatly.
He shouldn't have talked so much shit, said
Taliqq.
We *tole* y'all all we knew! You're outta
touch, Queen! Troll's and him was bes'
friends, *dammit*, he would *never* hurt the
Troll! He protected him!
But---said Isaiah.
He *loves* Troll like a brother! He's been real
depressed lately… off his anti-
depressants…Troll and him are on the outs
on account Troll turning *Jew-boy*…
Troll's not a *Jew*!
Look, we're wasting *time*---A few bean bag
rounds to the back of the head might *kill* a
man that size in his kinda health anyway!
And MaGoo's as *blind* as a bat and can't
swim a lick worth a *damn* to save his life!
He'll drown for sure, sobbed Leah. Goo!
Goo!
He'll drown or Texas *alligators* will get 'im!
Said Black Angus, *Get 'im out!*

Isaiah nodded.

Let's get 'im out! Called Isaiah; her soldiers spring into action.

MaGoo! MaGoo! Come back, ok? Listen to me! We mean you no harm! *MaGoo! MaGoo!* Pandemonium, then resignation took hold of them. They lit up the shore using their head lights. Bull all knew. Nothing could be found but traces of blood near the shore. Look as they might, the small body of Mister MaGoo was not found.

The devil river took him, said Taliqq. Isaiah and Mingo looked at each other with a dawning horror. Mingo noticed the mistrust with which she looked at Taliqq and him, and it broke Mingo's heart. Had they just murdered an innocent man? They looked at Big Black Angus. he looked sick and drunk. Eyes red, head reeling, he was staring at them with raw hatred, as thick tears streamed down his face; but he quickly averted his eyes, wiping away the tears.

Y'all jus' murdered my little buddy for no reason, he stammered.

Angus---started Mingo.

We jus' came out here for some brewskis,
cause we didn't wanna go to the 'hospital
with Willy talkin' crazy, said Black Angus
numbly.

He took Leah in his arms and with gentle
words soothed her into silence.

Then he looked at Isaiah and Mingo again.
Got your answers? Are you *satisfied*?
Silence.

Black Angus ---*dude*! Mingo began. We----
Lookit, *Queen? Mingo?* Us and *you*? From
here on? You get no love from us…We're
done…

MaGoo *baited* us! Said Isaiah. You *let'm*
insult us…you did too!

We *tole* y'all, said Black Angus …I lost my
little *sister*, and my brother in law *Troll*..now
Y'all jus' *murdered* my best friend for
something we didn't do…

Black Angus …Black Angus, said Mingo,
we're crazy with the Troll thing… we are
really sorry. Anyway…You haven't lost
your family…This was an accident…

You *murdered* MaGoo! Said Leah bitterly.
Anyway, do we know he's really dead? said
Taliqq. Leah….

Don't *speak* to me, sicario *scum*! She said.
Murderers!

We didn't *murder* anybody, said Mingo, we jus' needed answers…We'll make it up to y'all, y'heah?

How? Angus demanded, laughing.

What would make this right? Asked Mingo.

We *tole* you we didn't do Troll no dirt! Said Angus.

Come on, Black Angus, said Mingo, your *practical*…what would make this right?

Bring me back my little buddy MaGoo---- living, breathing, unhurt …Otherwise, you *can't make this right*.

Lookit, said Mingo, money can't replace your friend, but---

Don't! Don't say *money* to me! Don't *insult* me with your *money* either.

But---

Your *money's* no good, ok?

Well we're sorry…

Sorry? You *are*! *We'll* pay *y'all* back ----on *our* own terms. You ain't ever heard of a *blood feud* have you?

You *threatening* us? Asked Taliqq icily.

Black Angus spat on the ground.

Don't make no *mistakes*, said Isaiah. If y'all didn't shine us on….

kiss my *ass*, ok?

Taliqq knocked him down with the butt of his Ak-47.

Mingo and Taliqq put guns to his head.

Waja say? Mingo asked softly.

No, darling! said Isaiah. Let 'im be.

Get up! Said Taliqq, pulling Angus to his feet.

You watch your *filthy mouth, trash,* or I'll kill you, said Mingo. You're talking to my *wife, hill Billy trash*!

Black Angus shrugged indifferently, wiping blood from his mouth.

See how you jus did us? Said Black Angus, bullyin' us?… you gettin' away with this cause we was friends and we ain't *packin' gun*, but that's *over* with. We got guns too, but you'll be surprise what my crew can do with our knives.

Black Angus …said Mingo. You're talkin' crazy. You talking whiskey talk!

Ain't no whiskey out here.

We kick ass when we have to, ok? said Mingo.

Call me trash again, why doncha? Sneered Black Angus, I got *Choctaw* Warrior blood in me, and today feels like a good day to die!

You ain't no Choctaw Warrior, said Taliqq, you a drunk ass red-neck! Anyway, Choctaws couldn't fight for shit! That's why the white man took their land.

You ain't gonna catch us *slippin'* again...
Ok...We're done here, said Mingo.
Yeah, you're *done*, said Black Angus, we
ain't gonna do *shit* for you anymore. Tell
Willy I didn't *touch* her *motherfuckin'* nigger
Jew and neither did MaGoo, may he rest in
peace, but if she wants a *piece* of me? I ain't
no pistolero like her, but fam'ly or not, I'll be
waitin'. If she's feelin' froggy? She wants to
murder kin that ain't done *nuthin'*? Let her
jump, hear?
Tell 'er to bring an army, said Leah, cause
we'll be ready. And I *am* a *pistolera*!
If *y'all* wanna go to war, said Black Angus,
let's go to war. It's *on*! Blood *feud*, baby!
Let's get goin' y'all! Said Isaiah. The *river* is
rising and I'm not wearing rubber boots.
Yeah, whatever, said Leah, *we'll see!* It won't
be no fun went the rabbit has the gun!
Get your *asses* outta my *sight*! ranted Black
Angus drunkenly, as a matter of fact, *we're
at war*, ok? I lost my best *friend*, my *sister*,
and my *brother* in law, so I don't give a *fuck*
about *fuck* no more. This is *personal*, ok?
Then you jus made the biggest mistake of
your life, said Mingo evenly. You're talking,
but we're good at winnin' wars. We'll
slaughter you, Black Angus, Like the *sheeple*
that y'all are.

Move out boys, said Taliqq to his soldiers.
Guard the Queen!
We're at war, *bitches*, sobbed Black Angus.
You wanna take us out here and now, *go for
it*. You might find out what it means to fuck
with a crew of pissed off *redneck* bikers, fuck
with us again!
Taliqq snorted with contempt.
Choctaw Warrior blood in me, and today
feels like a good day to die!
Aww, shut up! Said Taliqq.
Sleep it off, Black Angus, Isaiah called back.
You're *drunk*. I *might pretend* I didn't hear
you.
Don't *pretend*! screamed Black Angus after
them, go on! *Run*! Play times over, don't
pretend nothin'!
Isaiah and her squad backed away in their
black vans, got on the road and sped away.

Chapter Sixteen

Take the G out of Black Angus, and waja
got? Asked Taliqq. Anus.
They all laughed.
MaGoo musta been the G, said Isaiah sadly.
They laughed again.
Lookit, she whispered to Taliqq and Mingo,
Considering everything? The way they
talked? We can't leave witnesses…

Who's second in command? Asked Mingo
in a whisper.

Little *Buddha*? Said Taliqq.

Is he leveled headed? Asked Isaiah.

Taliqq nodded carefully.

The best wars are those you avoid fighting,
said Mingo. Right Queen?

Isaiah nodded.

Reach out to *Little Buddha*, said Isaiah.
Everybody who was out there gotta
go…now.

Black Angus 's gotta *go* Queen, said Mingo.
No matter what…

I jus' said, *reach out* to *Little Buddha*, said
Isaiah. Didn't I? Everybody down there was
a *witness*. We shoulda done them then and
there. Get on the phone. Get the second van
back out there. Put the snipers to work,
they'll never see it coming. Tell'm to use
silencers. No mistakes. *Now.*

Yes darling.

Mingo whispered instructions into his
phone.

I know they didn't do Troll, said Mingo
when he finished on the phone, but two
wrongs don't make a right. I won't *allow*
him to disrespect you like that. And like you
said, no witnesses. End of story… Black
Angus 's gotta go….

Isaiah stared out of the window, nodding
approval.

And *any other* hot head in his set too who'll
be left, said Taliqq, nodding grimly.

The quicker the better, whispered Isaiah.
Pass word on the cell phones…we're at war
with the SWC. Mingo, darling, I gotta call
Romero.

She got on the phone and had a guarded
conversion with Romero. Isaiah got off the
phone quickly.

Call it off.

What?

Tell them to stand down and come back.

Why? Asked Mingo.

Romero.

Romey?

Yeah. He heard, and says he's certain
MaGoo is alive. Says we're being
suckered…maybe Black Angus is in on it.

How would he know?

I don't know…I jus believe him. Let's go
visit with Romey. We'll fort up there for the
night. Wants to talk to us….but let's not let
this escalate if that little *turd* MaGoo is still
alive.

You know what? MaGoo knows that area
like the back of his hand, said Taliqq, with
growing enthusiasm. That little *weasel's* a
survivalist…Been camping out around there
since he was knee high to a tadpole.

That little *maggot* MaGoo was *always* a
grifter, said Mingo, Might he be scamming
us?

We didn't see a body, right? said Isaiah.

Romey might jus be right, said Taliqq.

If that's true? Said Mingo, Big Black Angus
'll be begging apologies real soon…unless
he's in on it. But he still gotta go!

Isaiah turned and studied Taliqq and
Mingo. Both discreetly avoided her eyes.

What gives with this *Judaism* thing, darling?
She asked her husband casually.

Mingo stared at the floor and shrugged.

We have no secret, right? Asked Isaiah.

He nodded.

What don't I know? *Mi amor?*…Fine. We'll
speak privately…

Mingo swallowed and nodded wordlessly. He began to shake and wiped his forehead. He took her hand and kissed it, and held it to the side of his face with closed eyes. Somehow, more than anything that happened that night, that frightened Isaiah. It surprised her to note that he was trembling.

Taliqq, Isaiah said frostily, turning icy eyes on him, you and MaGoo have some *history*, huh?

Darling we knew they worked together once, said Mingo, his voice shaking. Used to be best friends once. You known MaGoo most of your life too.

Right, right, said Isaiah. So Taliqq...or should I say *Tal*?

Only Leah calls me that...I prefer Taliqq...

Fine. This *Leah* thing?

Taliqq looked embarrassed.

She was my lady before I went down to Huntsville, said Taliqq.

Do you love her?

I rather not discuss it----

Understood. I might need to know that, said Isaiah. Might make a lot of difference for her...I'm thinking she's gotta go.

Taliqq looked at her sharply, and then nodded sadly.

Yeah, I love her…and I don't want her harmed, Queen.

Understood. So? Talk.

I come back outta Huntsville when my conviction on murder was overturned on appeal and it seems my business partner and buddy MaGoo slipped his *shoes* under my bed…

Wow. And you were best friends?

Were.

A real *creep!* Said Isaiah, carefully studying him. *Isn't he?*

For her sake? I never did anything---yet.

If it comes to war…said Mingo.

She'll be in the middle of it, said Taliqq miserably. She's standup like that…good with a 9mm Uzi.

Maybe it won't come to all of that, said Mingo.

So, Isaiah said carefully, Taliqq…You sounded like a *Jew* back there…what's up with that?

Taliqq winced. Are you an anti-Semite, Queen?

Isaiah laughed.

I'm a good *actress*, said Isaiah.

So were you acting back there?

Isaiah said nothing.

That's not the point. We *thought* you were
with the *Nation of Islam*.
Does it make a difference?
It might. I don't want them thinking we're
raiding their believers.
Queen, with due respect, I'm jus' a
hireling—
No, do not go *there*! Said Isaiah. For all
intents? You're our *War Lord!*
You mean assistant to *you* two, said Taliqq
with a nervous smile.
Now you got *jokes*? Asked Mingo.
You're my *cousin-in-law!* Said Isaiah.
But Queen------
I don't *care, cousin or not*! Snapped Isaiah.
You are a brother to my husband which
makes you my brother too. You are *one of us.*
No secrets! I *expect* you to be honest!
I am!
Are you?
Yes!
No secrets, ok? We've *embraced* you…
And *I* embraced *y'all!*
Have you?
Yes! Me and my set don't do this for
money…you *know* that!
Esta bueno, ta bueno, said Mingo.
I understand, said Isaiah, but what *are you*
really?

A loyal friend. Family. I'd die for you guys.
Don't die for us, , said Isaiah, live and help
us change it up out here. Anyway? You got
Nation of Islam in your crew…we respect
them ……
So do I!
We trust you….You never have told us what
you believe in…
Truth.
What *truth* is that?
Taliqq can be a Muslim
name….or…Sephardic *Jewish*…
Meaning what?
Ok, he said, Queen, this may not be the time
or place…
Ok…Agreed. But just so you'll know? I
don't want *false flaggers* getting next to us.
Mes entiende?
False flaggers? Said Taliqq, looking
wounded.
Isaiah looked at him stonily.
Tu sabe que te estoy deciendo?
Entiendo, Reyna.
You'll need to *explain* yourself to us later,
y'heah? Ok?
Ok….
Mingo involuntarily cringed, then broke
into a sweat.

MaGoo is a common weasel…A common grifter since he was knee high to a tadpole, said Romero, pouring them their favorite drink, hot raspberry flavored tea. *Isn't he? Ain't that right, Juj?*

Julio nodded. Women sat on one side of the room, their laps covered by blankets. Men sat on the other side.

They sat on Persian cushions on the hardwood floor, atop Navajo rugs which covered much of the floor of the family room in front of a roaring fire. The golden, dancing fire was the only light in the room. With a rustic, hand carved, wooden mantel sitting elegantly over it, the adobe fireplace was arched and edged with flagstones. It was late so they spoke in whispers so as not to wake the children. The walls were covered with beautiful Texas impressionist paintings. Many were done by Julio and Romero, and were jointly signed.

It was the first time that Taliqq had been invited to such an intimate family gathering.

An immense bird cage held a few chattering
African Grey parrots; smaller cages held
and parakeets, and finches. Dogs, large sleek
German shepherds, and Rottweilers, a
veritable pack, sat in various parts of the
room dozing, or paying bored attention to
their surroundings and their masters. Even
so, the room was sparsely furnished and
barely filled.
The adobe walled room, with thick plank
doors bound by wrought iron, with dark
brown logs as roof beams, and even darker
Vigas seemed very elegant yet casual. A
beautiful stained glass, wrought iron
chandeliers hung from the ceiling in the
center of the room. Under the large arched,
uncurtained windows sat a profusion of
house plants in shiny brass and enameled
planters.
Though they sat on the floor in front of the
fire, the room was decorated with Mission
style furniture that he knew to be costly.
He's lived on the grift his whole life, said
Julio, right along with is folks. Did some
pump and dumps with penny stocks on the
Net, till the SEC came around, and he's been
on the lam ever since. Probably still doing it.
Used to forge art too…maybe still does….

We used to call 'im Wheezer back in the days, said Romero, looking at Mingo, who look clammy and shaken.
Pretended he had asthma. Inhaler and all, said Julio.
A pint-size con man, even then, said Romero, said some things about Julio once, I smacked the crap out him…MaGoo, or *Wheezer* beat us out of a lot of money for kids back then…
when he wasn't beggin' us out of all our cash, said Julio. Little turd… I shoulda shot him back in the day when I had the chance….
Remember the time he claimed I broke his glasses? Romero asked Julio.
That's when you slapped him, right Papi?
Yup. He was talking about you, so I smacked the crap out of him…swore he'd kill me…Glasses broke…
Wada we give him? Five Cs? Asked Julio.
Glasses, said Romero, held together by Super glue and duck tape, mind you!
Cat and Mouse laughed.
True story, said Julio.
He goes to the Lion's Club, said Romero, and gets the glasses replaced for nothing.
I remember this! Said Cat.

What about the cash y'all gave him? Asked
Mouse.

Bought Mota wholesale, from some wet
backs, said Romero wryly. What was he?
11? Word is, he mixed in a pound of old
Oregano, made a fortune selling it to local
weed heads. Then comes back and says we
should give him more money.

We found out? Started calling im the *Weasel*
instead of Wheezer after that, said Julio.

How come I didn't know about this? Asked
Isaiah.

At the time you didn't really think much of
us, said Julio humbly.

Isaiah looked into the fire unhappily.

Isaiah, you remember Mook? Asked
Romero. his Ma used to know Mami? She
was Doctor Nunez's nurse, right? She saw
MaGoo's Medical records. Say's he has
perfect vision. Those glasses are fakes. he
sees better than you or me.

Research I've done, said Rosy with a yawn
indicates that MaGoo is a member of a
group along with Leah called *Ejad*.

What is that? Asked Isaiah, sipping warm,
honey sweeten tea.

JDL splinter group, said Rosy. Promotes total Unity of what they call 13th tribe, *greater Israel*. They raise funds for Ultra radical Jewish settlers in the West Bank.
What? Asked Isaiah.
MaGoo is a *JEW*? Asked Mingo. They all laughed.
That nasty little anti-Semite? Asked Taliqq.
Remember, the little clown is a great actor, said Julio.
Leah turned him, said Rosy. Maybe he never formally converted. He gathers information on Anti-Semitic groups and raises funds by swindling them---among other things.
Turned him? Asked Taliqq. I don't buy it....MaGoo claims he's a *Christian*!
Conmen say what they gotta say, said Romero.
Didn't you know? Asked Rosy. Yeah, your *girl* Leah is a Jew and a fundraiser for several Radical Zionist groups, Taliqq. I'm convinced she's Mossad.
Isaiah was speechless.
So....We were *conned*? Asked Isaiah.
We heard a splash, said Mingo.
Isaiah scratched her chin and said, but no one saw him go in the water.....
Romero and Julio exchanged a knowing look.

The splash trick, said Julio shaking her head.
The *splash trick?* Asked Isaiah.
When we were kids? We'd sneaked down to
the River? Said Romero. We woulda gotten
our butts beat if Popi and Mami knew-----
but we loved going to the river....
Julio? Romey? said Mingo, *Focus*! The *splash
trick?*
Oh, said Romero, yeah, The *splash trick* ....
Little turd, mumbled Julio, lost in memories.
See, said Romero, we'd be at a spot, fishing
or swimming.
You and I would be fishing, said Julio
crossly, the rest of those butt wads----
Will you all please tell us what the splash
trick is? Snapped Isaiah, smiling in spite of
her impatience.
Mind your manners, sniffed Julio.
Juju, you tell them, said Romero.
See, we would be fishing? MaGoo would go
down further down the River, right? Said
Julio. He'd hide behind bushes, right?
Romero said, We'd hear a big splash and
thrashing and splashing and screaming for
help-----
I thought I was telling this? Said Julio
crossly.
Sorry, Mami! Said Romero.

No, no! Go on! If you wanna —--
Come you two, *please*! Said Mingo.
We'd think he was drowning and we'd run
over? Said Julio.
We'd get there, said Romero, and MaGoo
would be in the water swimming and
laughing at us.
See? The *splash trick?* Said Julio. Sometimes
he'd just throw a rock in to make a splash.
Wow, said Mingo. We been *conned---maybe*.
Maybe-----said Rosy, pensively. Dollars will
get you donuts that Black Angus will find
out that Mister MaGoo stole them blind.
This is just a vanishing act, said Risah.
MaGoo is on the run.
Yup, Leah will be too, said Isaiah.
Yeah, you got grifted, said Rosy, seems like.
Romero nodded. Just like Black Angus
was! And everyone else out there---
Except Leah, said Taliqq bitterly. She was
probably in on it...
In a few days, said Rosy, I'll place a call to
her, pretend I'm calling about MaGoo's life
insurance, a big check for her. We'll figure
her out and find MaGoo.
So, said Isaiah, we still don't know what
really happened to Troll-----

Who gives a shit? Asked Risah. That butt
wad is not worth all this hassle. He's not our
blood.

Darling, said Mingo to Isaiah, let's put that
on ice until we work things out with Black
Angus, don't you think?

Good idea, said Rosy. I think Romey should
reach out to 'im. You were friends since
elementary school, right?

Works on our Kawasaki bikes, said Romero.

I know, said Rosy. A total fool, but not a
bad person. Sounds like MaGoo conned
him. I'll tell him to take a good look at his
money.

Isaiah called Mingo, Taliqq, Rosy and Risah aside; she held them back when Romero and his family went to bed.

Lookit, let's go into executive session, said Isaiah, I know all y'all wanna get your sleep, but we need to review---or at least consider----

I'd like to call the inner mesa to order please.

Why come to us now? Asked Rosy.

Rosy---

It was one *bonehead* move after the other, Isaiah!

You don't understand----

What is the *matter* with y'all? Are you *cowboys*? huh? Asked Rosy furiously.

Right! *Humiliate* us! kick us, we're still wiggling, said Mingo angrily.

Get pissed off, ok Elder? said Rosy. See how much I care!

We're here for wisdom, not attitude! Said Mingo.

See if I give a shit! Don't you get it? You two are much more than gang leaders now! You two are *religious and community* leaders! You're the highest level of esta cosa nuestra! What in the *hell* do you think you're doing playing gangster on the street, huh?

Maybe we weren't wise, said Isaiah.
Quit acting like a buncha hood dumbasses!
That's what Taliqq should be doing! Right
Taliqq?
I agree, but---
But *nothing*, *Taliqq*! What the fuck?
I messed up, said Taliqq, I shouldn't have let
them ride with me, but I answer to them.
That's no excuse! You shoulda talked sense
to them. *They* shouldn't have been out there!
You do the rough stuff! I don't have the
words…. But at least you two got a chance
to *dance,* right, *Queen?*
Isaiah and Mingo winced.
Enough, ok Rosy? said Risah calmly. I'm
sure you three are already beating
yourselves up about this.
I agree, said Rosy, what's the point?
Mistakes were made, said Isaiah humbly.
It's obvious, said Rosy, that you didn't
think this through Isaiah. Why *were* you
three out there in the *first* place?
Anger, said Isaiah. Troll shouldn't be in a
hospital.
Never spill blood in anger, said Rosy. And
fuck Troll, ok? He's caused this family
enough grief! You're mom and dad are
wrecks!

Rosy, mammy, said Risah, please, eh?
Enough. By the way, he's fine, whatever you
were told.
I'm *sick* of hearing about him, said Rosy, It's
not your problem, ya'll.
Rosy----
No, This should have been *delegated*. Quit
playing *detective*, ok? A fool got jumped!
Sorry, but you don't run out and deal with it
anymore, understand? Fuck defending the
poor down trodden masses.
Why are my parents freaked out?
Isaiah, he's not our prob, ok? We ain't the
good guys, Isaiah! I been telling y'all:
delegate, delegate.
Look, kid, said Risah, you might wanna
listen to her. You allowed your heart to
overrule your street savvy.
I deny that! Said Isaiah. We're protecting
our reps!
Troll, Troll, Troll! You're freak out, aren't
you? Said Rosy. You're wondering if he's
you're----
Dammit, Rosy, I said stop! Said Risah.
No, Risah, this gets on the table!
What get's put on the table, rosy? Said
Isaiah carefully.

Nothing, said Mingo, nothing! We're not going to say stuff just for the sake of running our mouths, ok Rosy?

Ok, look, said Risah, Troll is like Romey to you minus complications, right? A big, loveable *monogamous* Teddy-Bear, right? Or is he? Willy is the little sister you never had, right? But is she? Or is she a grown ass woman with a complicated man and a complicated life? Fact is, she and Troll---- *guided* you straight into this mess….maybe a whole lot of people around you aren't really letting know everything they're doing.

Why? Asked Isaiah furiously. Rosy, I need to know what you are talking about.

Aw shit! Said Rosy. Just forget it.

Is it about the fellowship?

Risah, said Rosy, lookit, maybe that's an internal matter that we should stay out of?

That's *bull* Rosy! Said Isaiah. The Westinas and the Vipers merged into Westia. As to the Fellowship? You worship with us, you're on the board! Risah is a sister Queen. It's as much your thing as mines, ok? So you wanna *talk*? Talk. I'm *fed up* with y'all failing to tell me what's on your minds!

No one wants to piss you off, Isaiah, said
Risah. Maybe they're scared you'll 1902
them if they do.
Not so! I'm a *spiritual* leader! I'm----
A killer who no longer knows how many
people's she's killed? Said Rosy. You and
your little angel faced husband, the Elder
here, will kill anyone in a heartbeat!
Isaiah glared at her.
That's so unfair! Said Mingo.
You said yourself! Said Isaiah. We're
religious and Community leaders!
Business people, said Mingo, and urban
micro farmers!
Yes, said Isaiah, We're *leaders* in the tiny
house movement, our organization----
Save the elevator speech, Queen, said Rosy.
I know, ok? but you scare the piss out of
most people!
Well I'll be *very* pissed off if I end up
looking like an *idiot* out there because *no one*
is telling me what I should know!
My darling----Mingo said.
No, querido, we were *clowned* out there! We
got ragged and tagged by that turd MaGoo
publicly! And *you*? You *questioned* my
leadership!
Sorry…

No, you *should* have, but we *do-not* do that
publicly! United front, *remember*? We are
one!
We are *one*! Your right, amor, Mingo said
softly. I didn't want another body on you,
but I was wrong to question you publicly.
We are *one*!
We showed our *asses* out there tonight,
people! Said Isaiah. We looked *stupid*, and
weak!
Queen, said Taliqq.
We *did-not* have our act together out there!
We got dogged by that miserable, *ugly* little
runt. We looked like incompetent *amateurs*
out there! *All* of us! And we're *not*! Then we
walk away looking like bullies. We haven't
put *Nuestra cosa* together by being *bunglers!*
Bunglers! Right or *wrong*, if we meant to put
them down, why did we drive away
without doing it?
We almost got caught slippin' out there,
said Taliqq, holding down his head. True. I
apologize. My mess, ok?
We're getting' soft, said Isaiah, Elder Mingo,
mi querido, we're getting *soft*.
No, Queen! Said Taliqq. I take full blame.
No, *this* was a collective screw up! Said
Isaiah.

You're right. It was *boneheaded*, said Rosy.
You shoulda delegated, and brought Angus
in too you instead of going to him!
Shoulda, coulda, *woulda*, said Taliqq
dismissively. If we expect perfection, we'll
always be disappointed. Didn't you just say
chalk it off?
Rosy gave him a dirty look.
Upstart, mumbled Rosy angrily. Maybe if
you hadn't ben acting so *macho*---
Call me whatever you want!
I made my *bones* out here when you were in
diapers, young'n! said Rosy angrily.
Taliqq grinned at Rosy. You might've even
changed them.
You're right, Queen, said Mingo softly.
Maybe...maybe Rosy is right...we have too
much going on to do the street thing
anymore...maybe we should be---
delegating.
Ok, but it goes beyond that! Taliqq, said
Isaiah, I apologize on behalf of me and my
husband for putting you in an embarrassing
situation. At the same time? *You* screwed up
too, ok? We *should've* been told that state of
things between you, Leah, and MaGoo!
But----
But *nada*! Said Isaiah. We *should've* been told!

Be *quiet, young'n*! said Mingo to his cousin.
Jus' deal with the facts.
Queen---
Did you *not* hear my husband?
Sorry, ma'am! Sorry, Mingo.
That's better! I'm not through talking *to you
yet, mister*! Elder Mingo, my darling, we
need to discuss some things alone later,
husband, but as to you, Taliqq? If you're a
Jew? *Fine*! Tell us! Don't false flag us! I
shouldn't have to find out in the *middle* of
this *mess* I've *walked* us into out of the
mouth of some two bit con artist----a penny
ante *grifter*! By the way, *are* you?
Pardon?
Are you an Orthodox Jew?
See? I've lost my cred with y'all I
guess…said Taliqq. Why am I even at the
inner mesa? I'm not a carnal, I'm just
esquina, y'all, I should go…
Hey! I'm not hearing an *answer,* cousin!
Snapped Isaiah.
Lookit, I'm stepping aside from anymore
work I been doing----
Oh, *shut up!* Said Mingo. You don't get to
just go! You're one of us. Just *shut up*,
cousin!

You're family! Said Isaiah. We *need* you! Just *answer* the question! *Are you?*

See---well---I'm going through conversion…
Are you?

Yes … yes…I am.

Isaiah studied him and chuckled.

Ok. Well, was *that* so hard? You think that changes anything? I'd *love* to hear your reasoning…I know several others are going through the same… Why the secrecy?

Abruptly Taliqq bowed down his head and started to cry silently through gritted teeth.

What is wrong-----

Mingo signaled Isaiah to ask no more.

It can't be easy to make such a big change, said Rosy. I should know….I'm going thru the same.

We, said Risah. *We* are going thru the same conversion.

Taliqq looked at them with surprise.

Isaiah stared at her, but Rosy looked back at her coolly.

Mi amor, said Mingo, visibly shaking, mi *querida*, why don't we leave it at that for now? Ma-ma-many people in the fellowship are doing the same----I think I'll be better able to answer some of your questions when we have *our* talk….

Isaiah gave him an icy, baleful look.

Anyway, said Risah chuckling, nothing for nothing, but why are you holding *Willy* prisoner?

We are *not* holding Willy *prisoner, said* Isaiah. ….She wants to do an 1902 on Angus…. we can't let her go *murder* her own *brother*!

Why are you holding *Willy* prisoner? Asked Rosy.

Aren't you listening to me? We are *not* holding Willy *prisoner*! Said Isaiah.

Willy's in *protective* detention, said Mingo, to prevent her murdering that dimwit, Angus the *Orc.*

They all laughed—except Isaiah and Mingo; they looked at the others sulkily.

Even though *you* mean to murder him yourselves? Asked Rosy dryly.

We agreed that it's on hold for now, said Mingo. But if it as to be done? I'll do it myself.

Why? Asked Rosy. You like Angus.

Like has nothing to do with it. He disrespected my Queen…She wants dead? He's dead.

Taliqq scratched his chin.

What about Romey, he asked.

What about him? Asked Isaiah.

I think Taliqq means, said Mingo, didn't we promise Romey----
No, said Isaiah. This won't be capture or kill either. Just kill.
But....
Isaiah cleared her throat noncommittally and said nothing for a moment.
On reconsidering? Said Isaiah, Darling, I'm sorry----but I want Angus dead.
But----
No buts. As to MaGoo? Gollum? The hobbit? MaGoo is alive. I'm certain of it. He may come at us---especially at Taliqq. Kill or capture, ok? If we can catch 'im, let's do it. Otherwise, bring down the light on 'im.
As to Leah? Asked Taliqq unhappily.
Control her Taliqq. On account of *you* she gets a pass, but Angus is a *dead man.* Nothing fancy---a bullet in the heart if we can help it, but he's *dead.* It's not about anger either.
Whatever you want, beloved. But we told Romero we wouldn't----said Mingo.
Yes, I know, darling, but we got responsibilities. Sorry. It's not Romey's call. We can't let Angus run his mouth and get away with it. Ruins our cred and reps. Our cred and reps are priceless.
But, mi amor---

No! He *dies*, mi querido. Please darling, back
me on this.
Muy bien, mi amor, said Mingo.
Why not throw him a good ole fashion East
Redemption ass whoop? Asked Risah, a
1902 isn't always the best alternative…
Are we being a little bloodthirsty? Asked
Rosy. Murders are a pain in the ass---and
expensive.
Nahhh, said Isaiah. We gotta clean this
mess up. A beat down? It would only
postpone the inevitable. Let's do it. Dress it
up. My darling, I can't allow you to do it.
And you, Taliqq? Sit it out, ok? Put Wolf on
it.
No prob Prophet, said Taliqq unhappily,
but can I at least advice?
Sure, said Isaiah. Quarterback it, but the
hands on? MaGoo is too in your head.
Somebody else pulls the trigger. I'll tell you
something else: if we settling accounts? Did
you notice Deacon Navarro hangang out
with Angus, like real people? I can't let it
slide, how he hit on Mouse----
Aw come on Isaiah! Said Rosy. Angus is a
harmless twit. Honey Buns runs that outfit,
and she probably had that poor fool beat
down.

Isaiah stared at her.

Honey Buns?

x

Come on *nothing*!   And we all had to quit the church because of that mess. He embarrassed Romey. I will *not* allow my family to be punked! Navarro goes. Put a psycho on him, Taliqq. Cut his throat, and I want is hands cut off before he dies. Let im bleed out somewhere…let him think of what it means to cross my family as he dies. Put it out n the street that he died that way afterwards. People will know.

Jesus Isaiah! Said Rosy. This is getting out of hand!

Abruptly they all laughed.

I want to send a message to anyone who might want to try for one of Romey's wives: hands off my nephews Mommies. The bodies gotta disappear, and no-*witnesses*.

Right, said Mingo, I don't want it to look like we did it.

Look, let's put a sicario on it, said Rosy. Make it look like a cartel deal. Some one out of Mexico…let's keep our distance on this.

Good, said Isaiah, I was starting to wonder about you…

Hold up, said Rosy. MaGoo is a survivalist? Right? A River man?

Ok? said Isaiah.

Who better to hunt someone like that than another survivalist/River man?

Who you got in mind? Asked Taliqq.

Are you thinking Moon? Sleep would never allow it! Said Mingo.

We run it up the flag pole and see…said Rosy.

We can count on him.

knowing him? Said Risah, he won't do it for bounty.

He's family, said Isaiah, and he wants a full body armor. We give him that? He'll do it.

I'll reach out, said Mingo. Taliqq, you don't know him well enough.

No, said Risah. keep it out of our family. Let's go with a wetback Sicario.

Ok, Risah, sorry, said Isaiah, but I say we get Moon to do it. Rosy, get *somebody*. Tonight. But please keep it simple and humane, for Willy's sake.

Humane? said Rosy, laughing. Murder? Cutting off hands? A 1902 is *never humane*.

Which is why *we* don't want to get *ourselves* murdered by being *sentimental*, snapped Isaiah. This is part of what we do, ok? Quit being so self righteous!

A bullet to the base of the skull? Said Mingo gently. Small caliber? It's *humane*. Where is the cruelty in that?

It might seem different if it's *your* skull on the receiving end, said Risah.

Beats gettin' shanked or stringled, mumbled Taliqq. Or getting stomped to death...I saw a lot of that down in la Pinta....

A bullet to the heart? It's merciful too, said Mingo. I say leave their faces alone.

Yeah If you want them to have an open casket, said Taliqq...for their family, you know?

True, said Taliqq, But an ice pick at the base of the skull-------

Hey! Hey! *Enough* of the *shop talk,* ok? said Rosy. You're grossing out my wife...and it's kinda boring.

Should we be holding hands and singang kumbayaya, or We Are The Children? asked Taliqq dryly.

Mingo smiled and chuckled.

I'ma *slap your face* in a minute *asshole,* snarled Rosy, giving Mingo a dirty look, disrespect me again!

Hey! Hey! Said Taliqq, laughing. Sorry, sis!

What? *What*? You think I won't slap the shit out the tough ass contract killer "Taliqq?" You think I'm too soft to pull a trigger? I slapped many tougher guys than you!

Ok, enough! Said Mingo.

Mind your *manners*, Taliqq! Said Risah.

I think we're a little tired…But quit *preaching* at us, ok Rosy? Risah? *Please?* Said Isaiah.

We ain't blood thirsty *psychos*. We don't like doing this anymore than *you*, but *business* is *business*. It ain't like you two *never* pulled the trigger.

We're jus' sayin', said Risah. I done my share of dirt…plenty of it. Wouldn't be here if I hadn't. But since when *don't* we do beat downs anymore? I don't know when murder---1902--- became the only option in this kinda situation…Anyway, I'm semi-retired.

Isaiah politely refrained from commenting.

Rosy, pardons, ok? said Taliqq. Back on subject? Lookit, this may not be the time to put this on the table, but I say, let's create our own motorcycle club.

Risah laughed.

What are you talking about?

We need it bad.

They all turned and stared at him.

Why not? Continued Taliqq. Once Angus gets got? Let's absorb the Steel Wheel Confederates into it. In the long run? We either do that or they'll continue to be a buncha pain in the butt rednecks knifing people once we do what we're planning. Everyone stared at him.

Are you even *one* of us? Asked Rosy. Ain't you a *mercenary*?

Mercenary my butt, said Taliqq. Then y'all owe me a buncha money, don'tcha? Yeah, me and my crew work for bounty. I'm not ashamed of it. We gotta eat, right? We got nothing coming from the streets. Who we gonna rob? Only action out here is y'all.

That's not right, Isaiah, said Risah. We gotta hook him up. Him and his crew. We ain't hurting, so there is no excuse.

Thanks, but I ain't here begging, said Taliqq.

Understood, said Mingo, but Cousin Risah is right, Queen.

Rosy, please, set it up, said Isaiah.

I never taken on anything, said Taliqq. That didn't sit right with me. But this? Here and now? I never taken a *dime* from any of you. Me or my crew.

That's true, said Isaiah. So why do you do it?

I'm here cause I love my cousin. He's the only family I got.

Not true, said Isaiah. We're all your family now.

Right, said Rosy politely. Did your Mom go to our church back in the day?

Yes, said Taliqq.

And you never met your daddy? Asked Rosy. Don't know who he is?

Taliqq looked at them shyly. Mingo looked at Rosy sharply.

Rosy---you think---Pastor Molina? Asked Mingo.

Pastor Molina was a serial impregnator, said Rosy, who screwed any pretty girl in his congregation he coul get his hands on.

Turns out he's Mingo's daddy, my Daddy, and maybe your, Taliqq. For all we know, cousin, you're our kid brother!

Woh, woh, said Risah, laughing, this is too big a conversion for this situation. Taliqq, get with Rosy? Get a blood test? Now, let's stick to the topic at hand.

Ok. *Lookit*, stammered Taliqq, we need a *cavalry*. No great nation can survive without a cavalry. If we have our own MC? We can rule *ALL* of North Texas. We got enough riders to were right off the bat we'll have the biggest MC in Texas. On the strength of this organization? We patch over all the smaller clubs around here--- most will jump on board anyway.

Thoughts? Said Isaiah.

Sounds good, said Mingo. Taliqq, this can only happens if you and your crew officially become part of our thing.

We like our independence!

Get over that, said Risah.

You gotta be with us, said Mingo. Which means All of y'all give your loyalty to my Queen. Totally.

Taliqq looked at them all carefully.

Agreed.

Rosy? Risah? Asked Isaiah. Do you accept him and his crew.

Risah nodded.

We already have, said Rosy. Make sure it's what they want.

One minute your plotting on bringang down the light, said Risah. Now this. We really need to focus.

All the same, said Isaiah.

Look, said Rosy, esta cosa de nosotro? We
call all of this the game, but it's not a *game*.
It's all about *business*. Internationally? We're
bigger than Microsoft, Apple and US Steel
put together. We're part of an *Industry*! It
rules the West Indies, Mexico and most of
Latin America. We make the Mafia look like
a candy store. All this gang stuff is crap. It'll
mean wars. Bloodshed? War? It's not cost
effective. Far too risky. We're at a point at
which all of us need *out* of the gang crap,
other than for recruiting soldiers. We're
business people. We need out of the gang
stuff.

It's *all* about *business*, prima, said Taliqq.
You need *muscle*.

Do I?

You're a business woman, you're a spy,
Rosy.

I don't care for *spy*. I prefer the phrase Intel
acquisition specialist, said Rosy airily.
Espionage is just an aspect of sound
management.

Ok, said Taliqq. I know your big secret: You're the financier for a consortium of the Mexico city cartels. You do all their money laundering, and you're also Queen of Los Sicarios y *Assassinos aqui en el Sul Norte, o Tejas a lo menos.*

Everyone froze.

Excuse me? Seethed Rosy icily. Are you spying on me? You talking about *my* business? *How* in the fuck *dare* you?

Aw come on! I'm not *stupid*.

We don't openly discuss certain things, said Isaiah nervously. Look, Rosy, he's new to some of this....

You cover your tracks well, Taliqq persisted, but I know *you* got carloads of assassins. I wanted to work for you for the longest time, but in the end I started my own thing out of need. I'm not tryna kiss your butt, ok? But you're like my idol. It's a true honor to even be around you.

Rosy stared at him dryly.

Taliqq, your embarrassing her, said Mingo. He waived aside Mingo's objections.

But are assassins all you need? I know an army of assassins can do a whole lot. But you need more. Out here? Without muscle your nobody.

I don't know *what* you're talking about, said Rosy, what *assassins*? But for your information? Assassins *are* muscle---the best kind.

Ok, ok. Secrecy is important, but all the same? Every dick-wad with a gun out here challenges you if you don't have the right kind of muscle. We're talking *visible* muscle. This is about *power*, not gang crap.

Theatricality has its purpose, said Mingo. Exactly! said Taliqq, *Theatricality!* he more *visible power* you got, the safer your business, the more you grow your business. You wouldn't do all the gang drama with more visible muscle. How you gonna hing on to your business without visible muscle?

I see your point, said Rosy, studying him with appreciation.

True, said Risah. If, *if* we decide to proceed…can you do it, but do it low key at first? *Deceit and diplomacy* instead of brawn and bullets, ok?

Smart *Diplomacy* is *Deceit, mostly, said* Mingo.

Isaiah grinned wolfishly. Rosy laughed with delight.

True, said Rosy, True! Maybe you kids have paid attention to me!

We can do it just like we did with Westia, said Isaiah. *If*…We created a federation, or a Commonwealth, or a confederacy, or whatever you wanna call it, but all of the smaller gangs in the Communion are our puppets.

We don't want to start a war with Bikers by turning the Westia into an MC, said Mingo. It's got to seem independent from Westia. Maybe we pick an MC, turn it into our puppet, and build through it.

But a puppet of the Westia, said Taliqq.

Not a just our puppet, said Isaiah, a
hammer. Our sword.

I'm liking it, said Mingo. Let's think of using the Steel Confederates as our puppet---- whatever's left when we're through with it.

If we do it? Once it firms up? Said Isaiah, it won't matter if people know it's Westia. Anyway, in case y'all forgot? Westinas were an MC. Most Westinas and our men ride. I thought about it in the past. I agree Taliqq. We *need* an MC. It increases our reach. Simple *visibility* is not our friend, Taliqq, unseen *presence* is. At first it's gotta be…*anonymous*…

You mean *autonomous*? Said Rosy, suppressing a yawn, fighting a profound sense of boredom.

No, said Isaiah, *anonymous*…it'll be run by me---*if* we do it. I mean an MC that exist like the Mafia…secretly… *Anonymously*.
That's *it!* Said Taliqq. *That's* the name!
What?
Rosy lapsed into sleep.
When the bad boys start to feel it flex? We'll put it out. *Los Anonymous!* All black uniforms, with a black on white Skull and Cross bones in the middle of the worn on the inside of the cuts---or black suit jackets--- when the time comes we'll reveal it! People will think it's a Goth thing!
You're thinking of *appearance,* not *substance* now! Said Rosy impatiently, waking up abruptly.
We'll just *consider* it…for now, ok? Said Isaiah. No colors, no patches at first….Just a huge membership, and *only* members know who's a member. We deny that it even exist to outsiders. We'll turn all the other clubs around here into puppets----
If we do it, said Mingo.
Should we? Asked Isaiah.
I say yes, said Taliqq.
Yes, said Mingo. *Experimentally.*

Yes, said Risah, if the club president is appointed by you Isaiah, answers to you, and can be removed by you.

In other words, said Rosy, yawning, it can't be a separate entity. *Just* our cavalry. Isaiah?

Wait, said Mingo. *Just* our cavalry. No President. It's ruled by the Queen. Run by Generals appointed by the Queen.

Let's do it, said Isaiah. *Experimentally.* Taliqq? Set it up. I want Chink to train our riders---fast. Clubhouses in each of our big hoods, crews, captains, set leaders, ok? Safe houses for every crew. My husband controls it for me---my Darth Vadar. Rosy? Intel and gots, ok? You Taliqq? Field general and cavalry warlord. You're the face of this, ok? You answer to my husband. Risah? Advise them. Anything you do? Run it by Rosy and Risah. Any issues? Bring'm to me. No mistakes, ok? Agreed?

Everyone nodded.

Back to the subject on and, said Isaiah.

Wait, one more thing, said Mingo. Chinita's *gotta* to be in it---not just training riders either.

Why? Asked Risah.

See, said Rosy, she's an OG, an old school
biker gangster, and a wizard on a
motorcycle, and knows how to fight on one.
Body builders? Mc's around Redemption?
They love her. She's got an old school gym
called Hell…all free weights, temperature in
it always hot enough to bake cookies. Old
school hardcore biker body builders? They
love the place. They view Chink with mad
respect. We got Chink? Instant biker cred.
Taliqq, said Isaiah, Chinita is like… a force
of *nature*….can you work with her?
Sure. I already do. Chink mercs with me.
My teacher.
Ok, said Isaiah. As to MaGoo?
We need to debrief him before anything,
right boss lady?
Right, said Isaiah. Once we know what
MaGoo was up too, MaGoo is dead. I want
ALL our pistoleros out on his trail.
Queen, said Mingo, who leads out on
MaGoo?
You and Taliqq, but you two *only* arm chair
quarterback, ok? Neither of you is on the
street on this, savvy?

Yup, said Taliqq unhappily. All the same? Look, I want all of this as far as possible from you two. You're somebody...I really didn't want you two in this tonight, but who am I to say? You two have a life, you got stuff to live for. You need to keep as much of a distance as you can from the streets. Let tonight be the last time you two ever do anything personally on the streets, ok?

We'll seriously consider that, said Mingo.

If at all possible? MaGoo? I want 'im alive, said Isaiah, but if he drops any of our people? Bring me his deceitful ten gallon *head* in a cheap Wal-Mart *five* gallon pvc bucket with a lid on top. I don't want it stinking things up anymore than it already has.

Wow, said Risah, *head* in a cheap Wal-Mart *five* gallon pvc bucket with a lid on top...Are you serious? Wow!

Why? Asked Rosy. She studied Isaiah sadly.

Consequences? Said Isaiah impatiently. We're making a *point*, sending a *message*...don't *rebel!* And because I wanna know it got *done!*

Don't *personalize* it, said Rosy. It's gotta be *business*. Jus tryna say. Remember something: once Roja wanted *your* head in a bucket.

Isaiah didn't comment.

Anyway…What will you *do* with it? Asked
Risah with a nervous laugh.
Isaiah frowned.
I'd love to stick on the end of a pole and
leave it standing by the river, but I'll settle
for burning it. Ok? No more discussion on
it. It's on! Get to it, y'all! Let's wrap this up
fast.
Rosy yawned and stretched and rubbed her
face.
Well, before any blood gets spilled, let's cool
off, ok? said Rosy. Please? Let's see how
things shake out, ok? Now if it's all the same
to y'all? I'm going to sleep.
She despises Troll, said Rosy. She's a self
hating, high yellow red skank. Angus is
standing tall for his mother.

Chapter Seventeen

After his wives went home at his urging,
persuaded that all was safe, in the middle of
the night, Troll sensed that someone was in
his Hospital room, watching him. He
opened his eyes.
MaGoo stood at the foot of the bed.
MaGoo? He whispered. You little fool!
I thought your ladies would be up here
babysitting you. Mines would be.
I told them I'd be ok. I made them go home.
Why?
I want them out of harm's way if anyone
comes to finish the job.
That was stupid!

I'll take care of myself. I'm ready. What are
you doing here?
I had nothing better to do, so I figured I'd
come see you. Even up the score!
So you can't let bygones be bygones?
Amends, and all that?
No, I can't!
Dude! Your face! What happen to you?
Nothing! Shalom Aleichem, achi.
Aleichem Shalom, little achi.
Is it safe for you to be here?
Shhh! Said MaGoo. I came to finish the job!
Get Real! Troll laughed along with MaGoo.
You think I'm kidding? You think this is a
game?
MaGoo----
This is WAR, Jew!
MaGoo then pulled out a large black gun.
You little *weasel*----
Please take out the SIG your holding under
the sheet *slowly* and put it on the night table.
Slow! Slow, achi!
Troll followed his directions with a sneer.
I knew I'd be seeing *you*!
Where you going to run to now, big man?
Tell me, Jew!
You have no shame have you?
MaGoo smiled wickedly.

War is *war*, buddy! And now, *this* has been coming for a good while now!

MaGoo squirted him the face with his water gun twice.

I'll get you for this!

MaGoo laughed. You'll have to catch me first!

Have you no shame? I'm in a *sick* bed, you little nit!

Since when is getting your ass kicked sickness?

Turd!

You had your ass *kicked*! So have I! So you're not sick! There's a difference.

Is that a new one?

Neat, isn't it?

May I see it?

Sure! MaGoo handing him the gun. I bought it at HOBBY LOBBY---

Troll took it and squirted him the face twice.

Ahhh. MaGoo sighed. That was *very* immature!

You squirted *me* first!

You could be article Twelved for that! That was a violation of the rules, since you asked to see it!

Dude, I'm lying here *sick*!

Getting an ass whoop is *not* sickness!

Your *despicable*, MaGoo! This is why you
came here, isn't it?

Hey! The water gun war waits for no man!

They both laughed.

Dude! I know what really happened,
MaGoo.

Tell me!

Five of them, dude. They wore masks, but I
know who sent them. And I know who led
them.

I know who sent them too, Goo.

I got suckered, big man, said MaGoo, they
called me, told me Angus and the boys were
about to be bushwhacked, so I jumped on
my little hog, and I'm speeding, and trying
to reach them on my cell at the same time. I
get to the club house? They're their playing
Cards.

Do you know who called you, Goo?

Bro, do you have to ask?

No. Who led them?

That zit Navarro.

Are you sure?

Yes.

I'll try to handle it as soon as I'm able, and
I'll pass that on to Moon.

Don't. Forget it. I may be in this hospital
bed, but I think some of them are in a bed
hurting too. Something snapped in me,
dude.
Wadaya mean?
I pulled my Khukuri out and I took out
three---
You *killed* them dude!
Wow! Bummer. Anyway, they beat my ass
good with two by fours. I think they found
out I'm no cream puff, though.
Fatally, said MaGoo.
Guess what they kept saying, Goo?
What?
Stay away from Willy or we'll come back
again! I told them, you're gonna have to kill
me! I got hurt, but you wouldn't know they
won if you had been there!
They didn't win.
I protected myself.
Good! You killed three! Dude, I'm being
blamed for the bushwhack.
Wow! Why would anybody blame my little
pocket size devil? They know you're my
besty!
The club cleaned up the mess for you. The
cops won't be an issue. Them boys were
probably up here without papers from south
of the border.

Say thanks to them for me!

They think *I* want to kill you.

I'm shaking in my boots, MaGoo!

Hey, I'm no cream puff either, dude!

I could take you down with one hand tied
behind my back, buddy!

Oh, shut up, you big lump!

MaGoo came to the side of the bed.

They think I did this to you, buddy!

I know it wasn't you.

Are you sure?

Troll snorted.

Get Real!

MaGoo kissed his forehead. He patted
Troll's head affectionately.

Had to check on you, big man. I didn't come
sooner because word has it Willy's blaming
me. Are they treating you ok in this dump?

Yeah.

Didn't you fix this sty up?

Why don't you shut up?

It looks like a Juarez Whorehouse.

So you risk your life to come sell the wuff
ticket?

I'm jus sayin'. Callin' it as I see it! This is a
little ornate for a recovery facility.

What would you know, Goo? Y'all live in a
cave!

A cave city, you clot! It's a beautiful place!
How are you, brother?
I'm ok. MaGoo…MaGoo, why are you
crying?
Are you still my friend, big man?
Of course! Always! We're *brothers*! Why
shouldn't I be?
I let y'all down, buddy, said MaGoo, with a
quaver in his voice.
Oh, stop it!
I let you down, dude! I shouldn't have left
you alone!
You did a great job watching my back little
brother. Now I get why you left in a hurry!
You got fooled!
I made a huge mess of everything…
Stop it, dude! This is not on you.
You shoulda been   packing, big man! I
shoulda made you see that!
Well, from here on I will be!
I tried to protect you and Angus…but I
failed, dude…I failed…
Oh, stop, little bro! You're not responsible
for this!
The two surviving boys that did this? They
already slipped on a banana peel and fell
into a hole…they ain't around anymore. I
tracked them down and finished them,
brother. They were not SWC.

Who were they?
East Communion Sicarios.
Will they be coming after you?
Maybe, but I doubt it. They were
independents. But I didn't keep you safe,
and they hurt you!
I don't hold you responsible. Nobody
should. I shoulda been packing. But that
Khukuri was as good as a gat for me.
Good. Keep it close.
I got it and a SIG under my pillow.
Dude, I pretended to hate Jews, to cover up
tonight. I actually pretended to be a *Christer*!
I feel----*dirty*!
You have *got* to be shitting me! *You*?
I hate myself for that. The Converts? They
think I threw them under the bus.
But none of us should hide our faith, said
Troll. Ain't that right, MaGoo?
Absolutely, bro.
They're all afraid of Isaiah, said Troll.
Maybe you did us all a favor though.
How?
All the secrecy needs to stop. It's whack! But
we're kinda afraid of how she'll react.
Well, Troll, you shouldn't be. She loves you
and Willy a whole lot.

I know, said Troll. That's what we're afraid of losing. We love her and Mingo too.

Does she really know who you are?

Troll said nothing for a moment.

Maybe I don't know who I am either. You and your ladies, Willy and my ladies are my only family.

Aw, listen atcha!

I mean it dude!

Ok, said MaGoo, should I tell you what I think?

Can I stop you?

Hey! Quit being a dick wad, you lump!

Troll laughed.

Ok, what?

You got family. You know who too, don't pretend you don't.

Who?

Ramiro and Romero. Two letters worth of difference! Strange, huh? Both of you have the same last name, right? Martinez. You're identical, right?

Coincidence.

Yeah, right! Need I go on, Troll?

What are you getting at, MaGoo?

Troll, you and Romero are identical twins. Monozygotes.

Troll wanted to laugh, but couldn't.

What? Why would you say that?

Isaiah is your kid sister.

Yeah, whatever!

Why does she look so much like you?

Troll could say nothing.

That's why she loves you so much.

Somehow, without knowing it, she knows it.

Then why was I not raised with them? How could that be, MaGoo?

I thought a lot about that. I've even did research, and I think I've figured it out!

MaGoo! Come on! If you have an idea say it!

Superstitions.

Huh?

About twins.

What?

There are tribes around the world that think that twins are evil. In some cultures they kill both. In some they kill one. Romero's mother---maybe you're mother---is Kiisi, from Kenya. Nobody will probably admit this, but I bet they're superstitious about twins. You'd be surprised how many die *accidentally* early on.

My understanding is that she is a well educated woman, and so is Romero's father.

And?

She wouldn't be superstitious.

Don't be so sure. Yeah, your father---

I'm an orphan dude. I have no mother or
father!
Ok! I'm chop liver, right? I'm not family?
Pardon me, blood brother, whispered Troll.
Alright then! Yeah, Mister Martinez is very
well educated, but a man will do anything
for his wife. So, they're devout SDA, right?
Right. Dude! *I* was raised….I was raised by
an SDA lady cousin!
Kiisi, right?
Troll stared at him wordlessly.
Yes….
See what I'm saying? I've checked. She was
cousin to Romero's Ma. See what probably
happened?
No! Maybe I'd rather not.
You grew up around Kenyans?
Yes….not really. I was sort of isolated.
How many twins you ever met among
Kenyans?
Troll said nothing.
You're Mom is a good hearted person.
I have no Mom!

Sure. Assume for the sake of what I'm
saying that Romero's folks are your parents.
Ok? She wouldn't let them harm you, but
they may have persuaded her to separate
you two completely, for your safety. Maybe
they do that in some places instead of
harming either one. Maybe her people were
freaking her out about twins. Maybe she
gets really frightened. So she chooses. Her
husband loves his wife, and like most of us,
he gets railroaded by a scared wife and goes
along. And maybe they have been dying of
guilt ever since. How do they make up for
it? They lavish all the attention on Romero,
and ignore their little daughter. Maybe they
did her a favor. Isaiah---She's tough as nails,
smart, develops a steel trap mind, and a
steel spine, she's a charismatic leader, a
natural born preacher---she becomes the
remarkable person Isaiah is. Isaiah might
see you as the brother who wasn't favored,
but got treated even worse than her, and
knowing how that feels, she goes overboard
for you.
Troll began to cry.
Shut the hell up! Ok MaGoo? I don't wanna
hear it.
No! Dude, maybe I'll be dead real soon!

Not if I can help it! Said Troll.
Hear me out, ok?
Fine. Tell you the truth, MaGoo?
Yeah?
I've felt like if part…part of me was missing
most of my life.
I think twins separated at birth say they
have that feeling.
If this is true, why does Romero hate me?
He doesn't hate you.
Why the attitude?
Jealousy of how Isaiah likes you. He doesn't
like competition from any one where his
little sister is concerned! And he's scared for
his mom and dad is all. I think for real for
real? He's scared of you!
Whatever! Scared of What?
He's scared of what you'll do to them----
I wouldn't harm a fly!
They don't know you.
I would love to know if I have family! I
would just love to see them, at least
once…I'd like to…I liked to hug Romero, if
he's my twin just once, you know?
MaGoo patted his head softly.
Maybe it will happen, dude, said MaGoo.
Dude, I'm Troll the nobody. Rich people
don't want anything to do with a pauper
like me.

You are not a pauper, so quit that crap!
They'd think I want money from them or
something…..MaGoo.. How would they
have chosen?
What?
Why didn't they choose me? Didn't they
love me?
Looks I guess.
Do what?
Dude! They figured as ugly as you are…
Kiss my butt dude!
They both laughed.
Who knows? It's a Devil's choice. I can only
guess.
Why did they love him more?
MaGoo thought for a moment.
Do you remember Romero at all?
I've always had a weird feeling….
You might have been separated at birth…or
later. They probably loved you
both…You're stronger than Romero…more
muscular. She let her cousin raise you, but
she keeps the weaker twin, if I'm right.
Troll stared at him, and wiped tears from his
eyes.
I guess I hate them all.

Nah, brother, don't be bitter. Why would you hate Isaiah? You don't know the whole story.
All of that is crazy mad speculation.
If we could get some of his hair!
Why?
DNA test.
You really should shut up now MaGoo!
Screw it, I don't care.
MaGoo tried to smile.
Right, big man. Anyway...I'm on the run...I probably won't make it till morning.
What are you talking about, little brother?
Isaiah and Elder Mingo? They tried to murder me tonight, brother. I think I'm being hunted, but I had to check in on you.
For G-d's sake! Why are they after you?
I tried to protect Angus, but it wasn't any good. See my face? She beat the crap out of me! They blame me!
What did you do?
Once I knew that Angus was safe? I escaped into the forest across the river.
Dude! Sit down, you're on the verge of falling! Are you hurt?
MaGoo tried to laugh.
A little.
Dang, dude!

First she pistol whips me, then they shot me
on the back of the head with a bean bag
when I ran for it….I nearly passed out, but
the cool water revived me.
MaGoo! I'm so sorry, buddy! Why didn't
you just tell them the truth?
And destroy Willy's family?
MaGoo, does Angus or Tiffany-Dawn
know?
He knows, but what is he going to do? She's
his blood!
Willy hates her, and now I don't blame her.
That woman is evil!
Does Willy think it was him? Asked MaGoo.
She knows it wasn't but she's putting on an
act to avoid letting anyone know that she's
figured out the truth.
Will she hurt Angus?
Of course not. Isaiah's keeping her at
Romero's house!
Jus' as I expected. An extraction team is on
their way over there. We gotta get her out of
there!
Why?
How will Isaiah react if she finds out about
our conversions?
Oh My G-d! Maybe we need to get Mingo
and Taliqq out of there too!

They wouldn't come. He won't leave his
wife, even if she kills him and Taliqq won't
leave him.
Who's Taliqq?
Leah's man. Probably Mingo's kid brother.
Maybe one of Pastor Molina kids.
Pastor Molina?
Serial impregnator. Knocked up more pretty
girls at the Redemption SDA Spanish
Church than you can count.
What?
Long story, dude. Redemption has a very
twisted dark side. Taliqq? He muscles for
Isaiah, but nobody knows, we're frien-
emies. Thinks I took Leah from him, but he
doesn't know she's my kinswoman through
marriage. Marigold's cousin.
Troll smiled. So are Sage and Thyme, dude!
What? You think I'd hit on a buddy's lady?
Chill out!
I don't hit on a *friend's* woman, dude!
I know!
I never once have checked out those fine
Red head girls of yours! Or that pretty little
Chrysanthemum! And I'd never even think
about Ivy or Safflower.
Watch it MaGoo!
They laughed.

I've been taking care of Leah, tryna talk her into going back to him. She walked out on him when he started running with the fruit of Islam. I happen to know he was just building an alliance, but she thought he was selling out Judaism.
So what happened?
I put on a good act of taking her from him tonight.
Why?
To keep them all confused about the truth of who did this to you.
Telling the truth woulda been simpler.
MaGoo sighed wearily.
Maybe, maybe not. Well, Troll, they're hunting me now, I think…and I'm hurt. My head feels awful! I better get going buddy.
Let me help you, little buddy! MaGoo, let he call for the nurses…let me----
Isaiah owns this place. I won't be safe here. The security here is shitty! I got by them easy. I snuck up here up a stream in my canoe…I'll get back to the river and hide, before light. I'll doctor myself…
I can't let you do this!
I wish my ladies were with me…if I'm not found tell them I love them…
Dude, let me get a nurse!

No! Tell Moon to come help me! Tell him to look for me in the old haunts in case I pass out…Once I get well? I go back to the hidden city.

When will we see you guys?

We'll always see you in the forest….My head is spinning. I'm really not well, but I had to come see you, buddy! I'll be in the shelter by the log near river---what are you doing?

I'm coming with you!

Stay in bed, you lump!

Shut up, MaGoo! I'm coming with you, blood brother!

Dude, you're hurt! You can't!

Help me on with my clothes!

Troll----

You're my *family*, dude! Sneak me out of here!

Troll, you can't, you're hurt---

MaGoo, quit arguing, little fella! You're my real family. I'm coming with you!

But---

Don't argue! I won't let you go paddling down the River alone with a head injury, especially in the dark, family.

No Troll----

I can walk. I'll help you row. We'll take care
of each other, buddy. Moon will come and
help us!
Troll, you're crazy!
Wait! We can call on Willy and Tiffany-
Dawn. They know this area. All we gotta do
is find a place to hide and they'll come get
us. She lives with us, along with Chryssie.
My shop isn't that far from here! We'll row
down the stream near my shop, and it'll be a
short walk for us from there. Maybe she'll
get us in her car.
You sly dog! Said MaGoo trying to laugh,
found a second wife, huh? Don't think I
don't know!
MaGoo, you haven't met Chrysanthemum---
or Ivy and Safflower, Have you?
Who are they?
A Chrissie's black hippy girl. I adore her.
The others were Slope's family. Dude, I'm
going to marry all of them.
You'll have a beautiful family.
I learned about polygamy from *you*! Said
Troll, chuckling.
Will they help us?
Yes! She's ---they're my ladies. She'll bring
the cabin to the river with us in it and we
can hide! It'll be a shorter journey.

You'll be a Patriarch, Troll! You have many
sons!
Help me grab my meds! Now let's go!
I don't know that I could've made it down
the river, said MaGoo. Thank you my
friend.
Once they get Willy she'll help take care of
us too… We'll send a messenger to
Cavernton for healers!

Chapter Eighteen

Moon man! Said Mingo. Waddup!
Waddup! Waddup!?
Elder! It be what it be!
They were in the cubby hole of an office that
Mingo and Isaiah used at the Westia
Fellowship Hall on Corinth Street in the
Redemption.
Thank you for coming on such short notice,
brother.
It's all good! Said Moon, how my nephews
doing, kinfolk? How's the tribe?
We're all doing great!
I know this has got to be important? said
Moon, or it coulda waited for the afternoon
family get together, right?

It's important, Moon.

I don't like leavin' Lil alone in the Forest, since it's harvest time.

Sorry for any inconvenience, said Mingo.

Are you hungry? Thirsty? How about a hot cup of chocolate? I know you love chocolate!

Nahhh, little brother, I'm good. Where's the Prophet?

At Romero and Julio's house. Said Mingo. Romero's down with an injury.

Really?

He'll be fine. I wanted to talk to you about this alone.

Is this about that situation at the River?

How did you know, Moon?

How could I not know?

Lookit, I'll cut right down to the chase, ok? Said Mingo. First of all, the body armor you want? Done deal. Same with the AA 12 gages, ok?

Wow! Cool! Not that I really have much use for it anymore.

Fantastic! Said Mingo. You are really getting into micro urban farming huh?

Not to mention eco-forestry! Said Moon.

They both laughed.

How goes the wilderness grow-op?

Better and better! No small thanks to MaGoo!

Organic wild high grade herbal relief
business is good to you, huh? Said Mingo.
It's a lot of work, but I love it! Said Moon.
It's a lot safer than rippin' and runnin'.
I hear you got partners. Forest people?
Well you know Lil is always gonna be down
with me!
Word! By the way? Congratulations! I hear
both Lil and Sleep are expecting!
Yes sir! You wanna get a woman pregnant?
Get with a second woman at the same time.
I don't know about all that, said Mingo,
smiling shyly.
I never thought I do the polygamy thing, but
I'm loving it. Romero is ahead of his time.
Me? Said Mingo, I'm strictly a one woman
man!
You'd better be, mumbled Moon, with the
woman you married!
They both laughed.
We need a favor, Moon man.
Really?
Moon, you ready to put in a little work for
us?
Who?
Did you hear what happened the other
night?
Tell me.

Bluffer? Big ole wolfhound? Romero's dog? Really, he's Rosannah's dog, but when she gave Julio and Romey the house, she left him there. He's turned into Romey's guardian angel. Everybody say's get rid of that animal. He's too big, eats too much. Romero loves that dog, said Moon. He should keep him.

Trust me, nobody'll ever complain about him again. It follows him around all the time. The other night, according to Romey, Bluffer goes in his room, growls in his ear until Romey wakes up. He knew something was wrong. He got Julio's 12 gage pump action?

Romey using a gat? Asked Moon.

I'm tryna tell you! Followed Bluffer through the house without turning on lights and guess what he finds? Three men trying to jimmy open the patio door.

What about the alarm? Motion detector? Jimmied! Said Mingo. They got to the phone line, and their alarm system. Dudes are wearing masks, right? The Bluffer knows when not to bark.

Killers? Asked Moon.

Sure. Maybe worse. Maybe second story men who were going to come in here, kill Roe, then rape and kill the women.

Huh! Fat chance of that! What happened
then?
Romero took them out. Took a bullet
through the thigh, but it was just a flesh
wound.
Dang! How is he?
He'll be alright. Bluffer goes through the
broken glass? Rips up two of them, but the
women are down stairs by then, right? They
questioned the last one as he was dying.
Says Navarro sent them. Romey's like, are
y'all alright? My dog! My dog is dead!
Mouse checks the dog. Turns out he cut his
ear. Mouse checks him out? After it's all
over? She says it passes out. I think he
suffers from panic disorder.
Panic Disorder? Said Moon. Dogs suffer
from panic disorder?
They might. Anyway, Julio is like, Papi,
everything's fine! Everything's fine! He
lucked out though. An artery got nicked, but
he didn't do much bleeding. His mom
stitched him up. Navarro was behind it. I
guess he figured this is a good time to get
some payback.
Wow.
Navarro, MaGoo and Angus gotta go.
Moon said nothing.

Look, can I have some water?

Sure! Mingo poured him a glass of water.

After that incident between him and Romey? said Moon, Navarro's been on my list.

Ok.

Done deal, you feel me? I won't let any one dis my little sister Mouse. But them other two?

Will you help a brother out, yo?

Elder, do you know what you're asking?

My wife---we want it done.

Moon looked at him carefully.

Come on, now! Your *wife* wants it done!

Mingo sighed and rubbed his face.

Can you do it?

You're not happy about it, are you Elder?

No.

Why do it?

You know the secret of a good marriage, Moon?

What is that?

Learn to know when to give way.

It don't always work. You gotta respect your conscience.

Still.

Here's my problem. MaGoo is a good friend of mines! Willow Kingdom Blood brothers.

Huh?

Crazy stuff between me him and Troll, but
we take it serious. And MaGoo's a partner.
He put me unto the forest thing. Saved my
life by doing it, I bet you, and the forest has
changed my life, too.
Moon---
Hold up! Ain't done yet! And he ain't the
one that hurt Troll.
Are you sure?
Absolutely, Elder. Angus? His Momma?
Honey Buns?
I don't know her, said Mingo.
First cousin to my Momma. See what I'm
saying? He's *blood kin* to me and Mouse. I
ain't gonna kill my kin over that fiasco at the
River. You feel me?
Moon---
Elder? Grow some balls where your Queen
is concerned. You know I had to with that
little dragoon I call my legal wife, right?
I'm *one* with my wife!
One ball?
Let's stay focused, Moon!
Son, please! You're Queen is a young
woman with too much pride and power.
Hold on-----
We're kin! Let me say this to you, ok? That
entire thing at the river was a cluster fuck!

You don't know all the facts, Moon.
They tried to tell you the truth and you
didn't listen.
And what is the truth? Mingo asked tiredly.
They didn't hurt Troll. They're his friends.
Especially MaGoo. They're like family.
Tighter than whale pussy. MaGoo would
rather die than hurt Troll.
MaGoo is a---
MaGoo is a half blind stand up G, like us,
who's done a lot that he ain't proud of. So
have we. I'm blind in the one eye, so I guess
I'm half blind too. He's scared shitless of
admitting he's a Jew to outsiders. So are we!
But there's a lot that you don't know about
him.
He dissed my Queen, yo!
Aw come on now! So what? If I'd kill
everyone who called my she devil a ho-ass
bitch, half of Cedar Crest would be dead.
Learn to ignore name calling. Y'all nearly
murdered that poor kid based on
misinformation. He threw smoke in your
eyes to prevent you from killing Angus, or
finding out what we all suspect!
Which is what?

It's a no win situation! Willy doesn't wanna tell, you, or Angus, or MaGoo because they'll know what'll happen. Y'all frighten the shit out of folks.

Will you tell me what you're talking about?

Cousin Honey Buns is the real voice with SWC. You know who she is, right? Willy's mom? She's the real voice over there. Has been, even before Angus became President. They're red skinned, red haired, but they're black, you feel me? So is Miss Willy.

Miss Willy? Said Mingo. I thought she and Angus are white!

I'm tryna tell you. She gets with Troll? Honey Buns hits the ceiling.

Why?

She doesn't like Troll. She hates dark skinned people, even though she has some black in her. Calls'm darkie.

Mingo sighed wearily. See me? People think I'm Mexican. Fact is I'm mostly black.

Do tell, said Moon.

Are you saying she's behind Troll getting hurt?

She's angry at Willy and Troll. Refused her blessing. Never wanted them together. Now Tiffany Dawn---

Who?

Willy's sister? Now she moved in with them a few months ago? She and that little crazy chick? Chrysanthemum? Well, they're up in there doing the nudist thing, living in that compound, and all that naked flesh makes for sparks, you feel me?

So Troll is now a polygamist? Asked Mingo dryly.

Do you understand now? Said Moon. Cousin Honey Buns hits the roof when she found out all that. Reached out to Navarro, who's tryin' 'n find a way in with any one which ain't Westia, you feel me?

MaGoo is taking the hit trying to protect Willy's family, said Mingo slowly. Angus is tryna protect his momma, even if he has to take the hit, or let MaGoo take it.

Exactly---sorta. Angus didn't want MaGoo being blamed. Angus has been good to MaGoo. Willy's Troll's lady, and a friend to MaGoo. So how do you get any get evens in this situation by hurting their mama?

Go after whoever did the actual beat down? Said Mingo.

And trigger a blood feud in the same
family? Asked Moon. Cause you know SWC
will stand up for their soldiers, and you
know what that will trigger. Willy and
Angus might end up dead. And if you kill
Angus or Honey Buns, Mouse will go to war
with you, and Mouse is my sister, you feel
me?

They stared at each other.

You'd go to war with us?

Elder, Elder! Said Moon. You kill either of
those two boys? You're committing a cold
blooded murder over what? You're reps?
Pride?

Our reps----

You're reps ain't worth murdering two fools
that don't have it coming!

You'd go to war with us, Moon?

Elder, my dear brother, we can't *allow* you to
murder our friends and kin. I'm speaking
for Myself *and* Mouse, My wife, Lil, and the
Cedar Crest Crew.

They stared at each other.

You ready to go war with us, Moon man?

If I have to. But dude, we're kin! Why we
gotta do this? Y'all need to big up and let'm
make it.

Moon looked him unflinchingly in the eyes
and sipped his water.

What's the solution, here Moon? We're
family. I stood *G-d-father* to your son Beryl!
I know! We're kin! But y'all might be drunk
with power, Elder. You can't just *murder*
folks because you can if there are folks that
will stand up to you. Come on! Please?
MaGoo and Angus get a pass. Ok?

Mingo and Moon wiped tears out of their
eyes.

Angus was drunk, Worried about Troll, and
your little muscle man Taliqq was up in his
face.

Mingo laughed and said, A little of Taliqq
goes along way.

Then Angus thought you killed his buddy,
MaGoo. So he lipped off a little. Come on
now! Give him a pass. You put out the
word, he apologized, paid damages, and
you look like statesmen instead of
murdering psychos.

Mingo dry scrubbed his face.

My Queen ordered me to kill them all.

She's your *wife*! You got *some* privileges!
Don't you? Appeal. Ask her to rescind.
Anyway, how you gonna let her order you
around like that? *Big up!* Man *up*! Stand up
to her, for *Christ* sake! *Argue* with her! You
gotta quit letting her be your G-d!
She *is not* my *G-d*!
Prove it. Prove it to yourself. Learn to say no
to her if she's wrong. Anyway, my hunch is
that MaGoo is on his way to Israel.
Is he really a Jew?
Why not? You're a convert, and I'm a
convert too, right?
All that Anti-Semitic hate he put out?
He was creating a smoke screen the best
way he could! You're real prob is the Troll.
How?
Don't you know who he really is?
What are you talking about?
You're lady knows, but she don't know that
she knows.
Moon, what are you talking about?
How come he looks so much like her and
Romero? Don't you know why Romero is
scared of him? Why are you're in laws
falling apart? Why haven't your Mother and
Father in law been going out lately? Why is
Romero so torn up with depression?

Why?

Because he knows.

Who is Troll?

Go to Rosy. I guarantee you your half sister---yeah, I know who she is to you---I betcha she knows. Isaiah knows. In her heart she knows. That's really why she wants to go on a killing spree over Troll. You don't mess with a lionesses kin. Like, maybe she thinks Troll has been through enough.

So who is he?

Talk to Rosy. This Neighborhood has a lot of secrets. A buncha y'all was children of Pastor Molina, but that ain't the only secret out here!

What am I gonna do, Puppy?

Moon smiled.

Now we *really* kinfolk if you calling me that. Troll told you. Nothing. Treat it as a crazy family squabble. Maybe y'all let Cousin Willy give her Mama a good ass whoop! That would balance things.

Beat her own mama down?

Why not? Beats shooting her. Hell, I should know. I killed mines, and ain't been right in the head since. Some Mamas need they ass whooped. Maybe the actual doers of the beat down? They get their throat slit up the road when they least expect it.

Maybe could be, said Mingo, that would go a long way to solving all this, if it could be arranged!

Maybe could be, said Moon, part of it has already happened. But MaGoo? Angus? Honey Buns? Let'm be. Or just spin it so it's all about Navarro. Word is? Navarro led out on the beat down.

Ok, will you handle Navarro?

Why you stressing on it?

When will you do that Navarro thing?

Might could be it's been done.

Mingo sat staring at him. Really?

I hear tell that he possibly picked up two foxy black she-male looking mamas to party hardy with in a gay bar…caters to bi-sexual too.

Are you saying Navarro was bi?

You ain't gotta be bi to enjoy letting a gay boy suck you off! They don't play! They love sucking dick!

Moon, that's way too much 411!

Cool. Maybe Navarro is looking to party in celebration of the mess he saw at the river, or they came unto to him. Maybe could be he was celebrating this whole cluster fuck. Confusion on your enemies and all that…Maybe these two foxy black she-male looking mamas comes on to him. You know the drill? Hey big papa, you wanna party? Navarro might-a been half drunk and was too stupid to ask why two fine looking bulldagga-maybe-she-males would wanna party with him.

Blue and Midnight?

Elder, why you asking all that for? You might could wanna pay out to them on the papers you had on him, if you see my meaning.

Done deal.

Anyway, he might could be gone missing. May could be he got knifed. Maybe could be his tongue got cut out and his hands cut off like your Queen wanted. Could be someone don't allow his little sister to be rolled on like that. That might make it easier for you to calm your Queen down.

Thank you.

Why you thanking me for Elder? I said
Maybe, and if I'm right, I don't know a thing
about it, kinfolk. Now, talk to Rosy about
Troll. By the way? Willy's in the wind!
What are you saying?
If you called your wife? You'll find out that
room Willy was in? Is as empty as a
restaurant kitchen if you holla la migra!

Chapter Nineteen

A dry dusty wind was blowing. It was cold. Autumn was getting nippy. It was the part of the day when evening turns into night. The spectral figure walked slowly, up the dirt road where Wilhelmina once lived, wearing a black hooded shirt that flapped in the wind. It was several sizes too large.

A neighbor saw her face.

Willy? Willy is that you?

No answer.

Wachu you doing up here, gurl? I thought you moved in with that colored fella a yers! Where you going?

Out of my way, Mister Jensen!

Aw come on, Willy, he said, struggling to hold on to his cowboy hat, don't go getting' riled at the man who used ta fix yer bicycle fer ya! *Wow* now! Don't go in there!

Me and my family own this place!

Ain't you fell out with your Mama?

She's here right?

Willy----

Go home to your wife and mind your own business, Mister Jensen! Said Willy, entering the yard of her mother's house, where she grew up carefully. She let herself in.

Willy entered her former home, and bolted
and chained the door. Her neighbor, an
SWC member, whipped out his cell phone
and called both Angus and Tiffany-Dawn.
Well, well, well! Said Honey Buns. The
Prodigal has returned!
How are you mama? Asked Willy.
Aw well, these old bones…fair to middling.
Fair to middling.
Mama, you know why I'm here?
So! You come to your senses? Are you
coming back home?
Get real!
No, Willy, I guess I don't know! I don't
know nothing about nothing.
Sure you do, you old darling, said
Wilhelmina. We got issues to resolve.
This place looks like hell….Angus hardly
stays here, Tiff stays with you now…Soon as
I finish this beer and a smoke? I was about
to do some dishes!
There's a first time for everything Mama.
Honey Buns laughed.
You were always my little *rattler*, Willy. My
little Willy! You know you're my favorite,
don't you?
Don't, mama. We got issues to deal with!

Her mother sitting at the kitchen table
having a beer.
What issues are those, darlin'?
You tell me.
I been waiting on you Willy! I was hoping
you'd come to your senses!
Wilhelmina approached her slowly.
Woe Willy! Stop right there! All right, you
stop right there.
You crossed a line, mama!
You nearly scaring me to death! She
laughed. Now let's be civilized! Ain't you
got a kiss for your ole Mama?
Wilhelmina looked surprised, then coldly
kissed her mother's cheek.
How you wanna do this mama?
How I wanna do *what*?
You gonna answer for hurting my
Ragamuffin. Me and you, ok?
Oh, you gonna *fight* your old mama? Never
mind your pregnant and I suffers from
arthritis?
I don't wanna hear it mama!
Ain't you supposed to be some kinda gentle
Jew now? Whatever happened to honor
your mother?
Who said you're a real mother? Don't *play*
with me!
I'm *warning* you, Willy!

You loved our Daddy, didn't you? He was
black! What changed you, Mama? Texas
filled you with hate!
He ain't nothing but a darkie *troll!* You
hear? They tried to give him a good hiding
is all---
They busted his ribs! Said Willy. They made
him a killer!
It coulda been worst! I *chose* not to have him
lynched! We just wanted to put him in his
place! He's a nigger *troll, Willy!*
Why you keep talkin' mama?
I *brought* you *in* this world and if I have to?
I'll take you *out, gurl*! But I'd rather not do
that to my own child....
Take me out? You and what *army*, mama?
I've *warned* you, gurl! I ain't one of them,
drunk ass stick up nigger boys you've
killed, you heah? Turn and walk away, and I
won't give you the *hiding* I should a gave
you years ago!
Come *give* it to me, you *slut!*
He mother laughed and shook her head.
That might *could* be the knife that cuts the
butter! I'm a one per center all the way! You
ain't *ready* for this, gurl!
How do you wanna *do this* Mama?
Well, alright, said the older woman.

Honey Buns sighed with resignation, took a slow final drag on her Camel cigarette and stubbed it out on a coffee cup saucer. She blew out the smoke slowly, studying her daughter through slitted eyes. She spat a speck of tobacco on the floor. She got to her feet slowly, stretched, threw off the leather SWC biker's vest she wore, and pulled out her Bowie knife.

Ok now, Willy. I sharpen this here with a *strop*. You know what that means? This thing is sharper than a razor. Do I need to do some street surgery on you, child?

Wilhelmina spat with disgust. You wanna do that, mama?

You take me on, you fight *mister blade too*. Mama's a *surgeon* with this!

She began to slowly circle her daughter, going into a knife fighters crouch, making a few feints, almost playfully.

You don't wanna know how many time mama's business here has been used, do you? I won't waste no bullets on you, gurl.

Wilhelmina took a few steps back.

We can do it like that if you want, Mama!

Gurl, I *warned* you! Daughter or not, step to with me, swing your hand, draw back a nub!

I'm tired a talking, mama! Come on!

Don't *make* me cut my own Chile! I will if I
have to, Willy! You know that, right? So help
me *G-d*, gurl!
Wilhelmina pulled out a Smith and Wesson
38 Special and smile fiendishly.
Her Mother straightened up and looked at
her expressionlessly.
If you don't put that away, you brought a
knife to a gun fight, Mama!
Her Mother hesitated and laughed. She
stood straight.
You gonna gun down your ole *mama, Chile*?
I prefer to just kick your *ass*, but I will if I
have too!
You see me packing?
You should be, old woman. The day of the
knife is passed, Mama. You in the land of
the gunfighters!
That ain't a fair fight, gurl!
Fair? You were jus' fixin' to slice me! Wachu
know about *fair* Mama?
I'm an ole woman----
Whatever! You're not even forty!
Be fair, chile!
 How many men you put to beating my
Troll? Five? Was that fair?

That *nigger* put down three of them with one
of them there Khukuris! *Good* SWC friends,
not members, but still! And the others are on
their way! I could almost admire him! He
gave as good as he *got*, I'll give him that!
How fair was that, mama?
Can't you put away that popper?
And let you cut me, huh?
Didn't I refuse my blessings? I *warned* you
on that, gurl!
Why we talkin' Mama?
I shoulda known you'd be too *chicken shit* to
fight *right*, Wilhelmina. You *always* have
been chicken shit!
Ok.
Wilhelmina pulled out a Khukuri.
Why you little black *bitch*!
You want a knife fight? I *knew* you'd pull
your little pig sticker, mama!
Never leave home without it, baby gurl! I
always keep it close!
You wanna do it with knives, mama? Fine!
See that kukri? That's the devil's right
hand! That ain't no knife!
Yeah! I'ma cut you to ribbons, old woman!
Aww come on Willy!
By the time I'm through, mama, the only
thing that won't be cut will be the bottom of
your boots!

Are you listening to yourself? All he got was an old fashion ass whoop! What's *wrong* with you gurl?

Whyja hurt my Troll, mama?

You was *warned*! You did not have my *blessing*!

Why couldn't you jus' respect my choice? I wan'ned you to be *somebody*!

I *am* some*body*, *mama*!

And who is that, gurl?

I'm am *Wilhelmina Smith-Martinez!* Troll's lady!

No! You're one of that *filthy* nigger pimp's *womin*! One of his *whores*! Yeah, I know he has a stable of five! You and your own *sister*! *Shame* on you, Wilhelmina! *Shame*!

Whores? Wilhelmina laughed. You don't know what you're talking about!

I wanted you to be *better* than me! Said her mother. I *tole* you I didn't approve of that darkie!

Well on account of that darkie this *darkie's* gonna whoop your red *ass*, Honey Buns! I'ma give you a West Redemption *darkie* ass whoop, you darkie *bitch*!

You and that big chopper? Said Honey Buns, Still ain't no fair fight, gurl!

Why we talking, mama? Let's just *do it!*

Wait, gurl! You jus' wanna murder me? That Khukuri ain't no knife---it's practically a sword!

Fists then, said Wilhelmina, putting away her Khukuri, but not her gun.

Put up the Popper, why doncha?

First throw your knife in the sink!

Her mother snorted and laughed. She threw her knife across the room into the sink. It landed with a splash.

Now put up the Popper!

Wilhelmina holstered her gun.

You think I needed that *knife* for *you, gurl*? *Look* at you! *Look at you!* Dread locks on your head! Dressed like Hippy *scum*! Five of you fucking that *NIGGER PIMP! You* turned into a *nigger*, gurl! You're *nothing to me now*!

You're *nobody, Willy*!

I'm waitin' Mama!

Gurl, you *really* think you can take *me*? You gonna best *me*?

Why you still talking, mama? To scared to do your own fighting? Chicken, huh?

Don't no true mother wanna hurt her own chile...

You ain't no mother!

I beat down *men* twice your size!

You still talking!

I got arthritis, ungrateful *murderous* little
nigger *bicth*! You was never any good,
unless you had that ole wheel gun! You ain't
woman enough to beat down your Mama,
little Missy.
Show me!
I *been* wanting to whoop you candy ass!
Come on, mama! *Whoop!*
You gonna pull out that popper again, or are
ya to yella to fight me fair?
Wilhelmina snapped the retention strap on
her gun. She pushed it into its holster
grimly. They briefly glared at each other.

Aaaaaargh! They both screamed, hurling themselves at each other's throat. Her mother tried to throttle her, but Wilhelmina grabbed her Mother's denim shirt by the collar and began to systematically to punch her grimly in the face with all her strength. Her Mother's face grew swollen and bloody, as her nose and mouth bled. One eye was blackened. Her Mothers grip slackened, and abruptly she broke away and dove for the sink. Wilhelmina jumped on her back, and grabbed around the throat from behind with a forearm and began to throttle her, but the momentum only propelled her mother forward. She grabbed the knife out of the soapy water. Gagging, she tried to stab her daughter's side, but could not, as Wilhelmina wriggled away. She tried to slash Wilhelmina's arm. The knife hilt was slippery with soap water, and she only managed to give her a superficial cut.

The pain was enough to make Wilhelmina
slacken her hold and her mother broke
loose. She spun, and tried to stab her
daughter in the side, but Wilhelmina
jumped aside and pulled out her Khukuri.
She slashed at her Mother's throat, but,
Honey Buns, barely avoiding the blade,
ducked back and slashed at her daughter's
face. Wilhelmina jumped back and slashed
her Mother's under the arm, then shallowly
jabbed her Mother's right thigh.
Ahhh! Screamed her Mother, dropping her
knife. She grabbed her wounded arm and
looked at her daughter in terror.
Willy, *listen*----You gonna murder your own
mama? I *carried* you tucked under my *heart*
for nine *months*, gurl!
Wilhelmina swiftly put away her Khukuri
and tackled her. Her Mother fell to the
ground, and Wilhelmina fell on top.
Straddling her, pinning her arms to her
sides, she grabbed a fist full of her mother's
hair and grimly began punching her on the
face again, until her mother went limp.
That was for my Troll, *ya bitch!*
Then she took out her Khukuri and held the
edge to her Mother's throat.
She panted, almost out of breath.

Mama, I could cut your wrinkly throat right here and *now*! And you *know* I will!

My throat ain't wrinkly!

Whatever! Shut up!

Please, gurl, *please* don't!

I'd rather not dirty my hands anymore than I already have! So do as I say, and I'll let you be!

Alright! Wadaya want?

Give me, Wilhelmina Esmeralda *Martinez* and Ramiro Job *Martinez* your blessings! Go on! *Say it!*

Who is that?

MY Troll!

I can't do it! Said her Mother. Black *bicth*!

Your *blessings* Momma!

Go to *hell*, damn *you*!

Now!

You *hate me* don't you Willy?

Yes, *I always have, for being untrue to my father, for the murders, for all the men. YOU MURDERED OUR UNCLE* ...but I love you too.

Oh, Willy, listen----

Now, bless my marriage.

Or what?

I'ma slice your throat...

Then how you gonna live with yourself?

I won't. I'ma cut my own throat too and
we'll bleed to death together!
For G-d's sake don't be insane, Willy! You're
PREGNANT.
You'll die knowing you were murdered by
your own favorite child and how you killed
her with your choice! I *mean* it, mama!
She glared at her daughter wrathfully. Her
eyes were red and filled with tears, love and
hatred.
A pounding started at the door. Angus
kicked the door in and ran to stop the fight.
Angus, stop right there or I'll slit her neck
right now, so help me!
Willy, for G-d's sake, *don't*!
Don't rile a pregnant red head favorite!
 She's our mama!
Stay out of this Angus, or I'll cut her *throat
and mines right now!*
Aww, don't little sissy!
*Can't you see? The next time they'll kill my
Troll! All I wanted was to be left alone. I wanna
have my baby…*
I warned you Willy!
Now Mama, *LISTEN. This has gotta end!* I'ma
ask you for your blessing *one last time. I love
you mommy,----*
LIAR!

*I don't lie. Now bless me or we'll soon be in hell
with the devil!*
I'm looking at the devil now!
Mama, said Angus, for G-d sakes! *Do what
she wants!*
Honey Buns slyly picked up her knife,
without Wilhelmina seeing.
Alright! You wanna be with your pretty
darkie troll pimp?
He's not a pimp.
*Take a p from pimp -and your left with imp, and
that's what he is, it's impious for me to bless
your union with that nigger imp.*
MAMA!
Fine! You have my *blessings and be damned!*
And now, burn in *hell*, nigger *bitch---*
She tried to plunge her knife into her
daughter's side, but her son kicked it out of
her hand.
No, Mama! That's *enough! Willy, stop now!
Stop! She gave her blessing!*
Mama were you about to murder me?
Let her go, Willy! It's over! It's over!
Wilhelmina got up stiffly, and scabbard her
knife.
She stood glaring at her mother as Angus
helped her Mother to a chair.
Angus, can you clean my mama up for me?
I'd kill for some black Olives, said Willy.

Do what?

Cravings, snarled Honey Buns. I used to crave them too when I carried y'all.

You two have so much in common, said Angus.

Shut up Bow-bow.

There's jar in the fridge, said her mother. Take'm. Angus, bring me the first aid kit. Come here rattler.

She bandaged her daughters arm.

 Now go.

Wilhelmina took the Olives.

Bow-bow, we good?

Sure Willy, it's all good!

Please take care of her for me Bow-bow. Now I'm doomed I guess, but I can't say I'm sorry! I'm evil without hope for harming my own mama, but you left me no choice. Bow-bow mama's bleeding. She'll need a Doctor!

Ok, sweety! Ok.

She tried to kill my Troll, Angus! She said, gasping for air. Understand? I had no choice.

I had nothing to do with it, Willy!

I know! I know it wasn't you, brother. I always knew.

I would never hurt him! Said Angus. I wouldn't have allowed it! I had no idea!

Ok, Bow-bow. Now Angus Cromwell-
Smith, Can't you accept me and Troll being
Jews?
Why?
If you can't I guess this is goodbye.
He looked at her, and wiped the sweat from
his brow.
No. No. I been thinking on this. You two
really wanna be Jews?
We already are, said Wilhelmina.
Ok...I don't wanna lose my little sister.
I know you didn't know about any of this,
said Wilhelmina. You won't set the boys on
us?
Never. Go get some rest.
We got no quarrel, ok?
Absolutely.
Will y'all let us make it?
I would never hurt you, Willy! Mama din't
do that through me!
You heard her? said Wilhelmina. You heard
her? She gave her blessing! Ain't that right
Mama?
I gave my blessings! Now go to *hell out my
house*!
This ain't your house, *old woman!*
Never let me lay eyes on you again in this
world, damn you! Go on!

See? Said Wilhelmina. She'll snitch me out,
Bow-bow. Tell the cops I'll be at my Troll's
home.
You'll have no problems outta me, said
Honey Buns.
No! she won't, said Angus. Whatever mama
is, she ain't a snitch Willy!
Tell her, Angus, said her mother.
Angus, you Tell them all, tell them all *she
gave her blessings*! Now tell them to let us be,
Bow-bow! So help me, I'll kill her or
whoever she sends if they comes after us!
Tell them all to leave me and my Troll be!
Ok Willy! I'll tell them! Now go, sweet
heart! Mama needs an ambulance!
And strangely neither mother or daughter
wanted to part.
See you in hell mama!
Not if I see you first...You was my *favorite*!
Screamed her mother after her. You was my
favorite!
I shouldna been. I'm evil made flesh. I
wasn't born to be nobody's daughter,
mama.
You were never any good, Willy, said
Honey Buns, her eyes filling with tears. You
was my *favorite*!
I'll always love you, mama!

Go on! Run to your nigger! *Damn you!* Now you're dead to me! *DEAD!* See you in *hell!* Yeah old woman! I'll see you in hell only if you see me first!
Run to your nigger! Damn you! Now you're dead to me! DEAD!
Wilhelmina walked warily, wearily away. Outside the wind seemed to howl madly, accusingly, and the dust devils swirled like dancing demons around her joyfully welcoming her to their ranks. She felt so alive. In the distance she heard the wail of police sirens. She walked away slowly, knowing not to run. Willy pulled up the hood of her hoody, and walked into the raging storm heading, home through the maddening swirling dust.

THE END,
BOOK ONE–

pg. 615

www.ingramcontent.com/pod-product-compliance
Lightning Source LLC
Chambersburg PA
CBHW052342020726
47503CB00001B/66